ENCHANTMENT

CAMILLE PETERS

D1518318

ENCHANTMENT

By: Rosewood Publications

Copyright © 2020 by Camille Peters

Rosewood Publications

Salt Lake City, Utah

United States of America

www.camillepeters.com

Cover Design by Karri Klawiter

To all who need to discover their own inner beauty—may you know how beautiful you truly are.

CHAPTER 1

*D*awn began to lighten the sky, dispelling the darkness from the night I'd spent wandering. By now my maid would have discovered me missing from my bed. I smirked even though the only witnesses to my satisfaction were the thick trees I'd been traipsing through for the past several hours; Father would most certainly be surprised when he discovered me missing.

My smile quickly faded. Perhaps I should have planned this excursion better by taking the time to arrange the blankets in such a way to make it appear as if I were still burrowed beneath my covers; that would have given me a few extra hours before anyone discovered my flight. Father had undoubtedly learned of it by now and was likely already searching for me.

Regardless, he wouldn't find me; I'd make certain of *that*.

Humming, I pulled my cloak more tightly around my shoulders as I continued trekking through the trees. The early morning sunshine penetrated the leafy canopy and warmed my body, which had grown numb with cold from the long, chilly spring night. But the cold was a small price to pay for my current adventure, as were my torn, muddy skirts and the scratches marring my hands and face from the branches the moonlight had failed to illuminate—battle scars earned from finally taking charge of my own life.

The forest grew brighter as the sun rose higher in the sky, dispelling the last of the shadows and my shivers. I paused to look around. Trees stretched out in every direction. I hadn't the faintest idea where I was. I grinned. *Excellent.*

Perhaps it was time I came up with a more solid plan. Running away had seemed much more simple when I'd focused solely on the *running away* part. My intended destination had always been rather vague, save for: *as far away from Father as possible.* And really, *that* part of running away was going quite nicely...even if I now found myself lost at the moment.

But being lost aside, things were still going rather well.

I rummaged in my hastily packed satchel for some bread and cheese I'd stolen from the kitchens. As I ate my makeshift breakfast, I ventured deeper into the trees in a random direction which promised to get me even *further* away from where I'd come.

My grin grew with every step. Father was certain to be furious. I had no doubt he'd come looking for me, but I refused to be found. Which meant I had to find both a hiding place and a new future for myself, one that was solely of my own choosing. For the first time since sneaking out my bedroom window, I frowned slightly. If only I knew *what* future I wanted. How could a previously caged bird know where to fly when she hadn't seen much of the world?

No matter, I'd find something; in that I was determined.

I finished my breakfast and licked my fingers—a gesture that would have put my now former governess into a fit for my wild, unladylike manners—and paused to take in the woodland surroundings more closely. I must be miles from my hometown, but considering I was hopeless with directions, I couldn't say exactly where I'd wandered to. I'd been traveling in what I thought was south in hopes of nearing the outskirts of Malvagaria, where it seemed unlikely Father would search first.

But was it the best place for me to settle? Should I remain in the kingdom, or try and find my way to Draceria? Better yet, perhaps I could travel to the coast and sail to Bytamia— Father loathed the sea and likely wouldn't think to look for me there, at least not immediately.

Fire flared in my breast at the thought of Father, his ships, what he'd done...I balled my hands into fists, trying to dispel my anger before it became a roaring blaze, as it was often prone to do. Today, my first day of true freedom, was too fine to ruin, not to mention I'd need a level head for whatever lay ahead. The more I imagined his fury at discovering I'd run away, the more my own slipped away until I was grinning once again.

This will teach you to use your only child for your advantage. Oh, but revenge was quite delicious.

I slowed my traipsing through the trees and thick undergrowth when I spotted something in the distance. I shaded my eyes and squinted. Was that...yes, it was a castle, a foreboding fortress of grey stone, gothic architecture, and sharp turrets jutting formidably against the morning sky. Of all the places I'd expected my wanderings to lead me, it hadn't been *here*.

I furrowed my brow as I studied the castle's architecture, as if it could provide clues to where I'd ended up. The royal family was known for their extravagance, which included half a dozen castles scattered throughout the kingdom. The question was: which palace was *this* one?

Considering the surrounding woods, it likely wasn't one of their primary residences...at least I *hoped* it wasn't, for unless it was abandoned, exploring the grounds would be quite risky. But taking risks was one of my primary pastimes. Because really, one couldn't come across a palace and *not* take a closer look.

My curiosity propelled me closer, causing my skirts to further tear in my haste as they caught on loose branches and thick undergrowth. The trees thinned before opening up to the towering wall that enclosed the castle...a wall without a gate. Two large stone columns stood yards apart, indicating the place where the gate should have been. But that area was swallowed up by thick vines blooming with yellow, white, and magenta flowers—honeysuckle, jasmine, and a type I couldn't identify.

The vines began to rustle as I parted them, searching for a way in. But I discovered only thick greenery as far as I could see, which was a peculiar puzzle. What type of castle had no entrance?

Undoubtedly one full of secrets. I simply had to see for myself. The missing gate, rather than deterring me, provided a challenge, and I never backed down from a challenge.

Perhaps the entrance was hidden within the foliage. With a determined lift of my chin, I brushed aside the vines, thrusting my hands and body deeper and deeper. The vines instantly stirred, the pink-floral ones snapping against my hands.

I gasped at the biting pain and stumbled back to stare at my hands, where several cuts lined my palms. I glared at the vines, but they simply rustled in a breezy way that almost sounded like laughter before they rose up to take a rather defiant stance. Ah, so these were magical vines. It appeared the rumors surrounding the Malvagarian palace gardens held some truth. Well, if I could handle a dark forest at night, I could certainly handle these.

I stepped closer for a better look. The pink-flowering

vines had thorns along the stems where the leaves grew, thorns which stood upright at attention in preparation to attack again.

"Ah, I see," I murmured. "You're guards. It appears the palace isn't abandoned at all. Fascinating." But my fascination quickly faded as the heat in my chest swelled. I held up my hands so that the stinging, bleeding cuts could clearly be seen. "This was completely uncalled for. A simple warning would have sufficed."

The vines did nothing, only continued to hover and watch to see what I'd do. I'd heard whispers that the royal family's gardens were enchanted. These vines—as pesky as they were—were likely only one of many marvelous wonders to be found within the walls. I simply had to explore the grounds to discover more, which meant I had to figure out how to get past these mischievous guards...and then there was also the issue of the missing entrance.

But no vines, magical or not, would deter me. Perhaps a bit of persuasion was in order. "My name is Maren," I said. "I mean no harm. It's only that I've just run away from home and was hoping for a place to rest before I continue my journey."

While the pink-floral vines remained still, the honey-suckle stirred, a sign I'd aroused its curiosity, whereas the jasmine rustled, as if inquiring *why* I'd run away.

Heaviness pressed against my chest. "That's quite a long story. You see, my father—well, he—"

No, I couldn't say the words out loud; it would make my situation all the more real. Besides, surely these plants wouldn't understand about debt and neglectful fathers and the disadvantages that came from being an unwanted merchant's daughter, especially one who had nothing to recommend her.

But the vines were still awaiting an answer. I sighed.

"Father did something cruel, but I shan't say any more. Won't you please help me? I simply can't let my father find me."

The vines began to rustle almost excitedly before gathering together, as if to converse privately; the whispers of wind almost sounded like hisses which grew steadily louder, as if the vines were arguing. I waited with bated breath, hoping they'd concede to let me pass, for I simply *had* to see what lay beyond the wall. Not to mention I was growing tired from my late-night excursion.

The whispering breeze suddenly ceased. Before I could inquire after their decision, the vines immediately parted, wriggling and twisting to form themselves into a giant archway.

I stared in wonder before turning my awe towards the vines, watching me almost expectedly, as if seeking a compliment. I happily humored them. "How clever of you."

They bristled rather smartly.

My heart lifted as I turned my attention towards the palace grounds. "Does this mean you'll let me stay and rest for a while?" Surely they'd only allow such a thing if the royal family wasn't in residence; I didn't want to risk encountering anyone that Father could later question as to my whereabouts.

At their bobbing nod, I took a step forward, but some of the honeysuckle vines blocked my way, allowing the jasmine to creep forward to search my skirts and muddy boots to ensure I wasn't armed. When they didn't find anything suspicious, they caressed the cuts they'd made on my hands. At their touch, I thought I sensed faint whispers of an indiscernible language, one that faintly tickled my thoughts with what sounded like an apology.

"It's quite alright," I assured them. "I'm used to scrapes and bruises. I get them a lot when I let my curiosity get the better of me."

I lightly touched one of the pink flowers and a name caressed my thoughts: *bougainvillea*. Hmm, that must be what it was called. Perhaps its proper introduction and apology meant we could be friends...and surely my new friends would allow me to pass through.

As if sensing my thoughts, the honeysuckle and jasmine vines retreated into the giant archway, beckoning me to enter. It was all the invitation I needed. After a grateful smile, I stepped into the magical palace gardens.

I froze in the entrance and looked around wide-eyed, trying to take in all the vibrant colors and variety of plants that greeted me. I heard rustling behind me and turned to see that the vines had once again morphed into the palace wall. I faced forward. The gate opened up to a twisting path that looked to have been formed from fallen leaves. I hesitantly stepped onto it, expecting the path to crackle beneath my feet, only to discover it was made up of cobblestones.

The path twisted and turned in several different directions, with the main one leading up to the steps to the castle's front doors...but I didn't dare venture there. Instead, I turned my attention to the other paths. Trees, hedges, and wildflowers lined each one, with the trees forming a canopy of branches over the paths—some laden with colorful blossoms, some dipped in autumn, and yet others comprised solely of vibrant green leaves. Vines wove around the trunks, and flowers grew in a halo around the bases. Each enchanting pathway promised infinite possibilities.

I excitedly started down the first path I came across, one lined with shrubs whose leaves were the colors of spring, twisting and turning as if guiding me to a picturesque garden where the flowers were arranged in ornate patterns that grew in bright hues, many of which I'd never encountered before. It took my breath away.

I explored first this garden, then another just as

wondrous, each like a dream, a place where time itself seemed to stand still. So it was quite shocking when I eyed the sun slowly rising higher in the sky and realized several hours had passed.

The spell cast by the surrounding enchantment broke. As marvelous as these gardens were, I began to question my trespassing through the royal grounds and arriving at the palace uninvited. Despite the guards' permission to enter, it would be foolish to linger, which meant I had to leave if I had any hope of staying ahead of Father. Already my explorations had wasted most of the time and distance I'd managed to put between us.

So foolish, Maren.

I began to make my way back to the gate, but paused when the hedge I'd been walking alongside suddenly shifted to inch across the path, blocking my way.

I pressed my hands to my hips. "What are you doing? I must be on my way." But my complaint was halfhearted, for despite it being the sensible thing to do, I didn't really want to leave.

The tall hedge refused to move, so I searched for an alternate exit. I caught sight of a long path to my right, overgrown with wildflowers. As if my noticing it had been a signal, the flowers parted in invitation. The path twisted towards a weeping willow, whose lilac and rose-colored dangling branches swayed gently in the breeze, a lure that beckoned me closer.

Curious as to what lay hidden beyond, I heeded their invitation and pushed the branches aside to step into a vast clearing. My breath caught. The entire grove was aglow, a ballroom for the waltzing sunlight, which glistened off the plants and leaves that appeared to be made of colored gems. While the jeweled fauna was enough to seduce me into exploring further, my attention was immediately captured by the rosebush growing in the center.

It was unlike any I'd ever seen—roses blossomed in a rainbow of colors, aglow as if light radiated from each petal. Transfixed, I stepped closer and brushed the glittered petals with my fingertip. They shimmered and glistened at my touch, vibrating with magic.

I had to have one of these roses, a memento not only of my time in these wondrous gardens but of the day I took control of my own life, a gift offered by the garden itself. I examined each one, searching for the perfect one to pluck. Rather than selecting a rose blooming in a rare, almost mystical color, I chose one of the deepest red—beautiful, yet common enough not to be missed.

The garden made no move to stop me; in fact, it seemed to be holding its breath in anticipation as I reached a hesitant hand out towards the beautiful flower. My fingers grazed the petals as I ran them along the thorny stem before hooking them securely near the base of the rose several inches below the blossom. With a wavering breath, I gave it a sharp twist and snapped it off.

The moment it broke free, a fierce breeze blew around me, causing glistening magic to rise from the flower and twirl through the air before seeping into my chest. Instantly, I felt as if an invisible thread had woven itself between me and the rose, connecting us together.

The feeling vanished almost as quickly as it had appeared. The breeze settled and the magic faded, leaving nothing but the flower cradled in my hand. But before I could tuck it safely away, a fierce roar echoed across the grounds.

My breath hitched as I spun towards the sound. It appeared I wasn't alone after all.

CHAPTER 2

My heart beat in an unrelenting tempo as I looked wildly around for the source of the roar, fear trickling up my spine for the first time since I'd run away.

"Who's there?" My trembling voice became trapped in my throat as my gaze settled on a man standing at the entrance. I gasped and stumbled back; he certainly hadn't been there moments before.

He was tall and broad shouldered, dressed in a red velvet tunic lined with gold. His black hair was tousled as if he'd just been running, and his dark eyes were narrowed at the rose I clutched in my shaking hand.

He took a menacing step closer. "What did you do?"

I took a steadying breath to summon my courage and straightened. "I plucked a rose." There was no use lying, not when he could clearly see the evidence before him.

The fury already lining his expression hardened. "So I see." He advanced another limping step, drawing my attention to the dark crimson blood staining his trousers from a large gash in his shin, which appeared to still be bleeding.

"What happened to your leg?"

He didn't answer as he crouched in front of the rosebush and lightly traced the severed stem, sadness filling his dark eyes. He tightened his jaw and turned the force of his anger back on me.

"You plucked a rose." His hardened tone made it sound as if I'd committed a grievous crime. I stilled. I hadn't...had I? My blood chilled. Perhaps I had. After all, these were royal gardens, and taking one of their roses without permission was no different than stealing from the royal family themselves.

I shifted guiltily. *Maren, you do get yourself in the most thorny predicaments.* An apology was definitely in order, which was rather unfortunate since I hated apologizing, but considering the offense, it was undoubtedly wise.

I lowered my gaze. "It is as you said. I'm sorry."

I waited for his response. At his silence, my gaze flickered upward to find him looking not at me, but at the rose I held, his expression grieved as if he'd just lost a dear friend.

"I appreciate your apology, although it can't undo what you've done, which is more serious than you realize." His tone, while still hard, had softened considerably. I studied him curiously before the realization of who this man was swept over me.

"Are you one of the Malvagarian princes?"

He gave a rigid nod. "I am."

I nearly groaned. Of course he was. It was just my luck to meet one of our kingdom's royalty in such a way—wearing a traveling gown marred by mud and tears, all while being caught trespassing and stealing; I ignored my prickling conscience that reminded me that these unideal circumstances were of my own making.

I knew a curtsy was in order, but I was too stunned and mortified to even move. He didn't seem to notice my faux

11

pas, for his attention had been recaptured by the rosebush's severed stem, as if he couldn't look away. After a moment, he slowly straightened and returned his attention to me.

"I am Briar, Crown Prince of Malvagaria and the keeper of these gardens."

Oh dear, he wasn't just a *prince*—he happened to be the *crown* prince and my future king. This just kept getting worse and worse. I finally stirred enough to bob into a rather inelegant curtsy. "I'm Maren, Your Highness."

Our introductions made, I awaited my inevitable punishment. While I'd heard our kingdom's crown prince was a mild-mannered man, I didn't expect mercy for my crime. If only I'd paid better attention in my studies of our kingdom's laws to know which consequences I could expect for theft.

I stiffened as he bridged the distance between us, favoring his bleeding leg, until he stood close enough that I could hear his anger-laden breaths. "I don't know where you come from, Miss Maren, but you are trespassing on royal property. Therefore I must ask what you're doing here." He spoke slowly, as if struggling to maintain his fragile hold over his displeasure.

I raised my chin. "I'm just passing through."

He lifted a dubious brow. "How did you get in?" He sighed before I could even answer. "The vines let you in, didn't they? Foolish things. I thought they were more trustworthy."

"I'm surprised you left a duty as important as guarding the palace to a bunch of vines." The impolite words escaped before I could stop them, but once again he didn't seem to notice my rudeness.

"The plants are more than capable, but I mistakenly believed they were more discerning." He gave me a pointed look and my cheeks flushed.

"There's no need to call my character into question," I said indignantly.

"I'm afraid that due to the circumstances, I have no choice: you've been found trespassing on royal property and plucking one of my roses. Those two actions are not points in your favor, Miss Maren."

Unfortunately, he was right. "If I might defend myself, Your Highness, I wasn't *trespassing* but *exploring*. I admit my actions were foolish, but one mistake doesn't make me a bad person."

He clasped his hands behind his back and studied me thoughtfully. "It doesn't, but you still have much work to do in repairing your unfavorable first impression." He faced the garden exit, his expression now more weary than frustrated. "I still don't understand how you entered the palace gardens in the first place."

"The vines seemed concerned for me."

He lifted a skeptical brow. "Concerned? You claim to understand the enchanted plants?"

"We had a conversation...of sorts, enough that we can now call ourselves acquaintances. They've treated me kindly." Unlike himself.

Even though I wasn't reckless enough to voice such an observation out loud, he seemed to have sensed my silent disapproval. He closed his eyes and took a steadying breath, as if fighting to regain his sense of calm. The rest of his anger faded, leaving only his exasperation.

"I'm surprised you felt inclined to return such a gracious reception with an act of thievery."

The heat in my cheeks deepened. "I can assure you that wasn't my intention. The gardens led me to this rosebush, almost as if they *wanted* me to pluck one of the roses."

He stilled and his expression paled. "What did you say?"

"The gardens led me to—"

My explanation was cut short when he stormed from the garden with long, agitated strides, despite his bleeding leg. I immediately scrambled after him as he headed up the path, all while ignoring the flustered rustling of the plants he passed.

He ducked beneath the weeping willow's overhanging branch and stomped to the ivy-covered entrance, where he stopped to glare at the vines, who stayed perfectly still, as if awaiting their scolding.

"What did you *do?*" he hissed.

They rustled guiltily. He waited, his ear cocked as if he were listening to each sway of the vines as they spoke in a silent language I couldn't hear.

"You know no one is allowed inside the gardens without my permission." He spun around to face the rest of the gardens. "And *you.*" His stern voice easily carried across the grounds, which all seemed to be listening intently to their prince. "Whose idea was it to trick her?"

My brow puckered. *Trick* me?

"Answer me." His tone was hardening with his impatience. "You know the consequences that come from plucking an enchanted rose. Whose idea was it?"

The garden remained still and silent—not a single branch rustled; even the birdsong had ceased.

I hesitantly stepped forward. "Forgive me, Your Highness, but what did you mean by the gardens *tricking* me?"

"I meant exactly what I said." He turned back to the vines, who rustled in a way that almost seemed...smug. "What do you have to say for yourselves?"

I didn't have to be able to understand them to sense their continued refusal to answer; the prince's hardening expression said it all.

"Are they always so defiant?" I asked.

"Pardon?" He turned back to face me...and stilled, as if

he'd only just now noticed my appearance. His lips twitched downward as he stared at my face. I bit my lip to suppress a sigh. I'd seen *that* look far too many times to count. I lifted my chin and stared firmly back, daring him to say something.

"Is something wrong?"

The prince blinked rapidly and hastily averted his gaze, his cheeks crimson—one of embarrassment, not of a man caught staring at a pretty girl.

"No," he lied before peeking up at me once more, as if he couldn't help but steal a second look to discern whether I was really as unattractive as I'd initially appeared.

I rolled my eyes, which likely marred my appearance even further, but I didn't care; I'd long ago stopped heeding my governess's attempts to supplement what I lacked in looks with social graces. Several snappy, sarcastic retorts burned on my tongue, but I bit on it hard to prevent them from escaping.

Instead I returned to the matter at hand. "Begging your pardon, Your Highness, but I'm less concerned about why your guards allowed me into the gardens and more concerned about leaving them. If you could please order your vines to open the entrance, I'll be on my way and not bother you any further."

His expression cleared as he regained his composure. "It's not so simple as that," he said. "Now tell me: why did you enter my gardens?"

It was more an order than a suggestion, and although he was a prince and thus very different than my father, I couldn't quite keep back my usual defiance whenever Father ordered me to do anything. "Forgive me, but my reasons for doing so are none of your concern."

His eyebrows lifted in clear astonishment at my disobedience, and remorse prickled my conscience that I was, as usual, being rather…*trying*, as my governess so often put it. Although I knew better than to be difficult for a prince, my apology lodged in my throat.

He sighed, as if this entire conversation had wearied him. "Considering you're on my grounds after you played off my guards' sentiments, it very much is my concern." His firm tone issued a warning I'd be a fool to disobey a second time.

I lifted my chin. "I stumbled upon the palace as I was wandering the woods. After hearing many marvelous stories about the enchanted palace gardens, I couldn't miss an opportunity to experience them for myself." It was part of the truth, at least.

For the first time since meeting this stoic prince, a shadow of a smile tugged on his lips. "Did they live up to your expectations?"

"Exceedingly. If only I could explore them further."

"Because of your foolishness, your wish will soon be granted." He folded his arms with another appraising look. "You've only given me part of your story. What were you doing wandering the woods without a chaperone?" His gaze flickered from my satchel to my torn and muddy clothes. "Ah, I see. You're obviously running away. But from what?"

Father's face filled my mind and I swallowed. "I can't tell you, so please don't press the matter any further. Just be assured that it was necessary."

Concern immediately softened his serious expression as he stepped closer. "Are you in some kind of trouble?"

I rapidly blinked to keep my burning tears at bay. I never cried, and I wasn't about to start now, in front of the prince. "I'm fine." It was an effort to keep my voice steady, and I knew by his frown that he'd seen through my lie. It was yet another offense against my future king.

But I was suddenly too weary to care. Thinking of Father had only reminded me how much time I'd lost. I glanced up at the sky. It was nearing noon. I had to hurry if I was to have any hope of staying ahead of him.

I forced a smile. "I truly am sorry I plucked your rose. I'd stay and continue to apologize, but I'm afraid I've already lost too much time and must leave." I dipped into a curtsy and turned to go, but I'd only taken a few steps before the prince's words caused me to still.

"I regret to inform you that you can't leave."

My heart flared as I slowly turned back around. "Why? Am I to be punished?"

"Not in the way you're likely imagining, but you'll receive a punishment nonetheless." His expression sobered. "I'm afraid you're trapped here, Miss Maren."

I stared at him. "What do you mean I'm *trapped?*"

"Exactly how it sounds: you can't leave the palace grounds."

I continued staring, my exhausted mind scrambling to comprehend his words. "Why? The vines let me in, so surely they'd let me leave as well."

He shook his head as he advanced a step closer, limping on his injured leg. "That would have been true...before." He gestured towards the foliage-covered entrance. "The vine archway is the only way in and out of these grounds, and it's controlled by the gardens, who've made it clear that they're forbidding you from leaving."

I gaped at him. "But...why?" My indignation swelled as he motioned to the rose I still held. "Because I took a rose?"

"An *enchanted* rose," he said calmly. "And don't look at me as if I'm responsible. Your offense was against the garden, and as such, they determine the consequences. I'm sorry, Miss Maren."

His apology was useless, for I had absolutely no intention of allowing myself to become a prisoner. Seeking freedom was why I'd run away in the first place, and I refused to trade one cage for another, even if this particular one was rather fascinating.

I set my jaw in determination. I'd found a way in, so I'd find a way out. I stomped past the prince and brushed the vines aside, searching for an exit, but the bougainvillea nipped me with its thorns.

I glowered. "Release me at once. I refuse to stay here." I made another attempt to push through the vines, but they only pricked me again. "*Ow.*" I drew back and sharpened my glare, but it had little effect, so I turned it on the crown prince instead, who watched solemnly. "Are they always so rude?"

"Only to thieves," he said wryly.

"Considering they tricked me into plucking that rose, such an accusation is unjust, so I suggest you order them to let me go."

"I told you it doesn't work that way, but since you clearly don't believe me, allow me to demonstrate." He turned to the vines. "I order you to release Miss Maren."

I waited with bated breath. The vines remained still and defiant. The prince glanced back at me.

"You see?"

My heart pounded wildly as the full implication of my situation settled over me, squeezing my chest with icy fear. "But...I don't understand. How can they not listen to you?"

He shrugged. "This is the garden's palace. I'm not the master here; *they* are."

The panic rose in my chest. "But...there has to be another exit—"

"There's only *one*," he repeated. "It's the archway the garden created for you to enter earlier. And as I've already said, the gardens have informed me they have no intention of releasing you."

"But *why?*"

He motioned to the flower I still held. "Magic has a set of laws, which you violated the moment you plucked that rose."

My breaths were coming up short. No, this couldn't be happening...I wouldn't let it happen. I spun on the vines. "Let me go! You have no right to keep me here after you tricked me."

They rustled in distinct refusal. I stomped my foot.

"Please don't do this. I just escaped my first prison. Are you really going to lock me away, too?"

The prince's eyes widened, and he turned to the vines with renewed determination. "I understand the conditions she's violated, but can't you make an exception?"

In response, an agitated wind blew roughly through the grounds. The prince's shoulders slumped as he turned back to me, his expression apologetic.

"They refuse to cooperate, which means you're trapped. I'm truly sorry, Miss Maren."

My frustration transformed into despair. I slowly sank to the ground. "This can't be happening."

My suffocating panic escalated, just as it had yesterday when Father told me what he'd done. I took a wavering breath in an attempt to calm myself. I couldn't give up. There had to be a way.

My gaze settled on the rose I still held. I extended it towards the garden like an offering. "Please accept this rose back as penance."

The plants stirred again as the breeze carried their whispers to their prince. I didn't need to understand them to know they were refusing my request; his hardening countenance said it all.

"Returning it now can't undo the damage you've inadvertently caused," he said. "Your action forged a connection to the garden, allowing it to lay claim on you."

My arm dropped limply to my side. "The magic...laid

claim on me?" For possibly the millionth time in my life, I cursed the curiosity that had led me to this. "What consequences come from plucking an enchanted rose?"

He nodded towards it. "A binding spell. You took something from the gardens, so they've connected you to them in its place." He looked out across the vast grounds with a pensive frown. "Such magic only occurs with that particular rosebush. The fact that the gardens led you there...I can't even begin to guess their motivation." He shook his head and returned his somber gaze to me. "The rose is like an hourglass. When the last petal falls..."

My heart beat wildly in trepidation. "What happens then?" I asked shakily.

He hesitated a moment, as if trying to figure out how much to tell me. "Then I'm afraid that the garden's punishment will be permanent."

CHAPTER 3

I stroked the velvet duvet of my new bed as I slowly took in my surroundings. I was in a *palace*, one as opulent and grand as I'd imagined...albeit gloomier.

I'd only caught glimpses of it as Prince Briar escorted me through the abandoned hallways, shrouded in shadows. Dozens of potted plants took up nearly every stoney surface, the only cheery details in the otherwise fortress-like structure; the exotic flowers' perfume clung to me along with the chill that seeped through my shawl.

Prince Briar didn't speak until we'd arrived at a door flanked by two potted miniature magnolia trees, who stirred as if to open the door, but the prince did it himself and bowed me through like a proper footman.

"Your room, Miss Maren."

I took a tentative step inside and looked around. Just like the corridors, the room was comprised of stone floors and walls, the only color coming from the forest-green rug, matching curtains, and the duvet, all patterned with a design of vines and roses. Despite my unexpected arrival, it was already clean and aired out, with a welcoming pot of red carnations atop the nightstand.

The room was simple yet lovely, but as beautiful as it was, it was still a prison. Desperation seized me again. I whirled to face the prince, who hovered on the threshold. "I won't stay here."

"Won't you?" Although his tone was calm, exasperation filled his eyes.

"No, I won't," I said firmly.

He sighed wearily. "Then would you prefer to stay somewhere else, perhaps somewhere less comfortable? The dungeon is also available."

I gasped and staggered back. "You wouldn't."

He instantly became repentant. "Of course I wouldn't. Forgive me, I shouldn't joke about such things. I understand you find yourself in a difficult situation, but allow me to assure you that this is one of our most comfortable rooms, and that while you're here, you'll be treated well."

"Regardless of your hospitality, I won't be staying. I refuse to believe that a bunch of enchanted leaves and branches can prevent me from leaving."

"Unfortunately, you don't have a choice." He folded his arms firmly across his chest and glared pointedly at the rose I'd plucked, still cradled in my hand. "I know my gardens. When they've made up their mind about something, there's no dissuading them."

Despair rose, pressing against my chest. "But if the curse isn't permanent already, isn't there a way to break it before the last petal drops and it becomes so?"

"It seems like there should be, but I wouldn't know. The gardens have never trapped someone before."

"But—"

"Every choice has a consequence. As much as the arrangement displeases me, I have little choice but to accept it."

I raised my eyebrow. "But you're a prince, are you not?"

"The *crown prince*," he clarified stiffly, as if I needed reminding. "And acting king, because Father—" He tightened his jaw and looked down the corridor, his gaze faraway. His expression had transformed from impatient to vulnerable so rapidly that I almost hesitated continuing to argue.

Almost, but unfortunately for him, I was nothing if not determined. "Well, as *acting king*, can't you control your own gardens?"

He returned his gaze to me with a wry smile. "I'm afraid it's not that simple. Now, is there anything you need?"

I glared at him. "I refuse to be a prisoner."

"You're not a prisoner; you're my guest, and as unwelcome as that arrangement is for both of us, you'll be treated as such." He started to turn away to leave but paused. "Is there anyone you would like me to notify of your whereabouts so I can reassure them of your safety?" Although his expression was nearly blank, I detected a flicker of curiosity.

"That won't be necessary," I said stiffly.

He frowned, clearly perplexed. "As you wish." He glanced at the rose. "I suggest you put that in water to make it last longer."

"Do enchanted roses really die?" I asked tartly.

"When they're plucked rather than given, then yes. It'll take several months, but eventually it'll begin to wilt, its petals will fall off one by one, and then..." Saying nothing more, he bowed crisply and departed.

I lingered in the doorway to watch him until he'd disappeared down the corridor before closing the door and leaning against it to slowly take in my new accommodations. As lovely as they were, it was still a prison. When I'd run away last night, I'd believed I was finally free, but my freedom had been fleeting considering fate had cruelly snatched it away again.

I sank onto the bed, exhausted from walking all night and from the suffocating emotions rising in my chest. The room seemed to be closing in around me. I took several steadying breaths, but it did little to lessen the rising despair, reminiscent of what I'd felt when Father had told me what he'd done.

I didn't want to remember it, but the memory returned unbidden—the one that had acted as the catalyst for my escaping in the dead of night...and leading me to the palace and my new prison.

"Miss Maren, what on earth have you done to your hem?"

I froze in my stealthy creeping down the hall at my governess's shriek and sighed. All hope vanished that I could sneak into my room and change without detection; luck had never been kind to me whenever I attempted to hide the evidence of my exploits.

I bit my lip to suppress another sigh as my governess hurried over, her horrified gaze riveted to the torn and muddy hem of my gown. "What happened?"

"I got it dirty." Obviously. Was any other explanation really needed?

She seized my arm to escort me not-so-gently back to my room to change. "Doing what?" By her darkening tone it was clear she didn't really want to know.

I filtered out some of my more wild afternoon activities and settled on the less condemning ones. "I climbed a tree, raced the boys next door, visited the horses in the stable..." None of which had been too scandalous.

She closed her eyes, as if praying for patience. "You know those activities aren't appropriate for a lady."

"Perhaps not, but they're appropriate for me."

She pursed her lips to keep her usual arguments at bay, ones she undoubtedly realized by now were a waste of breath. I'd seen that familiar look of hers enough to know that with my frequent mischief and lack of etiquette, she considered me a difficult charge.

It wasn't as if I were trying to be difficult...or perhaps I was. A little. It was an act of defiance for the years she'd spent trying to counteract my apparently unfortunate appearance by attempting to mold me into a proper lady.

But I didn't want to be molded into anything. This was who I was, and if I had to be a lady to make up for something I didn't consider to be an inadequacy, I wanted no part of it. But I'd been rebelling for so long that I was no longer sure whether I was still trying to fight against her expectations or if this was who I really was. It bothered me that I didn't know the difference.

The moment my bedroom door clicked shut behind us, she wasted no time in tugging the offending garment off and helping me dress in a clean one. I peered at my reflection and wrinkled my nose at the dress—one far too elegant for everyday wear, especially for someone like me who couldn't seem to keep out of mischief.

"Why are you dressing me in this?"

She yanked a brush through my hair. "Your father wants a word with you."

My stomach lurched. Oh dear...he never had anything pleasant to say, considering I'd always been a fierce disappointment to him. First I'd had the gall to have been born a girl rather than a boy, and despite my having been rambunctious enough to serve as a surrogate son, it hadn't been enough.

Then when mother had died without giving him any heirs, what had previously been indifference towards me had twisted into what I was convinced was actual hatred, which had only grown over the years as it became clear that with my lack of beauty I couldn't even be useful to him by securing an advantageous match that would increase his wealth and prestige.

As such, he treated me with cold disdain...when he didn't ignore me altogether. He only summoned me when he had something to tell me, and experience had taught me that whatever it was, I wasn't in for a pleasant conversation.

I gave a dramatic groan and my governess gave me a scolding tap with the hairbrush. "Keep your emotions in check, and don't slouch."

"Isn't it better for me to show my emotions now rather than later when I'm with him?"

She sighed but didn't argue against my logic, as I knew she wouldn't.

"Do you know why he's summoned me?"

"I'm not privy to the master's wants." She finished arranging my hair and set aside the brush to study me with a critical air, slowly turning me in order to observe the full effect of my appearance. Although I was dressed in a fine gown, it never made any difference to her.

She sighed wearily. "The dress is lovely and your posture is passable, but everything else...it's really such a pity."

There was no need to ask her to clarify—I knew what she was referring to. I stared into the mirror, trying to see the flaws in my appearance that everyone else seemed to notice, but I simply couldn't. My thick black hair had a wave I found quite lovely, and my copper-brown eyes were a unique and quite striking color. I also saw nothing wrong with my features, which everyone else deemed to be plain. It was simply a face, my face. Why did everyone else seem to think there was something wrong with it?

"I'm lovely," I said confidently.

She pursed her lips and said nothing, but it didn't matter what she thought. I gave myself a shaky smile, one that betrayed the nerves knotting my stomach at the thought of facing Father.

The anxious knots only tightened with each hesitant step I took towards his study. What could he want with me? Had he heard about the prank I'd played on the stablehand? Or about yesterday's mud fight with some of the younger male servants? Or—

I stopped in front of the study door. For a moment I remained *frozen before I managed to lift a shaking hand.* Keep control of your temper, *I scolded myself fiercely. With a final wavering breath, I knocked softly on the door.*

"Enter." Father's brisk tone was an order, one I didn't dare disobey. I entered his study, where Father sat at his desk, his fingers steepled and his dark eyes fixed on me. He jerked his chin towards the seat across from him, his wordless command to sit. I did with as much grace as if I were sitting in front of a king—or in this case a tyrant, one who'd ruled my entire life with an iron fist.

"I've finally found a husband for you," he said without preamble.

My breath caught. "A...husband?" Impossible. The only men I was well acquainted with were all lower class. Surely Father wouldn't condone a match with any of them.

Which meant this match was arranged, meaning I wouldn't like it. Although we'd spent little time together over the years, I knew enough about Father to know that whatever man he approved of would be one I'd detest.

"Yes," he said curtly. "One of my investors: Lord Brone."

Lord Brone? *The name meant nothing to me, but already my chest tightened as foreboding clenched me in its icy grip.*

"He's my wealthiest and most valuable investor," Father continued, oblivious to my escalating panic. "He's heard of my recent... difficulties, and has offered his assistance...for a price."

My heart thudded wildly as I sensed where this horrible conversation was leading. Several months ago, Father had lost his most valuable ship when it was en route to a very profitable trading post. The recent selling of some of our more valuable pieces had already told me our situation was dire; apparently it was worse than I could have imagined...and that I was the latest commodity Father would put up for sale.

"You've offered my hand?"

He nodded. "He'll pay generously."

"Isn't it normally the father who pays a handsome dowry to

persuade someone to marry his daughter?" Bitterness laced the respectful tone that up until now I'd fought—and was now failing —to maintain.

"In most situations yes, but this is being done as a favor to me. He's one of my most faithful clients as well as an old friend. He believes I'm only experiencing a minor setback and is investing in my business in hopes of a later profit. Yet he isn't a philanthropist; he wants something in exchange, as any savvy businessman would."

"And he wants me?" My tone was skeptical, for I highly doubted that. No one wanted me, and I wanted to keep it that way, at least in instances like this.

"I haven't informed him of your—" He motioned up and down, gesturing to all of me.

I folded my arms, too angry to mask my emerging scowl. "I'm surprised such a wealthy man who can save your business hasn't already married. Why hasn't he found a wife before now?"

"Because most men have been...hesitant to offer their daughters. It's been a source of great frustration for him."

Whatever had caused other fathers' hesitancy, obviously mine had no such qualms. I opened my mouth to retort, but he snapped his hand up, silencing my words.

"Further arguing is pointless. We've already signed the engagement contract. It's done."

It's done—my fate sealed with two heartless words. But I refused to go down without a fight. "And you don't worry he'll feel tricked when he sees me?"

Father shrugged. "He's a practical man more than a sentimental one. He's getting on in years and needs a caregiver and an heir. You should fulfill those responsibilities satisfactorily, which is all that matters."

My stomach twisted. I took several steadying breaths in an attempt to push the nausea away, but it only continued to churn.

"What if I'm too feisty for him?" Which I'd do everything in my power to ensure.

Father smirked. "Then it'd be prudent to warn you that his reputation precedes him as being a rather...harsh man. You'd be a fool to rile him."

Which meant only one thing. My stomach coiled in fear: I was being given to an abusive, heartless brute.

Father was surveying me as if I were up for auction. "It's a pity you don't look more like your mother."

It wouldn't have made a difference. It wouldn't have caused him to care for me, for seeing me would only remind him of how much he missed her.

I pushed away memories of Mother and lifted my chin. "You cannot make me marry him."

Father stood to glower down at me. "That's irrelevant; you'll do as I say and marry him if I have to drag you to the chapel and threaten you into saying your vows. Don't think I won't."

And he would. Panic swelled, clawing at my throat. Marriage... to a man I didn't know or love; even worse, he was an abuser. No, that wouldn't happen. I wouldn't let it. My defiance swelled within me. I tightened my jaw. "I won't."

His eyes narrowed dangerously, but I ignored the warning in them to hold my tongue, for I refused to be silent and submissive.

"I won't marry him," I continued firmly. "You can threaten me, but you cannot force me. I refuse to attach myself to such a beast of a man."

He glared and leaned in closer. "You seem to be under the impression you have a choice in the matter; you don't. It's done, Maren."

There was always a choice. "I do, and I've made mine." I stood to leave, but Father reached across the desk to seize my arm and yank me back down.

"Don't leave until I've excused you," he snarled. "And you won't leave until you've seen reason. You'll marry Lord Brone if it's the last thing you ever do. Do you understand me?"

Anger seared through me, hot and burning, until I was seeing red. I glared at him but said nothing.

"Let me be frank with you, Maren," he hissed darkly. "This is your last chance for security. Due to your looks and your rambunctious ways, you will never get another offer, so unless you want to end up on the streets, you'd best accept this one gratefully."

"I don't care if this is my only offer; I don't want to marry."

It was a lie—I did. But I didn't want to be forced into an arrangement; I wanted to find love...even though that wish felt impossible. For while I saw nothing wrong with myself, apparently everyone else did, especially men.

But even in these less-than-ideal circumstances, I refused to settle for unhappiness. Since marriage was a seemingly impossible dream, I'd have to settle for a life alone, one I was determined to fill with adventures. Being strapped to a horrible man who'd acquired me through a business deal with Father and who would undoubtedly make my life miserable was something I refused to tolerate. It was my life, and I refused to give control of it to anybody but myself.

The rest of my earlier panic gradually subsided, replaced with a sense of peace. I made up my mind right then and there about what I'd do should Father remain unyielding...which unsurprisingly he did. He spent a good hour yelling and threatening me, which I took calmly, my resolve for my chosen course of action giving me the inner strength to withstand his emotional blows.

"He'll come for you first thing tomorrow morning," Father finally concluded. "Until then, you'll be locked in your bedroom. Now leave."

He dismissed me with a disgusted wave of his hand. I rose gracefully, keeping my expression submissive so as to not allow him to detect any sign of my resistance, while inside I was defiant.

For once I was glad Father scarcely knew me, for he clearly

didn't realize that a bolted door couldn't keep me locked away, not when there was a perfectly good window that I could use to escape in the dead of night.

Father couldn't keep me a prisoner.

BUT APPARENTLY, the enchanted gardens of the Malvagarian palace could.

CHAPTER 4

A soft touch caressed my brow, stirring me from a restless sleep I hadn't realized I'd fallen into. I groggily opened my eyes, expecting to see a lady's maid hovering over me, but instead...I bolted upright with a startled gasp. The potted carnations on my nightstand hastily withdrew before swaying in apology.

Surely I'm still dreaming. But considering I was trapped inside a palace known for its enchanted gardens, that was unlikely. The enchantment must extend to the plants within the palace walls as well.

The carnations were still for a moment, as if suddenly shy at having been caught, before one tentatively reached out again to stroke my hair in a motherly way, its petals soft and almost tender. My hair was a tangled mess from my nap, and the leaves began to patiently work through the tangles, their touch gentle.

I yawned and rubbed my eyes. "How long was I asleep?"

They gestured towards the window, where through the slit in the drapes I could see the sun hanging low in the sky as evening neared. My stomach jolted. I'd slept most of the afternoon away, losing more time than I could afford.

I nearly tripped over the blanket someone had draped over me as I stumbled from the bed and tugged open the curtains to stare across the grounds, cast in a sheen of golden light from the sun hugging the horizon. My breath caught, for from my vantage point the grounds looked like a colorful patchwork quilt. My ever-present curiosity returned, pleading for me to explore...

No, there wasn't time for that. I had to leave as soon as possible. As soon as night fell I'd use the cover of darkness to sneak away; no prince or enchanted gardens could keep *me* trapped against my will. Surely there had to be other avenues of escape. My mind worked frantically as I planned, pausing only at the knock on my door.

I turned as it opened and a maid bustled in, an elegant crimson dress draped over her arm. She swept into a curtsy the moment she spotted me standing near the window. "Good evening, Miss Maren. His Highness has assigned me to tend to you for the duration of your stay."

Which will only be for a few hours more. I forced a smile. "How kind of him."

She came closer and paused to stare at me before she hastily blinked and bridged the remaining distance between us.

"His Highness has requested you join him for dinner, so I've arrived to help you dress." She held up the gown, made of satin and embroidered with designs in gold thread, a dress far too fine for me to run away in. "This gown belongs to Princess Reve, which he has graciously allowed you to borrow."

I longingly fingered the golden trim. "And she won't mind?"

The maid hesitated. "She—I'm sure not, considering she's

in no position to use her wardrobe."

I puckered my brow. How peculiar. But no matter; I couldn't accept such a gesture, as tempting as it was. I stepped away. "I won't be joining His Highness for dinner."

She gaped at me in disbelief. "But he's requested it. Surely you can't refuse."

I likely couldn't, for when it came to the royal family, *request* was a synonym for *command*. But the last thing I wanted was to dine with the man who, intentionally or not, was effectively my captor. Although he claimed it was his garden's doing, the fact he'd stood by and done nothing made it all too easy to cast part of the blame at his feet.

"I am refusing," I said clearly. "His Highness told me I'm to be his guest, and as his guest I have the right to choose where to take my meals, and I'd prefer to take them in my room."

She blinked at me. "But—"

"I'm afraid I must insist on this," I said. "You may thank His Highness for the invitation, but I will not accept it." I turned my back on her to face the window again. In the course of our conversation, the sun had sunk even lower, replacing the previous pools of light with shadows, which made the gardens appear almost spooky.

The maid hesitated before she took her leave. The moment the door clicked shut behind her, I relaxed my stiffened stance. My stomach growled in clear disapproval of my decision. The makeshift meal I'd eaten as I'd wandered the woods felt so long ago, and a lavish meal would have been most welcome. But I refused to be swayed; I wouldn't dine with the prince.

"No complaints," I firmly scolded my hunger. "We must be strong. We cannot allow His Highness to try to earn our good favor. Besides, we need to concentrate on getting out of here so we can be on our way."

My stomach gave another gurgle in objection and I sighed. Perhaps I shouldn't have been so stubborn, but it was too late now.

To distract myself from my gnawing insides, I returned my thoughts to my escape plan: I'd sneak away when it grew dark. Once I found a way outside the gate, I'd head north... no, south. Or was it east? Regardless, I'd head for the capital, which I remembered from my studies was only a mile or so away from this main palace. With a steady pace, I'd arrive before midnight and could have a nice hot meal at an inn, and then tomorrow I could begin looking for work and a more permanent place to stay. All would be well.

Another knock sounded at the door. "Miss Maren?"

I clenched my jaw. Prince Briar. "What is it?" I asked stiffly.

"I'm here to escort you to dinner."

Even though he couldn't see it on the other side of the door, I scowled. "I'm afraid I'm not going to dinner. I'm not hungry."

My stomach growled again in protest. I prayed that His Highness hadn't heard it. Then he'd know I was lying...but by his heavy silence, I knew he likely suspected it already.

He sighed, confirming my suspicion. "It's not in my nature to force anyone, especially a lady, but I must insist on your eating something. If you don't want to join me, then I'll arrange for a tray to be brought to your room." He waited for my reply. When none came, I heard his footsteps retreat down the hallway.

True to his word, a tray of food arrived shortly after. I half expected a small meal, but with the fine cuts of meat, fruits, and elegant side dishes, I'd clearly received a plate from the prince's own table. Guilt seeped over me at his thoughtful gesture, and for a moment I wavered in my resentment—perhaps I'd been treating him unfairly.

I gave my head a firm shake. No, I was treating him exactly how he deserved. He might be kind, but an honorable warden was still a warden.

I wrapped up the food I could easily take with me when I escaped before settling on the edge of the bed to pull the tray closer. I was delighted to discover that the food was still hot; the mouthwatering steam rose up to tickle my cheeks, and the delicious meal warmed my insides as I disregarded my manners and ate ravenously.

I paused mid-bite when something brushed against my ankle. I glanced down to find that a potted plant near my feet had reached out with its long leaves to brush against my ripped hem. It shook in clear disapproval; if it could speak, it'd certainly be *tsking*.

I reached out a hesitant fingertip to caress one of the leaves and words tickled my mind. *Dirty and torn. We must mend it.*

"Thank you for the gesture, but there's no need." After all, if I was about to escape, there was little point.

But the plant ignored me as it quickly procured needle and thread from the nightstand drawer and immersed itself in its sewing. I stared, my food entirely forgotten, as I watched it mend first the hem, followed by one of the holes in my skirt, then another.

The carnations suddenly brushed my hand, causing me to jump. *Eat*, they ordered, and I dutifully returned to my meal, finishing it in only a few more bites. I stood while the plant was still mid-stitch. "I'm going to explore the gardens."

The carnations tilted themselves towards the window, where the sun had sunk lower in the sky while I'd been eating my meal.

"I don't care that it's dark," I said, guessing its concern. "After all, I spent half the night traipsing the woods without incident." I started for the door but was blocked by another plant, this one occupying the space between the door and the wardrobe. Before I could protest, it opened the bureau and retrieved my shawl, which it draped gently across my shoulders.

I stared at the plants in wonder. They'd shown me far more kindness after a brief acquaintance than I'd ever received from Father or my governess. It almost made it difficult to leave. But I had to.

With a muttered thank you, I cracked the door open and peered into the shadowy corridor, half expecting guards to be flanking the door to prevent my escape, but it was abandoned. I clutched my satchel close and crept down the hallway, guided by the light flickering from the torches lining the walls.

My footsteps were muffled by the rugs lining the stone floors, making it easy to be stealthy. I kept my eyes peeled for any servants, but just like the journey to my bedroom hours earlier, I encountered no one save several plants, who stilled as I passed as if watching me attentively, although thankfully they made no move to stop me.

The corridors were a twisty labyrinth, but I'd paid careful attention to the route when Prince Briar had escorted me earlier, so I had no fear of getting lost. *Left, right, down that hallway, another right, another left...* The towering oak front doors loomed ahead. I slowed as I neared, warily eying the guards rigidly blocking my path, the first human inhabitants I'd seen within the palace other than the servants who served me.

"Good evening," I said brightly. "Might I have permission to take a stroll before bed?"

They eyed my satchel suspiciously but must have been told to treat me with deference, for they stepped aside without comment. I smirked as I flounced past them. Just like when I'd run away from the manor, escaping now was all too simple.

Outside, night had fully fallen, shrouding everything in darkness. The nearly full moon provided enough silverly light to easily maneuver my way down the steps and up the path that led to the exit. The plants lining the path bobbed as I passed, seeming both curious about this stranger and excited to make my acquaintance. Tempting... but I had to leave tonight if I had any hope of staying ahead of Father, lest he capture me and deliver me to Lord Brone as if I were nothing more than one of his commodities.

I reached the vines, who lifted themselves up in anticipation of a confrontation. But I was equally prepared for a battle of wits. I pressed my hands on my hips. "You can't keep me a prisoner. It's grossly unjust to punish me for a crime you tricked me into committing."

They didn't budge, but simply stared at me.

"Please, you must release me. I'm certain my family is worried." I wasn't above begging or lying in order to gain my freedom.

A honeysuckle reached out to lightly caress me. *We know you've run away, so we've granted you shelter.*

Drat, I'd forgotten I'd played off the sympathies of the vines on the other side in order to enter the gardens in the first place.

I switched strategies. "I could never impose on the crown prince; he has many duties to fulfill and I fear that my presence would only distract him. Besides, if I stay here, surely my father will come looking for me..."

We'll keep you safe. The honeysuckle gave my hand a little pat before withdrawing. Clearly, the vines had no intention of releasing me. Stubborn things.

I heaved a frustrated growl before looking around for another means of escape. Nearby stood a majestic willow growing near the wall, one I could easily climb in order to scale over the top. I grinned. Perfect.

I readjusted my satchel and started for the tree. The vines immediately began tittering, whether in agitation or worry, I wasn't sure. I leapt and grabbed the lowest bough to hoist myself up, but before I could climb any higher the tree *moved*, leaning away from the wall.

I gasped. "What are you doing?"

It inched even further away. I scrambled up the tree, hoping I could reach the top before I was too far from the wall to climb over...but the willow was faster. By the time I was level with the top of the wall, we were leaning several yards away, too far to jump.

I growled in frustration. "Your mischief won't discourage me. The grounds are vast. I'll simply find another tree, and if that one pulls the same trick, I'll find another way to escape. Don't think you can keep me trapped here against my will."

I began to climb down, but I'd only gone a few feet when a jasmine vine untangled itself from the others to coil around my waist and pull me from the tree. My stomach lurched as I gave a startled yelp.

"Put me down."

The vine obediently lowered me but made no move to release me, even as I stumbled and fell to the ground. The others snaked over and began to twist around my ankles. I tried to shake them off, but to no avail.

"Release me at once. You can't keep me a prisoner. I won't let you."

I struggled to pry away the vines immobilizing my limbs, but they held firm. My frustration mounted, as did my sense of helplessness, as suffocating as the vines entangling me.

Approaching footsteps sounded along the cobblestones. I didn't even need to turn around to know who was approaching. "Good evening, Your Highness."

The footsteps paused, and I reluctantly turned towards him. He held a glowing lantern, whose light illuminated his bewildered expression. I was undoubtedly quite a sight—ratty hair, tangled skirts, and held captive by vines.

He remained still, but a wry smile slowly appeared, as if he found my capture amusing. I released an annoyed huff. "A little help would be greatly appreciated."

He narrowed his eyes but made no move to assist me. "The guards informed me you were likely up to mischief. I can see that they weren't mistaken."

I sighed in defeat. I should have known the guards at the front doors would report my suspicious behavior.

The prince's look was far too knowing. "You tried to escape, didn't you?"

As tempting as it was, there was no use lying. "Can you blame me? I'd have thought you'd be in support of such a plan considering you don't want me here almost as much as I don't want to stay." I made another attempt to tug off the vines coiled around my ankle, but they only tightened. "Let me go," I snapped. Naturally they ignored me.

"As I've told you several times already," Prince Briar said, "you can't escape, not after you plucked a rose."

"It seems far too cruel a punishment for such an offense," I said.

"Might I remind you that *I'm* not the one holding you captive…or weren't you listening the other times I told you?"

"Unfortunately, listening isn't one of my strengths." I gave another futile tug on the vines before giving up and glaring at the prince. "Whether I'm your prisoner or the gardens', I'd prefer to serve my sentence free from being tied up."

"Although your current predicament is one of your own making, I'll heed your wishes." He stepped forward to give the vines a stern—if slightly indulgent—look. "Release her.

There's no need to keep her entangled; she can't leave the garden."

Of course the stubborn things refused to obey him. Instead they rustled, as if telling him something. The corner of his mouth twitched.

"She tried to breech the wall by climbing a tree?" He glanced towards the willow that had nearly uprooted itself in order to thwart my escape. "That explains why it's out of place." He gave me a inquisitive look. "So you're a lady who climbs trees?"

"Why shouldn't I climb trees?" I turned my scowl onto the vines. "Now are you going to obey the prince and release me or not?"

To my fierce relief they did, finally loosening their tight hold on my waist, wrists, and ankles. It felt as if I'd just taken off a corset; I released a whooshing breath. Prince Briar extended his hand to help me up, but I ignored it as I clambered to my feet and brushed off my ruined skirts, an excuse to avoid the prince's gaze. But I could only delay my obligatory gratitude for so long.

"Thank you for your assistance," I mumbled.

He nodded curtly before strolling past me to stand in front of the vines, which were slowly retreating back to their usual place. "Any word?"

They shook themselves in a distinct *no*. Frustration hardened the prince's previously concerned expression.

"No word?" Panic filled his voice. "That's unacceptable. Please, you have to find out *something*. You know she's not in her right mind. I can't bear to think of her wandering alone. If you hadn't let her out..."

My curiosity was immediately piqued as the vines drooped from their scolding. Prince Briar tightened his jaw.

"Inform me the moment the guards return so that I can speak with them."

Without another word, he returned to my side to offer his arm, which I took mutely so he could escort me back into the gloomy palace, which was just as dank and chilly as the crisp night air. I tightened my shawl more securely around my shoulders.

For several minutes neither of us spoke, the only sound being our echoing footsteps. I kept my gaze focused on the golden pool of lantern light leading us down one winding corridor after another.

"What were you discussing with the vines?" I asked when the silence had grown unbearable.

He said nothing. Clearly His Highness didn't wish to speak of it, but I was too inquisitive to let the matter drop.

"It sounded as if someone is missing. Who is it?" My mind immediately returned to the maid's strange reaction after I'd asked whether the princess would mind me wearing her clothes. "Is it your sister?"

He stilled, his breaths suddenly coming up fast. By his reaction, I knew my guess was correct.

"Where is she?" I asked. "What happened to her?"

"I don't wish to speak of Reve." He began walking again, his strides long and agitated; it was an effort to keep up with him.

"How did she go missing?" I pressed. "It sounded as if she wandered out of the grounds?" Why could she so easily do so and I was still trapped? It was most unfair.

"Please, Miss Maren, I don't wish to speak of her."

Ah, a mystery. With that, the enchanted grounds, and the rumors about the curse afflicting the prince, there was no shortage of things to investigate if I was forced to stay.

Speaking of that curse... "And what of the curse you're under? If we're forced to be companions for the unforesee-able future, surely I have the right to learn of it?"

"I don't wish to divulge those details either." His tone,

while polite, was underlined with impatience; I was clearly getting to him, just as I seemed to do with everyone eventually. "Please, Miss Maren, I'd appreciate it if while around me you at least attempted to quench your curiosity."

I gave a reluctant nod, but my attention was soon captured by the way the prince was limping, much as he had earlier, although he'd changed his clothing so there was no longer blood to act as evidence of his earlier injury. "Might you at least tell me what happened to your leg?"

We rounded a sharp corner. "*You* happened," he grumbled.

I swelled indignantly. "I certainly didn't cut—"

"There are consequences for every action," he said curtly.

I wrinkled my brow. "Are you suggesting that my plucking the rose cut your leg? That's not my fault. The gardens are the ones who led me to—"

"That might be true, but *you're* the one who chose to take a rose, not them," he said. "Every decision comes with inevitable consequences, many of which affect more than just you. I advise you to consider that more carefully the next time you're *curious.*"

I tightened my jaw to keep myself from retorting something rather disrespectful, and we spent the remainder of the short journey in tense silence. It was a relief to finally reach my bedroom, where he bowed and departed without even a *good night.*

I stared after him, my heart pounding wildly and my mind whirling with all the clues he'd revealed about the strange goings on in this palace—curses, magical gardens that he seemed somehow connected to, and now a missing princess.

Despite my predicament, a smile tugged on my lips. There were a lot of mysteries here, and if I had to remain trapped indefinitely, I was determined to solve them.

CHAPTER 5

I looked up and down the corridor lined with doors, each of which led somewhere that still remained unexplored.

The Malvagarian Palace was vast and gloomy, devoid of color in its architecture, but it made up for it in the variety of plants and vibrant flowers that filled each room and the fantastic treasures I'd already discovered. The walls were adorned with lavish tapestries and paintings, while the corridors were lined with well-crafted suits of armor and tables laden with gilded vases and curious decorations. Even after three days poking around every nook and cranny, I'd barely scratched the surface of all the palace contained; there was simply so much to see.

During my wanderings I'd stumbled upon the vast library, filled with towering shelves of books covering all manner of subjects, but after hours of searching I found nothing dealing with enchanted rosebushes or magical entrapments. Despite that disappointment, exploring provided the very distraction I needed from my hopeless circumstances, with the added bonus that it helped me avoid the prince. I hadn't seen or spoken to him since the day I'd arrived; I'd done my best to avoid him and was quite pleased I'd succeeded.

He wasn't the only one I was avoiding—I hadn't set foot on the grounds since my failed escape attempt. I'd awoken the first morning of my new sentence to rain, and although I normally didn't mind being outside during a storm, I gratefully seized the excuse to maintain my grudge against the gardens for what they'd done to me.

Despite my stubborn determination, curiosity tickled my senses every time I wandered past a window and caught a glimpse of the fantastic wonders of the grounds just awaiting my discovery, and this yearning only grew with each passing day.

But I refused to give in, so I redoubled my efforts to explore as much of the palace as possible, venturing anywhere that wasn't locked and avoiding the entire east wing, which was coated with dust and shrouded in cobwebs, as if it'd been abandoned for quite some time.

Surprisingly, I encountered very few staff in my wanderings, just the occasional servant going about their work and a few guards, all of whom looked at me in pity but none of whom offered to help me. The advisors I encountered who lived in a separate section of the palace also proved unhelpful.

The gates had opened on several occasions to allow ambassadors, nobility, and messengers in and out, but whenever this occurred, the garden would thwart me in some way, so that by the time I reached the gate, it was always closed, keeping me imprisoned. If I was going to escape—and I certainly *would*—it'd have to be accomplished on my own merits.

One afternoon nearly a week into my sentence, I came across a section of the palace that I hadn't yet explored. It didn't have the look of being abandoned, but the atmosphere was cold and dreary, with an unsettling feeling of neglect. There weren't any signs I *shouldn't* be here, which was as good as an invitation.

My footsteps echoed ominously as I ventured down the corridor. Despite the air of neglect, the furnishings and decorations were more lavish than I'd seen in other sections of the palace. I was drawn towards the partially open door at the end of the hall, one that was intricately carved and gilded in gold.

My breath caught as I peered inside. Past the spacious sitting room stood another open door leading to a bedroom with a large four-poster bed, where an elderly man lay, staring gauntly up at his canopy, his raspy breaths loud enough I could hear them even from the corridor. The royal insignia adorning the tapestries on the wall confirmed my suspicions: this was the King of Malvagaria.

I knew little about our kingdom's monarch, only that his health had been deteriorating for quite some time. But from what I could see from my vantage point, His Majesty was not just unhealthy, but dying.

I startled as the guard standing outside the door spoke. "You shouldn't be here."

I started to back away, but the king had turned at the guard's barking order and noticed me hovering in the door-way. I froze and held my breath. Would he get angry with me for being where I shouldn't?

He tried to lift his head. "Reve, darling? Is that you?"

My stomach jolted and the guard raised his eyebrows in question. I silently ordered myself to move away, but I remained frozen. The king continued to stare before a smile filled his wrinkly face. He reached for me.

"Reve?" A raspy cough shook his body, and before I could talk myself out of it, I crossed both rooms to the pitcher of water at his bedside. Ignoring the attending nurse's admonitions that I shouldn't be here, I hastily poured him a glass and helped him drink it. He managed a few gulps that dribbled water down his chin before he leaned back with a sigh.

"Thank you, darling." He closed his eyes for a weary moment before he reopened them to study me. His brow furrowed. "You're not Reve." His voice was weak from illness and disuse. "Nor are you Gemma."

I swallowed. "No, I'm not." My tone was apologetic.

"Where are they?" he asked weakly. "Where are my girls?"

"I don't know, Your Majesty."

"Please, you must find them. I'm so worried—"

His pleas were interrupted by another coughing fit that shook his entire weak frame and caused the nurse to hurry to his bedside, where she eased him into a sitting position until his coughing subsided. When it passed, he fell back against the pillows and began to ramble incoherently, repeatedly asking after Reve and Gemma, his entire expression distraught.

Helplessness pressed against my chest. "I'm sure they're alright." Unsure what else to do, I settled on the edge of his bed and took his hand, cold and clammy within mine. I gently patted it. "It'll be alright." I repeated the words several times, making my tone as soothing as possible, and gradually the king began to relax.

"What are you doing?"

I sprang from the bed and spun around. Prince Briar stood in the doorway carrying a tray. "I—" I had no explanation for why I'd thrust my presence onto the king.

The prince strode over in quick, agitated steps, his dark gaze narrowed at me. "Why are you in my father's room?"

"I—the door was open, and I was curious, and I—I'm sorry."

I expected him to get angry, but he looked far too

exhausted to summon up the emotion. Instead, he released a long breath. "Is there anything you're not curious about?"

"Not really."

To my surprise, his lips twitched, as if he was tempted to smile but thought better of it. He set the tray on the nightstand before taking the seat beside his father and reaching for his hand. "Father, it's Briar. Would you like some lunch?" His tone was incredibly gentle.

The king blinked. "Briar?" It took him a moment to focus on his son, but when he did he smiled. "Briar. It's wonderful to see you, lad." He affectionately patted his cheek.

"You too, Father. You're looking well." Prince Briar's voice was cheerful, masking the worry lining his features.

"Did you see that Reve finally came to visit me?" The king gave me a fatherly smile such as one I'd never before received, causing my heart to lurch. "She seems to be doing well. I'm so relieved. You know how worried I've been about her."

The prince didn't even glance at me. "You may excuse yourself, Miss Maren."

Despite his direct order, I couldn't move, the memory of the king's loving gaze keeping me rooted to the spot. Prince Briar gave me a look that clearly warned me to heed his command, and I dared not ignore his wishes a second time. I curtsied and slipped from the room, but I couldn't resist lingering outside the door, where the guard eyed me suspiciously.

Prince Briar brushed his father's wispy white hair off his damp brow, deep concern etching his entire expression. "How are you feeling, Father?"

The king didn't answer. Instead he looked around, his gaze lost. "Where's Reve? Why did she leave?"

"That wasn't Reve."

The king's brow furrowed in confusion. "Are you sure? She looked like my Reve."

"No." The prince's tone was patient. "Their coloring is similar and she was wearing her dress, but it wasn't her."

The king frowned, clearly disappointed. "Then where is she? She hasn't visited me in a while."

The prince swallowed, looking as if he could barely keep hold of his emotions. "She—" He hesitated, clearly not wanting to inform His Majesty that the princess was missing. "I'm sure she'll visit you soon. You know how she is—a bit self-absorbed, trapped in her own world…"

The king managed a breathless chuckle. "Dear Reve." His look became earnest. "And what of Gemma? Have you found her tower yet?"

"No, but I've spared no guards in the search. We'll find her. I promise." He gave his father a reassuring squeeze of his hand.

"And how is Drake and his new wife…now what was her name…"

"Rhea. They're both doing well. I just got a letter from them. Shall I read it to you?"

"I'd like that." The king settled back against his pillows with a weary sigh. "I just returned from my annual tour of the kingdom. This time I took young Briar with me. He was so excited, especially to meet the people. What a dear boy he is. He just turned twelve…" His eyes fluttered closed and the prince's composure faltered, revealing the fierce concern he'd been masking.

"I'll read the letter to you after lunch, for I want you to eat first. We can talk about this trip you took with Briar while you do so. Can you sit up?" He tenderly helped him scoot upright before picking up the soup he'd brought to spoon-feed his father.

I knew I needed to move away and leave them to their

privacy, but I was riveted to the scene. I watched the entire visit, unable to look away from the gentle way the prince fed his father, the animated way he read his brother's letter, the serious way they discussed his duties as acting king in his father's brief moments of lucidity, and then the way they both lit up as Briar related stories from the prince and his siblings' childhood.

The king mostly listened, save for occasional interruptions asking where his daughters were. Each time the prince soothed his father's worries, not seeming the least bit impatient with him, and His Majesty soon relaxed and allowed his son to resume their previous conversation.

When the king wasn't inquiring after his children, he listened to his son with rapt attention, the fatherly affection obvious in his entire manner. If I'd been born a boy, would my father have looked at me in such a way? But then I remembered the look the king had given me when he'd mistaken me for his daughter and I realized that such a look came from the man he was, one my father wasn't at all.

Soon the king's eyes began to droop. The prince rose with obvious reluctance. "I should let you rest, but I'll be back tonight."

In response, the king fumbled for the prince's hand and squeezed it weakly. "Tell Reve to visit me again."

"I will." Prince Briar leaned down and kissed his father's forehead before taking his leave, pausing near the bedroom door to give his father a lingering look before departing.

Too late I realized I was about to be discovered and had just missed my opportunity to leave undetected. I scrambled away and started down the hallway with rapid steps. Behind me, I heard the door to the king's sitting room open all the way and the prince step into the corridor.

"Miss Maren?"

Drat. I turned with a forced smile. "Good afternoon, Your

Highness." I swept into a curtsy. The prince stared at me for a long moment before sighing.

"You eavesdropped, didn't you?"

"I—yes."

I expected a reprobation, but the prince said nothing as he tugged the door all the way closed and rested his forehead on it with a weary sigh, as if his visit had drained him. He stood there for a long moment before he pushed away from the door and turned towards me. I expected him to be angry, but he only looked haggard. I still felt scolded all the same.

I shifted guiltily. "I'm sorry, I know it wasn't my place to watch you with the king."

"Then why did you?"

How could I explain? It had been more than curiosity, for watching the prince with his father...I'd never seen such tenderness and affection between a parent and their child. "I didn't expect...that is, I—" I lowered my eyes, unable to find the right words.

The prince sighed again and rubbed his temples, as if warding off a headache. "Regardless of your reasons, I'd appreciate it if you limited your curiosity to exploring the palace rather than disturbing my father."

"I didn't mean to bother him. When I saw I'd come upon the bedroom of the king, I started to leave, but before I could, he noticed me and called for me."

"He thought you were Reve."

It seemed hard to believe I could be mistaken for a princess. I eyed the worry filling the prince's eyes. "Is there any word—"

"I don't want to talk about it," he said brusquely, and I snapped my mouth shut.

I glanced towards the now closed door, where the King of Malvagaria lay beyond. I'd never thought I'd ever meet my king, and even if I had, I'd surely have imagined a meeting far more grand, one where His Majesty received me regally rather than on his sickbed.

"What's wrong with him?"

"He's ill," the prince said, and I was relieved that his tone had softened. "We've tried everything, but...now we're just waiting."

"Surely there's something that can be done," I said. "Are there any healing herbs to be found in your enchanted gardens?"

"There's nothing," the prince said. "While certain plants found in the gardens can preserve life, they're all for cases where someone is dying of unnatural means. As for Father... his time is simply coming. Unfortunately, magic can't solve everything."

In that moment, he looked as if he carried the heaviest burden—not only of his father's impending death, but also the responsibilities of the crown that would transfer to him when that day came.

He looked so vulnerable in that moment, so *human*, that I couldn't resist bridging the distance between us to rest my hand on his arm. He startled but didn't pull away. "I'm very sorry," I murmured. He gave a rigid nod. "I hope you find your sisters before—"

"That's my greatest wish, but I fear I'll be too late."

My heart wrenched at the thought. I nibbled my lip and glanced towards the king's door. "Would it be alright if I visited him? I know I'm not Princess Reve, but if he thinks I am...or will that only make the situation worse?"

The prince considered for a moment before offering a shadow of a smile. "You'd do that for him? Really?" At my nod, his small smile fully emerged. "Thank you. You're truly kind."

Kind was not often a compliment I received, but in this instance I didn't deserve his praise. Guilt tightened my chest that I'd led him to believe my offer had been made out of the goodness of my heart rather than my own selfish desires.

"Please, there's no need to thank me, not when my motives aren't entirely selfless. I simply like him very much." Not to mention I wanted to know what it felt like to have a real father...even if he was one who was ill, both in body and mind.

"Regardless of your motives, I appreciate the gesture all the same. Thank you."

Something changed in the prince's countenance, and he looked at me almost as if he were seeing me for the first time. My cheeks warmed as I dipped into a hasty curtsy to take my leave, but I'd only taken a few steps when he spoke.

"Please wait, Miss Maren."

I glanced over my shoulder. "Yes, Your Highness?"

"I wanted to know if you—" He hesitated, embarrassment darkening his cheeks. He cleared his throat and straightened. "I was about to go down to luncheon. I know you've been enjoying taking your meals in your own room, but I was hoping...would you please accept my invitation to join me?"

I blinked in surprise. "I—" I stopped, unsure how to answer.

He shifted from foot to foot. "I know you're upset with me, and you have every right to be, even though I assure you I hate the thought of your being trapped here and would free you if I could. But since you're here..." He peered up at me with a shy, hopeful look.

My first reaction was to adamantly refuse, but my usual hot anger had no sooner flared than it dimmed.

You know it's not his *fault*, my conscience whispered. *It's the gardens'*. Thus it'd be unjust to harbor a grudge against the prince, especially after what I'd witnessed—only a good man would be so attentive and loving towards his father.

His Highness was still awaiting my answer. "Would you really want to dine with an unwanted guest?"

He flinched at my biting tone and I instantly felt remorseful. "Regardless of how you came to be here, you're still my guest, and I'd enjoy your company, especially considering my family isn't here, making the palace rather...empty."

I heard the words he didn't say: he was lonely. Despite my reservations, compassion swelled within me, as I was all too familiar with such an emotion. While I'd stayed out of Father's and my governess's way back at the manor, I'd spent a lot of time with the servants. But now I had no one to talk to save the plants that tended me in my room and occasionally the maid the prince had arranged to assist me, none of which were adequate companions.

"Thank you for your invitation. I'll gladly accept."

He relaxed and after a moment's hesitation offered his arm. I looped mine through his and allowed him to escort me through the hallways, which we walked in silence. My attention was quickly captured by the ornate decorations we passed. The Malvagarian Palace truly housed many treasures, each one unique and incredibly fine.

"Your collection is quite impressive," I said.

He smiled. "It's a collection many generations in the making and has no parallel. I hope to add extensively to it throughout my life."

"Is that simply to carry on the tradition, or are you an appreciator of treasures?"

His dark eyes lit up. "Both...but there's another reason. I thoroughly enjoy scouring the surrounding kingdoms looking for priceless objects to add to my collection. I used to spend most of my time researching where certain treasures could be found and planning expeditions to retrieve them, but that was before—" He immediately fell silent.

My interest was immediately piqued. "Before...what?"

He sighed and didn't answer, so I tried to decipher one myself. I'd heard many stories over the years about our kingdom's wandering prince, but it had been so long ago that part of me had wondered whether they'd been merely rumors. Apparently they hadn't been.

"I heard of your excursions," I said tentatively. "But it's my understanding that it's been several years since you've embarked on one. What changed?"

I expected more silence, but to my surprise he responded with a wry smile. "Many things. My parents didn't approve of my wanderlust, particularly my mother. They encouraged me to be more devoted to my royal duties rather than focusing my time on the treasures of generations past." He frowned. "They weren't wrong. I was irresponsible."

"So you've given up your treasure hunting?"

He hesitated before nodding reluctantly. "My mother can be rather...persuasive. As such, I doubt I'll ever go on such an expedition again. I scarcely even leave the palace."

"Does that upset you?"

He slowed to take in an antique vase resting on a nearby table, his expression wistful, before he shook his head. "I know my duties, Miss Maren." His voice was stiff, although not unkind.

"Do you ever resent them?"

"Not at all, but that doesn't make it any easier to let go of a part of oneself, nor prevent one from mourning for something that can never be again." He reached out to stroke the rim of the vase with his fingertip, almost longingly.

"You have other treasures you can focus on," I said. "Especially your people. And perhaps doing so will help you come to better appreciate your current collection rather than continuously seeking to add to it."

His expression became thoughtful. "That's a very wise approach: to be grateful for the beauty around me rather than seeking more elsewhere." He didn't even glance at me as he made his comment, his attention remaining riveted to the vase, causing my heart to lurch. He clearly didn't consider me a beauty to appreciate.

I bit my lip. "Do you consider yourself a connoisseur of beauty?"

"Certainly."

Even though I scarcely knew Prince Briar, disappointment tightened my chest all the same. He was just like everyone else. Even though I had no interest in the prince, part of me always hoped I'd meet a man who was different from everyone else, but it was clearly a foolish wish.

His brow furrowed as he finally lifted his gaze and surveyed my expression. "What's wrong? Did I say something to offend you?"

"Of course not," I lied. Really, I was overreacting; his all-too-common reaction certainly wasn't worth getting upset about. Besides, I didn't care what he or anyone else thought.

He appeared doubtful, but thankfully he didn't press me. We continued to the dining room, walking in silence until we neared the staircase that descended to the grand foyer. I stopped suddenly, my attention captured by an ornate tapestry depicting a gruesome battle, almost grotesque in its depiction.

"How awful," I breathed. "Can you really call something like this beautiful?"

He answered without hesitation. "Yes." He caressed the scarlet threads depicting the blood in the carnage scene. "Beauty isn't always obvious. In this case, it's the craftsmanship that is beautiful rather than what's being portrayed, as well as the lesson that can be taken from the story it's telling." He pointed me towards a beautiful landscape hanging on the opposite wall. "I can't deny this piece of art is more beautiful to the senses, but that doesn't mean the other piece lacks its own special type of beauty."

I tilted my head as I studied first the painting, then the tapestry, and after some thought I could see what he meant. The tapestry's craftsmanship was exquisite, the needlework so fine that the emotion from the battle emanated from each thread; the expressions captured by the weaver of each individual made them so real that they seemed to jump out of the tapestry itself. I felt I'd been directly transported to a moment in Malvagarian history.

"Yes, I think I see what you mean," I said. "Perhaps the tapestry is beautiful, too."

"I agree." He gave me a gentle smile before continuing down the stairs. Even though we'd left the tapestry behind, it lingered in my thoughts.

We entered the dining room, where a lavish meal had been spread. The prince helped me with my seat before settling across from me. I waited to take a bite until he began eating, giving me permission to enthusiastically cut into my roast beef. The meat was tender and incredibly juicy, bursting with flavor. I moaned in appreciation and eagerly dug into my potatoes next.

"I haven't seen you around the palace...or the gardens," the prince said after we'd dined for some time in companionable silence. "Where have you been hiding?"

"I've been exploring," I said almost hesitantly, suddenly wondering if I'd been wrong to assume I could look around the palace as I pleased.

The corner of his mouth lifted, as if he'd expected nothing else. "Did you find anything interesting?"

I sipped my wine thoughtfully as I considered everything I'd seen these past three days. "The east wing," I finally said.

He lifted an eyebrow. "The abandoned one? I'm surprised such a place has captured your interest."

"Certainly, for it leads one to wonder *why* it's abandoned."

"I see." He leaned back in his seat to take a long sip from his goblet. "I'm afraid the answer isn't as exciting as you likely think. It was my mother's section of the palace, and now that she's...not here, I find no reason to maintain it, at least when the staff is so low."

"And why is that?" As the crown prince, couldn't he have as many servants as he wanted?

"Many of the servants have been here my entire life. Rather than hire new ones to fully staff my brother's palace, I allowed him to take those closest to him, while several who've remained here are part of the search for my sisters, leaving the palace rather empty. Thus it seemed pointless to have them maintain the unused east wing when there are other areas of the palace that require far more attention."

His explanation made sense, but it also invited more questions. "What became of the queen? There are whispers that she hasn't been seen in public for months."

He swirled the contents of his goblet without meeting my eyes. "That's something I don't wish to discuss." He set his drink down and returned his gaze to mine, his own inquisitive. "Is exploring all you've done here so far?" He seemed surprised at my nod. "Really? Surely exploring can't occupy all your time, especially once you've found everything there is to find. What are your other hobbies?"

My cheeks warmed. "Nothing that's worth mentioning." It wouldn't do to tell His Highness about all my unladylike interests. While I wasn't ashamed of them, it was one thing to pursue them with the stablehands and other servants, and quite another to discuss them with royalty.

"Really?" His curiosity only deepened. "Do they have to do with your climbing trees?"

Oh yes, he already knew about that particular habit. There'd be no harm in sharing the others. So I told him of

58

my riding horses, and the mischief I'd gotten into with some of the servants, and my tendency to get dirty, and the afternoons I often spent with the gardeners or the cooks helping them with their tasks. As I spoke, I eyed him carefully, expecting him to be scandalized...but he only seemed amused.

"From what I know of you already, your interests don't surprise me in the least." I relaxed at his open and friendly expression...until he spoke again. "You've made no mention of your family."

I automatically stiffened, as if the prince's tone had been accusatory rather than kind. "What of them?" I asked shakily.

"I simply wondered, especially after you didn't want me to send word to anyone...is everything alright with them?"

I concentrated on swirling the food on my plate. "Not... exactly. My mother died many years ago and I'm an only child."

"And what of your father?"

I went rigid before narrowing my eyes suspiciously. Why did he want to know? Had the gardens told him I was running away from him? Did he mean to turn me over to him? Considering I was still unmarried, legally Father had a claim on me, not to mention he and Lord Brone had signed a betrothal contract. I doubted His Highness would approve of my breaking it by running away.

All the more reason not to inform the prince of the truth behind my circumstances, else he'd be obligated to side with the law rather than me.

It was time to end this conversation before it wandered deeper into forbidden territory. I set my napkin aside and stood. "Forgive me, but I'd like to go to my room now."

He hastily rose as well. "I'm sorry, have I—"

I curtsied, cutting off his fumbled attempt at an apology

for which he undoubtedly didn't understand the reason. "Thank you for the meal."

I turned and left the room before he could offer to escort me. Despite my hasty departure being the wise course of action, I couldn't help regretting my time with the prince had come to a premature end, a feeling I didn't quite understand.

CHAPTER 6

I softly closed the king's bedroom door behind me following my latest visit, my fourth this week, during which His Majesty had only been semi-coherent. In the moments he'd been alert, he'd seemed confused by my presence, alternating between believing I was his daughter and that I was a stranger. But he'd held my hand and seemed to enjoy the stories I shared about the mischief I'd frequently gotten into with the stablehands at my manor—stories which had caused the attending nurse to murmur in disapproval— and by the time sleep had claimed him, he'd worn a peaceful smile.

I wandered to the window at the end of the corridor and peered out. The rain had finally stopped, and the sun penetrated the grey clouds swallowing the blue sky, its golden light dancing against the colorful patchworks of the garden below, whose wonders I could only capture hints of from my vantage point.

The familiar, ever-present yearning swelled within my breast. I pushed the window open and leaned against the wet sill in an effort to get a closer look. There was so much to see, but my gaze was quickly captured by a topiary garden to my right, whose magnificent topiary animals appeared to be *moving*. The allure of seeing such a thing up close was too strong to continue to resist.

Grudge against the gardens or not, I could no longer ignore their gentle whispers, promising me fantastic discoveries and new adventures. I pushed away from the window and hurried through the corridors to the front doors.

The moment I stepped outside I became awash in the fresh, earthy air that smelled of rain and blossoms. I tipped my head back, relishing the sun's warmth and the gentle breeze caressing my face. It felt so good to finally be free from the stifling stone walls of the palace. After several deep breaths, I pattered down the steps and turned in the direction I thought I'd seen the topiary garden.

However, finding it proved more difficult than I'd anticipated, especially since the gardens' layout seemed different from when I'd last explored. I paused to look around. I was certain I'd been in this section before...but the plants were different, as were the paths twisting amongst the foliage. Had they changed on a whim?

The enchantment behind such a feat only strengthened my curiosity, which guided my explorations. I strolled the paths slowly so I could take in every detail of the ornate arrangements of the flora, some of which bloomed out of season while others were unique flowers I'd never before encountered, all of which only added to the gardens' splendor. It truly was a feast for the senses.

I slowed when I caught a glimmer of light glistening across something burrowed between a clump of dahlias and irises. I crouched down for a closer look. It looked like... something metal, perhaps? I dug away the dirt around it to reveal a tiny iron key, floral in design. I lightly traced it. What could such a key possibly open?

I grinned. Whatever it was, I was certainly going to find out. I eagerly hooked my fingers around it and gave it a tug. It didn't budge. I tugged again, harder. It remained unmoving. I dug further to investigate and saw that several roots from the nearby plants had grown around it, keeping it securely burrowed in the earth.

I carefully worked them loose; it took some time, for they were rather entwined, as if the garden didn't want to give it up. But after a silent tug-of-war battle with the roots, I eventually succeeded in pulling it free to cradle it in my palm. What fun it'd be to explore the palace to discover which door it opened. Perhaps one of the rooms in the abandoned east wing?

Something gently brushed my shoulder. I gasped and hastily swiveled around, keeping my hand clutching the key firmly behind my back. Had someone seen me take it? I relaxed when I saw that it had only been a branch from an oak, which held out a bouquet of peculiar looking flowers.

"What are these?" I asked as I safely tucked the key away in the pocket sewn in my petticoat.

The branch gently nudged my shoulder, imploring me to accept the bouquet. I cautiously did, and the moment I touched their stems the flowers began to glow, bathing me in the sweetest perfume.

"They're beautiful," I murmured. "But why—"

The branch brushed against me again; at the contact, the tree's whispering voice caressed my senses. *Forgive us.*

I blinked in my surprise. "Is this an apology?" I smiled as I sensed the tree's affirmation. "Thank you." Hope flared in my chest. "Does that mean you'll let me go? Surely there's a stipulation to the curse binding me here." I heaved a frustrated sigh as the oak's branches drooped; the gardens' silence told me that if there was a loophole, they refused to divulge it. "Why are you so determined to keep me as your prisoner?"

The daisies near my feet brushed against my ankles. *Not a prisoner, but our guest.* The oak gently caressed my cheek with one of its leaves, affirming the daisies' words, but I refused to be won over so easily.

"If I really weren't a prisoner, you wouldn't have taken away the only door leading out of here." I threw the flowers to the ground, causing them to immediately stop glowing. "Keep your apology gesture; you are *not* forgiven."

I stomped down the path, but before I could round the corner, a vine tangled around my ankle, causing me to nearly trip. I spun back around.

"What is it now?"

A breeze gathered the fallen bouquet to return it to the oak's branch, which then extended it back to me, more earnestly than before, its plea that we might be friends. I hesitated before heaving an annoyed sigh and accepting it.

"Fine, I'll accept your gift. But this doesn't mean I'm not still angry; it'll take quite some time to earn my good favor."

The surrounding plants seemed to straighten, as if eager to begin immediately.

Hmm, perhaps they could be useful after all.

"Could you show me where the topiary garden is? I saw it from the palace window and was hoping to explore—"

An excited breeze immediately rustled across the grounds as the surrounding plants urged me forward; I happily accepted its guidance. We passed the entrances to many intriguing-looking gardens that tempted me to pause and venture inside, but the garden's breeze pushed me past them towards the topiary garden.

In a short time the path opened up to reveal a tall hedge wall, with a floral arch that served as the entrance to the hedge garden. Glimpses of the large topiary animals found within peeked over the wall. I wasted no time entering.

It was more lovely than I could have imagined. The paths

leading to the variety of topiary animals twisted around hedges, which were cut into various ornamental shapes— some were groomed to resemble different plants and flowers, others more enchanting shapes, such as rainbows, suns, and stars, all of differing colors rather than the evergreen leaves found in ordinary hedge gardens; there was even a large hedge maze on the far side.

But it was the topiaries resting on several stone pedestals that stood out. They moved as I approached them, causing me to stop and stare in wonder as hedge animals of all types hopped down to explore the garden—rabbits, squirrels, cats, peacocks, turtles…there was even a swan floating across a lake located in the center of the garden. I released a breath of awe. It was all so exquisite.

I'd begun to wander towards the lake for a closer look at the hedge swan when a tiny squeak caused me to pause. A small topiary peeked out from behind a clump of hibiscus flowers.

I crouched down. "Why, hello there."

The little face immediately ducked away.

"Don't be frightened, I'm not going to hurt you." I extended my hand encouragingly. Two green eyes peered out, followed by a nose, sniffing cautiously, as if checking for danger. When it deemed it safe, the rest of the topiary slowly edged out from its hiding place.

My breath hooked in wonder. It was a hedgehog made from a lilac shrub, with a white, fluffy leaf underbelly. My grin widened.

"Oh, you're adorable." I stroked it gently, marveling at its texture, which seemed to be a mix between shrubbery and fur. He leaned against my caressing touch before squeaking again and venturing closer.

It was fascinating to watch it move and feel it nuzzle against my hand; from what I could tell, it was clearly alive. I continued petting it, and would have spoiled the plant indefinitely, but a *clink* suddenly filled the air, causing my head to snap up in the direction it had come from.

What was that noise? I slowly stood and tiptoed towards the edge of the garden to investigate, the hedgehog following closely behind. I pressed my ear against the leafy hedge, but the sound was too muffled to discern, although it sounded like...a clink of a trowel.

I brightened. It must be a gardener, which was excellent news. Not only had I enjoyed the company of the gardeners back at the manor and had often helped them with their more simple tasks, but a gardener working these grounds undoubtedly knew them well enough that they could perhaps help me find a way to escape.

I walked the length of the hedge wall in search of the entrance to the maze, and even after I'd found it, it took quite some time to navigate its twists and turns. I kept to the outer edges so as to avoid going too deeply inside and inadvertently becoming lost. The hedgehog topiary scurried ahead of me, as if it knew the way, and with it as well as the sound of digging as my guides, I soon came to a small enclosure within the maze.

I gasped in surprise, for kneeling in the dirt wasn't a gardener at all. "Your Highness?"

Prince Briar didn't pause in his work, but he did glance up with a half smile. "I thought I heard you on the other side of the wall. I should have guessed you'd come to investigate."

I continued staring, slowly taking the prince in from head to foot. Gone were his fancy velvet tunics, replaced with much simpler attire. His hands were burrowed deep into the earth, with a large pile of weeds beside him.

"What are you doing?"

He sat back on his heels and motioned to the weeds with his trowel. "Weeding."

"I can see that, but why are *you* weeding?"

He shrugged. "I've finished my duties for the day and decided to take advantage of the break in the storm, plus I enjoy the task."

I ventured closer, taking in the dirt stains on his knees and sleeves. "I admit I'm surprised. I didn't expect the crown prince to be a gardener."

He leaned over to yank out a rather firm, stubborn weed. "I'm not afraid of hard work, and I especially love the gardens. It's quite satisfying to do my part to bring beauty to the world."

His gaze was almost reverent as he slowly took in our surroundings. It truly was a lovely place, with flowers not only growing around the circumference but also woven throughout the hedge wall, making it feel as if we were entirely immersed in blossoms, which filled the air with their intoxicating perfume.

Despite the beauty of the garden, I was quickly distracted by the prince's appearance. Sweat dampened his face and hair, while dirt covered his hands and burrowed beneath his fingernails—there was even a streak across his cheek, which in no way detracted from his handsome features; if anything, it enhanced them. My cheeks warmed to have noticed and I hastily looked away.

He clearly misinterpreted my fluster, for when he next spoke, it was an apology. "Are you still upset about lunch the other day? Whatever I said to offend you, I hope you'll forgive me."

I peeked up at him and immediately softened at the earnestness filling his wide, dark eyes. "You did nothing wrong. I simply don't like to talk about my father."

He nodded his understanding and thankfully didn't inquire further. My shoulders relaxed with relief and I offered him a small smile, which he returned before resuming his weeding. But I wasn't ready to depart from his company just yet; there was something soothing about his presence, not to mention stumbling upon him gardening invited all sorts of questions about the mysterious prince.

"May I stay? I could do with some company."

The prince smiled again but said nothing more. I settled on a stone bench tucked into a small alcove formed by the floral-hedge walls, where I pulled my legs up and arranged them beneath my skirts before resting the garden's bouquet on my lap.

Prince Briar's eyes narrowed. "Please tell me you didn't pick those flowers."

"No, they were an apology gift from the garden."

He slumped in clear relief before returning to his task.

"Would it bother you if I watch?" I asked. "I have quite a bit of experience keeping gardeners company."

"Did you often talk to the gardeners at home?"

They were some of my only friends, for while the upper class seemed to revolve solely around appearances, the servants at the manor hadn't judged me for lacking something I had no control over.

"I enjoyed their company, as well as hearing their knowledge on the various plants they tended." I gave him an expectant look.

"Ah, so I'm to provide you with knowledge in addition to company?"

I stiffened, suddenly worried I'd been too presumptuous and had offended him...but I relaxed when the corners of his mouth twitched, as if he ached to smile but was fighting the impulse. He sobered at my reaction.

"Are you alright?"

"Yes, I'm fine." I hesitated, unsure whether I should say more. "I...sometimes forget that you're the crown prince, which is ridiculous."

"Not at all, especially considering I'm currently weeding and covered in dirt." He started to return to his task, but paused, suddenly looking quite weary. "Unfortunately, I don't quite have as much vigor as I used to, so perhaps a short break is in order." He stood and carefully brushed off some of the loose dirt clinging to his clothes before approaching the bench. "May I?"

"Of course." I scooted over to give him room and he sank beside me. I immediately became awash in his earthy warmth that caused my insides to give a peculiar shudder, something I'd never experienced around anyone before, especially a man.

Desperate for a distraction, I returned my attention to the weariness weighing on the prince as he leaned back and closed his eyes.

"Are you alright?"

He managed a nod. "I'm just tired. I don't have nearly as much energy as I did before I left for my extended trip to Draceria several months ago. Although I've gained back some of my strength, I haven't yet fully recovered."

He reached out to weave his fingers in the flowers and leaves of the hedge behind him and took a long, steadying breath. My brow puckered as I watched. It was almost as if he were gaining solace and strength from the plants them-selves. My senses tingled with excitement. It was another mystery.

The prince remained still and silent for several minutes, and I did my best not to disturb him. Finally his eyes flut-tered open and he glanced sideways at me. "I'm surprised I haven't seen you in the gardens before now. Have you had a chance to explore them further?"

"Not until this morning."

"Oh? Did the rain scare you off?"

"No, my anger did." He lifted an incredulous brow,

inviting me to elaborate. "I'm afraid I was holding quite a grudge against the gardens for trapping me."

"So you finally believe that I had nothing to do with it?"

I felt a blush creep across my skin. My behavior towards His Highness had been rather abhorrent. "I do. I'm sorry I was so angry."

"It's understandable." His look was so kind, and for some reason I felt the heat in my cheeks deepen again, though I wasn't sure why. "Does the fact that you're outside again mean you've also forgiven the gardens?"

"Not so much *forgiven* them as become too curious about all they contain to remain annoyed and distant. Besides, the gardens have offered penance." I fiddled with the bouquet of blossoms in my lap, which glowed at my touch, drawing the prince's gaze.

"Ah, those are extraordinary flowers. To receive such a gift means the gardens have taken a liking to you."

"Nonsense, they were simply apologizing." I rubbed one of the soft petals between my fingers, pausing when the gesture caused my skin to tingle. "What was that?"

A secret flashed in the prince's eyes. "Those flowers are special, but I'll leave you to discover for yourself why. Only know they don't bestow such a gift on just anyone."

Much like they apparently didn't lead *just anyone* to the enchanted rose bush or lock them away within their walls. I examined the flowers more carefully. Each uniquely shaped blossom was comprised of two different colors, with a thin layer of glitter on their glowing petals.

I lightly traced one. "They're exquisite. Do the gardens contain more plants such as these?"

"All kinds, but I'll leave you to discover them, else it'd ruin the surprise."

I gave him an innocent look. "Perhaps I want the surprise to be ruined."

He shook his head. "Although we're barely acquainted, I feel I know you well enough to confidently say that it's the *thrill* of discovery that drives you more so than the discovery itself. Am I correct?"

I couldn't resist the smile tugging at my lips. I was flattered that a prince had taken the time to discover such a thing about me.

"Perhaps a bit," I allowed. "But I can't deny I also love discovering fantastic things." My gaze once again took in the lovely enclosure where we were currently sitting. "I can't imagine how long it took for the gardeners not only to create such a paradise, but preserve it. I can't wait to explore every bit of it."

"You'll have plenty of time to do so." He stood to return to his weeding; the moment he left I immediately missed his presence beside me. "And as for the gardeners, other than myself, there aren't any. The *garden* tends itself, and only humors me with occasional tasks because it knows how much I love to garden."

"Prestigious tasks such as weeding?"

"Exactly." He smiled, causing his eyes to crinkle in a rather appealing way. He returned to his task, but I didn't want our conversation to end quite yet.

"I noticed that the garden layout has changed since the first time I explored it."

He chuckled. "Yes, it's always rearranging itself. It reminds me of Reve, who constantly changes her clothes throughout the day, unable to settle on a single outfit because she loves so many." At the mention of his sister, his entire manner twisted in pain, and I felt the strangest compulsion to do everything I could to rid him of such a heart-wrenching expression.

"I visited your father again," I said gently. "He often thought I was the princess. Is it wrong for me to confuse

71

him? I'd hate to hurt His Majesty."

Prince Briar was silent a moment as he considered my question. "No, I don't think so. I imagine it gives him comfort." His expression softened. "Thank you for visiting him. I can't express how much it means to me. Your kindness is even more appreciated considering you didn't ask to be trapped here."

His dark, sincere gaze seeped into mine, and for a moment I couldn't look away. The moment I realized I was staring I hastily did so…but I couldn't resist almost immediately stealing another peek. His hair was rumpled and falling across his damp brow into his eyes, and his features were not just fine, but kind and gentle.

My stomach fluttered rather pleasantly, even though it felt wrong to be drawn to the prince's appearance when I'd always loathed others dismissing me for mine. But it was impossible *not* to notice.

I'm such a hypocrite.

I tried not to look at the prince again, but my gaze was drawn to him anyway…only to find him staring at me as well. Was he analyzing my own appearance and finding it distasteful? Even though I'd spent a lifetime dealing with others' negative stares, for some reason it rankled me more to have His Highness do it, too.

"Please don't," I whispered.

His brows furrowed. "Don't do what?"

"Please don't look at me like that."

He blinked and tore his gaze away with a blush, as if only just realizing what he'd been doing. "I—I didn't mean to offend."

I sighed and he was immediately apologetic.

"Forgive me, I've upset you."

I pulled my legs up and rested my chin on my knees. "I'm simply tired of it all—of people looking at me and immediately judging me not by who I am, but by what they see."

He was silent a moment as he perused my face a moment more, causing me to shift nervously, especially since my appearance was more unkempt than usual, especially my hair, which hung loose and wild in tangles around my face.

His gaze lingered on my hair before his expression softened. "You're not unattractive, Miss Maren." And he returned to his weeding.

I gaped at him, unsure whether I'd heard him correctly. "You must be in jest. No one has ever said such a thing to me."

"Then people have done you a great injustice."

I stared at him blankly, unsure what to say to that. But even though I'd spent my entire life convincing myself that I didn't care what others thought of me, warmth blossomed in my chest and seeped over me, my body's betrayal that his words had affected me more than I wanted to admit.

The prince pulled the last weed before he straightened, wincing as he stood. Guilt seeped over me as he rubbed the leg that had been injured when I'd plucked the rose. "Does it still hurt?"

"Only a little." His look was reassuring, which somehow only made me feel worse. He gathered his tools before standing and offering me his arm. "Might I persuade you to dine with me again?"

I grinned widely as I stood and looped my arm through his, but we'd only taken a few steps before the prince paused and crouched down.

"Hello, little topiary."

The hedgehog I'd discovered amongst the hibiscus flowers was nestled in another batch, his nose wriggling as he fixed his dark green eyes on us. I crouched beside the prince and extended my hand. The hedgehog sniffed cautiously before scurrying over to crawl into my palm. I picked it up and nuzzled it against my cheek.

"He's adorable."

Prince Briar smiled. "He seems to like you, which is high praise as the hedgehog topiary is notoriously shy."

I stroked his leafy fur and melted at the way he leaned into my touch. "You call him *the hedgehog topiary*? That will never do, Your Highness. Such a delightful creature needs a name."

"Christening him will only further endear him to you, so by all means, proceed."

I considered the matter. What sort of name would suit such an adorable magical creature? The perfect one came to me. "How about…Hibiscus, for that's where I found him. Do you like that, Hibiscus?" I tickled beneath his chin.

The hedgehog crawled up my arm and rested on my shoulder, where he nestled against my dark hair, his clear agreement. The prince's eyes crinkled as he watched.

"Despite your shaky start with the gardens, I knew they'd like you. Before I know it, you'll have charmed them all."

I brightened at the prospect, and my joy only grew when I linked my arm back with the prince's. Perhaps staying at the palace wouldn't be such a terrible fate after all.

CHAPTER 7

I awoke early the following morning, eager to try my hand at gardening. Hibiscus, who was curled up asleep on my pillow, stirred as I crawled off the bed and tugged on the dress I'd worn when I arrived at the palace, wrinkled from when I'd thrown it haphazardly into my wardrobe.

I froze halfway through brushing my hair when I caught sight of the enchanted rose I'd plucked from the garden— although it remained in full bloom, a single petal had already fallen off. My heart beat quickly as I lifted it to examine it. The prince had warned me that each petal served as a measurement in an hourglass that, when it ran out, would trap me here permanently. Already my time to escape was slipping away. I'd need to come up with a plan to leave, and soon.

My mind worked frantically as I finished getting ready, but as before ideas for escape remained elusive. After splashing water on my face and taking a stack of toast from the breakfast tray on my nightstand, I turned to my topiary hedgehog, who watched me attentively.

I extended my hand. "Would you like to accompany me on my first gardening adventure?"

He crawled up my arm to perch on my shoulder, where he stayed as I hurried out into the balmy and bright morning. I paused on the top steps to survey the gardens, which looked quite immaculate. But the prince had said it purposefully left him tasks to perform, which meant I'd surely find something if I searched diligently enough.

After some poking around, I discovered a greenhouse, which contained all manner of tools and seed packs. I grabbed some gloves and a trowel before choosing a packet at random, then began to wander in search of where I could plant them. After a quarter of an hour I finally stumbled upon a patch of untouched dirt tucked away in a seemingly ordinary garden. That suited my purposes—I couldn't inadvertently mess anything up, and if I did, hopefully the gardens could fix my mistakes. They were magical, after all.

I knelt in front of the plot of earth and tugged on my gardening gloves, pausing to allow Hibiscus to crawl off my shoulder so he could explore the surrounding flora. I watched him for a moment before I eagerly turned to the empty flowerbed. There was something so magical about an untouched plot of earth—it contained endless possibilities to become anything with just a few seeds. There was such power in that thought.

I pressed my fingers into the damp earth to check the soil and picked up my trowel. Before I could even dig a hole to plant the seeds, a fierce wind blew it right out of my hand. I blinked in astonishment at where it'd landed several feet away before glaring at the surrounding plants, rustling in clear agitation.

"What did you do that for?"

As usual, they didn't seem inclined to explain their

mischief. I rose to retrieve the trowel, but before I could, a nearby fern seized it with its leaves.

I glared again. "Do you think I'm so easily dissuaded?"

I reached for it, but my fingers barely grazed the handle before the fern handed it to the one beside it, who handed it to another. Faster than I could believe, the trowel traveled across the garden, where a nearby elm extended a branch down to pluck it out of reach.

I pressed my hands to my hips. "Is this some sort of game, or are you forbidding me from trying my hand at gardening? You let His Highness do it." Admittedly, that was rather a poor argument, considering he was a prince who could do anything he wanted, and I was simply Maren. But still, the gardens' favoritism was clearly unfair.

The plants continued to rustle angrily. I tightened my jaw.

"Fine, I'll just dig with my bare hands." I returned to the plot, but before I had a chance to carry out my plan, hurried footsteps sounded in the distance, pausing at the garden entrance. I didn't even have to turn around to know who it was.

"Good morning, Your Highness," I said dully, swiveling on my heels to face his disapproving frown. He cocked his ear towards the rustling plants to listen to their angry account. Tattletales.

"Is what they're saying true, Miss Maren?"

I shrugged. "I have no way of knowing, considering they haven't granted me the honor of even hearing their complaints."

Prince Briar wandered to the elm, who handed him the trowel it had confiscated. He examined it for a moment before giving me a disappointed look. "They say you're trying to garden."

"I'm only following the example of my future king," I said.

"Or is such an activity forbidden to the prisoner?" I knew I shouldn't goad him, but I didn't like the way he was scolding me like a child.

He pursed his lips. "You know you're not a prisoner but my guest, but that doesn't mean you have the right to garden without my permission. If you desired to try it, you should have come to me first."

Shame pressed against my chest and burned my cheeks. He was right. I'd been impulsive and disrespectful. I pushed through my pride to summon the apology I knew I needed to give, however reluctantly.

"You're right, I'm sorry. I'm used to having free reign to do as I please at my manor rather than being a guest to a prince, where I can't so easily get my way."

"You do strike me as the sort of woman to consistently try anyway." To my fierce relief, his tone had lightened, meaning his anger was ebbing, much more quickly than I could believe.

"Still, it was wrong of me." I glanced longingly at the empty plot with a sigh. "I suppose my gardening ambitions are dying before they've even a chance to grow." Such a shame.

"Let's not be too hasty." As he approached, he gave me a half smile that made me realize he'd already forgiven my offense. He settled on the ground and patted the spot beside him, inviting me to sit. Once I'd settled, he held out the trowel. "Would you like a second chance, Miss Maren?"

By the earnestness in his eyes, I knew what he was really asking: after his harsh reaction, he wanted a second chance as well.

I accepted the trowel with a smile, which caused him to relax. "Will you really allow me to plant?" I asked eagerly, unable to quell the excitement filling my voice at the prospect.

He chuckled. "Most women would shy away from such an activity, but I should have suspected you wouldn't."

"My governess always said I took any opportunity to get my hands dirty."

He tilted his head. "Was she correct?"

I responded with a wicked grin, and to reinforce my point, I made a show of tugging off my gloves. "Shall we get started?"

"If you wish." A frown creased his brow as he studied the seed packet. "Where did you find these?"

"In the greenhouse." I bit my lip. "I am allowed to go there, aren't I?"

"Yes, that's not my concern." He tipped a few seeds into his palm to better examine them. "Do you know what seeds these are?"

"Of course not," I said. "That's the thing about seeds—you can't see what they become until they've been planted."

"That's not entirely true—you can always see a seed's potential before you even plant it." He flipped the packet over so I could see its label. "These seeds come from the aqua asters that grow in the water garden, and thus have no place in the transformation garden. A seed must be planted in the right soil in order for it to grow and thrive."

"What did you call this garden?"

"The transformation garden."

I wrinkled my brow as my gaze slowly took in the garden that, while beautiful, seemed otherwise unremarkable. "It appears to be just an ordinary garden."

"Because you're not looking hard enough; you must dig deeper." He motioned to the empty plot of soil. "Even if you'd acquired the right seeds, you couldn't plant them here, not when there are already other plants growing here."

I frowned. "But *nothing* is growing there."

He smirked in challenge. "Don't be too hasty in

dismissing the possibility. The palace grounds are something truly special; if you wish to garden in them, you must first understand them."

I very much did want to garden, so I straightened in determination and turned back to the seemingly empty plot, but no matter which angle I scrutinized it from, it seemed to be nothing more than an empty plot of earth.

"I don't see anything," I said. "Are you certain there's something special about this?"

"Just because you can't see something doesn't mean it's not there," he said. "You must learn to see deeper. This is a very special plot of flowers. I'll show you."

He reached out to demonstrate, robbing me of my opportunity to discover it for myself. I seized his wrist. "Wait."

His eyebrows lifted in shock at my overly familiar touch. My cheeks burned as I hastily released him.

"Please don't show me. I want to figure it out myself."

His mouth curled up into a grin. "Be my guest, milady." He grandly gestured towards the flower plot, and I turned back to it with renewed determination to unearth the mystery of the garden's secret, the prince's earlier words filling my mind: *You're not looking hard enough; you must dig deeper.*

After a more thorough examination, I noticed something I hadn't before—plant-shaped *shadows*, a strange phenomena considering no plants grew here...or *did* they?

Excitement swelled in my breast as I glanced sideways at the prince's encouraging expression. I eagerly accepted his silent invitation and lightly caressed the top of one of the shadows. At my touch, a flower appeared, one that was so clear I could see straight through it. I lightly touched the one beside it, then another, causing a crystal-like flower to reveal itself each time.

I released a breath of wonder. "They were invisible."

"They are only one of the transformation garden's splendors. They only appear when gently touched, and then it's only for a few minutes. See? They're already disappearing."

I looked in time to watch one fade away until it could no longer be seen. "Incredible." My awe quickly melted into horror. "I almost dug these up!"

"You didn't see them."

That was no excuse. My governess had always warned me that my impulsiveness would one day lead me into trouble. It appeared she'd been correct. What if she'd also been right about other things—like how improper my hobbies were, or even worse, how my supposedly plain appearance would never attract a man?

I gave my head a little shake. I mustn't think that.

I watched until the last blossom became invisible once again before I stood and glanced around the garden with renewed interest. What previously seemed entirely ordinary now seemed ripe with possibilities, possibilities I was eager to discover. "This is a transformation garden, you said?"

Prince Briar grinned. "It's become much more interesting to you, hasn't it? Have your desires to garden been eclipsed by your need to explore?"

"Temporarily."

I began in earnest, examining each area carefully so I wouldn't miss any of this garden's secrets. Every new discovery was wondrous—there were flowers whose petals broke into tiny pieces of light when touched before raining gently to the ground, flowers that transformed into butterflies before turning back into plants, and several patches of flowers that, according to the prince, changed their color and shape depending on the time of day and weather. I was eager to return later to witness that particular phenomenon.

As I explored, the prince watched me with a gentle look,

seeming pleased with each of my delightful exclamations as I discovered another of the garden's wonders.

Eventually I'd seen everything I could and found myself once again kneeling in the dirt next to the invisible patch of flowers, ready to finally try my hand at gardening. The prince gently caressed his fingertip across the plants so each reappeared. He searched carefully until he found a small patch of earth where none were growing.

"I hoped there was an empty spot. Now all we need are the correct seeds. I'll return in a moment." He stood and departed with a bow, leaving me with a strange sense of loss without his gentle and kind companionship. Thankfully he wasn't gone long before he returned with a packet of seeds, which he presented with another bow. "Your seeds, Miss Maren."

I accepted them gratefully, my smile teasing. "Does a prince usually play the role of a footman?"

"When it comes to gardening, I take it upon myself to perform whatever duties are required of me, for it's my greatest passion." His entire manner became reverent, softening his already handsome features. My stomach gave a strange flutter before I suppressed it.

No, I wouldn't be swayed by his looks. It went against everything I stood for.

But the prince was so kind...

No, Maren. Stop it this instant.

I picked up my trowel, desperate for a distraction. "Where do we begin?"

"Dig a hole a few centimeters wide in diameter and just as deep," he instructed.

I obeyed, digging a few in the small patch of earth we had to work with. When I'd finished, the prince tipped several seeds into my palm, which I placed into the earth; dirt embedded in my fingernails as I covered them up, humming cheerfully as I worked.

"Did you often take it upon yourself to do servants' work?" he asked as I planted the next seeds. "Surely you had servants at your home."

"There were many servants at the manor," I said as I firmly patted the dirt on top of the newly planted seedlings. "I often helped them with their work. Not only do I like to keep busy, but the servants were…friendly." The only ones out of all of my acquaintances who'd exhibited any kindness towards me, but I kept that particular observation to myself.

"What were your favorite chores?"

I peered sideways at him to gauge whether or not his interest was sincere. It appeared to be, which only increased my puzzlement. Why would a prince care to learn such trivial details about a mere merchant's daughter? "I enjoyed helping the cooks in the kitchens, tending to the horses, and working in the gardens."

"So this isn't your initiation to the world of gardening?"

"It is to *planting*," I said. "The gardeners at the manor only ever let me weed."

His lips twitched. "And would you consider yourself an experienced weeder?"

"Are you looking to hire another servant, Your Highness?"

He chuckled and shook his head. "No, you're safe from that particular scheme, but I do have a question." He leaned back on his elbows, his look teasing. "Since you're apparently an expert weeder, what did you think of my skills when you witnessed them yesterday?"

I pursed my lips to keep from smiling. "They were passable."

"Only *passable*?" His brows shot up in mock offense. "That

will never do. You must teach me all you know and allow me to become your apprentice until I'm an expert."

The apprentice prince? I bit the inside of my lip, but it did nothing to prevent my giggle from escaping. "While the art of weeding has many coveted secrets, perhaps I shall humor you in gratitude for teaching me to plant." I covered the last of the seeds and sat back on my heels to survey the three small bulging mounds in the ground, quite satisfied with my work, however small.

"Might I ask another question, Miss Maren?"

I glanced back at the prince, who was suddenly looking quite serious. "Besides that one?" I asked, my teasing a mask for my escalating heartbeat. What did he want to ask? Surely he wouldn't inquire after my father again, would he?

"Why do you refer to your home as *the manor*?"

So he'd noticed. I should have suspected he would before long. "I call it that because that's where I lived, yet it never felt like home."

Compassion filled his dark eyes. "I understand that sentiment." He glanced at the formidable stone castle looming over us. "Although I mainly grew up here, it was just one of many palaces we lived in. If it weren't for the gardens or Father...this likely wouldn't be home at all."

The palace did seem more like a fortress than a warm, cozy place to grow up in. Yet although my manor had seemed more inviting on the surface, it had been just as cold.

"You mentioned your father and the gardens, but not your siblings or mother," I said hesitantly. "Weren't you close to them?"

He frowned. "My relationship with them has always been...complicated. Since I'm the heir, I had little time free from lessons and duties to spend with them. It didn't really matter, for Drake and I have never really gotten along, and

Gemma has always been quite sickly. I was closest to Reve...
before she began to change."

I ached to ask *how* she'd changed, but I had so many other
burning questions, and I was certain he wouldn't answer all
of them before he decided to stop sharing. "What about your
mother? Were you close to her?"

He gave a hollow laugh. "Not exactly. She's always been
too busy trying to get her way to be close to anyone."

"There are rumors going around about her..." I hesitated,
wondering if it'd be too presumptuous of me to ask whether
Her Majesty was currently residing in a mirror; it was a
rather ridiculous notion, even for the most outrageous
gossip.

He studied me for a moment before managing a tight
smile. "I know what you want to ask; I can see that the question is practically bursting to break free. So I shall humor
you: she is indeed trapped in a mirror."

My mouth fell agape. "Surely she can't be."

"She is." He attempted to school his expression into one
that was more serious, but his lips twitched, ruining his
attempt to mask his amusement. "Forgive me, it shouldn't be
funny, for it doesn't make me a very good son."

I leaned back on my elbows, dirtying the sleeves of my
dress. "Then I'm not a very good daughter, for I'd be quite
thrilled if my father ended up in a mirror. You must tell me
how you managed it."

"That's quite the story," he said. "And one my brother and
sister-in-law should be the ones to share during their next
visit."

If I was still here when that time came. I was still determined to escape, although admittedly I hadn't been thinking
about it much during the past few days as I should. That
oversight had absolutely nothing to do with the prince...or
so I told myself.

I tugged out a weed and twirled it between my fingers. "What about the rest of your family? Are your sisters cursed too?"

His expression immediately closed itself off again. "Yes."

I waited for him to elaborate but he didn't. "Please, I'm dying to know. There are so many rumors about your family..."

He lifted his brow. "And what are they saying?"

"That all of you are cursed. They say that Prince Drake is in a mirror—"

"Not anymore," the prince offered.

"—and that your sisters..." I paused, waiting for him to elaborate if he wished to. He didn't answer for so long I feared that once again he wouldn't. But finally he released a heavy sigh and leaned back on the lawn to stare up at the cloudless blue sky.

"You might as well know. You're correct in that all my siblings are cursed, except for Drake, whose curse has already been broken. Gemma has been trapped in a tower for several years, but no one except for Mother knows where it is, and she's not divulging any details as to her whereabouts. And Reve"—emotion choked his voice—"she's...disappeared."

My breath hitched. "*Disappeared?*"

He leaned forward and the remainder of the story tumbled out, as if it'd been bottled up for so long he couldn't keep it in a moment longer.

"Her curse affects her mind, and it's only been growing worse. Last autumn, Mother and I went to Draceria so I could make a match with Princess Rheanna. I pleaded with Mother to allow us to take Reve with us, for she'd been becoming quite...confused. Mother refused, for she's all about appearances and feared the rumors that would spread should another kingdom see her condition, so we left her behind." Despair filled his face. "I should have stood up to her and insisted she be allowed to come, but I didn't. And because I didn't..." He swallowed and said nothing more.

"What happened?" I prompted.

"I returned from Draceria to find her missing with no idea what had become of her. Our only clue is from the gardens, who claim she slipped past them...and never returned." He clenched his fists. "I can't bear to imagine her wandering out there all alone in her condition. The moment I realized she was missing, I sent every guard that could be spared out to search. A group had already been looking for her the moment they discovered her disappearance. It's been six months with no sign of her. I fear she's lost forever." Anguish marred his expression. "I'm her older brother. I should have protected her. And I didn't. I failed her."

"Of course you didn't," I said. "You didn't know she'd disappear. If anyone is to blame, it's the gardens." It seemed rather foolish to leave an entire palace's security to a bunch of vines, magical or not.

He gritted his teeth. "They let her out."

"And me in."

His jaw tensed as he stiffly nodded. "I don't know why... the gardens have always loved Reve. Why would they betray her, betray *me*? And they've offered no explanation. I don't understand."

Tense silence followed his story. I nibbled my lip as I considered the matter. "If she's been missing for half a year, I'm surprised she hasn't returned on her own."

"She likely can't. When I last saw her, she was losing portions of herself. How can she return if she doesn't even know who she is?"

"But *you* do," I said. "You must join the search and find her. You know her best and are likely to know where she might have gone."

"It's not so simple as that," he said, sounding weary and... broken. "I can't leave the gardens."

I frowned. "What do you mean you can't *leave?*"

"I mean exactly what I said." He looked across the grounds, his gaze unseeing. "Not all prisons have bars. Though I'm the future king, I'm still dependent on the whims of the gardens, and they have very specific conditions for me, which I've already violated once and can't risk doing again, not when I haven't yet fully recovered from the first time." He sighed. "Even if I could join the search, I can't do it now. Father's health is precarious and I'm serving as regent. All I can do is hope."

Exhaustion lined his features. Now that I considered it, he often seemed tired. Did it have anything to do with his curse or his connection to the gardens? I'd have to investigate further. I thrilled at the prospect; I loved a good puzzle.

The sun had now fully risen in the sky and beat down on our necks. My stomach growled, reminding me I hadn't eaten anything in hours since my meager breakfast of toast.

Prince Briar heard it and rose. "Won't you join me for lunch? I'd enjoy your company before I have to lock myself away in my study."

"Are you sure you haven't tired of me?" I asked as I took his offered hand and allowed him to pull me to my feet. He gave my hand a squeeze before looping it through my arm.

"Not at all."

My cheeks warmed at his look. I hastily looked away and whistled for Hibiscus, who'd spent the morning napping in the shade of the trowel-stealing elm. Once he was securely on my shoulder, we left the garden.

We were silent as he escorted me back to the palace, and it wasn't until we began ascending the front steps that I overcame my fluster enough to speak. "Thank you for teaching me to garden. I enjoyed my time with you, Your Highness."

He paused halfway up the stairs to give me an earnest look. "Please, I'd appreciate it if we could dispense with all formalities. *Briar* will suffice...Maren."

A strange thrill came over me to hear him say my name. "I could never go against a direct order from the future king; Briar it is."

I gave him a teasing smile, which he returned, and in that moment, it felt as if something new had been planted between us. I couldn't wait to see what it'd grow to become... if I was but brave enough to nourish it.

CHAPTER 8

I tried the iron key in the last door lining the dusty, abandoned corridor, but like all the others I'd attempted this past week, it didn't fit.

"It doesn't fit this one either, Hibiscus."

The hedgehog wriggled on my shoulder. I slumped against the wall with a disappointed sigh. I'd tried nearly every locked door I could find—at least the ones away from the attentive notice of the guards. The doors in the abandoned east wing had been the last ones to try, and I'd been so certain that I'd finally discover the door the mysterious key opened somewhere amongst them. But I hadn't.

Ever since finding the key, it'd burned a hole in the pocket I'd stitched in the underside of my gown. For every key unlocked a door, and locked doors held all manner of secrets, ones I was determined to discover.

I cradled the key in my palm to study it by the faint flickering light from my candle. A possibility tickled my mind as I lightly traced my thumb along the ornate floral pattern at the key's base: was such a pattern merely ornamental, or was it a clue as to which door the key opened? Perhaps its door was

90

not within the palace, but was hidden somewhere in the vast gardens. My senses tingled with excitement at the possibility.

I pocketed the key and picked up my candle to leave the wing, but paused when I spotted another door, slightly ajar, at the end of the corridor. Naturally, I went to investigate and peered through the crack to peek inside. All the furniture was draped in cloth, save for a single accent table at the far end of the room, where an elegant hand mirror rested facedown. I pattered closer and lifted my light to better examine it. Even beneath the thick layer of dust, I could tell it was made of gold, with a design of onyx gemstones embedded into the back. My finger tingled and dust clung to my fingertip as I lightly traced one of the black stones.

From somewhere beyond the east wing, a door opened and closed. I startled and yanked my hand away. Although Briar hadn't specifically forbidden me from being here, I suddenly had the unnerving feeling I was somewhere I shouldn't be.

I hurriedly exited the room and made my way through the gloomy, neglected corridor. I breathed a sigh of relief when I finally stepped back into the main part of the palace, where I blew out my candle. Other than the suspicious frown from a nearby guard who'd seen me slip out of the east wing, no one else seemed to notice me. I only hoped I hadn't done anything wrong that would cause the guard to inform the prince about my behavior; ever since our gardening session together last week we'd been becoming better friends, a relationship I desperately wanted to maintain.

I made my way outside, eager to test my theory that the key fit a door somewhere on the grounds. I paused on the steps to look over the many paths leading to different sections of the garden, debating about where to search next.

Since my arrival at the palace, I'd seen many of the spectacular gardens, but I knew I'd barely scratched the surface in my explorations. And considering I had yet to see a locked door in any of them, it was undoubtedly well hidden. Whichever garden the enchanted grounds kept locked away behind it was surely a spectacular one, even more so than the wondrous ones I'd already discovered. I simply had to find it.

Hibiscus's nose tickled my neck as he wriggled on my shoulder. I reached up to stroke his leafy body. "If a secret garden existed somewhere on the palace grounds, do you have any idea where it'd be?"

Hibiscus froze, while the surrounding flowers immediately straightened before rustling in clear agitation, as if knowing exactly which garden I referred to but desperate to keep it a secret, a promising sign that the place I sought actually existed.

I chose a path at random and began my search. The plants must have passed down the news that I was looking for a secret garden, for every hedge, tree, flower, and greenery I encountered seemed unusually restless and attentive, as if they were monitoring my every move. Their strange reaction only further piqued my interest—whatever the secret garden contained must be quite spectacular. I became more determined than ever to discover it.

There was something guiding me more than mere curiosity; I felt as if I was being led by an invisible force, as if I was meant to discover this hidden garden. The lure was tantalizing—seductive whispers brushing against my thoughts, beckoning me to further explore until I found the object of my quest.

After nearly an hour, I paused at a crossroads, finally noticing something promising: while the path I was on continued to meander alongside the hedges until it twisted out of sight, the path beside me ended abruptly at a towering hedge wall swallowed in vines, one that stretched so high above me I had no hopes of peeking over to see what lay inside. I crouched down to examine the cobblestones, which the wall cut in half, suggesting that rather than ending here, the path continued *beyond* it.

Excitement fluttered in my chest. "This must be it."

All around me the garden's agitation intensified and Hibiscus wriggled on my shoulder. The moment the seductive lure pushed me forward, he scurried down and placed himself directly in the middle of the path, blocking me from going any further.

I frowned. "What is it? Is something wrong?"

He squirmed. Peculiar, but I wouldn't allow him to distract me from my impending discovery. I stepped around him and he immediately darted in front of me again. I slowed, suddenly hesitant, and studied the hedge wall more closely. It appeared entirely ordinary, with faint traces of light filtering through the thick growth of leaves, revealing that something awaited on the other side.

"Hibiscus, why are you so apprehensive? This is what I've been searching for. We must explore it."

I ventured forward and pushed aside the vines, which immediately tangled around my hands much like the ones who always guarded the outer palace walls. I managed to tug myself free and stepped back with a glare.

"What was that for?"

The vines gave another angry rustle before making another attempt to coil around my wrists, while Hibiscus futilely pushed against my ankle with his nose in an attempt to keep me away from the door. Rather than hinder me, they only stoked my burning need to see what lay beyond the wall. I fought off their tightening hold enough to brush them aside...only to discover that no door lay beneath them.

I heaved a frustrated sigh and stepped back to examine the wall again. If a secret garden really lay beyond it, it made sense that the entrance wasn't obvious, and thus wouldn't be conveniently located at the end of the path. I stepped off the cobblestones to walk the circumference of the outer hedge, picking my way through the thick undergrowth that repeatedly caught on my hem, as if trying to thwart my efforts to find the garden's entrance.

I circled the wall three times before pausing at a section I'd repeatedly passed without thought. I examined it more closely, compelled by the magic to take a closer look. Not only did the vines grow thicker here, but it was the only section of the hedge almost impossible to access with the obscuring way the trees grew in front of it, as if they were standing guard over...something. My anticipation tingled, for I strongly suspected what that *something* was.

I tried to find a way to access this section of the wall, but the trees served as impenetrable obstacles; the only solution was to climb them and hop down on the other side. I hiked up my skirts and held them in one hand before expertly tugging myself up onto the lowest bough. The branches scratched at my skin as I carefully maneuvered my way higher before jumping down on the other side.

The moment I landed, Hibiscus—who'd faithfully followed me into the tree—scurried down and caught the hem of my dress in his mouth to tug me to a stop.

I gently shook him off. "What are you doing? I just want to see what's inside the secret garden. What harm can it do?"

Undeterred, Hibiscus made another attempt to grab my hem, but I ignored him and stepped closer to the wall, pushing aside the biting vines like a curtain. My stomach sank in disappointment when I was met with nothing but the leafy hedge. But if the door wasn't here, why was Hibiscus acting so strangely?

I squinted and examined the wall more carefully...and grinned when I finally saw it. It wasn't an ordinary door made of wood, but was part of the hedge itself, its outline so faint that it blended seamlessly into the greenery, only discernible when one looked carefully. My smile grew as I traced my fingertip along the edge. This was the door I'd been searching for; I was certain of it.

I crouched down to the tiny, almost completely hidden keyhole cut into the hedge leaves. There wasn't any handle, and the lock itself was nearly completely obscured by vines and the leafy hedge. A tingle of excitement rippled over me as I pried them away and lightly traced the keyhole. This was it. I couldn't wait to see what spectacular wonders awaited me on the other side.

I retrieved the key from its hidden pocket. It warmed and tingled in my hand, as if it sensed it was about to be used and was excited by the prospect. As if guided by some sort of enchantment, I hypnotically lifted the key and allowed it to guide my hand to the keyhole. In a last desperate attempt to interfere, the vines tried to snatch the key from my hand, but I succeeded in tugging it away and shoving it into the lock... but still hesitated before turning it.

A warning whispered in the back of my mind that perhaps there was a reason for the plants' and Hibiscus's apprehension. Could there be a reason this garden had been locked and its key hidden? Foreboding settled over me at the thought...before I dismissed it. In all my time here, I'd yet to encounter anything sinister on the royal grounds, so I highly doubted anything dangerous lay beyond this locked door, especially when I'd discovered its key half buried in the ground, just waiting to be found.

The lock's click echoed through the sudden stillness that had settled over the grounds as I turned the key, as if every plant were holding its breath in anticipation. At first nothing happened, but then the keyhole began to glow and the door opened with an ominous creek to reveal the mysterious garden hidden inside.

I stepped forward...and immediately stilled. The entire garden was shrouded in silver mist, which hung thickly in the air, obscuring the plants from view. While the other gardens I'd explored contained a feeling of enchantment, an unsettling feeling hovered over this one—one more ominous than mysterious—and caused a shiver to creep up my spine. My first instinct was to leave, but something more powerful than my own reservations compelled me to venture further in.

With each step the mist began to lift, gradually revealing the details that had been previously masked from my view: several jagged rows of tall, thick, prickly weeds, growing in grotesque shapes and looking as if they'd been stained black. I abruptly froze and stared. These plants were so different from the vibrancy and color of those growing in the main gardens—these hung limply, as if all their magic had been drained from them.

I reached out a hesitant finger and stroked the barbed leaf of the nearest one. The moment I touched it, the plant disintegrated into vapor. I gasped and stumbled back, tripping over my skirts in my haste and falling to the hard, dry ground. There I watched as the dark smoke rose from what had once been the plant and twisted in the air before vanishing.

For a moment I stared wide-eyed at where the plant had, until moments ago, been growing. Now it was nothing more than an empty plot. Before my mind could even scramble for an explanation, the plant residing beside it began to fade, gradually disappearing from view until it'd vanished completely. Moments later, the ebony weed beside that one began to melt into a stream of ink, which began to slowly slither towards the open door.

Foreboding squeezed my chest with its icy fingers, pressing tighter as more of the plants disappeared while others melted into an inky substance, as if they were all somehow connected to one another. I finally emerged from my stupor long enough to scramble to my feet and hurry towards the exit, pausing only briefly on the threshold to glance back. The entire garden was blanketed with fog once more, and the inky black liquid from the melted plants was trickling ever closer.

I escaped outside and slammed the door. I pressed my back against the closed door and fought for each ragged breath. I knew the moment the strange, eerie mist reached the door, for coldness seeped through it to spread across my back. I gasped and stumbled away, steadying myself with the trunk of the willow I'd climbed to reach the garden entrance. There I watched the vapor curl up over the top of the towering hedge wall with its smoky fingers before vanishing into the air.

It took a moment for my pounding heart to steady and my frantic breaths to settle enough to turn the key, locking the garden up once more; the click sounded more ominous than it had when I'd unlocked it minutes before. I shakily withdrew the key and stared at it. It was icy cold, just like the door had become.

I had to get rid of this. Immediately. I looked around for an appropriate hiding place and chose one near a protruding root from the nearby willow. I dug a deep hole near a distinguishable knot so that I'd easily remember where the key was buried, even though I had no intention of ever using it again. Relief washed over me the moment I covered it up, and, suddenly exhausted, I slumped against the trunk.

It took several breathless minutes before I managed to stir. I craned my head back to take in the hedge that I now knew guarded whatever dark plants resided in the mysterious garden...ones I'd inadvertently destroyed with a single touch. The vines and surrounding fauna were still and droopy, as if weary from their fight to prevent me from entering the garden, a fight they'd lost. Guilt twisted around the nerves already tightening my stomach; I'd been foolish to ignore their warning.

I had to tell Briar what had happened. My heart sank; that was the last thing I wanted to do. The friendship budding between us had been blossoming more each day. I'd never had a true friend before, and it was something I didn't want to lose. But if the prince discovered what I'd done...I shook my head. No, I couldn't lose his kind regard. I wouldn't.

Perhaps I could wait to see if my venture into the mysterious garden had any ill effects. I was sure I hadn't done any permanent damage, for not only were the palace gardens enchanted, but whatever I'd inadvertently triggered was safely contained behind the locked door.

I took a steadying breath before slowly standing and climbing the tree; it was a relief to drop down on the other side and put more distance between me and the garden door. I paused in brushing off the dirt from my skirts when I sensed all the surrounding plants eyeing me in clear disapproval.

I bit my lip. "I've buried the key and promise never to open the door again. Please don't tell Briar what happened."

It was a plea I was certain they'd ignore, for they had a duty to their prince. My conscience whispered that it would be better for him to learn of my mistake from me rather than the garden, but my stomach clenched at the thought of confessing. I couldn't bear to experience the same disapproval coming from him as was now coming from the gardens.

Above me, the sun had risen high in the sky, signifying the late afternoon hour. I'd already missed lunch, and if I didn't hurry back, I'd miss dinner too, which would invite all sorts of questions from the prince I didn't want to answer. I began to search for Hibiscus so we could leave...only to discover that he was nowhere to be found.

"Hibiscus?"

He didn't come at my call. I looked frantically around, scouring the thick undergrowth for a lilac topiary hedgehog.

"Hibiscus?"

At his continued absence, the icy fear I'd been struggling to keep at bay squeezed my chest. I hadn't left him in the secret garden, had I? I was about to turn around and return to the door when a nearby clump of quivering hibiscus flowers caught my attention. I crept closer and parted them to discover my hedgehog huddled there, shivering in fright.

I gently stroked his back. "There, there, Hibiscus. The garden is locked up. Everything will be alright." But the words felt like a lie. After all, the fact remained that I'd unlocked that garden and done *something* to its plants, but I tried to reassure myself that whatever I'd done was now safely trapped within the strange garden.

I slowly glanced around, as if I expected the black weeds to be hiding amongst the foliage, but there was nothing but the colorful vegetation. Still...I couldn't quite shake the worry that seemed to emanate from the silent plants, still watching me nervously.

I stroked the hedgehog quivering in my lap. "Calm down, Hibiscus. Everything will be alright," I again whispered assuringly, but my voice shook, betraying my underlining panic. What *had* happened in that garden, and would there be any consequences from my foolhardy adventure?

CHAPTER 9

"*W*hat's the name of this plant?"

Briar barely had to examine the unusual flower whose sunset-colored blossoms grew upside down from the leaves before he recognized it. "That's a *brugmansia*, also known as *Angel's Trumpet* or *Angel's Coral Sunset*."

Both names were incredibly fitting, considering the flower's soft-orange and delicate-rose coloring, as well as the way its trumpet-shaped petals dangled delicately from the leaves, as if the blossoms descended directly from the heavens.

"*Brugmansia*." I repeated the name slowly to commit it to memory, just as I'd been doing for all the other plants Briar had taught me about in the week since we'd started gardening together. I was certain that if I only befriended the whimsical gardens, they'd be more inclined to let me go.

The only problem with that plan was that the more time I spent here, the less inclined I was to leave...but perhaps that was more because of the prince than the enchanted grounds themselves. I glanced sideways at him. We'd spent time together every day this past week, and the more we did, the more I came to like the stoic but kind-hearted prince.

"Maren?"

I blinked rapidly, my cheeks burning when I realized I'd been caught staring at him. "What is it?"

The corner of his mouth lifted. "I asked if you were truly interested in learning the names of all these plants, only to receive a blank stare in return. Now I fear I've been boring you." Despite his teasing tone, vulnerability shone in his dark eyes, as if that was a genuine concern of his.

"Of course you're not," I said. "I'd tell you if I were bored."

He chuckled. "I daresay you would." For some reason, he seemed pleased by this. He glanced around the garden where we'd spent the past hour. "That's the last of the plants in this garden. Shall we adjourn to another? There's one in particular that I know you'll enjoy."

A bubble of warmth swelled in my chest at the thought that he not only seemed to enjoy my company but was finding excuses to extend it. It almost seemed too good to be true. "Do you really have time?" I asked.

"Certainly," he said. "My next meeting isn't until after lunch, and I'll spend the evening catching up on papers."

He stood and extended his hand to help me up. I waited for Hibiscus to crawl back onto my shoulder before accepting it. A strange thrill came over me to touch him, and another fluttery ripple quickly followed when he looped his arm through mine to escort me from the garden.

We walked in companionable silence as he led me confidently down the twisting garden paths, but my contentment faltered when we passed the path I'd taken a few days ago, the one that led to the mysterious locked garden.

I immediately froze. Briar glanced over, his brows furrowed in concern. "Is something wrong?"

My heart pounded as I stared down the path. I still hadn't

told Briar what had happened in that garden, even though my conscience had repeatedly urged me to. But I'd ignored its promptings to confess, simply because the more I remembered that day in the strange garden and the way its plants had transformed, the more certain I was that I'd done something wrong.

But if I had, wouldn't the gardens have tattled to Briar? The fact he hadn't brought it up caused me to hope that what I'd done hadn't caused any harm.

"It's nothing." Guilt tightened my chest at the lie. I turned away from the path and forced a smile. "Shall we resume our stroll? I'm quite eager to see which garden you want to show me."

Briar studied my face carefully, causing me to squirm. Would he be able to detect my guilt? After a tense moment he relaxed and resumed walking. "It's just straight ahead."

A few minutes later we stood at the entrance, where I stumbled to a stop once again, this time to stare around the garden in wide-eyed wonder.

This garden looked to be straight from a dream. Flowers grew not only from the ground, but seemed to grow straight from the air, hanging above us like a canopy to bathe us in their sweet, floral perfume. Sunshine filtered through the gaps between the petals and leaves, glistening off the other flowers which floated around like bubbles.

"Incredible," I murmured when I'd finally found my voice. "How is such a wonder accomplished?"

"Magic," he said simply. "I wish I knew more of the gardens' secrets, but perhaps the mystery only adds to the enchantment."

I tugged myself free from Briar's arm to wander through the flowerbeds, which grew so wildly and close together I had to watch my step so as not to trample on any of them. It was incredible how something so untamed could still be so lovely; it only enhanced its beauty, making me feel as if I were tucked in a cocoon of foliage, completely separated from the real world.

Briar walked beside me, seeming to take great pleasure in my reactions. "Do you like it?"

"I *love* it," I breathed. "I never want to leave."

"Then you may come as often as you like, but keep in mind that you can only access it during the morning hours. Come, there's one section in particular I want to show you."

He re-offered his arm and led me through the haphazard lines of flowers, which parted for their prince, offering a narrow path that forced us to walk close together. We settled beside a flowerbed of violet blossoms I couldn't identify, and I cast my gaze across the garden, tinged pink in the dancing rosy-golden light that caused the surrounding flowers to glisten.

"I see why you love gardening so much," I said reverently. "Especially when you have such a garden as this. It would be a pleasure to work in such beautiful surroundings every day."

"These gardens, as wondrous as they are, aren't the main reason I enjoy the hobby," he said. "There's something incredibly satisfying about nourishing a seed to help it grow into its full potential. I love doing my part to add beauty to the world."

He paused to subtly stifle a yawn, and paranoia immediately flared in my chest. "Are you tiring of my company?"

"Not at all. I'm simply...exhausted."

My relief quickly turned into concern as I eyed the dark circles beneath the prince's eyes. "Are you not sleeping well?"

"I'm sleeping fine, but it makes little difference. Ever since I left Draceria, I seem to be constantly tired, though not quite as weak as when I initially returned."

He'd alluded to this trip before, but he hadn't provided many details. "What happened in Draceria?"

He released a long breath. "Many things, but the worst was when I violated the conditions of my curse; I am now being punished for it. I knew how foolhardy the decision was, but it needed to be done. While at times the lingering effects become rather wearying, I have no regrets."

If anything, my curiosity only grew with such a vague answer, but there was another matter I found far more pressing. "And you were in Draceria for Princess Rheanna?"

He actually blushed. "That's correct." He suddenly became rather preoccupied with tracing swirls in the soft dirt. "We were to forge a marriage alliance."

I automatically stiffened, even though I'd already known this. The entire kingdom had, just as we'd also learned that the princess had instead married Briar's brother, Prince Drake. But suddenly what had been nothing more than royal news felt far more personal now that I was sitting so closely with the prince who'd become more my friend than my future sovereign.

"And...it fell through?"

He nodded. "We became good friends and at one point were even engaged, but in the end we didn't suit one another, so she married my brother."

He continued to avoid my eyes and looked around, as if desperately searching for a distraction, which he found in a nearby clump of weeds. My heart beat wildly as I watched him begin yanking them out with unusual fervor. Clearly he was more upset about his broken engagement than he let on. Had he been in love with the princess?

A strange burning feeling seared through me at the thought that he possibly had. "Did she break your heart?" I asked gently.

His gaze snapped up in surprise before he hastily shook his head, to my fierce relief. "Not at all."

I furrowed my brow. "Then why—"

"She couldn't break what she didn't have," he said, more adamantly. "I'm happy for her and Drake. How can I not be when my friend and brother found love together?" He frowned. "Why are you looking at me like that? Do you not believe me?"

"Forgive me, you just seem rather emotional when discussing the event. I assumed it was because..." I hastily looked away, feeling more foolish by the minute to be discussing such a thing with the crown prince.

"I'm not resentful my brother fell in love with my intended," Briar said. "While Rhea is a fine woman and would have made a wonderful wife, she was my mother's choice, not mine."

"Do you have someone else in mind?"

He shook his head, but the way he peered up at me was rather...soft. My cheeks warmed at such a look, and for the first time in my life, I felt...special, like I *could* matter to someone. I was almost afraid of both this secret wish and the seed of hope that had been planted in my heart at the prince's look. The last thing I wanted to do was nourish it, not when doing so would only lead to disappointment.

As if he realized he'd been staring, Briar hastily looked away, his expression almost...confused. I did too, unable to look him in the eye after the strange *something* that had passed between us.

I found a much-needed distraction from my suddenly fluttering heart in my mischievous hedgehog, who'd spent the entirety of our conversation quietly exploring the surrounding flora. I watched as he ventured closer to a group of cheerful-looking orange-and-white blossoms.

"What are you up to, you silly hedgehog? Come here." I reached out to pluck him up and Briar suddenly lurched forward.

"Be careful, that plant has—"

I gasped at the sudden biting pain and yanked my hand away. I gaped as blood quickly pooled in my palm to trickle down my wrist.

Briar carefully took my hand. "I should have warned you, but those flowers have hidden thorns that cut surprisingly deeply." He took out his handkerchief and began to gently dab at the blood staining my hand. Despite the gentleness of his touch, it caused me to stiffen, even though the last thing I wanted to do was to pull away.

The pain was becoming sharper, making me slightly lightheaded. I concentrated on each of Briar's movements and the crimson blood staining his handkerchief, breathing deeply in order to fight the dizziness slowly overcoming me.

He paused to lift the handkerchief and examine the cut, carefully running his fingers over it to check how deep it was. A strange shiver rippled up my arm as he touched me.

"Does it sting?" he asked.

"A little," I admitted, even though it was beginning to hurt more than a mere *sting*.

"Luckily it's not too deep, but we should put something on it. I know just the thing." He helped me up and led me from the garden. I obediently followed, but my steps quickly began to slow as my surroundings blurred together, even as the stinging cut began to burn.

Briar slowed. "Maren?" He lifted my hand eye level and cursed.

"What's wrong?" I stuttered.

"Your cut is starting to fester. I'd forgotten that the thorns are venomous."

My heart lurched at the word. "They're *what?*"

"Not to worry, it's not toxic enough to be fatal." But worry still clouded his eyes, which wasn't at all reassuring.

He walked faster, and in my attempt to keep up I stumbled, kept from falling only by Briar's secure hold around my waist. My vision continued to blur and darkness pressed against my senses, as if I was near a faint...but I wouldn't succumb; such a gesture was frequently used as ploy by beautiful damsels on prospective suitors and thus had no place here.

I gave a yelp of surprise when the world suddenly tipped as Briar scooped me into his arms. "What are you doing?"

"Carrying you," he said as he picked up his pace. "You're near a faint, and the medical garden is still on the other side of the grounds."

"That's inconvenient." I made a half-hearted attempt to wriggle free before I gave up the fight and slumped against him. While he was warm and smelled amazing, his chest was rather firm and not exactly comfortable. "I might prefer to walk. Your chest is too hard." I gave it a little poke.

To my surprise, he chuckled. "Your usual frankness means you're not fading away from your condition." He quickly sobered. "I pray you're not seriously hurt; I'm not entirely sure the effects of a cut from a poisonous plant, and a magical one at that."

I jostled uncomfortably as he took a sharp turn and ducked beneath an overhanging branch. "Do you really know so little about your own gardens?"

"It would take a lifetime to learn all of its secrets, and that's with it not constantly changing."

"Excuses, excuses." His quick stride was beginning to make me woozy. I closed my eyes and leaned against his shoulder. "I'm surprised there's even a poisonous plant found in these gardens. Is it for enemies of the crown?"

He chuckled again, but it sounded forced. "That's one possible explanation, but in truth it's one of my mother's plants. The queen grew many unusual kinds, and while most are contained in a separate garden, some can be found sprinkled throughout the grounds." His expression tightened in worry as he stared at my hand cradled close to my chest. "I should have warned you some plants could be dangerous. Now harm has befallen you while you're under my charge."

"Don't be ridiculous. I'll be fine."

But his concern warmed me all the same...or perhaps that delightful warmth came from his chest, which was becoming cozier the longer I lay curled against him. Then again, it could be from the fever I could feel burning my face as heat spread across my injured hand. It was hard to tell in my delirious state, especially as the pain steadily grew, enflaming my hand. I tightened my jaw, determined not to react.

But a whimper escaped anyway. Briar increased his pace. "Hold on, we're almost there."

And in a moment we were. Briar entered a garden whose scenery all blurred together and gently set me down on a bench. I missed his arms around me the moment he released me, but I was too weak to protest. A moment later I felt something cold on my hand.

My eyes shot open to find the prince kneeling in front of me, my hand gently cradled in his as he carefully spread a pasty green substance across my cut. The stinging pain lessened with each touch; whether it was from him or the salve I wasn't sure.

"How does it feel?" he asked gently.

I swallowed. "Better." I blinked at my cut. "My hand is orange."

His lips twitched. "So you've noticed."

Now that my discomfort was gradually slipping away and my fever was receding, this new worry fought for my attention. "It's not permanent, is it?" As if I needed anything else to mar my already unusual appearance.

"It isn't...at least, I don't *think* so." He nibbled his lip and dipped his finger in the salve to reapply it to my hand. "This is the garden's most potent healing balm. My siblings and I frequently used it while growing up. You'll be healed in no time."

I was already feeling better. As the pain continued to fade, my vision was gradually clearing, allowing me the opportunity to slowly take in the garden, sterile and plain compared to the others, with its muted colors and simple plants growing in rigid, tidy rows.

"Are all the plants in this garden medicinal?"

"Most of them. Some do various other things."

"Such as?"

His lips curved up, seemingly charmed by my usual unquenchable curiosity. "I'll leave that for you to discover when you're feeling better."

He dipped his finger back into the flower in his lap, whose petals formed a bowl, which automatically refilled itself with the green medicine whenever he took some. With each application the heat from my hand continued to fade... only to spread across my cheeks as I lifted my gaze to study the prince—the concentration lining his brow, his deep chocolate-brown eyes, the way his black hair fell untidily across his forehead.... My stomach gave a strange twist and I yanked my gaze away, only for my attention to be captured by his hands cradling mine.

He's so kind. I doubted I'd ever met someone as sweet as him.

Briar finished applying the salve and began to wrap my hand up in a thick leaf that cooled my hand and made me feel almost sleepy. He paused to peer up at me through his tousled bangs. "Are you feeling better?"

"Much," I said. "Whatever you put on my hand seems to have worked."

He tilted his head, a smile in his eyes. "Are you sure? Because you haven't asked many questions about this garden, and I'm worried the poison dampened your curiosity, which would be a rather tragic casualty."

"Never. Give me another moment and I'll pester you with a myriad of questions."

The way he smiled made me wonder if he was looking forward to it. He finished tying off the leaf bandage and placed my hand gently in my lap. He started to withdraw... but froze, his eyes narrowed at my wrist. He seized my hand once more and lifted it eye level to examine it more closely.

His jaw clenched. "Where did you get this?"

Drat, he'd noticed my scar, which would force me to reveal more about my past than I was prepared to explain. I swallowed. "Nowhere."

"I highly doubt that." He lightly traced the scar encircling most of my wrist with his fingertip, a gesture which strangely made me more compelled to confide in him. I tightened my jaw to resist the impulse and he released a frustrated breath. "Please, Maren, I must know. I can tell you've been cut. Tell me what happened."

His tone was more an order than a request, but I refused to allow it to extract my secrets from me. Unfortunately, my tongue had different ideas. "It wasn't intentional if that's what you're worried about," I said. "It was an accident."

The memories returned unbidden—my fight with Father several years ago—back when his temper had been closer to the surface in the months following Mother's death—the bitter way he'd yelled at me, the fear that had caused me to back away into a priceless vase. It had shattered before I could stop it, causing the hatred filling Father's eyes to deepen.

His fierce look still haunted me. I'd desperately tried to pick up the broken pieces so I could put the vase back together, frantically thinking for one crazy moment that I could perhaps fix it, that I could mend the disappointments that seemed a permanent obstacle between Father and me and thus fix our relationship.

But Father had stomped over to yank me away, causing me to drop the piece of porcelain, which slit my wrist as it fell. The scar served as a constant reminder of the decision I'd made that day as my governess tended to my wound: I'd never be able to please my Father, nor could I change him, so I refused to allow him to control how I felt about myself.

The story burned in my memory, but it was one I couldn't share, not with the prince. But he expected something, so I gave him the simplest answer I could. "I broke a vase after I backed into it."

Briar lifted a brow. "Should I put my own treasures under constant guard against such clumsiness?"

"Of course not." I hated needing to explain. "It was an accident. I'd been distracted because Father...was yelling at me." The words escaped before I realized it, and I immediately wished I could snatch them back.

Briar's entire manner hardened in a protective way I always imagined an older brother would look, if I'd had one. "Why?"

My cheeks burned but I forced myself to shrug in feigned nonchalance. "I've always been a disappointment to him."

And I had no doubt I always would. I'd wasted too much time trying to please him before realizing that his approval came at too high of a cost: that of losing too much of myself. So I'd instead focused my efforts on doing the opposite of what he expected of me. While I hated his negative attention, part of me thought it was better than no attention at all, and I hated that part of me that craved it.

I startled as Briar gently rested his hand over mine, his entire expression full of compassion. "How could you possibly disappoint him?"

I shrugged, even though I knew the answer to that all too

well. "I'm his only child, one who had the gall of being born a girl when he wanted a son. Mother never could have any other children and died several years ago. I look nothing like her." I gave Briar a pointed look to emphasize that point. "*Nothing*. And I'm unladylike and...everything I'm not supposed to be, making me useless to my father, until—" Searing anger sharper than the burn that the poisoned thorns had inflicted swelled in my chest.

Briar squeezed my hand. "What did he do that made you run away?"

I startled. "Who told you Father is the reason I—" But I already knew the answer. I slumped in defeat. "Apparently your garden isn't one to keep secrets." I should have known a bunch of enchanted plants couldn't be trusted. That would be the last time I took them into my confidence.

He gave me an apologetic look. "When you remained elusive about yourself, I couldn't help but ask them about you to find out what they knew. I wanted to know more about the woman living in my home."

I sighed. "I should have known the plants can't keep a confidence."

"They were solely motivated by their worry for you," Briar said. "After all, they like you very much; you've thoroughly charmed them." His dark gaze became prodding. "So why did you run away?"

This was a secret I'd been terrified of revealing to Briar since, as a prince who obeyed the laws of the land, he'd be forced to turn me over to my father. But the kindness in his eyes and the tender way his hand rested over mine compelled me to trust him.

"Because Father...sold my hand."

Briar's breath hitched before his face twisted in disgust. "He. Did. *What?*"

I hastily explained. "He's a merchant. A year ago he lost

his most valuable ship and all the goods on it, leaving us nearly destitute. His primary investor is in need of a wife, so he agreed to help Father if...he got me in exchange. Considering I'll likely never get another offer, Father agreed... without my knowledge or consent."

Briar gritted his teeth. "He has no right—"

"According to the law, he does." I lifted my chin. "But I refuse to allow myself to be sold to anyone, much less a man as horrible as Lord Brone. So I ran away, but because of the garden's imprisonment, I haven't managed to get very far. If Father comes looking for me..."

My gaze darted towards the garden entrance, as if I expected Father to appear at any moment. But of course he wasn't there.

"He won't get in," Briar said assuredly, accurately guessing my fear. "You don't need to be afraid." He gave my hands a comforting squeeze. "I won't allow your father to take you. You have my word."

I ached to embrace his promise, but I knew doing so was naive. "You can't promise me such a thing. Aren't you obligated to turn me over to my father if he should find me?"

"I won't," he said, his expression fiercer than I'd ever seen it before. "I'll figure out a way to free you. Please don't concern yourself with the legal details; I don't want you to worry. Just know that you're safe here. You have my word."

His promise enfolded me like an embrace, and for the first time since sneaking out of my window in the dead of night and into an unknown future, I felt...peace. I smiled. "Thank you."

He nodded curtly. "Of course. I can't believe your father... what kind of scoundrel would..." He clenched his jaw to suppress the words that would likely be too indelicate for a lady's ears before his gaze lowered to the cut on my wrist, which he lightly traced once more. "Did he ever hurt you?"

My eyes burned and I hastily blinked my tears away. Briar's expression crumpled.

"Maren? He didn't, did he?" Despite his barely suppressed fury at the thought, he was all gentleness.

"Not in the way you mean. Only in words and neglect."

"That is more than enough." He shook his head, his disgust deepening, before he squeezed my hand again. "I'm proud of you for taking charge of your own life and running away, and I want to offer my sincerest apology that I initially made you feel unwelcome here. Please be assured that I'm happy to have you stay with me."

I managed a watery smile. "I appreciate the sentiment, even though we both know that it's the gardens who are truly in charge of that decision."

His lips lifted into a small smile of his own. "They certainly are, but I welcome you all the same." He looked over the apothecary garden, his expression pensive. "I now better understand at least part of the reason why the gardens tricked you—they were trying to protect you, even if they went about it the wrong way."

"But will its protection last?"

"Of course. I'll do everything in my power to ensure that it does. I promise."

His promise lightened my heart, and for the first time, the burdens I seemed to have always carried alone lifted. I gave him another shy, hesitant smile, which he returned, causing another drop to nourish the hope sprouting in my heart that despite my being unwanted in the past, perhaps with Briar things would finally be different.

CHAPTER 10

I looked up from the book of poetry I was reading out loud to His Majesty when his wrinkled hand weakly squeezed mine. I immediately set the book aside. "Is there something you need?"

He didn't answer, simply stared up at the canopy of his bed, his eyes glassy and his breathing shallow. I pressed the back of my hand to his brow and frowned at the attending nurse.

"He feels warmer. I fear his fever is getting worse. Can you check?"

She bustled over to do so. By the worried way her forehead crinkled, I could tell I was right to be concerned. "I'll inform His Highness at once." She hurried from the room, leaving me alone at the king's bedside.

I wiped a cool rag across his brow, the helplessness pressing against my chest making my movements shaky. "You're going to be alright, Your Majesty."

He fumbled for my hand. "I'm glad you're home, Reve darling. I've been so worried for you." He lifted my hand to his lips to weakly kiss my knuckles.

My eyes burned but I bit the inside of my lip to keep my tears at bay. "Please don't worry," I said soothingly. "I'm safe and won't leave you again." My heart wrenched at the lie, especially since there was still no word about the missing princess, but the peace that settled over His Majesty made it worth it.

The king said nothing more, but his grip on my hand tightened, as if seeking solace from my touch. I studied his expression. Although I had no nursing experience, even I could see how quickly the king had faded in the month since I'd arrived at the palace, especially within the past several days.

I patted his hand. I basked in the feel of my hand in his, for in it I could feel his fatherly concern, concern which I'd always longed for from my own father. Even though I knew His Majesty was only giving it to me because he'd mistaken me for his daughter, I treasured it all the same.

A soft knock sounded on the door. The king weakly glanced towards it, his eyes lit with hope. "Gemma dear, is that you?"

The door opened to reveal Briar, the nurse hovering just behind him. "It's me, Father."

The king smiled, his eyes crinkling at the edges in the same way Briar's did. "There you are, my boy. It's good to see you."

He lifted the hand not holding mine to beckon his son closer. Briar lit up at his father's invitation. He hurried to his father's side and sat on the edge of the bed to take his hand.

"How are you feeling? I heard you have a fever." By his tone he sounded as if he'd only just found out about it, when in truth it'd been worrying him unceasingly these past several days.

"It's only a fever," the king said. "There's no need to fuss."

"You know there very well is a need," Briar said. "It's been a privilege to have the opportunity to fuss over you after all the loving fuss I received from you growing up."

His father managed a brief chuckle that quickly turned into a raspy cough. I hastily poured water into a glass and handed it to Briar, who helped the king take several small sips before he leaned his head back with a weary sigh.

"Are you alright?" Briar asked, his eyes swirling with concern.

The king nodded weakly. "Yes, but I need a moment." He heaved another struggling breath. "Stay with me."

Briar patted his hand. "I'll stay right here."

The king seemed to relax, although worry lined his brow. "How is the kingdom?"

"Faring wonderfully," Briar said. "It's been my greatest pleasure helping you until you're well enough to return to your duties." Although his tone was cheerful, the heartache in his eyes revealed the truth: his father would never be well enough to resume the throne.

"I've never doubted your abilities, my boy," the king murmured. "Did I interrupt your duties?"

"My next meeting isn't for another hour, and I was only going over documents when the nurse sent for me." Briar held up a thick stack. "I can just as easily read over them here if you don't mind the company while you rest."

The king smiled, and Briar settled the papers on his lap, not letting go of his father's hand.

I knew I ought to leave now, but I couldn't make myself do so. So I alternated between watching Briar—the concentrated way he studied each document as well as his frequent glances towards his father to check on him—and the king, who also alternated between staring gauntly at the ceiling and turning a rather loving gaze towards his son. In each look, I could see how proud of him he was and how much he adored him. A lump formed in my throat. How fortunate he was to have such a father.

Briar paused at a particular document and frowned as he studied it before turning to the king. "Father, if you're feeling up to it, might I ask what you think of this new proposal on raising the tax on imported goods?"

The king shakily accepted the document. He read over it carefully, looking far more alert than he had all day, as he usually did whenever Briar asked him his opinion on matters of state. Most visits Briar brought documents for his father—both those that required the king's signature after he'd carefully explained their contents, or those which he had questions about. Although frequently confused, the king seemed more himself when they discussed political matters, and even had a few suggestions for alterations, which the prince always carefully noted. Each time I watched these interactions, my respect for Briar grew. Despite his position as acting king, he always respected his father's position and never took advantage of the moments when his father was less than coherent, including now.

The king finished looking over the document and glanced up with a frustrated sigh. "What's Draceria?"

Briar's expression faltered, although his tone remained cheerful. "Draceria is our neighboring kingdom and our closest trade partner."

The king's frown deepened as he glanced over the document once more before shakily handing it back to the prince. "I'm afraid there's much about this I no longer understand. What do you think about the proposal, son?"

Briar hesitated. "I want your opinion. Despite my taking care of the more tedious tasks on your behalf, you're still the king."

"The time has come for you to make such decisions yourself. I'll sign whatever it is you need me to, but I trust your judgement."

Briar swallowed. "But what if your trust is misplaced? What if I prove incapable? I could never be as great a king as you've been."

"You're not meant to be like me. I hope your reign exceeds mine in every way as you become the king you're meant to be." He rested his hand on his shoulder. "You can do this."

A myriad of emotions passed over Briar's face before determination settled over him. "Thank you, Father. I'll do my best."

"I know you will."

Briar set aside his documents and the two began to converse quietly, their affection for one another obvious in each gesture, but it wasn't long before the king's lucidity began to fade.

Panic filled Briar's eyes as he desperately clung to the king's hand. "Please stay with me a moment longer, Father."

But the confusion that so often overcame His Majesty had fully settled over him. He blinked at Briar before his eyes narrowed. "Who are you?"

Briar stared, clearly stricken. Although I'd witnessed many of the king's confusions, this was the first time I'd seen him forget his son. "It's me, Father," he said shakily. "Briar."

The king's expression cleared. "Briar, you say? I have a son named Briar. A quiet and rather serious boy, but you'll never meet one kinder than him. He likes to sit on my knee during meetings and follow me around as I tend to matters of state. I've been teaching him sword training. Such a good boy."

Briar's eyes grew glassy as he listened. "Our afternoons sword training together are some of my fondest memories."

The king's brow furrowed. "No, we didn't do it together; I

did it with my son, Briar." He looked around, searching. "He was just here. Can you get him? I want to see him."

Briar sat staring at the king for a long moment before he rested his forehead on the king's chest, his hold on his father's hand tightening. He stayed in this position for several minutes while I watched helplessly.

The king made no move to push his son away; he was back to staring at the canopy. I gave Briar a few minutes before I summoned enough bravery to rest my hand on his shoulder. He reached up and brushed against it as he slowly straightened. His eyes were bloodshot, but there were no other signs of the emotion that had passed over him, for he'd gathered his composure and wrapped it securely back around him.

"I'll send for Drake and Rhea. Now rest, Father."

The king stared blankly at him for a moment before recognition filled his eyes once again and he smiled. "I'd like that, Son." He reached out to pat his cheek. "I'm so proud of you."

Briar swallowed. "Thank you." He dipped down to kiss his father's wrinkly cheek. "Take care. I'll visit again soon." He rose to leave, but the nurse stepped forward from where she'd been standing against the wall.

"A word, Your Highness?" My stomach tightened in worry at the gravity filling her expression.

Briar glanced at me, his silent request I leave them to their conversation. I obeyed and waited outside the door. He emerged several minutes later, his expression ragged. He quietly closed the door behind him and pressed his forehead to it for a moment, taking several deep, steadying breaths before looking wearily up at me.

"Thank you for sitting with him again. You've been so sweet with him."

"I've enjoyed spending time with him." And with the

soberness filling his eyes following his conversation with the nurse, I feared that my moments with the king were soon to come to an end. "What did the nurse say?"

Briar sighed. "That he's declining quickly. I need to write Drake and Rhea and inform them of the situation. I pray that they can arrive in time."

Alarm flared in my heart. "Could it be so soon?"

"I'm afraid so. I'm not ready to say goodbye." His entire manner crumpled. "He's never forgotten me before."

I stepped forward and rested my hand on his arm. "I'm sorry, I'm sure that was quite painful for you, but I don't believe he's truly forgotten you. He simply doesn't recognize you sometimes, but your memories together are still very much a part of him."

Briar slowly nodded but didn't lift his gaze, which was fixated on my hand resting on his arm. He covered mine with his and gave it a squeeze. "Thank you, Maren. I'm glad you're here. I don't think I could get through this without you." He took another steadying breath and straightened back up. "I shall write the letter at once. I'll see you later at dinner."

He stepped away, severing our touch, but the shadow of it lingered long after I'd watched the prince disappear down the corridor.

THE LETTER WAS SENT to the prince and princess within the hour, and their response arrived the following morning: they would leave immediately and arrive by nightfall. Although I knew the gates would open to admit them, I wasn't even tempted to seize the opportunity to escape; I couldn't leave Briar during such a time. He spent every spare moment with his father, all other duties temporarily suspended so he could tend to him.

The Malvagarian prince and princess were announced shortly after dinner. The footman admitted them to where we waited in the parlor and they entered hand in hand, looking weary from their travels but alert. Prince Drake shared Briar's dark coloring and similar features, although he more closely resembled the king, whereas Princess Rheanna was a golden-haired, blue-eyed beauty.

For the very first time, insecurity over my own looks twinged in my breast, but I hardly had time to dwell on it when the princess broke away from her husband to hug Briar, Prince Drake looking on with a somber expression. Neither even glanced in my direction.

"Thank you for coming so quickly," Briar said when he and the princess broke their embrace.

"How is he?" Prince Drake asked. "Has he grown worse since you wrote?"

"His condition deteriorated rapidly during the night," Briar said. "While he has moments of lucidity, they're becoming fewer and fewer. I'm grateful you came."

"Is he up for visitors? I'd like to see him now." The prince started to turn but paused when he caught sight of me. His eyes narrowed. "Who's this?"

"This is…" Briar hesitated, clearly unsure how to intro- duce me. "This is Miss Maren, who is here as my guest."

Prince Drake lifted an eyebrow but didn't ask further questions. "Miss Maren." He bowed before taking his wife's arm. She greeted me with a smile and curtsy before exiting the parlor with her husband to visit the king, leaving Briar and me alone.

"I'm relieved they were able to come so quickly," I said. Briar said nothing as he stared after the prince and princess, his expression unreadable. When his silence continued, I spoke again. "How shall we explain my presence?"

"Simply with the truth." Briar's gaze didn't waver from the closed door, and I finally recognized the emotion filling his entire manner: unease, as if something about his brother and sister-in-law's arrival unsettled him.

Fear suddenly squeezed my chest. Was it the princess? Did Briar harbor unrequited feelings for her? My stomach knotted at the thought, even as a strange, searing feeling seeped over me.

I lightly grazed his elbow. "Are you alright?"

He managed a nod. "I haven't seen my brother very often since his marriage to Rhea. We've never been particularly close, and I fear their visit will only escalate the tension that's usually between us. I have more than enough to worry about right now."

Relief washed over me, quickly replaced by guilt that I could feel such a thing midst Briar's distress. "Perhaps this experience will be just the thing to strengthen your relationship and bring you closer."

He managed a nod before giving me a half smile. "Although the task seems rather daunting, I'm glad I don't have to face it or Father's illness alone." He stepped closer, an intensity filling his eyes. "I feared you'd seize the opportunity to escape when the gardens opened the gate for Drake and Rhea. I'm relieved you're still here."

My heart swelled. "So am I." It would be an honor to stand by the crown prince at such a trying time, but I knew I was motivated by something far deeper than honor or even friendship, an emotion I was almost afraid to examine for fear of what I'd discover.

~

DUE TO THE lateness of the prince and princess's arrival, we didn't see them for the remainder of the evening, for after sitting with His Majesty they retired for the night.

I awoke early the following morning eager to check on the king. Despite the approaching summer, a chilly draft drifted through the palace. I wrapped a shawl around my shoulders and tiptoed through the silent passageways towards the king's chambers, as I did every morning. I expected to find only a nurse, but instead I found Briar asleep on the chair beside his father's bed, his forehead pressed against the covers and the king's hand enfolded in his.

I slowly backed from the room so as not to disturb either of them, but at the sound of my footsteps against the stone floor, Briar groggily looked up. "Maren?"

I hungrily soaked in his slightly disoriented expression and tousled dark hair before hastily averting my gaze with a heated blush. "Good morning, Your Highness."

"Briar," he corrected automatically as he yawned and stretched. "You haven't forgotten my insistence on disregarding formalities in quite some time."

That's because I hadn't needed them to remind myself that the flustered way the prince sometimes made me feel was entirely inappropriate, as I did now. "Have you been here all night?"

He yawned again before nodding to the empty chair beside him, urging me to sit. "Most of it. Drake and Rhea spent the first half with Father before becoming too tired to remain up with him, so they sent a servant for me so I could sit with him. We don't want him to be alone...and yet I fell asleep." Guilt marred his expression as he surveyed his father to ensure that his negligence hadn't harmed him, but other than the king's raspy breathing, he appeared fine.

"Don't blame yourself; tending him all week has made you exhausted. Couldn't the nurse have stayed with him?"

"I wanted to do it," he said fiercely. "Although I turned out to be a poor choice; I should have been more vigilant."

"You've been nothing but vigilant," I said soothingly. "Now you should go to bed. I'll stay with the king and will send word if there's any change in his condition."

Briar seemed reluctant to heed my suggestion. He stared at his father, his expression both loving and utterly helpless. I gave his arm an encouraging tug, and his perplexed attention lowered to my hand, just as it'd done the other times I'd been brave enough to touch him.

He hesitated a moment more before sighing in acquiescence. "Very well, you win, but don't look so smug about it."

I smirked. He rolled his eyes good-naturedly before standing, relinquishing the chair nearest the king. As I rose to take it, he brushed my hand with his thumb, causing me to instantly still.

"Thank you, Maren. Your support means everything to me."

My heart flipped at the tenderness filling his dark eyes. It began to beat wildly when Briar's fingers lightly caressed my wrist, sending heated tingles up my arm.

I glanced down at where his thumb lightly stroked my knuckles, his movements almost hypnotic. "What are you doing?"

Crimson stained his cheeks as he rapidly withdrew, and I silently cursed my burning need to ask questions that had pulled his pleasant touch away.

"I don't know. Forgive me." Puzzlement lined his brow as he flexed his hand, as if trying to dispel the feeling of my touch; my stomach sank at the thought. He cleared his throat. "I'm rather tired. Please excuse me."

He hastily left the room without a single look back, leaving me staring after him.

～

I SAT with His Majesty for an hour before Prince Drake arrived, looking both regal and rather unkempt, his eyes bleary as if he was still half asleep. He stumbled to a stop when he spotted me at his father's bedside. For a moment he simply stared, his gaze flickering between me and the king, before he slowly took in my appearance, which was undoubtedly poorer than usual due to this morning's haste in getting ready. He didn't say anything, but he didn't need to; I'd seen a look similar to his enough times to know exactly what he was thinking about me.

I rose to curtsy and he emerged from his stupor to bow in return. "Good morning, Miss...Maren, was it?"

"Yes, Your Highness. And you're Prince Drake."

He nodded in acknowledgement as he approached his father's bed. I hastily moved so he could take the seat closest to the king. Even after he'd sat, he didn't pull his suspicious attention away from me, causing me to wriggle beneath his perusal.

Words could always be relied upon to fill even the most awkward silence. "His Majesty has slept peacefully," I said in a rush. "Other than a worsening fever and more ragged breathing, his condition remains the same, but I hope—"

Prince Drake held up a hand and I immediately fell silent. "Forgive me, but I'm afraid I still don't know who you are. Briar said you're his guest...and yet you're tending to our father. Are you Father's new nurse? Her assistant?"

"I'm neither."

Prince Drake's brow furrowed. "Yet you're tending to the king as if you were." He frowned. "Might I ask what you're doing in my father's sickroom? Last I knew, Briar was sitting with him."

"He was, but then Briar grew too tired, and—Prince Briar, I mean." I hastily corrected my informal address at Prince Drake's eyebrow lift.

"I see." He surveyed me a moment more, his expression grave. "So you're a guest at the palace. How did you manage to be invited when Briar made it clear to me several months ago that he wouldn't extend invitations to anyone while our father's health was so precarious?"

My cheeks burned at his accusatory tone, but I lifted my chin defiantly. "It's not his doing. The gardens let me in, and now they've trapped me...for plucking a rose."

Prince Drake's eyes widened and he looked like he had a myriad of additional questions, but I was thankfully spared the tense interrogation by Princess Rheanna's arrival. Prince Drake's expression immediately cleared as he greeted his wife with a tender smile.

"Good morning, darling. How did you sleep?" The worry filling his eyes suggested he was inquiring after more than just how his wife had spent her night. She nodded to me before smiling warmly at her husband as she came over and kissed his cheek.

"I'm doing fine, dear; thank you for asking. How is your father?" She turned her concern to the king.

"The same as last night."

He rose to offer her the seat next to him, and I took her arrival as my cue to leave...especially since I wanted to escape the prince's questions should he feel the need to resume them. I was nearly to the door when Prince Drake called for me to stop.

"Miss Maren? I have many more questions for you, which will have to wait for a better time."

My stomach lurched, but I simply curtsied in response

before escaping both the princess's friendly smile and the prince's suspicious frown. Surely my evasion was only temporary, but I prayed the prince's interrogation would at least wait until after the king...no, I didn't want to think about his impending death.

Away from His Majesty's chamber, I had no distraction from the thoughts that had been haunting me for the past hour, where I'd thought of nothing except for Briar's soft touch. My confusion kept pace with me as I strolled the gloomy corridors, my stomach in a tangle, even as I yearned for him to touch me again.

CHAPTER 11

*I*t wasn't much longer. The family and a few select advisors gathered around His Majesty's bed as he struggled to take one rattly breath after another. Solemnity filled the chamber. Princess Rheanna sat beside her husband, her arms looped around his waist and her head resting on his shoulder, while Briar and Prince Drake each held their father's hands, watching each of his breaths with riveted attention. My throat clogged with tears as I watched the dear man I'd adopted as a father figure, the only one I'd ever known, slowly slip away.

He'd stopped speaking several hours prior, and now seemed entirely unaware of his surroundings. I alternated between watching the king and watching Briar, whose haunted look made me yearn to sit beside him and comfort him, but propriety kept me still. I was already out of place being here during such a solemn time, yet I was utterly grateful Briar had insisted I remain.

Time dragged, each second measured by the king's labored breaths, each one bringing the transition of the crown closer and closer. I was watching our future king when His Majesty took his final breath, so I witnessed the heartbreak fill Briar's eyes when his father finally passed, quickly followed by fear for the royal mantle now resting on his shoulders.

The physician leaned over to close the king's eyes before following the advisors' lead as they all knelt before Briar and bowed their heads in respect. "Your Majesty."

Briar's eyes widened slightly before he lifted his chin and nodded to them. Prince Drake and Princess Rheanna also dipped into a bow and curtsy.

"Your Majesty."

Briar swallowed and stepped forward to rest his hand on his brother's and sister-in-law's shoulders, bidding them to rise. Princess Rheanna promptly hugged him while Prince Drake patted his shoulder with an encouraging smile.

"You'll be a wonderful king. Rhea and I will support you in any way we can. You won't be alone."

Briar managed another nod as he stepped out of the princess's embrace and glanced towards me. Too late I swept into my own curtsy, my cheeks burning that I'd neglected to show our new monarch the proper respect. But he didn't seem offended; if anything, he appeared slightly over-whelmed.

Briar was still staring at me as I rose. I searched his expression, trying to discern his well-being. He already looked weary from the burden he now carried. I ached to go to him and comfort him, but I knew now wasn't the time in front of so many official noblemen.

The chief advisor stepped forward. "With your permis-sion, Your Majesty, we'll formally announce the king's death before beginning the arrangements for both the funeral and the coronation."

Briar didn't even glance at him as he nodded, so he missed his deep bow before he and the other advisors left, leaving the family alone. I knew I ought to leave now that my role as standing in for the missing Princess Reve had come to an end, but I couldn't make myself move.

Prince Drake and Princess Rheanna began quietly discussing details of the succession, but Briar broke away to return to his father's bedside and gently take his hand.

"I'll be a good king and do my best to care for our people, just as you did," he whispered. "I won't let you down. I promise, Father." After a lingering look at his father, he pressed a kiss to his brow before rising to walk to the alcove, where he stood regally with his hands clasped behind his back, staring unseeing out the window.

Before I could talk myself out of it, I went to his side. The window overlooked the grounds, currently shrouded in a thick fog, the plants droopy and their colors faded. Alarm flared in my chest. "What's happened to the gardens?"

"They're in mourning," Briar said hollowly. "As is tradition when a Malvagarian king passes." A tear trickled down his cheek but he made no move to wipe it away. Silence settled over us, during which I frantically tried to come up with something to say.

"I'm so sorry." I yearned to hug him, and reached out to do so, only to remember the prince and princess's presence. I forced myself to tuck my hands behind my back.

He managed a rigid nod, his jaw taut to contain his grief. "I can't believe he's gone. I'm going to miss him so much."

"He was a good man and a wonderful king." Unsure what else to say, I rested a hesitant hand against his stiff back. Rather than pull away, he relaxed at my touch.

"Despite my bearing many of the crown's responsibilities for over a year, it feels heavier now," Briar said. "No one will ever be the king Father was, especially me."

"You'll be a remarkable king," I said.

He swallowed. "Will I?"

"Of course you will."

He said nothing for a minute as he continued to stare unseeing out the window. "He had so much faith in me," he finally whispered. "I don't want to let him down."

"You won't. I know you won't."

Briar finally turned away from the window to look at me, a myriad of emotions in his eyes: hope, gratitude...and even fear. "How can you be sure?"

"Because of the man you are," I said. "If you treat your subjects the way you've treated me, then the kingdom is in excellent hands...so long as you don't let the gardens trap them."

He lifted his eyebrows. "The first piece of kingly advice I've received: no locking my subjects inside the enchanted gardens. Duly noted."

I managed a smile, which he hesitantly returned, as if he wasn't sure it was appropriate to smile so close to his father's death. The fact that he could reassured me that no matter what happened, he'd be alright.

I looked back at the king, lying so still and silent on the bed. "It'll be quite a transition, won't it?"

"Thankfully, not as drastic as it would have been had I not been helping him this past year." He reached out to lightly brush my hand, causing it to tingle. "Thank you for your encouraging words and constant support. I'll do my best to live up to your faith in me."

He didn't pull away. Instead, his fingers continued to stroke the back of my hand, his dark gaze penetrating mine, as if he was searching for something. The feeling that over-came me as he looked at me in such a way was a little fright-ening, so I hastily averted my gaze...only to notice the prince and princess had stopped conversing and were watching us closely, Prince Drake with a suspicious frown and Princess Rheanna with bright eyes focused on our touching hands.

My cheeks warmed and I hastily jerked away. What was I doing? I couldn't touch my new king in such a familiar way. Briar blinked down at our hands, as if he'd only just realized what we'd been doing. A blush tinged his cheeks as he cleared his throat and turned back to the window.

I took a steadying breath in an attempt to calm my wildly pounding heart. "When is the coronation?"

"Due to Father's prolonged illness, preparations for both his funeral and my coronation have been in the works for quite a while; they're both in a week's time, only a day apart." He glanced sideways at me, suddenly nervous. "With the arrival of so many guests, the gates will open."

I expected my heart to lift at this news, but I only felt disappointment. "Oh."

"I don't know what would happen if you managed to escape," he said. "There are consequences for plucking a rose, even if I don't understand what they are, considering I know little about how the gardens' magic works." He stared out across the dreary grounds, as if the answers could be uncovered there. "Although I advise against it, I don't doubt you'll want to take the opportunity to escape. This would be your only chance to do so, should you wish it."

My heart sank further. "Are you asking me to leave?"

"Of course not." He swiveled back to face me, his expression almost pleading. "I don't want you to leave." His blushed deepened and he hastily returned his gaze to the window. "Your presence is…soothing and gives me strength, which I desperately need this upcoming week. But it's selfish of me to ask you to stay."

My heart swelled—he wanted me here. It wasn't until I'd heard the words that I realized just how much I no longer wanted to leave. The enchanted rose had lost several more petals, but in this moment it no longer seemed to matter.

"You don't even have to ask; it'll be my greatest pleasure to stay, Your Majesty."

He flinched. "Please don't call me that."

I furrowed my brow. "Then how shall I address my king?"

"It's already going to be strange being 'Your Majesty' with everyone else, but with my family and you I want to simply be Briar, especially considering we're friends."

A strange thrill rippled over me. *Friends...* "I'll call you whatever you wish."

He relaxed. "Thank you." His somber gaze returned to the late king. "I wonder if I'll ever get used to bearing my father's title; it doesn't feel like mine, as it puts me on a pedestal I don't feel I deserve."

"No one really does," I said. His eyebrows rose at my frankness and I hastily continued, "but you're a man who'll continuously strive to be worthy of the title, making it fitting that you're the one wearing the crown."

He pondered that for a long moment before he smiled. "Your frankness is both insightful and reassuring." He stepped closer, making the remaining space between us tingle and hum. "I'm so grateful you've chosen to stay. I need someone like you to help ensure I never abuse the sacred responsibility entrusted to me."

My heart swelled at the great honor and trust he was bestowing upon me. Did he really deem me worthy of it? By the sincerity in his eyes, I realized he did.

"Then I'll promise to always be honest with you and inform you the moment I ever feel you're abusing your power." But considering the good man that Briar was, I knew I'd never have any need to.

He released a whooshing breath. "Thank you, Maren." He extended his hand to shake on our promise. I rested mine in his, marveling at the warm, comforting way his enfolded mine. I was secretly relieved when he didn't immediately release my hand. "Will you be at the coronation?" he asked softly.

"Would that be appropriate for a merchant's daughter to be among all that nobility?"

"Of course. Didn't we just establish that we're friends? Not to mention you'd be the distinguished guest of the king. Please, Maren, I need you there."

My heart pounded as I became lost in his gaze once again. Even if I had the freedom to leave, nothing would prevent me from supporting Briar. But deep down I knew there was another more personal reason that compelled me to stay, one I couldn't even admit to myself.

"It will be an honor to be there."

His stiff shoulders relaxed. He lifted my hand and pressed a soft kiss across my knuckles. "Thank you."

Heat rippled up my arm straight to my cheeks, lingering long after he released me. Flustered, I hastily turned away and caught the princess still watching us through narrowed, rather speculative eyes. She met my gaze with a friendly and strangely knowing smile.

My heart flipped. I'd seen such a smile before, frequently exchanged between women whenever they speculated about potential matches. I'd never expected such a look to be given to *me*. Surely I'd imagined it. For no matter my own feelings towards my appearance, others didn't find me beautiful enough to attract the romantic notice of a man, especially that of a prince now turned king.

My heart constricted painfully, and for the first time in my life, I felt a twinge of regret.

THE PALACE WAS a bustle of activity the week following the king's passing as the servants hastily prepared not only for his funeral but for Briar's coronation, as well as all the guests that would arrive to commemorate both events.

It was strange seeing the previously empty corridors filled with so many people, ones I felt had infringed on the world I'd created with just me, Briar, and the gardens, a world I wanted back. I avoided the guests as much as possible; I couldn't risk being recognized and having word return to my father about where I was hiding. If it hadn't been for my promise to Briar, I'd have remained locked in my room until everyone left.

With all the preparations, I hadn't had a chance to speak with him since our stolen moment following his father's death. Although he remained poised, I sensed it was merely a mask for his true emotions. I ached to ask after his welfare, but he was constantly swamped by his duties that came with his new title and role as host, so I did my best to discern his well-being through perusal alone.

Despite the regal way he held himself, tension stiffened in his shoulders, weariness lined his brow and sadness filled his eyes. Yet in spite of his obvious strain and heartache, he maintained his usual kind, easygoing manner, facing each of his tasks with grace and dignity...most of the time. Other times, the stress seemed to become too much for him, and he'd snap at a servant or storm away grumpily. It was these moments that I most yearned to go to him.

Every so often I could have sworn his gaze flickered towards me with a look that suggested he wanted to speak with me as much as I longed to speak with him, but there was never an opportunity until the morning of the coronation. The king's funeral had been the day before, but overnight the grounds had cast aside their mourning and become vibrant once again.

I seized the opportunity to escape into the cool morning air and into the gardens. Pink dawn tinged the sky and sunshine glistened across the grounds, the enchanted gardens' celebration that honored the crowning of the new king. I wandered down a random path, basking in being free from the stifling confines of the palace and the wearying task of avoiding all of its noble guests; as usual, the gardens were my refuge.

I paused at the familiar *clink* of a trowel. I lifted my skirts and hurried towards the sound, smiling when I entered the transformation garden to find Briar with his hands burrowed in the dirt as he weeded.

He didn't notice me at first, so I was able to linger at the entrance and study him: the dirt lining his handsome features, the way his black hair clung to his damp brow, the serious set of his mouth as he concentrated on his task, and the huge pile of weeds beside him evidence of his hard work. I wished the people could see their king now.

"So this is where His Esteemed Majesty has been hiding."

He swiveled around to face me and grinned widely. My heart lifted to see his smile after the soberness that had been cloaking him ever since inheriting his father's throne. "I'm not the only one who's been hiding—you've been lingering in the shadows all week."

"You've noticed?" I asked.

He sat back on his heels. "I certainly have, and it's driven me mad. We must remedy it at once. Come, keep me company for a bit." He motioned me over with a rather regal wave of his hand; he already wore his crown well, as if it had always been a part of him.

I settled on the ground beside him, as usual not minding the dirt. I expected him to immediately begin conversing, but instead he took a moment to stare at me before smiling again, this one softer than before.

"It's good to see you, Maren."

My cheeks warmed at the tenderness filling his tone. "It's

good to see you, too. I'm sorry I've been so elusive. Will you grant me a portion of your kingly mercy?"

His lips twitched. *"Kingly mercy?* How am I ever to take my new duties seriously with you?" He waved his hand with theatrical regality. "I might be persuaded to grant such a token if you tell me the reason."

I bit my lip. "I was afraid some of your guests would recognize me."

Understanding filled his eyes and his expression softened in compassion. "I promise I'll protect you from your father should he ever find you. You have nothing to fear."

Gratitude warmed my heart. "Thank you, Your Majesty."

"Briar."

I smiled. "Yes, that's certainly more fitting considering your kingship is playing in the dirt. I didn't expect to find you here mere hours before your coronation."

His good humor vanished, replaced with the weariness I'd caught so many glimpses of this past week. "Considering it's only a few hours away, can you expect me to be anywhere else? Besides craving some time alone, I need the strength of the gardens if I'm to have any hope of getting through the day. I can't believe it's already here."

"How are you feeling?"

He fiddled with a weed and sighed. "Nervous isn't quite the word...I'm terrified. After today, it'll be so...official. And I wish my sisters could be here." He lifted his gaze to mine. "I'm grateful for your presence. Thank you again for staying."

"I'll serve in whatever capacity you need me. What will that be at this moment?"

He considered. "Are you up for the challenge of helping me relax? I could really use a distraction from my nerves."

That would indeed be quite the challenge before such a momentous occasion. I tapped my lips thoughtfully before giving him a mischievous look. "I have a question first: how does His Majesty feel about using bribes to convince a certain subject to remain silent about his love for dirt?"

To my relief, he chuckled, and a twinkle filled his eyes. "I'd hate for such gossip to spread to the masses; it could embolden my enemies. Tell me, Miss Maren, what favor can I grant to persuade you to keep silent about my dirty little secret?"

I picked up one of the discarded weeds and twirled it by its stem, considering. "My request is a rather simple one: I don't want anything to change between us."

All humor left his expression. "Neither do I, Maren. Are you afraid things will now that I'm king?"

I shrugged. "Perhaps a bit."

He rested his hand over mine. "You have no need to fear. Shouldn't the fact that I'm weeding before my coronation assure you that while my title has changed, I'm still the same person? I won't lose myself to my role, I promise."

Fierce relief swept over me. "I'm grateful. It'd be quite a tragedy to lose such an amazing person." Our gazes lingered on one another's for a moment before he broke it first, his cheeks darkening.

"Unfortunately, my new role does come with certain obligations, such as presenting myself at my coronation in a way befitting a king. I should go and prepare."

"I suppose you must," I said. "But I suspect arriving covered in dirt would only endear you to the people as you show them who you truly are: a hardworking man with a good heart."

He managed another smile as he stood and offered his hand, but even after he'd helped me up, his hold lingered, tightening around mine as vulnerability filled his eyes. "You truly believe I can do this?"

I rested my hand over his. "I have no doubt you'll be as fine a king as you are a man."

He lowered his gaze to my hand. My cheeks warmed and I started to withdraw, but his fingers grasped mine and held fast.

"Thank you, Maren." But even though we were both due inside to prepare for this momentous day, neither of us moved, and despite the promise we'd just made with one another, I sensed something *was* changing between us...but whatever this confusing change was, it was one I welcomed with all my heart.

CHAPTER 12

"*W*ill you, Crown Prince Briar of Malvagaria, solemnly promise and swear under God and oath to govern the people of Malvagaria and rule over the kingdom in wisdom, according to our law and custom?"

The priest's voice echoed throughout the gilded throne room. Briar stood before him, draped in a velvet robe and clutching the ruby scepter steadily as he listened to each oath with the most solemn expression.

"I promise to do so," Briar vowed.

"Will you do all in your power to ensure that the law, justice, and mercy are executed fairly in all your judgements as king?"

"I will."

It was difficult to focus on the ceremony with my attention riveted on Briar. I analyzed his expression in an effort to discern his well-being on the most momentous day of his life. Whatever nerves he'd displayed earlier in the garden were masked. He stood confidently and regally, sincerity filling each word as he vowed to serve the people of Malvagaria to the best of his ability.

"All this I solemnly promise to do."

Briar knelt before the priest, who placed the jewel-encrusted crown on his head. It looked quite heavy, but Briar was steady as he lifted his head and rose, wearing the crown as if it had always been a part of him.

As Briar turned to face his subjects, his gaze briefly flickered not to his people or his brother and sister-in-law standing near him but to me, as if seeking strength. I offered him an encouraging smile and assuring nod, which caused him to relax his shoulders and lift his chin.

An advisor stepped forward. "I present His Royal Majesty, King Briar of Malvagaria. May his reign be long and prosperous. All hail King Briar."

The crowd stood to dip into bows and curtsies. "All hail King Briar."

As I sank into my own curtsy, I stole another peek at our new king and was surprised to find that his gaze remained riveted on me. Warmth blossomed in my chest at the intensity of his look; despite the promises we'd made one another in the garden this morning, something was indeed changing between us, a change that made me feel strangely fluttery and...happy.

After the priest presented His Majesty with the ceremonial regalia and spoke several more flowery phrases, the ceremony concluded, and the crowd approached the new king to pay their respects. I wanted nothing more than to join them, but the pressing throng of nobles made it impossible. I sidled to a corner to watch Briar greet his subjects with his usual courtesy.

It was there Princess Rheanna found me several minutes later. "There you are, Maren. I've been looking for you. What are you doing way over here?"

"I didn't want to interrupt—"

"Briar was asking after you." Her lips twitched into the

same knowing smile she'd worn several times this past week whenever she'd witnessed Briar and me together. "He insists you sit with us at the feast. He'll likely be swamped with conversation, but at least you'll get to be near him, as well as have an opportunity to meet the visiting royalty."

I was to meet the other royalty? Panic knotted my stomach. "Please, I couldn't—it wouldn't be proper." Despite my presence at the palace, I didn't belong in Briar's glittering world and would undoubtedly meet with disapproval from those who did.

Princess Rheanna pursed her lips at my refusal before mischief filled her eyes. "I'm afraid your resistance is futile, for His Majesty desires it. You dare go against the king's wishes at his own coronation?"

Even I wasn't *that* foolish, which meant I had no argument. How had I managed to get myself so entangled with the King of Malvagaria? But the moment the crowd parted and my gaze settled on him, my stomach gave a strange flip, and I knew nothing would make me regret our friendship.

"Hmm, how interesting." The princess sounded rather pleased about something.

"What is?" I couldn't tear my eyes away from Briar and the regal way he stood, looking so distinguished in his formal uniform. He really was quite handsome, but it was more than that—kindness filled his features, even when he looked solemn.

"I'm simply pleased you're here. I've been worried about Briar ever since our broken engagement, but it appears I no longer have a need to be."

My gaze snapped to hers, aglow with intrigue. "Whatever do you mean?" For there was only one meaning I could construe from such a comment, but surely she couldn't possibly think—no, I was definitely mistaken.

"I know you understand perfectly what I meant. Although

we haven't interacted much since my arrival, I've already concluded you're a clever one."

I sighed in defeat. "You're mistaken. There's nothing between us except friendship. Whatever traits I may possess are of little value compared to other more important ones required of any woman." I gave her a pointed look.

The princess's brows scrunched together. "Is that what you're worried about? It shouldn't be." She looked me over and smiled. "That gown is perfect on you; its coloring brings out your flawless complexion and beautiful eyes. And that hairstyle really suits you, especially with your gorgeous dark hair."

I reached up to touch one of the elegant curls my borrowed lady's maid had done for my fancy updo. "Does it?" I'd never worn my hair in such a way.

She nodded. "You look very lovely, Maren."

I resisted the urge to snort, for a beautiful gown and hairstyle could only do so much.

We slowly worked our way through the crowds to Prince Drake, who immediately looped his arm around the princess to nestle her against his side. "There you are, darling. I was afraid I'd never find you in this throng." He kissed her cheek before wrinkling his nose at the nobles surrounding his brother. "Look at them, already groveling for his favor. I don't envy him one bit. Thank goodness he's the eldest rather than me."

"It does look rather overwhelming," Princess Rheanna said. "You must rescue him when it becomes too much for him."

"And deprive his new subjects the pleasure of meeting their king?"

Even though I knew he was teasing, the urge to defend Briar rose in my chest and compelled me to speak. "It would be in your best interest to intervene, for if his subjects smother him too much, Malvagaria will be in need of a new king, and who's next in line?"

I gave the prince a pointed look. He raised his eyebrows before bowing in acquiescence. "An excellent point, Maren. It's admirable to meet someone who has no qualms about speaking her mind."

He looked like he wanted to say more. I braced myself for the interrogation he'd promised me a week ago but which the funeral and coronation preparations had so far helped me avoid, but I was spared by the announcement of the start of the coronation feast. I released a whooshing breath of relief.

The crowds began to disperse as the guests made their way to the vast dining hall where the celebratory feast had been prepared. Like the throne room, the vaulted hall was adorned lavishly with flowers from the gardens, whose sweet perfume mingled with the tantalizing smells of the feast. Music from a nearby string quartet provided the backdrop for the hum of conversations.

Briar sat first at the head of the table and we all followed. I was seated several seats away beside Princess Rheanna, with the Sortileyan crown prince and princess on my other side. The Princess of Sortileya, Princess Seren, took her place beside them and looked around the room with a sour expression.

"Do you see the Bytamian crown prince?" she quietly asked her brother, whom I'd heard referred to as Prince Aiden. He paused in conversing with his wife and glanced around the dining room before shaking his head.

"I'm afraid I don't."

Princess Seren scowled. "Unbelievable," she said in a hushed whisper. "Our arrangement is only a few months away and I still haven't met my intended. As his kingdom's crown prince, it's his duty to attend the coronation of Malvagaria's new monarch."

Prince Aiden frowned. "I agree. I wish I could offer an explanation for his absence."

Princess Seren picked up her spoon with an elegant huff before dipping it into the soup the attending footman had just placed in front of her. "I'll still perform the duty expected of me and forge this alliance, but I'm not impressed he's chosen not to attend such an important event. As crown prince, Ronan should—"

"Seren, please." Prince Aiden's voice had lowered. "I know you're frustrated, but don't allow your emotions to get away from you. This isn't the time."

She pursed her lips and nodded curtly. Prince Aiden sighed and turned towards the three Bytamian princes sitting across the table.

"Prince Jaron, do you know if Crown Prince Ronan will be joining us? My sister is eager to better acquaint herself with her intended."

A handsome man with strawberry-blond hair glanced over with an arrogant tilt of his head. "Unfortunately, Ronan is busy at sea." His sea-green gaze flittered towards Princess Seren. "My apologies, princess." He bowed his head before resuming his conversation with his brothers, leaving the princess with her jaw taut in displeasure.

Prince Aiden gave her an apologetic look. "I'm sorry, Seren."

She merely harrumphed and took another dainty sip of soup, her shaking hands the only outward sign of her frustration. She caught my staring and narrowed her eyes. "I don't believe we've been introduced."

"This is Miss Maren," Princess Rheanna said. "Maren, this is Seren, Princess of Sortileya, and this is Crown Prince Aiden and his wife, the Crown Princess Eileen."

Prince Aiden and Princess Eileen acknowledged me with a smile, but Princess Seren watched me with a rather calculating look. "*Miss* Maren, was it? I'm curious to know how you came to find yourself sitting amongst the royals and so closely to the new king, or how you even procured an invitation to the coronation at all." Her gaze flickered towards Briar, now deep in discussion with the princes of Bytamia. "Or perhaps I do understand, if the rumors are to be believed."

"Seren..." Prince Aiden's voice was low with warning. After giving me a final smirk, she tossed her head elegantly and returned to her meal.

I frowned and leaned towards Princess Rheanna. "What did she mean by—"

"I'm sure she meant nothing by it," Princess Rheanna said hastily, but the worried look she exchanged with her husband contradicted her words. My stomach knotted and my simmering curiosity pleaded for me to ask for clarification, but unfortunately now wasn't the time or place. Later.

I avoided eye contact with the sour Sortileyan princess for the duration of the seven-course feast. Thankfully her brother and his wife were much more friendly, particularly the crown princess, and they kept up a steady conversation with me whenever I wasn't conversing with Princess Rheanna. I kept information about myself vague and focused our topics on them, asking for details about their forest kingdom, their nearly two-year-old son, and the happy news Princess Eileen shared about the upcoming birth of their second child.

Although I didn't have a chance to talk to Briar, our gazes met several times, each one accompanied by his soft smile. His frequent looks and the pleasant conversation with my dinner partners were almost enough for me to ignore the

CAMILLE PETERS

heated stares from the other nobles and the pressing fear that one would recognize me.

By the time the grand meal concluded several hours later, I felt fit to burst and definitely not up for dancing, but I still followed the guests into the glittering ballroom for the coronation ball to be held in the king's honor.

A majestic diamond chandelier hung from the vaulted ceiling, casting pools of golden light across the marble floor, where Briar had already taken his place with Princess Rheanna to begin the ball. At his nod, the orchestra struck the first note, and the two began the waltz. After several twirls, other couples joined them on the floor.

I wasn't surprised when no one asked me to dance, both for the opening dance and the ones that followed, leaving me with no distraction from the unsettling feelings twisting my stomach as I watched the king dance with one beautiful woman after another.

Until one came in the form of a golden-haired prince. "You must be Miss Maren."

I turned towards the cheerful voice that was accompanied by a handsome face and a charming smile. The prince adjusted the baby in his arms and bowed.

"My sister, Rhea, has asked I ensure you aren't neglected during the celebrations. I'm Crown Prince Liam of Draceria. And this beauty"—he motioned to the adorable infant in his arms—"is my daughter, Princess Anea." He presented the young girl, no more than a few months old, with the widest and proudest grin.

I smiled into the little princess's dark brown eyes, watching me curiously. "She's lovely."

He seemed to have been waiting for those very words and immediately swelled up with fatherly pride. "Isn't she the most adorable princess you've ever seen? She's supposed to remain in the nursery with young Prince Deidric, Aiden and

Eileen's son, but I snuck up to get her. How else am I to show her off?" He kissed her cheek.

My heart swelled at the affectionate display. "You're fortunate to have a distraction from the dancing."

He chuckled as he stroked her golden curls. "Perhaps there was an ulterior motive for retrieving her, but I'll also heed my sister's wishes and act as a charming companion for you on her behalf. How shall I begin my quest? Perhaps by providing you with your own distraction?"

"That would be quite welcome," I said.

"Are you not fond of dancing, Miss Maren?"

"Not particularly." In truth, I hadn't had the opportunity to do enough of it in order to form an opinion, but that was the last admission I wanted to make to a prince.

"I can't say I blame you. If my own partner weren't so charming, I wouldn't like it myself." He gently bounced his daughter in his arms, earning him a darling smile, to which he responded with another besotted grin before turning a rather mischievous look onto me. "Now that the polite pleasantries are out of the way, are we good enough friends for you to confirm or deny the rumors currently swirling around about you?"

My stomach lurched. "Rumors? What rumors?" Had news that I'd run away from an arranged engagement spread so far? Undoubtedly, if Father was offering a substantial reward for my return.

"You mean you haven't heard?"

Before I could respond one way or another the dance ended, and Princess Rheanna returned to my side and give her brother a stern look. "I recognize that look in your eyes, Liam. You'd better not be badgering dear Maren."

"I'm doing nothing of the sort, merely trying to find a good story." His eyes widened with innocence, but by his sister's frown, she clearly wasn't fooled.

"She's Briar's special guest and deserves to be treated as such."

Prince Liam's lips twitched. "I know who she is. That's why I was asking whether or not it's true that—" His words cut off at Princess Rheanna's glare and he held his hand up in a conceding gesture. "Very well, you win. I shall cease my questioning and simply die of curiosity."

"Good." Princess Rheanna gave me a rather strained smile. "Are you enjoying the ball so far?"

I wouldn't be so easily dissuaded. "Do you know what he's talking about?"

She hesitated. "I...no, of course I don't. Oh look, it's Anwen. You simply must meet her." She hooked her arm through mine and led me deeper into the crowd towards a woman wearing a golden-silk dress. By the adoring look she exchanged with Prince Liam and the kiss he bestowed on her, I knew she must be his wife.

Princess Rheanna immediately went through the proper introductions. Princess Anwen greeted me kindly before giving her husband an indulgent look. "Dear, I thought we discussed keeping Anea in the nursery during the coronation?"

"The coronation is over," he said, unabashed. "Besides, the nursery is boring compared to spending time with her papa. Isn't that right, sweetheart?" He gave his daughter a snuggle, which she returned by tugging on his ear, resulting in an even wider grin from the prince. My heart wrenched in longing; I'd never imagined a father could love his daughter in such a way.

"But a ball is no place for a child," Princess Anwen continued.

"Certainly it is. How can I miss the opportunity of showing her off to those who've undoubtedly never seen such a beautiful princess?" Prince Liam looped his arm around his wife's waist and drew her near him to kiss her cheek, as if seeking penitence, and Princess Anwen softened.

Princess Rheanna leaned towards my ear. "That girl is already the most spoiled child in Draceria, and before we know it, she'll be the most spoiled one in all the surrounding kingdoms as well."

Prince Liam's grin was unrepentant. "Challenge accepted."

Princess Rheanna rolled her eyes before holding her arms out. "Might I have a chance to spoil my niece?"

"In a moment." He made no move to hand her over.

Princess Rheanna sighed and gave me an exasperated look. "That means *never*. He's rather possessive of that girl and only lets Anwen hold her."

On cue, after a final kiss, Prince Liam handed Anea into his wife's waiting arms. She accepted their daughter with a tender smile, but she wasn't holding her for long when Prince Liam's gaze caught sight of someone in the crowd and lit up.

"It's Nolan. Excellent, he hasn't had a chance to meet our princess." He plucked Anea from Princess Anwen's arms and turned a wide grin to the approaching prince. "Nolan, have you met my Anea?" He made absolutely no acknowledgement of the princess at the prince's side, who looked nearly identical to Prince Liam's wife. Were the two sisters?

Prince Nolan smiled indulgently. "I haven't. She's quite lovely."

"Isn't she? She's a perfect child," Prince Liam continued with fatherly pride. "Not only does she look like her beautiful mother, but she also shares her temperament, the blessed girl."

"I'm happy for you both," Prince Nolan said.

The two began conversing, during which Prince Liam pointedly continued to ignore the princess standing at

Prince Nolan's side...until Princess Anwen gave him a gentle nudge and nod towards her.

Prince Liam heaved an exaggerated sigh. "It's a pleasure to see you again, Lavena." His sour tone contradicted his words.

Without turning her cold expression away from the couples dancing across the floor, Princess Lavena gave a jerky nod of acknowledgment but otherwise made no other response, which seemed to suit Prince Liam just fine, for now that his dutiful greeting was completed, his attention had returned once more to little Anea in his arms, who was now playing with his cravat.

His wife was much more polite. She smiled kindly at the princess. "Are you doing well, Lavena?"

Again, the princess didn't respond. Instead she turned towards Prince Nolan, watching her with a disapproving frown. "Am I expected to dance with King Briar?"

"Of course. You know Mother and Father hope for a match."

I'd just taken a sip from a glass of punch offered to me by an attending footman and nearly choked on it at his words. My coughing sputters drew the princess's attention and she scowled. "And who is this?"

"This is Miss Maren," Princess Rheanna said. "She's a dear friend of ours."

Princess Lavena lifted an elegant brow and smirked in a way that caused my cheeks to burn. "That's not what I heard. I heard she's—"

"*Lavena.*" Prince Nolan's hiss caused her to obediently fall silent, but it didn't erase the smirk playing across her mouth. I ached to ask what the princess had been about to say, but if I'd been mistaken in my initial assumption, I had the horrible feeling I didn't truly want to know.

After Prince Liam was satisfied that Prince Nolan had

doted sufficiently on his daughter, he reluctantly handed her to the nursemaid, who'd been hovering anxiously against the wall waiting to take her young charge back up to the nursery.

Prince Liam watched his daughter go with a longing look before engaging the Lycerian prince in a discussion until the current dance ended, at which time Prince Nolan seized the opportunity to escort his sister towards Briar after he finished twirling across the floor with a dark-haired beauty I'd spent the past several minutes trying—and failing—to ignore. But before Prince Nolan could reach the king, another matchmaking noblewoman arrived at his side with her daughter in tow. Both dipped into an exaggerated curtsy until Briar bid them rise and accepted the beautiful woman's hand for a dance. I gritted my teeth.

"Poor bloke, I don't envy him." Prince Liam's voice tore my attention away from analyzing every feature and simpering smile of the auburn-haired beauty currently in Briar's arms.

"Envy him what?" I asked stiffly.

"The tedious task of trying to find a wife," Prince Liam said. "Most noblewomen are vipers only seeking the position of queen. It'll be quite the challenge for Briar to find someone who's genuinely interested in him."

His words caused my heart to pound furiously, and it was quite an effort to appear calm. "Briar deserves better. Perhaps you can give him some advice?"

"Unfortunately I don't have any, for I'm lucky in that my perfect match fell right into my lap." He looped his arm back around Princess Anwen and nestled her close.

My attention was once again captured by Briar's dance, particularly the way he stared at his partner. He clearly appreciated her beauty, for his look demonstrated more than mere politeness; his frequent smiles revealed he clearly enjoyed her company. My insides burned at the sight, a puzzling reaction. Why did I care so much what he thought of his dance partner, or the fact that he wasn't dancing with *me*?

"Have there been any potentials?" Prince Aiden arrived with Princess Eileen, both their gazes on Briar and his dance partner. "He seems quite taken with this one."

The knots in my stomach only tightened at his words.

Prince Liam shrugged. "No more than he was taken with his previous partner. We've been paying close attention." He turned to me. "We're shamelessly placing bets on who will become the next Malvagarian queen. Perhaps you'd like to join us?"

I most certainly did *not*.

"You really shouldn't bet on such a thing," Princess Anwen gently scolded.

"Why not? It'll be a fun game. Come on, darling, I know you secretly want to play." He wriggled his eyebrows.

Princess Anwen hesitated before giving him a mischievous smile. "While I have no interest in placing bets, I admit I do want to join in the speculating, for I'm quite curious who Briar will choose."

"Excellent, you can be on my team." Prince Liam brushed a kiss across her cheek before returning his attention to Prince Aiden. "What are your thoughts on the matter?"

The Sortileyan crown prince pursed his lips in thought. "It's hard to know, for Briar is rather difficult to read. As for potential matches, there are several woman in attendance who are from wealthy and prestigious families, connections which would only strengthen the Malvagarian royal bloodline. Whomever he chooses, he's under pressure to do it soon, not only to give Malvagaria a queen, but to secure the succession as soon as possible."

My stomach continued to twist until I was certain I'd be sick. The blood rushed to my head as I glared at the woman dancing in Briar's arms before looking away with a scowl. I caught the speculative look of Princess Anwen.

"Perhaps I will place a bet," she murmured to her husband. My cheeks warmed. Whatever bet she placed concerning me was one she'd undoubtedly lose.

The next dance ended and another one began, with me still remaining without a partner, leaving no distraction from Briar's next partner, the sour Princess Lavena. His goal accomplished, Prince Nolan returned to us looking weary.

Prince Liam frowned at him. "What made you decide to play matchmaker?"

"My parents' insistence, and the task is as tedious as I feared it'd be." He rubbed his temples, as if warding off a headache.

"I'm surprised Lavena was allowed to come at all," Prince Liam said. "Since the *incident*, I'd hoped she was kept under lock and key."

"You're not too far from the truth," Prince Nolan said. "She's still being punished for allowing your match to fall through, but our parents couldn't resist the opportunity to have me bring her here to try to win the hand of the new Malvagarian king."

My fists clenched again.

Prince Liam's eyebrows rose, his eyes lit with intrigue. "Indeed? I hope you're not offended if I do my best to persuade him against such an alliance."

"There's no need; he's already informed me he's not interested in the match."

I hadn't realized how stiffly I'd been standing until I relaxed at the prince's words.

"Sensible man." Prince Liam looked like he had plenty more to say, but he snapped his mouth shut when Princess Anwen laid a hand on his arm in warning.

I returned my reluctant attention back to Briar's dance.

He and Princess Lavena danced stiffly and without speaking, causing me to relax further. Clearly, there was no need for me to be concerned he'd align himself with Lyceria.

Prince Nolan seemed to think so too, for he frowned as he watched the dancing. "I have no idea what we're going to do with her. King Briar isn't the only one who's made it clear there will be no match with Lavena; the Bytamian princes also have, as well as many Lycerian nobles. We fear we won't be able make any arrangement for her." He heaved a heavy sigh. "She's not even upset about the situation. I'm actually beginning to believe she wishes never to marry."

Prince Liam snorted. "Unsurprising, for marriage would force her to give up some of her...habits.—"

Prince Nolan's frown became pensive. "I don't think that's the reason; I believe it's because of Kian."

Prince Liam's mouth fell agape in surprise. "My brother? But he's been dead for—" The rest of his response was lost on me, for at the moment the current dance ended and Briar escorted Princess Lavena back to her brother. My heart lifted when he shifted his attention to me and bowed.

"Might I have this dance, Miss Maren?" And he extended his hand.

CHAPTER 13

or a moment time seemed to stand still as I stared at Briar's outstretched hand as he waited for me to place mine in his. He'd asked me to dance. Surely this was a dream. No one had ever asked me to dance before, and now I was being invited to dance with the *king*.

No, I corrected myself, I was being invited by *Briar,* and I couldn't think of a better man to dance with than him.

At Princess Rheanna's encouraging look I curtsied and placed my hand in his. A warm ripple trickled up my arm at the contact, causing me to smile, which he readily returned.

As he led me into the center of the ballroom, I tried to block out the heated gazes and the tittering whispers of the nobility already spreading amongst the crowd, but I still caught snippets.

"Who is she?"

"What a plain thing."

"How has she managed to capture the king's attention?"

My embarrassment only deepened when Briar gave my hand a reassuring squeeze, a sign he'd also heard the horrible whispers. I kept my eyes lowered to my gold satin slippers poking out from beneath my crimson-satin gown until Briar's arm wrapped around my waist, the heat pooling from his touch immediately dispelling the iciness prickling my heart.

"Please don't take their words to heart," he murmured. "You're the one I've been wanting to dance with all evening."

Kindness filled his eyes, making it easier to bravely lift my chin. I wouldn't allow the opinion of strangers to dampen my usual confidence, and I most certainly wouldn't allow anything to ruin the wondrous fact that I was about to dance with my new king.

The notes of the music swelled as the orchestra began to play. To my delight, it was a waltz. Briar noticed my surprise and grinned. "Although several overly eager noblewomen made it difficult to ask you to dance sooner, I must admit I also delayed asking you until I knew the next dance was a waltz."

My stomach flipped, but before I could fully analyze the meaning of his words, I became distracted when he gently pulled me closer, stealing my breath. The dance began, and I became lost in the steps, my focus less on them and more on the feeling of Briar's arms around me. I'd never been held by a man before and was amazed by how wonderful it felt...but that was likely more due to the fact it was *Briar* holding me than anything else.

We didn't speak for the first several measures until Briar leaned down to my ear. "You look lovely, Maren, although I must admit I prefer you covered in dirt."

I laughed, a rather inelegant sound which carried across the gilded ballroom and caused more titters from the scrutinizing onlookers, but I didn't care anymore. How could I after such a sweet comment from my dear friend?

"If only my governess could hear you make such a statement; she's spent my entire life scolding me for my unlady-like love of getting dirty."

"I shall send her a letter immediately following the ball, complete with the royal seal. My esteemed approval for dirt should hopefully keep you free from her disapproval in the future." His eyes were teasing, but even so I didn't doubt he'd make such a gesture should I earnestly ask him. The thought warmed me through.

"Or perhaps your first act as king could be to pass a law banning all governesses from scolding their charges for such an offense?"

He laughed and my heart lifted at the sound. Although he'd danced with several beautiful women—many of whom had made him smile—none had caused him to laugh. I knew, for I'd watched each of his dances closely.

"Done. I'll see to it first thing in the morning." He winked and I grinned.

"Your seeing to such a grave atrocity is much appreciated, Your Majesty."

"Briar," he immediately corrected with a smile.

I couldn't call him that when we were at risk of being overheard by so many people, no matter how much I wanted to.

Seriousness replaced his previous amusement. "All jesting aside, despite not arriving with at least one dirt splotch on your cheek, you still look very nice."

Very nice wasn't the same as beautiful, but the compliment was sweet all the same, even if the gesture had undoubtedly been motivated by his desire to combat the whispers coming from the watching crowd.

"Thank you, Your Majesty...Briar."

He gave my hand a gentle squeeze and our dance continued.

"I'm so relieved I finally get to see you," he said. "I've

wanted to speak with you ever since the ceremony, but we were seated too far away at dinner, and since then I've been swarmed."

"As the king you have many admirers."

"Or ones pretending to be," he said wryly.

"While I'm sure there are many willing to flatter you in an attempt to forge a beneficial royal connection, you'd do yourself a disservice if you ignored all the praises bestowed upon you, for you deserve them."

He frowned. "How can I when I've yet to prove myself? My reign has only just begun."

"You can't discount the good you accomplished when you were still only the acting king," I said. "Nor can you discredit your admirable character."

His expression softened. "I greatly appreciate your reassurances. Thank you, Maren."

I was pleased I could help him in any way, especially after his thoughtfulness in asking me to dance. A comfortable silence settled over us as we continued to twirl across the ballroom floor. This really was the most lovely waltz. It no longer mattered that I'd never been invited to dance by anyone else; Briar was enough.

But the experience quickly soured when we waltzed past another couple and Briar's gaze flickered towards the blonde beauty. My stomach immediately knotted at the obvious appreciation in his eyes. Despite his sweet compliments about my appearance, he hadn't looked at me like *that*.

The burning envy that had been my nearly constant companion since the ball began quickly returned, sharper than ever. "There are many gorgeous women in attendance," I said stiffly. He'd have his pick of a bride when the time came.

That thought only tightened the knots inside me, and the

one that followed soured my stomach: when that inevitable day came that Briar married, I'd still be trapped at the palace, a curse that would be made more torturous as I was forced to watch Briar live his life with someone else.

He grinned even as his gaze caught sight of another woman dancing nearby. "Indeed. The court is very fortunate." Although his gaze didn't linger before returning to me, it had still wavered too long. Tears stung my eyes. He noticed and concern immediately replaced his previous appreciative distraction. "Are you alright?"

I tried to school my expression, but my emotions pressed against my chest, making it difficult to breathe. "It's nothing." My voice shook, betraying me.

He frowned, clearly unconvinced. "You're rather terrible at lying, or perhaps I simply know you too well for you to get away with it. Please tell me what's wrong. We only have a few more moments before the dance ends, and I can't bear to spend the rest of the ball wondering."

I pursed my lips. The last thing I wanted to admit was that I was jealous that it was his duty to find a beautiful wife. It was absurd that I even cared, but I did all the same.

"I admit your unusual secrecy has only made me more curious," he said. "Shall I command you to tell me?" Although his tone was teasing, his words still struck me. As my king he *could* order me, leaving me no choice but to confess my ridiculous vulnerabilities.

"Is that to be your first act as king?" I asked sourly. "Forcing me to share something I don't wish to divulge?"

His amusement immediately vanished. "I—of course not, Maren. I didn't mean—I would never—I'm sorry."

I tightened my jaw to stave off the anger clawing at my heart, begging for release. I mustn't allow it to escape. There were only a few more measures left to get through to what had started as such a beautiful dance but now was nothing but torturous. I determined that I'd get through them with as much poise as I could muster.

"Maren?" Briar's tone was pleading.

"I have no idea why you danced with me," I stuttered. "But I wish you hadn't asked."

He flinched. "I asked because you're my friend."

My bitterness tainted the word, for a mere *friend* was clearly all I'd ever be. Goodness, what was wrong with me? Friendship was something to be treasured, not resented. But I resented it all the same, simply because when it came to him, it wasn't enough. I'd never before wanted anything *more* in my life, and this sudden new desire frightened me, even more so considering I'd chosen the *king* to attach this absurd wish to. I was far more sensible than that.

But my head and my heart were in clear disagreement, for something was stirring within my breast, and if it was what I suspected it was, I was a bigger fool than I'd initially believed. It'd be in my best interest to weed out the ridiculous sentiment as quickly as possible before it could take root...which meant I should keep my distance from the king.

The music mercifully stopped, finally ending the torture of being cradled in His Majesty's arms. I dipped in the shallowest curtsy I could get away with, and walked off before he had a chance to escort me off the floor as was proper. More tittering whispers hummed in the crowd but I ignored them, just as I ignored the king calling my name before a scheming mother thrust her daughter upon him for the next dance.

I took refuge in an abandoned corner, masked from view by a large potted fern. There I pressed my back against the wall and closed my eyes to take several deep breaths, but they did nothing to quell my suffocating hurt. I quickly lost the battle and my tears escaped.

"Are you alright, Maren?"

Princess Rheanna had arrived, obviously having seen my flight before I'd managed to secure my poor hiding place. I straightened and hastily brushed away the evidence of my tears, but by the sympathy filling the princess's expression I knew she'd already seen my wavering emotions.

"What happened?" she asked gently. "Did Briar do something?"

"What makes you think he did anything?"

She bit her lip. "With the emotional way you hastily left after your dance...it appeared that the king had offended you. Everyone is whispering about it."

Guilt pierced through my anger, immediately followed by horror at what I'd inadvertently done. This was Briar's coronation, and because of my jealousy and unruly temper, I'd made him look bad in front of his subjects.

Some friend I was. "I didn't mean—"

"I know you didn't." Princess Rheanna sidled into my tight corner until she was at my side, where she took my hand, her blue eyes steeped in concern. "Will you tell me what happened?"

I released a wavering breath. "He—well, we were dancing, and during it he kept noticing other women, and I—" I couldn't finish. It sounded so stupid when I voiced the reason for my anger out loud. "I was wrong to get upset."

"You feel what you feel, Maren, but I know Briar well enough to confidently assure you that he meant no offense. He's an honorable man."

I knew that. It made my childish reaction even worse, especially considering it wasn't his fault I wasn't beautiful. "I know."

"Yet it still bothers you?" Her tone was so gentle.

"No, of course not. I don't care that I'm not—" I swallowed my denial with a frown. Although that *used* to be true,

I realized that it no longer was. What had accounted for this change?

The princess's expression was so kind. "Obviously, you do a *little*."

My cheeks warmed. "I didn't used to."

Compassion filled her eyes. "I wish you still wouldn't. You have no reason to doubt yourself." She grazed my elbow and turned me to face the wall, where a gilded mirror hung. "See how lovely you look?"

I gaped at my reflection. While I'd never minded my appearance, even I had to admit I looked different...*regal* even, just as the princess had said. Although that was undoubtedly due to the gown I'd borrowed from Princess Reve and the administrations of my lady's maid to tame my unruly hair, yet there was something more...something I couldn't quite pinpoint. It was as if my elegant presentation had slightly altered my features—not changed them, but somehow refined them.

But even if the princess and I could see this, that couldn't make anyone else notice, particularly the king whose attention was so easily captured by the myriad of beautiful women surrounding him.

As if she sensed the melancholy direction of my thoughts, Princess Rheanna rested an assuring hand on my arm. "A mirror's reflection is an interesting thing, for it only shows what's on the outside of a person while completely ignoring what's within. Beauty is not always easily discernible, but I know Briar truly sees you, Maren. You must believe that."

I shook my head. "It wouldn't matter if he did, for there's nothing like *that* between us." Even though with each passing day I realized that I foolishly wanted there to be. I'd always secretly yearned for love, even if I'd long ago given up the hope of ever receiving it. I quickly shook my head. No, surely whatever I felt for Briar wasn't *that*.

"I believe you're wrong," Princess Rheanna said. "He's a good man who possesses the ability to see deeper than most. I'm sure—"

"Maren?"

My heart leapt treacherously at the sound of Briar's voice. I spun around to find him hurrying over, his expression frantic. Despite the crowds and vast ballroom, he'd somehow managed to quickly find me after his dance.

I stared at him, scarcely noticing Princess Rheanna quietly slipping out of the alcove where we'd had our private whispered conversation. "Did you need something, Your Majesty?" I asked coolly.

"I—" He blushed before he set his jaw in determination. "I clearly offended you and must make amends. Please, tell me how I can do so."

"You have more important things to worry about than my feelings—your noble guests and an entire kingdom to name a few."

He frowned. "So I'm not allowed to worry about you?"

"I see no reason why you should."

"Because we're friends, and as such you must allow me to apologize for whatever I did to hurt you...but not here."

He warily eyed the crowds hovering nearby, who were pretending not to notice us but were clearly trying to eavesdrop all the same. Dread pooled my stomach. I was only worsening the awkward situation I'd created with my reckless behavior following our dance.

"I must apologize," I said hastily. "When I left you in the middle of the dance floor—I didn't even consider how it'd make you look. I—"

He waved off my apology. "That doesn't matter. I know you meant no offense; I'm sure instructions on how to behave after the King of Malvagaria inadvertently hurts you at a ball weren't covered in your decorum lessons."

"But—"

"It doesn't matter what they think," he continued. "All gossip eventually dies down. It matters more to me what *you* think. Which means I must speak with you now. Please." Before I could answer, he took my hand and began leading me back towards the dance floor.

Alarm flared in my chest. "What are you doing?"

"Dancing with you again. I can't leave in the middle of my own coronation ball to talk with you, but I can't bear to wait until afterwards. This is the only way we can have relative privacy in order to converse."

Even though I wanted nothing more than to dance with him again, I knew we couldn't. "But Briar—I mean, Your Majesty—you can't. Everyone will notice you've danced with me twice." I tried to tug my hand away but he held firm.

"Let them notice."

"But it's inappropriate—"

"As king I'm allowed some indulgences." He paused and glanced worriedly towards me. "But if you're too angry…"

I managed to shake my head and his shoulders slumped in relief.

"Then we'll dance." He led me back onto the ballroom floor where no one had been dancing as they awaited the king. My cheeks burned at the pointed attention. I took a steadying breath and lifted my chin, trying to appear more confident than I felt. I could do this.

This dance was entirely different from our first. We'd no sooner begun it than he pulled me close, his grip almost possessive. "Now Maren, please tell me what happened between us so that I might apologize."

I glanced around. Although others had begun to dance, many were still staring. "*Here?*"

He sighed. "I wish there was somewhere more private we

could go instead, but I'm afraid this will have to do. Now please, tell me what's wrong."

I hesitated, but his eyes were so pleading that my resistance melted, as did the rest of my anger. I'd been wrong to get so upset. Years ago I'd decided to not be bothered by things beyond my control, for doing otherwise only made me miserable, and yet I'd done just that tonight. How could I recapture my previous confidence?

"You've done nothing, Your Majesty. It was only my own insecurities that made a mess of everything. I was wrong to choose to be hurt. Please forgive me."

He frowned. "Of course I forgive you, but please allow me to inquire further. What do you have to be insecure about?"

My cheeks heated and I hastily looked away to avoid his gaze, only to find every eye still upon us. I lowered my gaze to the floor.

He was silent a moment, but he must have sensed the words I didn't say. "I see."

My heart lurched. "Do you?" I both wanted him to understand and was terribly embarrassed to be having such a conversation with him in the middle of a ballroom.

"I believe so."

I peeked up at him. His look was incredibly gentle, albeit slightly confused.

"I thought I'd assured you how lovely you look this evening. Forgive me for the oversight, and allow me to remedy that. You look—"

"It wasn't that." It was the fact he'd been distracted by those who were *more* lovely. "You gave me many lovely compliments."

"Then how did I hurt you?"

Even as he made his inquiry, a couple dancing nearby accidentally brushed against him, briefly pulling his attention away from me. The beautiful woman immediately batted her eyes flirtatiously. "Forgive me, Your Majesty."

He smiled and nodded his head in acknowledgement, his gaze lingering on her even after she danced away, causing me to blanch. He noticed my expression and seemed to realize what he'd just done. His attention snapped fully back to me and remorse twisted his expression.

"*Oh*. I'm so sorry, Maren, if I made you feel...I didn't mean to. You're truly a lovely person. So kind, curious, supportive..."

But not beautiful. No matter; the other traits he'd listed were far more valuable, for they were ones I *could* control. I felt silly for having forgotten this, however briefly.

I was ready to put this conversation behind us, which meant a change in topic was in order. "I don't wish to discuss this anymore, especially since we have little time remaining before our dance ends and I desire to spend it talking of more pleasant things."

He still seemed reluctant to drop the topic, but sighed in acquiescence at my determined expression. "Very well, I shall indulge your desires."

I heaved a sigh of relief. "Thank you. Now tell me how you are and what you thought of the coronation. Do you feel any different?"

He considered. "I did...but for some reason, I don't now. Perhaps because I'm with you. You make me feel..."

I paused mid-twirl, suddenly quite desperate for his next words. "What?" I whispered.

His look became searing. "With you, I feel as if I can do anything."

My heart soared...only to come crashing back down as my fierce joy at his words caused a horrible epiphany. For in that moment I fully understood what was happening between us: the seed of affection that Briar had inadvertently planted in my heart—one he'd been gradually nourishing with every interaction—had blossomed into something more, something that was both beautiful and terrifying at once: I was falling in love with him, and I needed to stop immediately.

But the emotions had already grown roots deeper than I'd realized, and it was likely too late to uproot them now.

CHAPTER 14

It took several days for the coronation guests to depart, but they finally did, leaving the palace quiet and abandoned save for the servants and advisors, just the way I preferred it. With each guest's departure the gates opened, but I allowed each escape opportunity to pass. Other than the torturous thought of being trapped here with the man I was growing to love as he eventually married someone else, my foolish heart wouldn't allow me to leave. It had chosen to fall in love with someone it had no business caring for, keeping me bound here beyond the dictates of the garden's sentence.

I hadn't had many opportunities to see Briar as he accustomed himself to his new role and spent most of his leisure time with his brother and sister-in-law, who'd chosen to stay a few extra days. I quickly grew restless without the companionship of the man who, ridiculous feelings of my heart aside, had become a dear friend. While he was often too busy during the day, we'd taken to spending evenings together, which I looked forward to with far more eagerness than was likely wise.

This evening I headed for Briar's study in hopes he'd want to go into the gardens for a stroll. The study door was ajar, and from within the room I could hear Briar's and the prince's low murmurs. I slowed and hovered outside the doorway to peer inside, not exactly *eavesdropping*, but admittedly doing nothing to announce my presence.

The room was shadowy, lit only by the flickering firelight and the scattered glow of several candles arranged on the desk, where a map of Malvagaria was spread. Briar's forehead furrowed as he leaned over to study it closer, while his brother hovered over his shoulder.

Prince Drake pointed to a place on the map. "This area looks promising. Have you searched there?"

"Yes. The regiment I sent returned only a few weeks ago without having found any sign of her."

Prince Drake scanned the map again and pointed to another section. "What about here?"

Briar shook his head. "I doubt she could have traveled so far, or been foolish enough to attempt this treacherous pass." He traced his finger along it.

"She could have done anything," Prince Drake said. "You know she's not in her right mind; the curse has undoubtedly only enhanced her usual recklessness."

"You're right." Briar pressed his hands on either side of the map and slumped over it, looking as if the entire world rested on his shoulders rather than simply the kingdom and his missing sisters.

"I know Reve has been gone a long time," Prince Drake said. "But we must try not to worry."

"She's been missing for *months*, Drake," Briar said, his voice strained. "And our searches have recovered no trace. What if she—"

"Don't say that," Prince Drake said. "We mustn't panic."

Briar didn't look up, the anxiety lining his features deepening as he slumped further over the desk. "I've failed her." The despair in his voice wrenched my heart.

"Don't talk like that," Prince Drake said firmly. "You can't allow your worry to get the better of you. You're normally more sensible than this."

Briar didn't stir for a moment before straightening with a resigned sigh. "I know. I don't know why...I've been having a difficult time controlling my emotions lately."

"Stress," Prince Drake said. "But don't let it inhibit your logic. Now, let's focus on the problem at hand and try to determine—"

"What good will discussing the problem over and over do?" Briar's voice escalated as his patience began to falter. "Reve is lost, and even if we could find her, there's still the matter of her curse, which has slowly been stealing her from us as it robs her memories one by one. If she doesn't remember who she is—"

"Calm down, Briar."

Briar ignored his brother. "And it's not just Reve; the search for Gemma's tower has led to nothing except dead ends. I curse Mother for making it invisible."

Prince Drake sank into the desk chair with a sigh. "It definitely presents an almost insurmountable obstacle. At least with the tower's enchantments she's not left completely unprotected, not to mention she has her guard."

Briar's jaw tightened. "Guard Quinn only adds to my worries concerning her safety."

Prince Drake frowned. "Why? He's an excellent guard who's devoted to his duties in protecting our sister; he values her life above his own."

"His devotion is the crux of the problem."

Prince Drake rolled his eyes. "But he's a man of honor and would never hurt our sister in such a way. You know this. Since when did you become so untrusting?"

Briar sighed. "I don't know." He rubbed his temples wearily and I had the urge to wipe away the worried furrows lining his brow. "Now, back to the problem at hand. Do you have any more ideas about where we can look?"

The prince didn't answer. Briar looked up, his dark eyes peering through the bangs hanging over his forehead.

"Drake?"

Prince Drake blinked and glanced over. "Hmm? You're asking for ideas?" He leaned forward in his chair to take in the map. "We can try the woods again; it would be the perfect place to hide a tower..." He trailed off, his gaze faraway as it drifted back to staring out the window once more.

Briar straightened with a frown. "You're distracted and have been for days. Is there something wrong?"

"Of course not." Prince Drake's gaze snapped back to the map. "Now, perhaps you should send out a regiment to the eastern woods. There are no nearby villages, making it a more logical place to hide a tower." His hand shook as he traced out a circle surrounding the area, stilling when Briar rested his hand over his, his expression concerned.

"What's wrong, Drake?"

Prince Drake jerked his hand away. "Nothing. I just have a lot on my mind, primarily my worry over our sisters."

"It's more than that. Something has been bothering you ever since your arrival...as well as Rhea."

"Rhea is fine," Prince Drake said, but his voice wavered, betraying his lie. "We both are. Wait, what are you doing?"

Briar had begun rolling up the map. "This can wait." He set it aside before leaning against the desk in front of his brother. "Please confide in me, Drake."

"Don't you have more important matters to worry about than me?" the prince asked sourly. "Your kingdom and our lost sisters, for starters."

"Just because I have many other things to worry about doesn't mean I can't also worry about you."

"And what makes you think I'll take you into my confidence?" Prince Drake asked.

Briar sighed. "Please don't do this, Drake. I thought that after what happened in Draceria we'd agreed to try to be friends."

"Just because we agreed to get along doesn't mean I want to bare my soul to you," Prince Drake snapped.

"You don't have to," Briar said gently. "But I would appreciate knowing what's going on. You're my brother. I may be powerless to help our sisters, but I can at least try to help you."

"There's nothing you can do to help me. The situation is beyond your control...and ours."

"Even so, I'm willing to listen."

Prince Drake snorted. "What good could that possibly do?"

"So you're not even going to let me try?"

Prince Drake remained stubbornly silent. I bit my lip from where I hovered in the shadows. I knew I ought to leave, for surely this wasn't a conversation I was meant to overhear. But not only did my curiosity compel me to stay, but retreating would only alert the brothers to my presence, so I remained, as still and silent as possible.

"Please, Drake," Briar repeated earnestly. "If you don't want my help, please at least allow me to extend it to Rhea."

"She doesn't need your help either," Prince Drake snapped. "She's not your wife, she's *mine*."

Briar sighed. "There's no need to be defensive whenever I show her any kindness; I'm not trying to infringe on your role as her husband. My feelings towards her don't extend beyond friendship. Our previous arrangement was made out of political duty and nothing more. You know this."

Prince Drake folded his arms firmly across his chest and didn't answer.

"I only care for her as a friend and now sister, just as I care about you. Please confide in me, Drake."

Prince Drake searched his brother's expression for a moment before his stubborn resistance melted away, revealing the devastation he'd been fighting to mask. "Very well, you might as well know. We were expecting a child but lost the baby."

Briar's mouth fell agape. "Oh, Drake."

The prince's shoulders slumped. "This is the second time. Rhea gets pregnant easily enough, but after only a few months..."

Briar rested a hand on his brother's shoulder. "I'm so sorry for you both."

Prince Drake buried his face in his hands. "We're both heartbroken, but her especially. I don't know how to help her except to be there for her, try again, and hope the next pregnancy succeeds."

Both were silent for several minutes, each at a loss as to what to say. "I'm so sorry," Briar said again, his voice quiet. "When did this happen?"

"A few weeks before we arrived. We'd been planning on announcing the good news during our visit...but in the end there was nothing to announce."

Briar frowned. "But you've been here for nearly two weeks. Why didn't you say anything before now?"

Prince Drake shrugged. "What with Father's death and your coronation...it was never the right time. It was mostly Rhea's insistence that nothing dampen your succession; you're only crowned once. Besides, you've had more pressing worries: your adjustments to the crown, finding our sisters, dispelling the foul rumors about—"

Prince Drake immediately snapped his mouth shut but it

was too late. Briar's eyes narrowed. *"Foul rumors?* What are you referring to?"

By his expression, it was clear Prince Drake wanted nothing more than to snatch back his hastily spoken words. "Nothing."

Briar's entire manner hardened as he rose from his chair and advanced a step to stand directly in front of his brother, towering over him in his seat. "Answer me, Drake. What rumors?"

The prince furrowed his brow. "I spoke in haste. It'd be best if I didn't tell you what—"

"No, you will tell me. *Now.*" I startled at Briar's yell, as well as his expression, twisted and fierce. From my hiding place I stared at the king in disbelief, baffled by the foreign ferociousness lining his normally gentle features.

The prince's eyebrows rose in shock and he too gaped at his brother. "What's gotten into you? There's no need to be so testy."

Briar clenched his fists, his breathing coming in short, heavy spurts. For a moment he said nothing, simply glared at his brother. Then all at once he relaxed, the anger fading from his expression to be replaced with...confusion.

"I—yes, you're right. I shouldn't lose my temper."

Prince Drake studied him carefully, as if he expected him to explode again if he pushed him too far. "I don't think I've ever seen you lose your temper."

"I'm sorry, it was inexcusable. I'm not sure why I..." Briar blinked rapidly. "Forgive me."

He slowly walked around the desk to collapse in his seat. There he closed his eyes and took several steadying breaths; with each one, his tension melted away, until the calm, good man I cared for returned.

Prince Drake watched his brother, his look having shifted from perplexed to concerned. "Are you alright?"

With his strange mood, I half expected Briar to snap again, but instead he pressed his hand to his forehead and took another wavering breath.

"I think so. I'm sorry, I don't know what—" He opened his eyes and straightened to give his brother a piercing look. "Now tell me: what rumors are you referring to? I have the right to know what is being said about me and my rule."

Although his temper had faded, his tone was still hard and dangerous, a warning that his brother would be foolish to disobey his request again. The prince hastily obeyed.

"It's not about your reign but a more sensitive manner." Prince Drake hesitated before Briar's glare compelled him to speak. "The rumors concern your *guest*."

My stomach lurched. Briar went rigid in his seat. "Maren? What about her?"

"Well, I'm sure you can imagine…" The prince gave Briar a knowing look but his eyes only narrowed.

"Fill in the blanks, Drake. I want to hear it all from you."

Prince Drake sighed. "Well…there are questions as to why a merchant's daughter is staying at the residence of the unmarried king without a chaperone…well, *you know*."

Briar's entire manner hardened as he slowly rose to his feet. "*Excuse me?*"

Looking regretful, Prince Drake nodded. "And with the pointed attention you gave her at the dance…well, I can see why the court is whispering. Many are wondering what exactly her role in the king's household is or even if she's being kept here against her will, but the general consensus is that they believe she's your—"

I couldn't quite stifle my gasp. Prince Drake whipped around to squint into the dark corridor, but my attention wasn't on him but Briar, who'd surely be angry to have caught me listening in on his private conversation.

I braced myself for his reaction, but to my surprise and

fierce relief he actually chuckled—a humorless sound that did little to dispel the tension in the air, but a chuckle nonetheless.

"Of course. I can't say I'm surprised. You may come in, Maren, especially considering the topic now concerns you."

I remained hovering in the doorway, the prince's disapproving look enough to keep me frozen. Gentleness softened Briar's previously hardened expression as he glanced towards me.

"It's alright, Maren."

My cheeks warmed as I tentatively stepped inside, keeping my eyes lowered in remorse. "I'm so sorry, I shouldn't have—I'm so sorry."

Prince Drake frowned sternly. "How inconvenient, Briar, that your guest not only causes all sorts of lewd rumors, but interjects herself into affairs that don't concern her."

Briar gave a low growl in warning and the prince said nothing more, but the look in his eyes said he clearly wanted to.

"You will not speak of Maren in such a way," Briar said. "She's my guest and will be treated as such."

"I know what I did was wrong, but I meant no harm," I explained hastily. "I merely wanted to see if Briar would like to stroll the gardens with me, only to find the door conveniently open, so I just..." I shrugged helplessly.

The corners of Briar's mouth twitched, and I hoped that was a sign that whatever strange, dark mood had previously settled over him was finally dissipating. But his amusement faded almost immediately, replaced by a vulnerable look. "How much did you overhear?"

I knew he referred to the uncharacteristic temper that had briefly overcome him. I hesitated. "Since you began discussing possibilities of your sisters' whereabouts."

Crimson stained his cheeks. "I—Maren, I have no idea why I—"

"You don't need to explain, but I do want to know whether you're alright."

Briar sank back in his seat and wearily rubbed his eyes. "I don't even know anymore. But I have no wish to discuss it, for I'm not the main concern." He straightened and gave me a serious look. "From your reaction, I take it you understand the implication of the rumor currently spreading?"

I lifted my chin defiantly. "I'm no one's mistress."

Briar's blush deepened and Prince Drake gave an awkward cough. "Yes, well...*we* know the rumors are just that: rumors. But you must admit how it *looks*..."

He was right. Guilt tightened my chest that my presence was hurting the man who'd been nothing but the kindest friend to me. I'd been so worried about being recognized that I hadn't even considered how my presence at the palace would look like for the gossiping court.

I pressed my hands on the desk and anxiously leaned forward. "How can I help? I couldn't bear to do anything to harm your reign."

My breath caught as he rested a gentle hand on my arm, immediately silencing my words. "None of this is your fault, Maren; people will always find things to gossip about the crown. The rumors will eventually die down."

"I'm not entirely sure that they will," Prince Drake said solemnly. "The problem will persist so long as Miss Maren remains unchaperoned under your roof."

"Perhaps a maid can serve as a chaperone..."

"I doubt that'll do much good," the prince said.

Briar sighed. "We'll figure something out. In the meantime, we'll simply ignore them." He caught sight of my expression. "Are you alright, Maren?"

A horrifying thought had just occurred to me, causing my

heart to hammer wildly. Other than how it would affect Briar's reputation, the rumor itself wasn't what concerned me—it was almost humorous considering no one in their right mind would believe the king would fall for someone like me—but who was *hearing* the rumors.

"Do the rumors refer to me by name?"

Prince Drake's brow puckered, but Briar immediately understood. He arose and walked around the desk to take my hand, his entire manner protective. "Please don't worry, I promise I won't let your father find you."

"Or Lord Brone?" I squeaked.

"Nor him." He squeezed my hand assuringly. "As the king, I'll do everything in my power to protect you. You have my word."

His thumb lightly rubbed the back of my hand, undoubtedly a gesture of comfort and friendship, but it escalated my settling heartbeat all the same. I expected him to caress my hand once and pull away, but his touch lingered, his fingertips trailing not just across the back of my hand but along my wrist, almost hypnotically, as if he wasn't aware of what he was doing. He paused only to peer up at me, and for a moment the most intense and beautiful feeling tiptoed between our connected gazes…

Prince Drake cleared his throat, breaking the spell. Briar startled and stared down at my hand resting in his, as if he didn't know what to make of it. He hastily released me, causing my heart to sink.

"Why are you looking at us like that?" Briar asked stiffly at the prince's indiscernible look.

"No reason, but…if you wish to dispel the rumors, you shouldn't allow anyone to see you holding Miss Maren's hand like that."

"What are you implying?" Briar's tone had become dangerous. "I would never misuse Maren in such a way."

"*I* know that, as does Rhea, but should the servants witness such a display…"

"I don't need your advice, Drake," Briar snapped, his earlier bad temper creeping into his voice as it slowly overcame him once more.

Prince Drake held up his hands. "Fine, then I won't give it. There's no need to jump down my throat; I'm only trying to help."

Briar took several heavy, frustrated breaths. "You're right. I'm sorry. I don't know why I…I just hate the thought of anyone hurting Miss Maren or thinking badly of her."

The look in his eyes as he gazed at me was so gentle, so kind, and…something else. No man had ever looked at me in such a way. Although I had no name for it, I loved its effect on me: it not only ignited my insides, but made me feel almost…pretty.

The prince once again spoiled the mood. "The only way I can think of for you to dispel the rumors is to find a proper wife, one who's suitable to become queen."

I flinched, the prince's implication obvious: as a merchant's daughter I was deemed entirely *unsuitable*. My chest squeezed at the thought. This was why I needed to weed out the deeper emotion I'd allowed to take root in my heart before it led to nothing but pain and disappointment.

I turned to leave, unable to bear hearing the king and prince discuss potential marriage candidates. "I see you two have more important things to discuss, so if you'll excuse me, I'll take my leave."

"Must you go?" Briar's fingers twitched near my hand, as if he was tempted to take it but thought better of it.

I nodded. "Please let me know if there's anything I can do to help make up for the foul rumors my presence has caused, as well as any way I can aid you in the quest for your missing sisters."

At their mention, Briar slumped. "I wish there were something you could do, but I'm afraid there's nothing. I'm so worried for them."

The devastation filling his expression pressed against my heart, compelling me to take action—anything to erase his distress and make him smile again. "I could help you look."

"You can't leave the grounds," Prince Drake said.

"Not to mention your father may still be searching for you," Briar said. "We don't want to take any chance of him finding you."

Drat, they were right. I nibbled my lip. "Then perhaps you can join the search, Your Highness."

"I will as soon as I'm able, but I can't right now." Prince Drake sighed. "I feel as if my loyalties are torn between my sisters and Rhea, but she is always my first priority, and she's in no position for me to leave her. I'm sorry, Briar."

"I understand." Briar released a sigh. "I've never loathed my curse more than I do now. I feel so helpless being stuck here when they need me. But I just can't be away from the gardens for that long."

I stared at the heartache filling Briar's eyes. The longer I did so, the more my need to take action rose in my chest. For the first time in weeks I desired to escape, but not for myself —for Briar. No matter the potential risks for myself, I couldn't sit idly by without trying to help the man who'd stolen my heart.

$\mathcal{I}$ finished penning my note to Briar and hastily folded it before I could change my mind about leaving it. He was going to be very displeased when he discovered it, but I couldn't allow the thoughts of his worry to dissuade me from my decision.

I left the note on the desk beside the bouquet of glowing flowers that the garden had given as an apology gesture, still as fresh as the day they'd been gifted to me, whereas the enchanted rose beside it had lost over half its petals. My time to help Briar was rapidly slipping away.

I hastily retrieved my shawl and quietly made my way to the entrance hall, where servants bustled about, loading the prince and princess's trunks into the carriage waiting outside.

Briar was already there speaking to Prince Drake, both wearing rather somber frowns. "Have you decided whether you're going to tell Mother about Father's death?" the prince asked.

I slowed, intrigued to learn more about the story of the

queen trapped within a mirror. Briar considered. "I know I must eventually, but I'm dreading the conversation."

"Are you afraid she'll try to influence you now that you're king?"

Briar set his jaw. "I refuse to allow her to have any sway over me. I'll tell her about Father when the time is right. There's no need to rush; you know as well as I do that there was no love between them."

Prince Drake nodded, conceding that point. "While I know her help would be unwelcome, the offer for my own is still extended. Are you sure you don't want us to stay longer?"

"I'll be fine," Briar said crisply, the exhaustion filling his eyes contradicting his words. "I must learn to stand on my own eventually, but I appreciate the offer."

Although the prince looked fiercely relieved, he continued to hesitate. "Are you sure? Because it's really no trouble for us to—"

"I'm sure," Briar snapped. Prince Drake blinked before his shock settled into a concerned frown.

"You've been unusually grumpy of late. Your stress only convinces me that you *do* need my help."

Briar glared a moment more before the frustrated lines of his expression softened. "Forgive me, I'm not meaning to..." He closed his eyes and took several steadying breaths before resting his hand on his brother's arm. "Perhaps I am a bit stressed, but not enough to force you to remain here longer than you want to. I know for the time being you'd much rather focus on Rhea than your princely duties. You take care of her, and I'll manage here."

The prince searched Briar's expression to gauge his sincerity before he sighed in clear relief. "If you're in earnest then I won't press the issue, for I do want to be there for

Rhea. I hope that things go well for you...with *all* your problems." His gaze flickered towards me.

I lifted my chin. Little did Prince Drake realize that this particular problem would be taken care of the moment they left...if they'd ever get on with it.

Unfortunately, the servants were still loading the trunks, so the brothers lingered, their conversation turning once more to the missing princesses and the best places for the fresh regiments to search. I was tugged from my eavesdropping by Princess Rheanna's approach.

"It's been a pleasure spending time with you. I'm sad we're leaving before I've had a chance to get to know you better." Her expression was so open and friendly that I regretted not spending as much time in her company as I could have.

"And you as well." I studied her expression; sadness flickered through her smile. I hesitated. "I'm sorry about—" I paused, unsure whether it was appropriate to bring up the conversation I'd overheard concerning her difficulties.

To my relief, the princess didn't seem upset over my nosiness. "Drake told me you and Briar know of our struggles." Her cheerful mask faltered as her smile dimmed and the heartache filling her eyes deepened. "I admit it's been devastating. To have two failures in a row...I fear the pattern will only continue. What if I'm incapable of carrying a child?"

I gently squeezed her hand. "I'm so sorry."

She forced another smile, this one more genuine. "As difficult as it's been, I won't allow it to break me." Her gaze softened as it drifted to her husband. "Perhaps it's because I found the man who's my rock in any storm. Life isn't without difficulties, but weathering them with someone you love makes all the difference." She stared tenderly at her husband a moment more before turning a rather knowing

CAMILLE PETERS

smile towards me. "I hope you find such a man for yourself... or perhaps you already have."

A heated blush enveloped my cheeks. "Of course not. I doubt anyone ever will..." I couldn't finish, but from the compassion filling the princess's expression, I knew she understood the words I hadn't spoken.

"I wouldn't dismiss the idea completely," she said. "Whatever you've been led to believe about yourself, there are men who will see deeper and cherish you for who you are; I doubt you have to look very far to find him."

This time when she looked towards the brothers, it was *Briar* who captured her attention. I immediately understood her silent implication. "No, it's not like that between us." No matter how much I was realizing I wanted it to be.

"He's a very kind man who sees what others don't, and I've noticed the way he looks at you. Open your heart to the possibility that the future you long for is just within reach, and I'm confident you'll find yourself pleasantly surprised."

My heart pounded almost painfully at her words, words I wanted nothing more than to be true.

Prince Drake appeared at his wife's elbow and I silently thanked him for his timely intervention. "Are you ready to depart, darling?" At her nod, he lightly rested his hand on her waist. "I've ensured that the carriage has extra pillows and blankets for your comfort."

She cradled his cheek. "Thank you, dear, but please be assured I'm well. It's just sadness that ails me."

"Then I'll spend the entire journey making you laugh."

He brushed a kiss across her cheek before glancing at me. I braced myself, for we'd never gotten around to the interrogation he'd promised me. To my surprise, he simply nodded and turned to leave.

The princess grabbed my hand. "Goodbye, Maren."

"Safe travels, Your Highness."

Prince Drake escorted the princess through the front doors, which closed behind them with a resonating *thud*. Finally. Now I could put my plan into action. I prepared to sneak away to retrieve my hidden satchel, only for Briar to stop me.

"Might I have a word, Maren?"

Now? Normally I welcomed any time spent with him, but time was rather pressing at the moment. I bounced restlessly on the balls of my feet. "Of course, but...is the matter urgent? There's something I need to do first."

He searched my expression, his look suspicious, as if he were trying to extract my secrets. He very well could have ordered me to stay, but Briar wasn't that type of king. "Very well," he finally said. "I shall be in the library."

Guilt seeped over me as I watched him disappear down the corridor, but dwelling on it would only waste time, which I didn't have.

I hurried towards the servants' quarters, pausing only to retrieve my satchel, which I'd hastily packed the night before and hidden behind a large vase. It was stuffed to the brim with food, maps, and anything else I might need to help locate an invisible tower or a wandering princess without her memories. I refused to sit idly by when there were cursed princesses to locate, especially when their absence caused Briar such pain, pain which had wriggled its way deeply into my heart, compelling me to act. I wasn't sure what would happen if I left, but it was a risk I was willing to take for Briar.

I made it to the servants' quarters and hovered outside the kitchen to cautiously peer inside, which was abustle with dinner preparations, making this exit impossible to take without anyone's notice. Instead I chose the one just off the abandoned larder, where I was able to slip away undetected.

Outside the early morning light cast the garden in a

lovely golden sheen, but I resisted the temptation to admire the gardens' beauty; there wasn't time for that. I hooked my satchel more firmly on my shoulder and hurried down the pathways that wove through the flower plots and hedges. The plants perked up in attention as I passed before rustling in clear agitation, as if they'd detected my scheme and wanted to put an end to it. A few even attempted to grab my ankles with their leaves as I passed, but I shook myself free from their leafy grip.

A stitch had formed in my side by the time I reached the vine wall that would transform into the garden exit. There I crouched behind some shrubbery to await the opening of the gate, and I was just in time, for moments later I heard the prince and princess's carriage clattering closer. When it was only a short distance away, the foliage slowly rustled to form the exit.

I hastily straightened as the vine archway rose and the carriage began to roll through, but I'd no sooner begun to creep out from behind the shrub than I was tugged to a stop.

I startled and glanced down. While I'd been waiting, the vines from the nearby wall had slowly slithered undetected through the undergrowth to coil around my ankles. I gave a futile tug, but they'd wrapped themselves several times around, immobilizing me.

I groaned. Not again. I glared at them. "Let me go."

Their confining hold only tightened, their adamant refusal.

"You don't understand," I said. "This time it's different. You must let me leave. Haven't you heard the rumors surrounding the king that I've inadvertently caused with my presence? My staying will only hurt him." Which would be a disastrous way to repay him after his many kindnesses.

They continued to ignore me, stubborn things. If they

gave a reason for their mischief, it was in whispers too quiet for me to decipher.

I tried to pry myself loose, but the more I dug my nails into the vines, the more confining they became. I growled in frustration and frantically glanced towards the carriage, nearly all the way through the exit. I had mere moments before I lost my only opportunity.

"I promise to return," I said as I made another futile tug on the vines. "I'm only going to look for the princesses. For Briar. Please."

The vines held firm; apparently these were guards that let nothing dissuade them from their orders. Aggravating.

The carriage exited the grounds and the vine gate begin to disappear. *No!* I scrambled towards the exit, only to trip and fall into the dirt. "Wait, please don't—"

Too late. I helplessly watched it vanish before turning my glower onto the vines.

"Thanks to you I've lost my only opportunity to help the king. Some friends you are."

They only rustled, as if laughing in amusement at my failure. My glare sharpened. For this offense, an indefinite silent treatment was in order...as soon as I persuaded them to release me, that is.

"Now that you've thwarted me yet again, I'd very much appreciate it if you would let me go."

To my surprise they didn't, even though they had no incentive to keep me trapped now that the gate had vanished. I growled in frustration and once again tried to wrench myself free.

"Release me at once, you stubborn—"

"What are you doing, Maren?"

I closed my eyes as burning humiliation seeped over me. I should have known Briar would come upon me in my latest predicament; after all, he had a knack of discovering me

189

whenever I found myself in any kind of embarrassing trouble.

Briar was awaiting an answer, which due to my awkward circumstances I didn't particularly want to give. "Ask these enchanted nuisances; they're the ones who've trapped me."

Briar glanced at them but they remained uncannily still, offering no explanation for their behavior. His eyes narrowed at their lack of cooperation before his questioning gaze flickered back to me. It appeared that as part of my punishment I'd be forced to confess my offense.

But I refused to humor the vines' annoying whims. "As you can see, I'm currently being harassed by the garden you claim likes me."

While the vines did nothing to loosen their hold, one of the honeysuckles did reach out to gently stroke my cheek, its apology faint but distinctive. I harrumphed. I wouldn't forgive them so easily; I had every right to remain annoyed with them indefinitely.

Briar watched my predicament with a solemn expression, his twitching lips the only indication of the amusement he was enough of a gentleman to suppress. "I believe the garden is quite fond of you, but the vines do serve as my guards, and as such they have obligations to fulfill. You've obviously done something to warrant your restraint."

I made another attempt to wriggle free and winced at their tightening hold. "A little help from His Majesty would be greatly appreciated."

"*Briar*," he muttered. He stepped forward to aid me but paused when he noticed my satchel, which I'd haphazardly dropped during my struggles near a plot of azaleas. His brows squashed together as he bent down to retrieve it. "What's this?"

"That's *mine*," I said hotly. "And I'd appreciate it if you didn't look through it."

Mischief lit his eyes as he peered up at me. "Unfortunately for you, it's within my rights as king to search the belongings of anyone caught by my guards, and any item in your possession at the time of capture is confiscated by the crown. Besides, I'm afraid I'm too *curious* to resist. You understand such a sentiment, don't you?" He winked and I scowled before watching helplessly as he searched my satchel.

His face fell during his perusal. "Food, supplies…you were trying to leave? I thought you wanted to stay."

"No, it's not like that. I merely wanted to help you search for your sisters."

His relief was instantaneous, and his previous hurt was immediately replaced with a teasing glint. "So that's what you were up to. I'm sorry I doubted." He rummaged even further. "I see you've packed for a long trip; you've even stolen several of my maps."

"Borrowed," I hastily amended before my vine wardens could cling to the word *stole* and extend my current sentence further.

His expression softened before he became serious. "As much as I appreciate the gesture, I must emphasize to you again: *you can't leave.* I don't fully understand the consequences of your taking that rose, only that it connected you to the gardens, and I can't risk your safety should you do anything to sever that connection by venturing away."

I sighed. "I don't understand how merely leaving the grounds would hurt me in any way."

He gave me a wry smile. "Trust me, I speak from personal experience." He turned back to the vines. "Now release Maren."

The plants made no move to do so. Briar sighed, muttering something that sounded like *stubborn.*

"I suppose it's up to me to rescue you." He carefully examined the vines to figure out the best way to begin freeing me.

"How did you know where to find me?" I asked.

His lips quirked up. "We've come to know one another quite well. From the moment of Drake and Rhea's departure, I could see that you had a plan. Naturally, I was interested to discover what your mischievous mind had concocted."

"So you followed me." I slumped in defeat at his innocent shrug. "Well, I suppose I must be grateful, else I'd remain entangled in these vines forever."

It was his cue to assist me. He pushed up his sleeves and stepped forward to begin gently untangling me from my viney prison. I was immediately immersed in his earthy warmth, which not only made me strangely lightheaded but also ignited feelings that I tried and failed to extinguish.

"I'm grateful your prestigious kingly duties extend to assisting your prisoners," I managed airily, struggling to speak midst my pounding heart, pattering rapidly from his nearness.

"I care about all my subjects, even the mischievous ones."

He set to work on the thick vine wrapped securely around my waist; I shuddered at each touch and prayed he didn't notice—my predicament was humiliating enough. In no time at all he'd freed me from that vine...only for it to recoil itself around me.

He frowned. "What are you doing? Don't re-tangle her." He sighed when the vines unsurprisingly ignored his order, and went back to work on once again freeing me from the one encircling my waist. "My apologies for the trouble my disobedient garden is causing you. I can't even begin to guess what it's up to."

From its whispers I could faintly hear and with the way it was insistently trying to push me closer to Briar, I had a vague idea, but it was too ridiculous a thought for me to entertain long; the garden didn't seem the matchmaking type.

Briar worked in silence for several moments, his concentration distracting him from speech, which was perfectly fine considering I couldn't have spoken even if I'd wanted to, not with the fluttery way he was making me feel with each careful touch. If the garden meant to torture me in punishment for trying to escape, it was doing quite a thorough job of it.

Briar finally managed to unwind the vine from around my waist, and after glaring at it in warning not to wrap itself back around me again, he went to work on the one encircling my wrist. "It was unwise of you to try to leave the grounds."

The pleasant feelings which I'd been experiencing with each of his gentle touches quickly soured into annoyance. "I was only trying to help," I said indignantly.

"I know, but it was still foolish...and unnecessary, for I doubt even one as stubborn as you could succeed when my guards have failed to find my sisters in the seven months they've been searching. Besides, there's your father to consider; I can't bear the thought of him finding you."

My stomach clenched. "I only wanted to make up for the trouble I've caused."

He paused. "You haven't caused me any trouble."

"I have, what with the rumors..." My face burned, but for a very different reason than the lingering effects from our close proximity. He stilled, his own cheeks turning crimson.

"Oh." He cleared his throat awkwardly and avoided my eyes. "Yes, there have been whispers...but not to worry, I'll succeed in quieting them. Somehow. And even if I can't manage it, I don't want you to worry. They're not your doing, especially since it's not entirely your fault you're trapped here."

He managed to free both my arms and crouched down to work on my legs. "I should be the one apologizing. While there's always gossip surrounding the royal family, I hate the thought that you've become entangled in it simply due to your association with me."

"There's no need to apologize to me, not when the consequences are more dire for you. What if the gossip prohibits you from finding a suitable match?" My gut wrenched at the reminder of that not-so-distant event.

Briar shrugged as he straightened. "Any woman who allows gossip to blind them to my true character isn't one I want to marry, nor would she be deserving of becoming queen." His eyes narrowed, not at me, but the vine slithering back around my arm. "What are you doing? Stop it at once, you pesky vines."

He tugged it away before it could take hold, and in his distraction, another one worked itself into my hair. His fingers brushed my face as he worked to untangle me from the gardens' latest mischief, causing another shudder to ripple over me.

"My apologies once again," he murmured. "I can't figure out the gardens' motive to entangle you in such a way."

Undoubtedly to embarrass me, for the longer he stood so close, the more frantic my heart pounded; with each continued touch, it was even becoming rather difficult to breathe.

He freed one vine from its tangle in my hair and moved to work on the last, his fingers grazing my cheek, causing me to shiver yet again. He paused and his dark brown eyes—which this close I could see were filled with golden flecks—met mine. For a moment he simply stared before his finger twirled almost hypnotically around a strand of my hair.

He visibly swallowed and his blush deepened as he hastily looked away. "I've almost freed you." In his haste, he gave my hair a painful pull, causing me to wince. "I'm sorry." He slowed his movements. After a moment more of working silently, he spoke. "Your eyes are lovely, Maren."

My breath caught. "What?"

"Your eyes. Their color is rather unusual...they're quite pretty."

I was unsure how to respond to such a compliment. "No one has ever said such a sweet thing to me before," I managed.

His shy smile settled into a rather somber frown. "Then my subjects have done you a great disservice. You have lovely eyes, and not just that, but you yourself are—" His fingers froze.

"What is it?" I asked.

His attention was no longer on me, but was focused else-where. He stepped away, taking with him the warmth that had come from his nearness. He'd disentangled me enough that I could twist around and follow his movements with my gaze. I watched as he walked towards the wall and paused in front of the foliage.

"What is—" The remainder of my question was swal-lowed up in my startled gasp as I finally noticed what had captured his attention.

Between his fingers was not a vibrant and leafy vine, but one that was brown and dry. It snapped as he broke off a portion and lifted it to examine it with wide eyes.

He traced the dead vine with his fingertip. "Impossible. The garden doesn't die...it *can't* die. Could the gardens still be in mourning?" He swiveled to face the other vines, now watching him warily. "How long has this been dead?"

They lifted themselves in a way that resembled a shrug. He pursed his lips and returned his concern to the vine, his brows furrowed, before he began following its trail, wandering further and further away.

I gave a futile tug to follow him, but my ankle was still trapped. "Briar!" He didn't seem to hear me. I raised my voice. "*Briar!*"

He paused and glanced back, blinking as if emerging from a trance. His eyes widened as he hurried over. "Maren! I'm so sorry, I didn't mean—here, allow me." He hastily went back to work freeing me from the remaining vine.

It took me a moment to find my voice. "Did you truly forget about me?"

"I—no, of course not. I just got...distracted."

Whatever beautiful feelings had just transpired between us evaporated, leaving my heart stinging. Briar was just like everyone else—forgetting me when something more interesting captured his attention.

The moment he tugged me free from the last vine I jerked away, unable to be near him any longer. "I'll leave you to your dead plants." With a trembling lip, I turned back towards the palace.

He reached for my hand to stop me. I immediately stilled, my breath catching in my throat as his fingers grasped mine, feeling far more wonderful there than they had in my hair.

"Please Maren, don't leave yet." His tone was pleading, compelling me to look at his remorseful expression, showing he not only knew his offense but regretted it.

"I thought you were different." I felt so foolish saying the words out loud, for I wasn't being fair to him. As king, he had far more worthy things to bestow his attention on than me, no matter how much I ridiculously wanted it.

"Please forgive me for abandoning you when you were in need of my assistance. I was just so...startled. Nothing in the gardens has ever died before. They must still be in mourning; it's the only possible explanation." His brow creased in concern and I felt even more foolish for my childish reaction.

"Your worry is understandable. I shouldn't have gotten so upset. Might I help?"

"I'm not sure what can be done. I must investigate the matter." He cast me an uncertain glance. "Would you like me to escort you back before I—"

I slowly pulled my hand away and forced a smile. "That won't be necessary." He'd caused me to feel so many emotions in such a short amount of time that I needed distance to sort them all out...as well as to give my heart a rather firm scolding. "I shall see myself back. I wish you luck with your investigation." I curtsied and spun around to resume my trek towards the palace's looming front door.

"Mari?"

I froze at the nickname. Only my mother had ever called me Mari, and that had been many, many years ago, before she'd died. Hearing it again made me both happy and achingly sad, causing me to miss not only her but Briar, even though he was only a few yards away.

I slowly turned. "What is it?"

He seemed as if he wanted to say something, but couldn't quite find the words. He opened his mouth, hesitated, then slumped in defeat. "Never mind. Will I see you at dinner?"

"Of course, Your Majesty." Speaking his title out loud added an extra layer of protection to my rebellious heart, which was reacting a bit too strongly to Briar's new nickname for me.

He winced. "Please don't call me that."

I didn't answer. He sighed.

"I'm really sorry for earlier; I didn't mean to hurt you." With that, he bowed and returned to the vines hugging the wall, leaving me staring after him, wondering how I could possibly stop whatever was happening between us before my inevitable disappointment caused me any more pain.

CHAPTER 16

*J*restlessly paced the corridor outside the room where His Majesty was meeting with his advisors. I hadn't had an opportunity to speak with him since yesterday when he'd freed me from the vines, for despite our plans to spend dinner together, pressing news had arrived in the form of an urgent missive which had locked Briar in his study for the remainder of last evening and into this afternoon. I ached to see him and find a way to help ease some of his burdens, but I hadn't had the chance, for he'd skipped breakfast and gone straight to his meetings, where he'd been cooped up the entire day.

It was now late afternoon. I paced the hallway outside his study so that I could see him the moment his meeting finished, ignoring the confused looks coming from the guards standing rigidly in front of the doors.

My pacing took me to the end of the corridor to a door I didn't recognize, which meant that whatever lay beyond it remained unexplored. Desperate for a distraction, I inched it open, allowing the golden lantern light from the corridor to pour inside and illuminate the walls, which were filled with frames. I'd discovered a portrait gallery.

I was eager for a closer look. I cast a tentative glance towards the guards at the other end of the hallway. When they made no move to stop me, I grinned and pattered inside. The curtains were drawn, keeping the room shrouded in darkness. I tugged them open and sunshine poured in, bathing the dozens upon dozens of portraits lining the walls of past royalty.

The current royal family's portrait hung in the place of honor at the center. I ventured closer. It appeared to only be a few years old. My attention lingered on Briar's handsome face before brushing over his brother to take in the familiar friendly features of the king and the cold beauty of the queen before settling on the two missing princesses.

I wasn't sure which was Princess Gemma and which was Princess Reve, for both shared similar features, although if I had to wager a guess, the pale, sickly looking princess was Princess Gemma. I took in the princess whom I'd inadvertently impersonated—she was quite a beauty. Despite our similar coloring, it was a wonder the late king had mistaken me for her.

Footfalls sounded behind me. I spun around to find Briar, his expression haggard with exhaustion. "I'm sorry," I said hastily.

His eyebrows rose. "What do you feel the need to apologize for?"

I motioned around the gallery. "The curtains were drawn. I shouldn't have...I'm sorry. I was just curious."

His perplexity gentled, a welcome sight after the strain I knew he'd been under since yesterday. "It's quite alright. You're free to explore any part of the palace that isn't locked."

I raised an eyebrow. "Is that so? What secrets does Malvagaria's king feel the need to keep behind locked doors?"

His lips quirked at my teasing before he sobered. "Not my secrets." He said nothing more as he glanced around the room, his expression wistful. I ached to see him smile.

"Are there any dramatic stories you can share with me from your family history?" I asked.

He frowned. "Most are rather dark, and unfortunately my family has only added to that legacy."

Did he mean the curses that plagued both him and his siblings? "I find I'd love to hear these stories all the same." The stress lining his eyes only deepened and I silently scolded myself for adding to his distress. "Although if you're not in the mood, my curiosity can wait for another time; I'm sure you have more important things to do than entertain me."

"Not at all, Mari. I always have time for you, not to mention I must make up for reneging on my promise to dine with you last evening. Please forgive me."

My heart fluttered at his second use of my nickname, spoken as naturally as if he'd been using it from the moment we'd met.

He bridged the distance between himself and his family portrait, which he stared at solemnly, his hands clasped behind his back. After a moment he reached out a hesitant hand towards his sisters, as if he meant to touch them, but his fingers paused several inches away, as if he couldn't actually bring himself to do so.

"Reve...Gemma." He said the names quietly to himself, heartbreak filling his eyes. A horrifying possibility suddenly bombarded my mind.

"That missive that arrived yesterday...was it about your sisters? Are they hurt?"

"No, it didn't concern them. Thank heavens. But I'm afraid the news is just as sobering." Rather than elaborate, he continued to hungrily stare at his missing sisters, as if he couldn't make himself look away. "It's almost painful to see them; I haven't been in here for so long."

My chest squeezed with guilt. "I'm sorry, I shouldn't have—"

"You have nothing to apologize for, Mari," he said gently. "Just because I avoid this room doesn't mean it's forbidden. Perhaps I should come more often, but seeing them...it reminds me how helpless I feel, how I'm failing them. I'm constantly pulled in so many different directions I'm not sure how to balance it all."

His expression was haggard, as if he carried the entire kingdom solely on his shoulders. I missed the crinkle lines that surrounded his eyes when he smiled and ached to ease his worry. "Perhaps a short reprieve from your duties will help," I said. "Can I trouble you for a tour of the gallery?"

He slowly nodded, but it was another full minute before he managed to tear his gaze away from his sisters and offer his arm. I accepted it and allowed him to lead me alongside the portraits. Rather than regale me with stories from his family history, we walked in a comfortable silence. There was something about simply *being* with him; each moment spent in his presence only deepened whatever strange workings were occurring within my heart. It was both exhilarating and terrifying.

We'd circled the room twice and were just beginning a third time when Briar finally relaxed beside me. I took that as my cue to speak.

I motioned to a nearby portrait of a past Malvagarian queen. "I see that beauty has a long history in the royal family." The reminder made me feel entirely ill-suited to be walking on his arm.

Briar's gaze flickered towards the portrait in question and

he scowled. "She's one of my more infamous ancestors; her beauty was nothing more than a mask for her cold heart and her cruel misdeeds."

He hastily led us past her, but not before I stole a final glance. Briar had inherited her large, dark eyes, but while his were full of warmth and compassion, hers possessed a hardness which distorted her otherwise flawless features.

"She suddenly doesn't seem as beautiful as before."

"External beauty isn't everything, Mari. There are far more valuable traits...although based on your behavior at the ball, I fear you place undo emphasis on it." He lifted a questioning brow.

My face flushed with heat. "I didn't used to, but being here...I admit I find myself thinking about it more than I ought."

He paused in our stroll and frowned, his eyes serious. "Have I done anything to make you feel—"

I quickly shook my head. "Of course not."

At least not directly, but I couldn't deny that being with him made me yearn for beauty in a way I never had before, and I was ashamed of this new part of myself. I didn't want to feel this way, yet the feelings came unbidden at every opportunity. Had this vulnerability always been a part of me that until now I'd simply chosen to ignore? If only I could bury it back deep inside me where it belonged.

He tilted his head, his brows drawn in concern. "Are you certain?"

I forced a smile. "Of course."

He frowned, clearly not convinced. I nibbled my lip, at a loss over how to explain that while *he'd* never made me feel inferior due to my lack of beauty as others so frequently had, he'd still inadvertently made me yearn to be beautiful all the same, simply because...

My heart lurched. *No*, I firmly scolded myself for the

dozenth time since these ridiculous feelings had first stealthily crept into my heart. *You mustn't be so foolish. Remember, he's the king, and you're simply...Maren.* Yet despite my firm orders to depart, the unrequited emotions lingered.

"Mari?" Briar was still watching me with his usual sweet concern.

"It's nothing," I lied.

He pursed his lips thoughtfully before his eyes lit up with an idea. "There's something I want to show you." He re-offered his arm and led me to a tucked-away alcove at the far end of the room, where several stands bearing different relics were arranged.

I paused to admire them, lingering on a vase whose jewels artistically depicted a floral scene, reminiscent of some of his own gardens. "Are these part of your collection?"

"Yes. I have many throughout the palace."

"Are all of them this exquisite?" His nod caused me to marvel. It'd likely taken him many years to acquire so many rare finds, all created with incredible craftsmanship. The effort required to gather such an assortment of treasures... Briar clearly appreciated fine things. The reminder was bitter.

"Every piece has a story," he continued. "And I value each in a different way, but there's one that's a particular favorite I want to show you." He gently led me by the elbow towards the end of the row, where he paused in front of a rather plain wooden box with absolutely nothing extraordinary about it.

I gaped. "*This* is your favorite?"

"One of them." He eyed my frown in surprise. "I'm surprised you've so easily dismissed it; I expected more from you. Why don't you take a closer look?"

He handed it to me so I could better study it. The wood was smooth but old and worn, with several chips marring its surface. I lightly traced my fingertip along each nick. "It's clearly seen better days."

"Each scar has a story, but they're not as important as its contents."

My forehead furrowed. Its contents? Was there a secret to discover? "I don't see anything special."

"Perhaps you haven't looked hard enough."

My usual curiosity swelled within me and I began to examine the box more earnestly, turning it over in my hands and running my fingers along its marred surface.

After considerable inspection I noticed a portion of wood on the bottom that was slightly lighter than the rest. I pushed this aside with my thumb to reveal a tiny knob shaped like a rosebud carved into the wood. By Briar's lit gaze, I knew I'd found what I was looking for.

I eagerly pressed the knob and gasped in delight as the box's lid opened like a music box to reveal the most beautiful rose I'd ever seen. The delicate flower was made of pure gold with tiny rubies coating each petal and emeralds lining the golden stem and leaves, jewels which glistened in the sunlight tumbling through the windows.

I stared in wonder. "*Oh.*"

"Isn't it lovely?" His tone was reverent. "It took some time to discover its secret, but now that I have I can only see it for what it contains. Most who look at this piece never discover it, which is unfortunate, for if they knew what's inside the box they'd realize that although it appears entirely ordinary on the outside, its value and unique beauty make it one of my most priceless treasures."

I couldn't speak, my awe still captured by the flower's intricate details. I lightly traced each of its exquisite petals, unable to believe that such a wondrous thing had been hidden from sight.

"Although I love my entire collection," Briar continued,

"the ones I find the most special are pieces like this—ones whose beauty isn't so obvious, whose value must instead be discovered. That principle applies not only to treasures but to the people I govern. I hope that seeing them for who they truly are will make me a better king for my subjects."

I had no doubt that it would, but his words did more than cause me to better admire him as my sovereign; they also caused me to hope that if he had the ability to look deeper into seemingly ordinary things, perhaps he could see something in *me*, something no one before him had taken the time to look for.

I admired the rose a moment more before reluctantly closing the box and handing it back to him, but he shook his head. "I want you to have it."

My breath caught. "No, I couldn't—it's one of your most precious treasures. I couldn't possibly—"

"You should keep it." He enfolded my fingers over the box, causing my heart to leap at his touch. "May it be a reminder that you, too, have something beautiful hidden inside, and lucky is the man who discovers it."

He lifted his hand and, after a moment's hesitation, brushed aside a strand of my dark hair and tucked it carefully behind my ear. His fingers lingered to graze my cheek, his gaze boring into mine, as if he were searching for something…but what? Whatever it was, I desperately hoped he'd find it.

His whisper broke the spell. "Would you accompany me to the gardens? There's one in particular I want to show you."

My heart beat rapidly, robbing me of my voice, but I managed a nod. He lowered his hand and withdrew, making me long for his touch. He offered his arm and I slowly accepted it, holding it more tightly than normal. The moment between us had only caused my buried feelings, impossible to fully suppress, to rise to the surface yet again.

Briar took one final look at his sisters' portrait before leading me from the gallery, down the twisting corridors, and outside into the sunny spring afternoon. Briar's usual guards followed us from a discreet distance, but otherwise we were alone...except for the plants, which seemed to watch us with far more attention than usual as we passed. I wriggled beneath their perusal.

"So where is this mysterious garden you're taking me to?" I asked.

"It's one that the gardens have assured me you haven't yet seen, which is a shame considering it's one of my favorites. As eager as I am to show it to you, I admittedly have an ulterior motive for taking you there."

"Does it have anything to do with your meetings?"

He sighed with a weary nod. "I must commend you for your patience in waiting this long to inquire what they've been about. I don't doubt you've been fit to burst with curiosity."

"I have been, but I managed to refrain; you seem to have enough trouble without my adding to it with my persistent nosiness."

He managed half a smile. "To my surprise, I find I've missed it. I'd appreciate another perspective other than those of my advisors, so I'll apprise you of the situation in hopes you'll provide the insight I need." He turned us onto a path lined with translucent flowers. "Last night I was informed there's an even graver problem than the discovery of the dying vines, which were already cause for concern."

"Have you deduced what caused them to die?"

He shrugged. "I'm at a loss. The gardens are magic, and magic can't just cease. It's certainly a puzzle."

I studied the furrows in his brow and ached to smooth them away. "And now you've been presented with yet another problem."

His frown deepened as we turned onto another path, whose blossoms appeared almost...droopy, as if whatever news Briar had received caused even the gardens to worry. "As you're aware, shortly after I discovered the dead vines yesterday I received a rather disturbing missive—the crops growing in two of the most fertile areas of the kingdom are suddenly starting to die."

I froze, tugging him to a stop. *"What?"*

His expression darkened. "We're at a loss as to what could have caused it, for there's been no extreme weather nor any known pestilences in either area of the kingdom. For previously thriving crops to suddenly wilt away is...disturbing, to say the least."

I nibbled my lip, considering. "It must be some kind of sickness."

"I previously thought so...until I realized that the two affected areas are on opposite sides of the kingdom, meaning that they have no relationship to one another. What sickness could affect two areas so far apart while leaving others untouched?"

Hmm, that was quite the riddle. "Do you think the two occurrences are connected, the dying vines and the dying crops?"

He shrugged helplessly. "It doesn't make sense that they would be, but I can't ignore that both are occurring at the same time. I'm sending out scouts to investigate the other areas of the kingdom to see if anywhere else is likewise affected, while having my agricultural advisors study the yield from the still-thriving crops to ensure the food is evenly distributed amongst the people so that no one starves."

"And in the meantime, you're investigating the other palace gardens to see if anything else is dying."

He nodded. "The one we're visiting is closest to where I

found the contaminated vines. I pray I don't find anything suspicious, but after today's grave news I have little reason to hope."

The worry filling his eyes deepened. My heart reached out to him. "This is a rather daunting problem to have so early in your reign. I'm sorry."

His shoulders drooped, as if he was already tired. "I hope this isn't a sign of what's to come; I've already exhausted myself weeks in. My people deserve better."

My heart warmed. He was such a good man.

We soon arrived at a garden just off the path near the vine-covered entrance. Briar unhooked a white-iron gate engraven with musical notes and held it open so I could enter. I stepped into the garden and froze.

"*Oh.*"

He beamed, the first real smile I'd seen all day. "I knew you'd like it. Just wait until you've further explored."

It took me a moment to stir from my wide-eyed wonder in order to do so. I'd seen many incredible and enchanting things on the Malvagarian royal grounds, but nothing quite like this. Petals shaped like musical notes floated gracefully through the air, as if engaged in a waltz, while the flowers themselves formed various instruments; trills of music filled the air as they softly played, sounding as if they were part of the wind itself. I knelt in front of a bed of strings to better examine the flowers, whose petals were arranged in such a way to resemble miniature violins and violas.

"Remarkable," I murmured.

The flowers wriggled excitedly at my attention and immediately launched into a lovely aria. The music was sweet yet unfamiliar, as if the garden's magic possessed its own otherworldly style. Each note the plants played seemed to tell a story, this one of earth, growth, and beauty, as befitting the enchanted gardens. With each tranquil note, the tensions that had been building inside me from my own insecurities and worry seemed to melt away, as if each musical measure healed my heart piece by piece.

"The music is so soothing," I whispered, as if the current piece deserved the utmost reverence.

Briar sat beside me with his eyes closed and his shoulders relaxed, looking more at peace than he had since his coronation. He smiled softly but didn't open his eyes. "Nothing quite relaxes me as much as the garden's music. While I'm here, all my worries and responsibilities fade away."

He listened for a moment more before he opened his eyes and met my gaze. Slowly, as if hypnotized by the music, he reached out a finger and lightly touched the back of my hand. My breath caught but I didn't move, especially when he began to lightly trace up and down each of my fingers, his touch incredibly gentle.

"Are you enjoying the garden, Mari?"

It took me a moment to find my voice. "It's enchanting." But it wasn't the fantastic garden and its soul-stirring music I thought of when I spoke the words, but Briar himself. My pulse erupted when he slowly laced our fingers together.

Briar is holding my hand. I never imagined anyone would ever do such a thing, let alone my *king*. But whatever his reason, I found I loved the comforting and fluttery sensation of Briar's hand wound with mine. It took me a breathless moment to summon enough bravery to tighten my fingers around his.

His breath caught and his gaze flickered down to our hands, but he made no move to withdraw. Instead he peeked up at me, his eyes shy. "Is this alright, Mari?"

I managed a nod, even as my fingers wove more securely around his. His thumb began to caress the back of my hand, each touch incredibly soft and gentle, causing my heart to crack open and all the budding feelings I'd been trying to suppress to tumble free.

Briar watched me, an indiscernible look filling his eyes. No one had ever looked at me in such a way. It was the same reverence that had filled his gaze when I'd discovered the jeweled rose hidden inside the seemingly ordinary box. Could it be that in this moment, he saw something deeper within me, just as I'd found the hidden rose?

Suddenly he stiffened and his gaze snapped away to over- look the gardens. "Did you hear that?"

I listened intently, but the only thing I could hear was the lovely melody coming from the surrounding floral orchestra. "Hear what?"

He didn't answer, simply listened, his forehead wrinkled in concentration. Suddenly, a jarring note penetrated the air. Briar flinched and yanked his hand away, leaving me longing for his touch.

"That." His gaze frantically searched the garden, as if expecting to find the offensive sound with his eyes. "It was a wrong note." His voice had lowered, as if he didn't want the nearby instruments to overhear his worry. "The plants have never…"

He slowly stood and began to wander the garden, keeping his ear cocked. I sat still and watched, the shadowy feel of his hand wound through mine lingering, the effects of his touch still manifest in my frantically beating pulse.

When my heart had gradually settled back to its normal rhythm, I stood and joined Briar's search, even though I wasn't entirely sure what we were looking for. It was diffi- cult to focus on the task when my thoughts were so occupied by not only Briar but the musical garden itself. I wanted nothing more than to let my gaze linger on each fantastic flower or sit and listen to the new song that had begun to cheerfully play; clearly the garden wasn't as worried about the wrong note as their king.

I paused in front of a second bed of strings, this one containing cellos and basses. I listened intently. Was it my imagination, or did the music coming from this section sound a bit more...strained? I crouched down to carefully examine each plant instrument.

And then I saw it. I gasped and swiveled around on my heels. "Briar."

At my frantic call, he was by my side in an instant. I pointed to one of the bass's strings, which was clearly broken. His breath hooked, and for a moment he stared in stunned disbelief. "But...how?"

"I take it magical musical plants don't break their strings?"

He shook his head, his forehead furrowed in clear worry. "No, they don't." He began examining the other plants in this plot, several of which also suffered from minor damage. He chewed his lip. "It seems to be limited to only this section. I doubt it's a coincidence that the plants closest to this garden's entrance are the ones suffering. But what could have caused it? It frustrates me that I have no idea what it is."

"Have you asked the gardens?"

Briar cocked his ear, as if expecting an explanation from the musical flora, but none came. His expression hardened, our previous contentment we'd found in our beautiful moment within the garden ruined. I ached to smooth out the serious lines of his face, but not as much as I wanted to hold his hand again. As if he longed for the same thing, his gaze flickered down to mine.

Taking courage from the invitation, I took a wavering breath and rested my hand over his. "I promise we'll figure out what's tainting the gardens. I'll help you."

He flipped his over beneath mine to stroke my palm. "Thank you, Mari. I don't know what I'd do without you."

His fingers laced through mine, as if he found solace in my touch, just as I found it in his. Whatever was happening between us, I never wanted it to end...even though my fears made me afraid it inevitably would.

CHAPTER 17

$\mathcal{I}$ frowned as I paused on the garden path to look around. Where was Briar? He'd told me last night he was planning on spending the morning in the gardens, but I'd been searching for nearly an hour without any sign of him. Perhaps he'd been locked away in another meeting, where he'd spent the majority of his time this past week.

I gave the plants a sidelong glance. "Have you seen His Majesty?"

Normally they were quite helpful...when they weren't being mischievous. However, lately they hadn't been as communicative, something that hadn't escaped Briar's notice. This additional mystery only added to the worry furrowing his brow, lines which seemed to become deeper with each passing day as the duties of his crown weighed heavily upon him.

Desperate to help ease some of his burden, I'd conducted my own investigation of the gardens in hopes of determining the cause of its condition, but other than discovering a few more dead plants sprinkled throughout the grounds and noticing the prolonged uncanny silence of the ones which were still alive, my search had yielded nothing.

I sighed and walked deeper into the garden on the off chance that Briar had ventured to one of the smaller ones contained in this section of the grounds. It only took a few moments for me to recognize where this twisting path led. My heart flared to life and I immediately stilled.

I nervously glanced at Hibiscus resting on my shoulder, whose sudden quivers only confirmed my suspicions. "Are we near that secret garden?"

He didn't answer, but the thick, unsettling feeling suddenly filling the air confirmed that we were indeed near the mysterious locked garden. I hadn't ventured this close to it since the day I'd opened it, and I wasn't keen on doing so now. My heart tightened in guilt when I remembered what had transpired there, and that due to my fear of losing Briar's good favor, I'd remained silent about it.

But this was the only area I hadn't searched for Briar, so I straightened my shoulders and walked further into the thicket of dense trees and shrubbery, growing so thick they blocked out the sun and cast everything in ominous shadows. I shivered.

I finally found Briar several minutes later, hunched over something just off the edge of the path, still quite some distance away from the locked garden. I released a breath of relief. "I've been looking everywhere for you. What are you doing in this section of the gardens? Conducting an important meeting with the plants?"

I hoped my teasing would earn me a smile, something I'd been trying to excavate from him at every opportunity in an attempt to soften the seriousness constantly filling his countenance.

He looked up, eyes gaunt, and for the briefest moment annoyance flashed across his face, as if he was frustrated by my interruption. Startled, my heart lurched, but the look faded almost immediately, replaced with the worry that seemed his constant companion, the transition so quick I wondered whether I'd imagined his initial reaction.

I took a hesitant step closer. "Is something wrong?"

He said nothing as he returned his gaze to whatever had captured it before I'd arrived. I leaned closer to peer over his shoulder and gasped sharply.

"What—" The rest of the words lodged in my throat, for I was unprepared for the sight that greeted me. I assumed they were plants...or used to be, but now they were black and wilted, oozing an inky liquid that slowly stained the surrounding soil.

"I have no idea what happened. I just found them like this." Heartbreak filled Briar's voice as he took in the dead plot, looking as if he'd lost dear friends; he'd known the gardens his entire life and undoubtedly considered them as such.

I crouched down beside him so that I could better examine the plants. I'd seen dead flowers before, but these weren't just wilted but almost...decayed. I reached a hesitant finger out and touched one of the shriveled dark leaves, which disintegrated at my touch until it was nothing more than ash.

My heart pounded furiously as I gaped at the pile of soot where the plant had been only moments before. "What could have caused this?" For I'd only seen such a phenomenon once before...back in the locked garden.

Briar gave a helpless shrug. "I wish I knew. This isn't the only unexplained mystery: plants are dying or slowly losing their magic throughout the gardens—the music of the orchestra garden is fading, the plants in the transformation garden are no longer changing, the health garden isn't producing its herbal remedies..." He trailed off.

"What can be done?" I asked.

"I have no idea. I wish the gardens would tell me what's wrong, but they've remained stubbornly silent. I don't understand their behavior." He heaved a heavy sigh and rubbed his eyes with the palms of his hands, and I fully noticed how haggard he looked.

"Have you been getting any sleep?"

"Not much. I've been up late catching up on paperwork after all the emergency meetings I've attended about the failing crops, and then I tossed and turned most of the night trying to sort out the puzzle about the gardens."

My mind drifted to the locked garden. Could it be...but no, I'd sealed it; I was certain of it. "I'm sure we'll come up with a solution soon." But my promise sounded empty compared to the daunting problem that lay before us.

"How?" he whispered helplessly. "I don't know what to do. I wish Father were here."

I was at a loss as to how to respond, so I simply rested my hand on his shoulder. With a wavering breath he rested his over mine. We hadn't held hands since our time in the orchestra garden a week before, and yet his fingers felt so familiar around mine, his touch comforting.

Briar began to gently play with my fingers, almost absentmindedly, as if his thoughts were far away. But mine were very much present—each caress from him ignited my heart and sent it pattering wildly.

"Are there any additional sections of the garden where strange things are occurring?" I managed despite each touch from him robbing me of breath.

He blinked, as if I'd torn his thoughts from somewhere far away. "There are many others, one in particular that's quite disturbing. Come, I'll show you."

He stood and offered his hand to help me up, not releasing it even after I'd stood. Instead, his fingers laced securely through mine. I gaped down at our connected hands before stumbling after him as he led me further down the path. Trepidation crept over me the moment I recognized it. Were we heading towards the mysterious garden?

To my fierce relief, he took a side path that snaked in the opposite direction. He paused several paces down it to point to the flowers growing alongside the cobblestones. Midst their fading colors, a black, jagged weed grew, slowly twisting around the blossoms.

My heart clenched. It looked like one of the weeds from the locked garden. The plants seemed to sense the sinister presence in their midst, for they leaned away from the weed, as if trying to put as much distance between it and them as possible, but it only slithered closer, like a snake after its prey.

"This morning I discovered several scattered throughout this section of the grounds," Briar said. "And look over there." He pointed further up the path, where another weed grew, this one twisting itself around the nearby plants, whose colors were slowly melting away as the weed choked them.

Horror rendered me temporarily speechless. "Have you tried pulling them out?"

"I have, several times. They won't budge." His forehead creased. "They're strange weeds, almost like the ones from... but it can't be." My pulse hammered as his gaze flickered in the direction of the locked garden.

I swallowed. I needed to tell him I'd opened that garden. Now. "Briar, I—"

He held up his hand to silence me. "Shh, listen. Can you hear that?"

I paused. The garden itself was silent, yet I sensed its great uneasiness. "What is it?" I asked nervously.

His frown deepened. "Someone is here, even though I'm not expecting any visitors. If you'll excuse me, I'm going to check on the gate." He lifted my hand to press a soft kiss on the back of my fingers, causing a shudder to ripple up my arm before he released me and headed up the path.

I watched him until he disappeared before turning my attention to the opposite direction, the one I knew led towards that mysterious garden. I nibbled my lip before glancing at Hibiscus perched on my shoulder.

"It's just a coincidence, isn't it? Surely the weeds aren't from *that* garden...are they?" Because if they were...then everything was my fault.

His nose quivered but he gave no other response. Even though it was the last place I wanted to venture, I knew I had to return to the garden and ensure it was still locked. With a determined breath that did little to quell the anxious knots tightening my stomach, I hesitantly headed towards it.

My pulse pattered in trepidation with each step closer to the tree and hedge wall that masked the locked garden's hidden entrance. I wouldn't go inside, but would only check to see whether anything appeared to be amiss. If it did, then I knew I needed to tell Briar about the day I'd gone inside.

I paused when I caught sight of the towering hedge that guarded the strange black plants within its walls, a sight which caused Hibiscus to immediately scurry down my arm and take refuge in some bushes far away. Even though it had been weeks, I still remembered where the entrance was hidden, as well as where I'd buried the key to get inside. The undergrowth appeared thicker than I last remembered; it snagged at my skirts as I poked my way through it towards the entrance.

I found the secret door that blended seamlessly into the hedge, only to discover it had been swallowed up in vines, so thoroughly that even the keyhole was covered with the thick, thorny stems. Had the garden grown over the door in order to prevent anyone from entering it again, or had it done so to keep the strange plants contained within it out?

I circled the entire hedge wall to ensure that is was still sealed tight. The tension pressing against my chest slowly eased. All appeared in order, and with the garden taking such precautions, I had nothing to worry about. There was no need to risk losing the man I cared for with an unnecessary confession.

Yet I couldn't quite shake the unease slithering through me, sharp and unsettling, as if my conscience were trying to warn me.

~

I WAS NEARING the stairs that led to the front doors when they burst open and Briar, hard-faced, stomped from the palace. I slowed, startled by the fury lining his countenance, which only slightly softened when he spotted me halfway down the steps.

"Mari?" He stared for a moment before rushing the rest of the way down to meet me.

"What is it?" I asked. "Has something happened?"

Warmth seeped from his touch as Briar gently took me by the shoulders, but it did little to comfort me with the almost frantic look filling his eyes. "Your father has arrived at the palace."

"*What?*" Alarm flared in my chest at his grave nod, and for a moment I couldn't breathe. "My father? *Here?* But how— did someone recognize me at your coronation and inform—" The fear clenching my heart robbed me of my voice.

Briar nodded solemnly. "I'm afraid he's aware of the rumors surrounding us and is demanding your immediate return."

My breath hooked sharply, and I could almost feel the

bars of my previous prison entrapping me once more. Deep down I'd known this would happen, despite my attempts to run. I shook my head frantically. No, I refused to return to him and Lord Brone. But the fear slithering its way into my heart made me feel it was inevitable.

Tears burned my eyes before I could stop them. "No, I can't go with him; I *won't*. Please don't make me—"

"Shh, it's alright, Mari. You don't have to." Despite the fierceness filling his eyes, Briar's tone was incredibly gentle, as was his touch as he began to rub his hands up and down my arms in a soothing gesture. "I'll take care of everything so that he'll never bother you again. I promise, Mari."

His gaze was wide and incredibly sincere, compelling me to trust him, although doing so didn't completely abate my fear. "How did he even gain entrance to the palace grounds?"

Briar frowned. "I'm not sure. The vines are supposed to protect the grounds from any intruders. It's just another mystery to add to the many others. But please don't be afraid, my dear; even though he's come, I'll still protect you." And to my astonishment, he leaned forward and softly pressed his lips to my brow.

I stilled in shock and my breath caught, even as warmth pooled from where his lips had touched my skin...in a *kiss*. Briar had *kissed me*.

He also froze, as if only just realizing what he'd done. He released me and hastily stepped back to put distance between us.

"I'm sorry, I—" A blush enveloped his cheeks as he lowered his gaze, suddenly finding the palace steps worthy of his prestigious attention. He cleared his throat without looking up. "Despite your father's demands, I refuse to allow him to take you from me, and will firmly tell him such. After all, I'm the king. For your protection, I'd prefer it if he didn't see you, but I have no doubt that you'll desire to see what transpires between us."

He knew me well, yet I was too stunned by Briar's sudden kiss to answer, a kiss whose shadow still lingered on my forehead. When I remained silent too long, he shyly peeked up at me and I finally managed to nod.

He relaxed. "I figured as much, but I won't risk him discovering you while you're eavesdropping, so I'll allow you to secure yourself in a secret hiding place within the throne room before I meet with him. It's behind a panel that contains a peephole so you'll be able to view the proceedings. Shall we go?"

He offered his arm, and although my mind still whirled, I managed to thaw enough to accept it. *Briar just kissed me.* The words repeated themselves over and over again in my mind, helping to alleviate some of my suffocating fear.

We walked to the gilded throne room in uncomfortable silence. When we arrived, Briar wordlessly led me to a panel that blended seamlessly into the wall and uncovered it to reveal a little cubbyhole lined with stone, with an assortment of pillows to make any eavesdropper hidden within comfortable.

Briar struck a match to light the candle occupying the tiny ledge at the back of the cubbyhole before helping me inside. I settled down and searched Briar's concerned expression. "You promise everything will be alright?"

"I promise, Mari." He gave my fingers a reassuring squeeze before stepping out of the cubby. The panel slid back into place, locking me inside. Even with the comforting light coming from the flickering candle, for one frightening moment I felt trapped and claustrophobic, as if I'd just sealed myself off in yet another prison. I took several steadying breaths and scooted closer to the small peephole just in time to see Briar regally settling on his throne.

He straightened in his seat and nodded towards one of the footmen flanking the doors. "Show the visitor in." His voice held an air of command he never used with me, reminding me that despite our deepening relationship, he was still the king.

The footman bowed as he exited the room. He returned shortly with Father. Terror immediately encased my heart, and even though I trusted Briar to protect me, the terror didn't loosen its icy grip; if anything it only squeezed tighter. Hatred seared through me at seeing Father's smug and hardened expression again. This flame only grew as he flounced in with his chest puffed out and a shrewd, calculating look filling his cold eyes.

"Your Majesty, it is the greatest honor." Father bowed deeply with a flourishing wave of his hand.

Briar lifted a single eyebrow at the exaggerated greeting before lifting his chin to a regal tilt. The king presented a formidable presence, which he'd undoubtedly need if the calculating look in Father's eyes was any indication.

"You arrived unannounced for a matter you deem pressing," Briar said, not even attempting to sound polite. "As king I'm quite busy, so state your business."

Father straightened with a slight frown, but he quickly masked it with a tight smile that didn't reach his eyes. "As Your Majesty wishes, I'll get straight to the point: nearly two months ago my rebellious daughter ran away from home. I've been fiercely worried for her, and have spared no expense in trying to find her."

I nearly snorted and betrayed my hiding place. Any expense he'd incurred had undoubtedly been done solely so he wouldn't risk losing his precious contract with Lord Brone and the aid he so desperately needed to escape the deep hole his debts had thrust him into.

Briar's jaw tightened but he didn't answer. Father waited

a moment before continuing, this time with a bit of hesitance. "Imagine my alarm when I was recently informed that my wayward daughter was, in fact, at this very palace. Naturally as her concerned father I had to come straightaway for her."

Briar's eyes narrowed. "You will not see Maren."

Father blinked. "Pardon, Your Majesty?"

"I need not repeat myself," he said cooly. "Maren will not be returning with you."

Father's eyebrow twitched, a telltale sign of his faltering patience which I knew all too well. "Forgive me, Your Majesty, but as the girl's father I must insist. You see, I've signed an engagement contract betrothing her to a Lord Brone. He has been most distressed by her disappearance."

Briar's jaw clenched further at the name but again he made no response.

"I'm afraid the contract is binding," Father continued. "I've already been placed in quite the predicament when she rebelliously ran away rather than fulfill her filial duty in honoring it, and I must do all I can to remedy the situation as quickly as possible. Surely you understand my dilemma."

"I do understand," Briar said. "But I'm afraid I don't sympathize. Maren will remain at the palace."

Father frowned before hastily smoothing it over with a tight smile. "Surely I've misunderstood Your Majesty, for I've heard tales of your benevolence and am certain—"

"Whatever you've heard, I must make it clear that I only extend such favor for those who deserve it." Briar didn't even bother to mask his disgust as he tapped the throne's armrest and surveyed Father coldly. "I've heard of this Lord Brone and am shocked that any father would betroth their daughter to such a man."

Father paled before quickly regaining his composure. "I can assure you that Lord Brone is the most respectable of men. He presented me with a very generous offer for my dear daughter's hand and I gratefully accepted."

Briar's frown deepened. "Regardless, I refuse to release Maren back to you. She is my guest and may stay here for as long as she wishes."

Father's composure cracked, revealing the scowl he'd previously masked. "Forgive me, Your Majesty, but as much as I hesitate to disagree with one as esteemed as yourself, I'm afraid I must. For I have more reason to worry about Maren's presence here than an unfilled contract considering there have been certain...rumors."

Briar's hardened manner deepened. "I've heard the rumors you're referring to and must inform you that they're not true."

"But Your Majesty—"

"I don't need to waste my breath nor my time defending myself to you," Briar said. "I've informed you of my decision and must order you to leave immediately." He lifted his hand, as if to summon his guards, but Father stepped forward, his jaw set in the determined way I'd seen him use whenever he was about to make a threat.

"As much as I want nothing more than to obey your wishes, I'm afraid I cannot do so considering it concerns my daughter. She's an engaged woman living alone with His Majesty, and thus her reputation is of my utmost concern."

Briar's mouth twisted. "I'm warning you: you're treading on dangerous ground with your insinuations."

"Forgive me, Your Majesty, but I must beg your indulgence. Maren is obligated to fulfill the contract between herself and her fiancé, and for the sake of her reputation she must leave the palace at once. As much as I regret the situation, I'm afraid my hands are tied."

Briar sneered at Father, not even bothering to hide his

disgust behind his usual royal decorum. "The solution is simple: you will release her from her contract."

"Unfortunately, that simply isn't possible," Father said. "I have no doubt that Your Majesty can clearly see the liability Maren has been for me. I'm indeed fortunate that Lord Brone is willing to make an arrangement that will be mutually beneficial to us both: he's in need of a wife and I'm in need of the money the arrangement will bring me. I can't afford to miss such a lucrative opportunity to unburden myself of a daughter who is otherwise unmarriageable."

I flinched at his sharp words. As if sensing my distress, Briar's own composure faltered as his concerned gaze briefly flickered towards my hiding place before returning his attention to Father, his countenance like stone.

"All contracts can be broken, and you will break yours, for I refuse to allow Maren to be handed over to a vile man for your monetary gain. This is my decision and I will not be dissuaded."

Father's eyes narrowed but he held his ground. "I must humbly protest, Your Majesty, for the law of the land clearly states that as her father, I have every right to marry her to whomever is advantageous to me. Even as the king, you cannot go against—"

Whatever fragile composure Briar had previously clung to snapped, and in one swift move he leapt to his feet. "How dare you," he thundered.

I jolted, startled by the sudden roar coming from such a mild-mannered man; I could see by the attending guards' wide eyes that they were just as surprised. Father stumbled backwards as Briar advanced a step, his fists clenched.

"You dare come to my palace uninvited to lecture me on the laws of *my* kingdom? You forget your place, merchant. I am the king."

Father scrambled back several steps more, his hands lifted in defense. "Your Majesty, I meant no offense—"

"And yet you gave it," Briar said coldly, not a single ounce of mercy in his dark eyes. "I *am* the law, and whatever I say is done. I most certainly will never hand Maren over to you, and don't you dare presume you can change my mind."

Father swallowed yet remained undaunted. "His Majesty is of course correct, but I shudder to think what your people would think when they learn their king not only willingly broke a contract of one of his subjects without provocation, but is holding someone's daughter as a hostage…"

A vein pulsed in Briar's temple. Father must have a death wish to speak to the king in such a way, although his argument was unfortunately valid. My heart sank. Briar wouldn't be able to protect me after all. By the frustration filling Briar's eyes, I saw that he knew it too—the king would be overstepping his authority to break one of his subject's legal contracts. But by the dangerous look darkening his expression, I feared he'd disregard the consequences and do it anyway.

Father's shrewd observation noticed Briar faltering. I caught a glimpse of his victorious smirk before he hastily masked it with an exaggerated sigh. "I don't wish to cause His Majesty any undue stress. I'm merely a man who finds himself in a difficult predicament with debts that must be paid. As Your Majesty can plainly see, Maren lacks any form of comeliness, and thus no one could possibly be persuaded to make me another offer for her…"

The look he gave Briar was calculating, and my stomach twisted at the sick game in which I'd inadvertently entangled Briar.

Briar's fury draped his regal posture as he took another menacing step closer. "How dare you say such horrible things about your own daughter," he hissed, his tone dangerous once again. "Maren lacks in nothing, least of all the beauty you fail to recognize in her."

My heart lifted in hope, even as surprise flickered over Father's features at Briar's defense, but his shock was only momentary before his expression shifted back to the cold shrewdness I knew all too well. I could almost see his calculating mind considering his options and the moment he came up with a new sinister plan.

"Perhaps I could be convinced to break the contract binding Maren to Lord Brone..."

Fire flashed in Briar's eyes. "Just what are you suggesting?"

"Nothing, Your Majesty," Father said smoothly. "I wouldn't presume to offer my humble suggestion to a mighty man such as yourself, only to offer a potential solution that would satisfy us both."

Briar's firm expression didn't change except for his deepening revulsion. "Go on."

Father smirked before smoothing out his own expression. "As a cunning merchant, I'm always open to a more advantageous offer." And he looked pointedly at Briar.

I clapped my hand over my mouth to stifle my gasp at his blatant insinuation. Father had some nerve to approach the king of the land in such a bold manner, but he'd always been a dauntless man—a trait that had led to both his success and his ruin. I waited with bated breath for Briar's reaction that would determine whether my father's current scheme had been cunning or utterly foolish.

Briar didn't speak for a long moment before he swiveled around and slowly returned to his throne, where he rigidly sat to look down his nose at Father. "Very well. I will pay off your debts in exchange for your releasing Maren from her contract."

My heart jolted. *No*, he couldn't make such a sacrifice on

my behalf. It was too much. I ached to protest, but couldn't risk Father discovering me.

Father tilted his head. "Only my debts? A man only has one daughter…"

Briar's decorum faltered once more as he rolled his eyes. "As well as provide you with a grand and fully-staffed manor house at the furthest end of the kingdom." Hardness filled his eyes as he leaned forward. "In exchange, you will agree never to see Maren again, nor inform anyone of our arrangement, nor reveal her location; you are to sever all ties from her. Do we have an understanding?"

Triumph filled Father's eyes. "His Majesty is said to be a wise ruler. I see the people aren't mistaken in their assessment."

Briar flicked his wrist dismissively. "I will have a contract of our agreement drawn up, after which you will leave immediately and never set foot in the palace again."

Father performed another exaggerated bow, unable to mask his victorious smirk as he took his leave. The door closed behind him with a resonating *thud*, but even after he'd gone I didn't stir from my hiding place. Instead I sat numb and in shock as the events that had unfolded before me whirled through my mind, jumbling my thoughts.

I startled as the panel suddenly swung open, revealing Briar peering down at me with concern. Despite the soft look filling his eyes, his expression was still hard, remnants from his confrontation with Father. "Are you alright, Mari?"

Too late I noticed tears burning my eyes, but unlike my past attempts to keep them at bay, they escaped unbidden. Briar immediately knelt before me and pulled me into a hug. I stilled in shock for a brief moment before I melted against him, burrowing my tear-streaked face against his warm chest.

"It's alright, Mari. You're safe. He can't hurt you anymore. I promise."

I shook my head and continued to cry, unable to stop even when he began rubbing my back so soothingly I felt I'd melt from his gentle touch.

"Mari?"

I hiccuped. "You shouldn't have—it was such a sacrifice—I'm not worth—" I couldn't finish.

"You *are* worth it, Mari." He pushed me away just enough so he could search my face. "What is tossing gold and a house at that vile man in comparison to your freedom from him forever?" He gently wiped the tears clinging to the bottom of my eyelids. "Now please don't worry. I was more than happy to do it. I'd do it all over again and more in order to protect you. You're special to me, Mari."

My heart swelled at his sweet words, made even more endearing by the tender way he'd spoken them. By the intense look filling his eyes I knew that he meant them, even if his possessing such feelings towards me didn't make any sense. But if he truly did...I almost felt like crying all over again.

Instead I burrowed myself back in his embrace and sighed with relief when he once again enfolded me within his comforting hold. There we sat together, even long after I'd stopped crying.

Gradually the reality of my new situation settled over me: Father was gone, Briar had protected me just as he'd promised, he found me special and worth caring about, and now he was holding me. Nothing had ever felt so right as being wrapped in his arms, and I fervently prayed that it was a place where I could remain forever.

CHAPTER 18

This garden was the most enchanting one we'd explored yet, but I could scarcely focus on its beauty with the way Briar held my hand as the boat in which we sat side by side floated gracefully down the stream. The water garden we currently explored was comprised not of cobblestone paths but of streams of different colors, which wove around miniature ponds and fountains where the flora grew in floating pots. With the lovely scenery and the beautiful way the sunlight glistened across the surrounding water, the scene was truly enchanting.

Yet I could only focus on the feel of Briar's fingers wound through mine and the warmth his touch caused to expand within my chest. I could no longer deny what was happening: not only was I *falling in love* with Briar, but my heart had already been completely stolen.

The realization was both thrilling and sobering considering my sentiments seemed foolish—a merchant's daughter who lacked in beauty and grace didn't belong in the arms of a king. Nothing could come from my feelings...could they?

But hope budded within my heart, for Briar was not only

holding my hand as we sat so closely our knees touched, but was attentively playing with each of my fingers, the wonders we gently floated past seemingly lost on him.

Each of his touches sent my pulse racing, quickly making our previously companionable silence increasingly more uncomfortable the longer it extended.

I reached out of the boat to graze my fingers across the surface of the golden water as we floated down the stream. "This garden is truly wondrous." It was almost a shame I was so distracted.

Briar didn't raise his gaze from where he currently brushed my knuckles with his thumb. "This garden has always been one of my favorites...as well as Gemma's; she finds the sound of the stream relaxing."

The tranquil sounds of the stream had been drowned out by my deafening heartbeat, which only escalated when his light and fluttery touch moved to stroke along my wrist.

He eventually paused his caressing and finally looked up to stare not at me but out across the water, his expression somber, just as it'd frequently been these past several days.

"Are you still thinking about the incident?" I asked.

He sighed. "I shouldn't have lost my temper with your father, as much as he deserved it."

He'd brought this up many times since Father's unexpected visit. Each reminder of Briar's sacrifice on my behalf tightened my chest with guilt, especially since it'd only fuel the rumors already surrounding Briar and me should anyone learn of what had transpired.

"You did what you had to," I said gently, praying he didn't regret his sweet defense of me.

Briar plucked a floating water lily from the stream and twirled it between his fingers, his taut expression thoughtful.

"I'm more bothered by *how* I handled the situation. Normally I have much more patience, even with men like your father." He frowned. "Instead I yelled, tossed my authority around, and used every tool at my disposal to bend him to my will. That's not how a king should handle his power, and it frightens me how easy it was to succumb to the temptation to do so."

I pursed my lips to stifle my inappropriate retort that someone like Father could only benefit from the humbling Briar had given him; his eyes were already haunted without my adding to his distress.

I squeezed his hand. "As much as we try otherwise, everyone has moments when they behave in a way they shouldn't—"

He shook his head. "It's more than that—it was as if a raging fire had been lit inside me, and I was determined to do everything within my power not only to stoke the flames, but unleash it. I relished putting your father in his place; it was such an incredible and *powerful* feeling—and that terrifies me." He squeezed his eyes shut, as if trying to block out the memory.

I frowned, not about what he'd said—for the feeling he'd described was one I'd felt far too many times, although perhaps not so strongly—but that it was *Briar* who'd said it, for he didn't seem the type of man who enjoyed another's distress. "You're only human." A reminder which was for myself as much as him.

"Surely being *human* is far below my kingly status." His teasing half-smile didn't reach his eyes.

"No, realizing you're human will only make you a better king. Being aware of this temptation is the first step in learning to control it." I flipped my hand over beneath his so my fingers could curl around his. "I'm grateful you defended me to Father. Thank you."

His melancholy softened, revealing the tender look I so

loved. "Perhaps that explains why it was so satisfying being angry with him—I loved being able to protect you."

His look became almost shy as his gaze seeped into mine, as if he expected the reasons for his feelings to be hidden within them. My settling heart flared to life again and gave a tiny *flip* when he cupped my chin and lightly stroked my jaw.

"Mari—"

Just as he started to lean closer, the boat gave a gentle lurch as it bumped against the shore. Crimson stained his cheeks as he immediately released me and lowered his gaze.

"Would you like to explore the rest of the garden?"

It took me a moment to emerge from the fluttery stupor he'd left me in and reluctantly nod. Normally I'd have found the prospect of exploring such an enchanting place magical, but even this most lovely of gardens couldn't hold a candle to the moment that had been interrupted; I ached to see how it would have unfolded.

But I couldn't resist the invitation to take his hand when he offered it. To my delight, he held it long after he'd helped me from the boat and led me up the shore. We walked along the bank of a glowing stream and paused on a crystal bridge to look over the railing down at the floating flowers, each sparkling in the sun's golden light. The blossoms were transparent, allowing us to see through them to the shimmery lilac-rose water below.

I sighed contentedly. "It's so beautiful."

The corner of his mouth lifted. "It is." But strangely he was looking at *me*, not our enchanting surroundings. The longer he stared at me in such a way, the more I felt almost... pretty. The feeling only increased when he tentatively reached out to tuck a loose strand of my hair behind my ear, lingering to carefully run his fingers through the strands, his gaze mesmerized.

My heart gave a pleasant lurch. *Briar is playing with my hair.* Ooh my, but this was an utterly incredible sensation.

"Your eyes are so lovely," he murmured. "They're not only an unusual color, but they're so expressive, constantly alit with your curiosity, confidence, mischief, joy...I never have to wonder what you're thinking." With each word he twisted and untwisted one of my escaped black curls around his finger.

I prayed that the current emotions filling my heart to bursting were absent from my eyes, for they were ones I wanted to hide from him: not only my love for him, but my secret wish that he never stop playing with my hair, a gesture that felt both intimate and...*romantic.* And with the tender way he looked at me...could he possibly feel such beautiful feelings towards *me?*

The memory of Princess Rheanna's words returned from the place I'd buried them for fear they'd give me false hope: *He's a very kind man who sees what others don't, and I've noticed the way he looks at you. Open your heart to the possibility that the future you long for is within reach, and I'm confident you'll find yourself pleasantly surprised.*

I'd locked my heart away years ago, terrified of allowing myself to hope for a future I didn't believe existed for me. But the way Briar looked at me now...could I be brave enough to open my heart and nourish this hope?

Briar's intense look was making it impossible to think clearly. I needed a moment to compose myself. I hastily tore my gaze away and noticed something that immediately pushed all thoughts of my blossoming love aside.

I leaned over the railing. "What's that?"

Briar seemed almost reluctant to look away from me, but the moment he joined me to peer into the water, he stiffened.

"What...?" For an inky substance slowly oozed across the

surface of the stream below, staining the rosy-colored water in blackness.

He gaped in disbelief while my heart pounded wildly—with this and the recent weeds, there was no longer any doubt: this was from the locked garden. I wasn't sure how the inky substance had escaped, but somehow it had, which meant I needed to finally tell Briar I'd opened it. Yet the words lodged in my throat as terror over his inevitable reaction squeezed my chest. I couldn't tell him. It'd ruin everything between us. But I could no longer remain silent.

Briar continued to stare down at the spreading blackness slowly tainting the water. "I don't understand. What could have possibly caused..." He paused as he caught sight of my guilty expression. "Mari," he asked slowly, his voice taut.

The walls guarding my secret crumbled. "I didn't mean to," I stammered.

His entire manner hardened in an instant. "Didn't mean to do *what*? What did you do?"

I shivered at the coldness already filling his voice. "I—" I swallowed, unable to form the words.

His jaw twitched, a sign that the sliver of control he held over his emotions was already on the brink of breaking. "Your obvious guilt indicates you've done something, and I demand to know what it was. Tell me, Maren. *Now.*"

Maren? He hadn't called me that in...quite a while. I tried to speak but the words clogged my throat, my heart's resistance to sharing the offense I believed would cause him to turn away.

Fire filled his eyes at my continued silence as the flames of his anger rose. "Tell me, Maren. That's an order from your king."

I flinched. He'd never used his authority against me, but his doing so now returned me to my proper place: in this moment we weren't friends, but simply a king and his subject.

I took a steadying breath and bravely lifted my trembling chin. "I didn't mean for it to happen. I swear."

His eyes narrowed. "What do you mean by *it?*"

"The hidden key...the locked garden...I was just curious, so I—"

His eyes widened in realization as he spun around and hurried down the slope towards the boat, his hurried footsteps resonating through the uncannily still water garden. I bounded after him, arriving just as he'd settled in the boat and prepared to push off from shore.

"Are you planning on leaving me?" I couldn't be in so much disgrace as to warrant such a punishment.

He paused briefly with a look like he was considering it... but surely I was mistaken, for despite his current temper he wasn't so heartless as *that.*

He jabbed his finger towards the opposite end of the boat as far away from him as possible. "Get in." The command was curt. I hastened to obey and nearly tripped on my skirts as I scrambled into the boat.

I'd no sooner settled than he pushed off the bank. The boat floated at a brisker pace than the leisurely way it'd arrived, as if the magic guiding it sensed our urgency and was eager to comply to avoid the wrath of the king.

I stole a hesitant glance at his expression, as rigid as his posture as he sat with the air of a displeased monarch, his stony look a warning that one wrong word would result in a dungeon sentence. Only my assurances that Briar wasn't such a man kept my rising panic in check.

Silence reigned as the boat continued to drift towards the garden exit. Briar cursed. "Go faster," he barked.

The boat's pace increased slightly, but not enough. Briar

heaved an annoyed sigh before his dark glare darted towards me. I automatically stiffened.

"Explain, Maren. I want to know the extent of what I'm about to face before I see it."

I shivered at the coldness filling his eyes, so unlike the Briar I knew. "There isn't much to explain," I stuttered. "I discovered the key—"

"When?" he demanded.

I scrunched my forehead, trying to remember. "It was the first day I explored the grounds. I noticed it poking partially out of the dirt alongside one of the paths on the way to the topiary garden, as if it wanted me to find it. But when I tried to take it, the roots entangled around it..."

Briar cursed again. "And you foolishly ignored such an obvious warning from the garden that the key wasn't for you to take? Did it not occur to you that there was a reason the key was hidden in the first place?"

My stomach lurched. No, it hadn't, nor had I recognized that the garden had been clearly trying to prevent me from stealing the key, but it seemed so obvious now...and I'd stubbornly ignored its warning.

"Furthermore, you then decided to use this key to snoop around in places you weren't supposed to go. Do you not understand what a locked door means, Maren? It means you're forbidden from entering it."

Shame burned my cheeks as I lowered my eyes. He took a deep breath, as if trying to quell his rising temper, but it didn't work, for his tone remained just as hard when he spoke again.

"When did you open the garden?"

I desperately tried to remember, but it was impossible with the way time here blended together, causing weeks to melt away without my noticing. I had no idea how long I'd been at the palace—two months? Three?—let alone when I'd discovered that garden.

"I'm afraid I don't know. I do remember your father was still alive, but that's all I can tell you."

He muttered another dark obscenity. "That's far too long."

Before he could say anything else, the boat arrived at the opposite bank, blessedly sparing me another harsh scolding.

Despite his fury, he was still enough of a gentleman to help me from the boat, although his assistance was more jerky than the tender way he'd rendered it before. The moment we were both ashore, he released me and hurried in the direction of the locked garden.

"I wondered if the garden had been breeched when I first noticed the weeds," he muttered as we took one twisted path after another. "But I've been distracted with more pressing worries to take my suspicions seriously, especially considering I falsely believed you'd never break my trust to enter such an obviously forbidden place. Apparently I was mistaken."

I withered beneath his accusing glare. "I'm so sorry, Briar, I—"

"I'm in no mood for your apologies, Maren."

My eyes stung as I snapped my mouth shut. How could everything between us have been ruined so quickly? It was impossible to believe that earlier we'd been having a *romantic* moment together, only for it to shift so drastically and so suddenly.

And it was all my fault.

The guilt squeezing my insides tightened with each step, for the closer to the garden we became, the more we could see the effects of the poison I'd inadvertently released—the plants lining the path were either infested with black weeds, slowly wilting, or being consumed by the inky decay, which had spread since our last visit, slowly swallowing each plant in its path. Before long, everything would be consumed.

Fear clenched my stomach. What had I unleashed and what were the lingering consequences of my actions, both from my mistake and the ones that had followed when I'd wrongly kept it to myself?

The moment we arrived at the garden, Briar didn't even hesitate in finding the location of the hidden door, now entirely swallowed up in vines. He climbed over the tree blocking the entrance and frowned as he studied the vines. "The garden was clearly trying to protect itself, but unfortunately it was all in vain."

He touched one of the dying vines, brittle from the sickness already invading the grounds, before tearing the vines away to uncover the door inch by inch.

I leapt forward. "What are you doing?" Surely he couldn't be *opening* the door, not when whatever was behind it needed to remain contained.

For a moment, an almost wild look filled his eyes, rendering him almost unrecognizable, as if he were desperate to see the garden for a reason beyond needing to check on it. The foreign look faded almost as quickly as it'd arrived, leaving him looking almost...confused. It took nearly a full minute of him staring blankly at the ripped-away vines gathered at his feet before he answered.

"The poison has already escaped, so such a protection is entirely useless."

I nibbled my lip. "Even so, is venturing inside still wise? Perhaps we should—"

"You're in no position to offer your opinion, Maren." His harshness immediately rendered me silent.

He tore more vines away until he'd uncovered the keyhole. He wordlessly extended his hand, palm up, for the key. Trepidation seeped over me as I knelt in the dirt near the knob in the root that marked where I'd buried it. I shivered at its icy touch as I picked it up and shakily handed it to him. Without even a nod in acknowledgement, he shoved it inside the keyhole, grasped the handle, and pushed the door open with an ominous creak.

My breath choked at the sight and smell that greeted us: the entire garden was black with decay, and a suffocating odor hung thickly in the air. All the plants had vanished, leaving nothing but oozing blackness staining the soil, with hundreds of weeds infesting the ash-covered ground. An ominous feeling filled the icy air, thick and foreboding.

"How did this happen?" I asked breathlessly.

"This garden contained dark magic," he said. "A magic that has now been unleashed...thanks to you."

My guilt pressed more painfully against my chest. "But I don't understand how it escaped. I checked on the garden to ensure it hadn't and it appeared sealed."

"You obviously triggered something when you first entered." He glared at me again and I flinched.

"Is there any way to reverse it?"

"I have no idea." He knelt in the dirt and ran his fingers through the dry, ebony soil, his expression darkening with each touch. "I sense a lot of sinister power. Whatever dark magic was locked in this garden has now been at force too long for us to have much hope of reversing the damage. We might have managed it if we'd caught it in time." His gaze sharpened accusingly. "Why didn't you confess what happened the moment you opened the garden?"

My cheeks burned. "I didn't fully realize—"

I stopped. No, that wasn't the entire reason, but I couldn't find the words to explain the terror that had consumed me when I'd first entered this garden all those weeks ago—not fear for the garden itself, but that my actions would cause me to lose all that was growing between Briar and me.

But hiding my mistake had been selfish, for in the end it'd only caused more damage, damage that Briar feared would be permanent. "Are the gardens going to die?" I shakily asked.

"Quite likely."

Jaw taut, Briar looked around a moment more before pushing us out of the garden and slamming the door behind us. He locked it and pocketed the key, clearly no longer trusting me enough to bury it again in a spot where I could easily retrieve it.

Arms folded, he turned back to me. "Do you fully understand the extent of the mess you've created?"

"I—" It took me a moment to find my voice. "I didn't mean to. I hadn't realized I'd done anything wrong, especially when the gardens didn't tell you what had happened—"

"Whatever dark magic is at work here is likely the result of a curse, and one of the laws of many curses is forced silence. The gardens didn't tell me what had happened not because it wasn't serious, but because they *couldn't*." His glare sharpened. "You, on the other hand, had no such spell of silence...yet you chose to remain silent all the same. The garden will *die*, Maren. And it's all your fault."

Tears burned my eyes. "I'm so sorry, Briar. I was just...curious."

His fury crackled as he advanced a step closer. "You destroyed a magical garden that has been alive for generations all because you were *curious*?" He spat the word out mockingly. "Curiosity doesn't permit you to do whatever you please. I would have thought you'd have learned from your previous curiosity after plucking the rose that trapped you here."

My tears finally escaped, but it wasn't because of his words or even my guilt, but the way he threw his accusations at me like daggers.

241

My heart broke further at the fire filling his eyes and the almost...beastly expression he wore. "This isn't you," I whispered.

He paused, his breaths heavy, and glanced down at this hands, seeming to only just realize his fists were clenched.

"I'm so sorry," I whispered.

He glared at me again. "Being *sorry* can't fix what you've done. I should have convinced the gardens to toss you out of the palace the moment you plucked that rose, for you've been nothing but a thorn in my side ever since you arrived."

He stormed off without another word, leaving behind the stinging memory of his fury and the horrible realization of what my mistake had cost me: not only the gardens, but the man I loved.

CHAPTER 19

"*H*ibiscus?"

Panic constricted my chest as I frantically searched the transformation garden...or what was left of it. Half the flowers were wilted, and the magic of those that were still alive had faded so that the plants could no longer transform as they once could.

I rummaged through a clump of weeds, but there was no sign of a lilac topiary anywhere. "Hibiscus?" But he didn't come at my call.

My hedgehog had been missing all morning. I'd scoured the palace—only avoiding the areas where I was at risk of encountering Briar—and the gardens that hadn't yet completely succumbed to the weeds' poison. But my hedgehog was nowhere to be found. It wasn't like Hibiscus to wander away. Where could he be?

"Hibiscus, where are you?"

I poked through a bed of wilted hibiscus flowers, searching...and froze. Nestled in the midst of the dead blossoms was my hedgehog, lying completely still, frozen mid-chew of the flowers he enjoyed so well.

My heart leapt to my throat. "Hibiscus?" I cautiously touched him with my fingertip, expecting to feel the familiar warmth of his body, but he was completely cold.

My breath caught. I touched him again, this time giving him a gentle shake with my fingers. Nothing. Tears clogged my throat. No, Hibiscus couldn't be...my denial wouldn't allow me to think the word, even though I couldn't deny that the magic which had given him life had faded.

How could this have happened? I'd taken precautions and kept him away from the gardens so he wouldn't catch the spreading sickness, but he must have wandered beyond my careful supervision, drawn to his natural home in a way impossible for me to quench.

I carefully scooped him into my arms and hurried into the palace, not stopping until I'd reached my bedroom, where I carefully set Hibiscus on my pillow.

"Hibiscus?" I stroked his lilac topiary fur in hopes that being away from the garden's poison would revive him, but still he didn't move, his open eyes staring glassily and unseeing ahead. The burning tears I'd fought to keep at bay escaped as I curled up on the bed and buried my face in my pulled-up knees, barely feeling the gentle way the nearby potted carnations stroked my hair in a futile attempt at comfort.

Grief washed over me in waves. I wasn't strong enough to face it while still battling my guilt over what I'd done to the gardens, more acute now that it'd cost me my only remaining friend. With these feelings and the suffocating loss of my relationship with Briar, I felt I was drowning with no hopes of resurfacing.

I hadn't seen Briar since our agonizing confrontation three days ago; he'd locked himself in his private quarters and now took all his meals there, clearly so disgusted with me he went to great lengths to avoid me. My heart broke the longer we were apart, a distance more torturous considering *I'd* been the one to cause it when I'd destroyed whatever had previously existed between us.

But while I knew I fully deserved Briar's wrath, I couldn't deny his reaction had been more intense than I'd expected from a man such as him…unless this was who he truly was. I gave my head a firm shake. No, I didn't believe that. And yet I could still see the anger twisting his hardened countenance, hear the coldness filling his voice, and feel his piercing glare, all signs that I'd lost the friendship I so treasured, one I'd give anything to get back.

And now I'd also lost Hibiscus.

My gaze settled on the enchanted rose on my nightstand, still in full bloom even though only about a fourth of its petals remained. Whereas before the thought of being forced to stay at the palace had filled me with joy, it was nothing more than a prison sentence now that I'd lost the favor of the man I loved. Without him, Hibiscus, or the enchanted gardens, I had no reason to stay. Would the gardens' weakened state finally allow me to escape?

For a brief moment I allowed my despair to entertain the idea before I hastily dismissed it. No, I wasn't one to give up so easily. I couldn't just abandon the fight, even when everything seemed entirely hopeless. But my renewed determination did little to dispel my heartache, so thick and suffocating I feared I'd drown in it.

I sat on my bed, staring unseeing out at the sky swallowed up by thick, grey clouds. Sharp pain squeezed my heart in its unrelenting grasp until a thought slowly penetrated my foggy grief: while there was likely nothing I could do about Hibiscus or the rest of the dying gardens, it wasn't too late to fix my relationship with Briar. Even if he was determined to hate me forever, I couldn't just sit idly by without at least attempting to make amends. Which meant I'd have to face him and risk subjecting my heart to more pain if he wanted nothing more to do with me.

I stood and made my way through the gloomy corridors until I reached his study, where I raised my shaky hand to knock...only to hesitate, my stomach clenched in fear. Maybe Briar would be angry at me for arriving unannounced, and I wasn't sure whether I was strong enough to face it again so soon. But face it I would. I bravely straightened my shoulders, took a steadying breath, and knocked. At Briar's invitation to come in, the attending footman opened the door.

Briar sat at his desk bent over disorganized stacks of papers, his expression haggard. He glanced up at my entrance and immediately leapt to his feet, his eyes wide in disbelief. "Mari..."

I relaxed my tense posture at the soft way he spoke my nickname as I frantically searched his face. His manner was absent his previous harshness, leaving only the exhaustion that lined his expression.

He began to walk around the desk towards me but paused halfway, as if afraid to approach me. He nervously searched my face, studying me as obsessively as I studied him. There was no sign of the fierce man he'd momentarily been only days before, only of the man I knew and loved.

In my fierce relief a tear trickled down my cheek. His breath hooked as he took a hesitant step forward. "What is it, Mari? Is everything alright?" By his own miserable expression, he clearly knew that things weren't...and that *he* was the cause.

I couldn't find my voice, for this reception was the complete opposite of what I'd expected. At the very least I thought I'd be received with distance and coldness, not Briar's usual warmth or even his shy hesitancy. Whatever temper had previously overcome him back in the garden, there was no sign of it now.

It gave me the courage to step forward. "It's Hibiscus. He—"

My lip trembled and I couldn't finish. In three strides Briar reached me with a look like he wanted to take me in his arms...only to hesitate once again. But I was in no mood for hesitation. He'd extended the invitation, however uncertainly, and I was going to claim it.

I flung my arms around him, relieved when he immediately embraced me. I became awash in the earthy scent I loved as I burrowed against his chest, basking in the feel of his warmth, his tight and comforting hold, and the soothing way he rubbed my back.

"I missed you," I stuttered when I managed to find my voice. "So much."

"I missed you, too."

How could he after what had transpired between us? How could he be holding me now so securely and cozily against his chest? I tipped my head back to search his gaze. "I don't understand. Don't you hate me?"

"No, Mari. I could never hate you...although I understand why you think I do." He sighed wearily, his dark eyes swirling with pain. "Might we talk? Please."

I was so relieved by his friendly reception I'd grant him anything. At my nod, he flicked his wrist, a silent command that sent his two guards from the room. The moment we were alone, he took my hand and led me to the desk, where he pulled up a chair and helped me sit before taking the one across from me.

He rested his elbows on his knees and gave me his full attention, his expression gravely serious. "I don't even know where to begin," he said. "Obviously with an apology, but that feels entirely inadequate compared to the pain I undoubtedly caused you with my anger."

I ached to deny he'd caused any, but there was little point. "You did hurt me."

He groaned and buried his face in his hands. For a long moment he remained in this position, saying nothing. "As much as I wish otherwise, I knew I'd done so. The moment I returned from the gardens, I felt as if I'd awoken from a horrific nightmare, and I realized the full extent of what I'd done to you. Since then, that moment has repeatedly haunted me. I'd give *anything* to take it back."

I searched his eyes, wide with sincerity. As much as he'd hurt me, his clear remorse as well as the love I felt for him made it easy to extend my forgiveness.

"I completely understand the wish to change a mistake," I said. "I ache to take back my own, especially since, unlike yours, mine is irreparable."

"Isn't mine also irreparable?" His entire manner was desperate.

"Of course not." I loved him too much to hold this one moment of temper over him forever, especially considering I knew the wonderful man he truly was.

"Then tell me how I can make amends. Will an apology even help?"

I managed a small smile, hoping it'd dispel some of the lingering tension so that we could return to where we'd left off before everything had fallen apart. "It's certainly a start."

"Then that's where I'll begin." To my astonishment, he got off his chair and knelt before me.

My cheeks burned. "Briar! Get off the floor. You can't kneel before me. You're the king."

"Not right now." He clasped my hands in between his and stared earnestly up at me. "I can't express how sorry I am for how I treated you back in the garden. I know I don't deserve your compassion or mercy, but I beg your forgiveness all the same." And he pressed his forehead to my hands, a gesture of humility that both touched and embarrassed me.

"Please Briar, don't do that." I shifted uncomfortably when he didn't budge; I didn't like seeing Briar kneel before me in such a way. I scooted off the chair and knelt in front of him, grazing his cheek to lift his gaze. "Of course I forgive you."

He gaped at me in disbelief before closing his eyes with a groan. "You can't, Mari. How I acted—"

"It's alright." I ached for him to believe me so he could stop hurting, for the pain filling his eyes was more agonizing than any he'd caused me.

He frantically shook his head. "But it's not. The moment I lost my temper, I was just so...*furious*. It seemed to consume me in a way that there wasn't room for anything else, least of all compassion for you. My complete lack of mercy absolutely disgusts me, especially since it came at the expense of the one who means the most to me. Thus I can never forgive myself for it."

"Please do," I pleaded. "Especially considering you were right to be upset with me after what I'd done." I hesitated before voicing the question I was terrified of asking for fear of how he'd respond. "Am I really a thorn in your side?"

His breath hooked and his hold tightened around my hand. "You're nothing of the sort."

I ached to believe him, but the wounds those particular words had carved into my heart hadn't yet healed. "But you said—"

"No, Mari." He squeezed my fingers desperately. "I've *never* thought that. I don't know why I said something so cruel, especially to you..." His voice broke, and in that moment he looked truly frightened. "What's wrong with me, Mari?"

"You're simply not yourself lately," I said soothingly. "Perhaps your father's death and the weight of your new responsibilities as king have been harder on you than you thought." I stroked his hair, a gesture that felt both forward and incredibly natural. My heart gave a pleasant lift when he made no move to stop me.

"I've never lost my temper in such a way, not even with your father," he said. "And what's worse: I didn't immediately apologize for the pain I caused you. I wanted to before now, but I was too ashamed to face you and too disgusted by my own behavior to summon the courage. But please believe me that I sincerely regret how I treated you and would do anything to take it back."

His apology warmed my heart, causing my lingering heartache to fade. "I'm relieved to know the real reason for your locking yourself in your rooms. I feared you were avoiding me."

"In a sense I was, but mostly to take precautions—I don't trust myself around you because I fear hurting you again." He frowned at the closed door. "Perhaps I shouldn't have sent my guards away."

"Don't be ridiculous; you would never hurt me."

"You can't say that, not when I did." He sighed and rubbed his temples. "But there's another reason I've remained in my study—I simply haven't had time to seek you out, not with everything that's happening."

Foreboding knotted my stomach. "What's going on?"

He collapsed back in his seat before wearily waving to the one across from him. "Please be seated and I'll explain."

I shakily perched on the very edge of the chair and pressed my palms to my bouncing knees in an attempt to still them. "Is it more than just the gardens?" I was almost afraid that asking about them would trigger his previous anger, but to my relief it remained at bay.

"I'm still not entirely sure of the effects of what happened, which makes everything much more complicated."

Guilt squeezed my heart anew, even as another apology burned on my tongue. Although I'd given it several times, perhaps now he'd finally receive it. "I'm so sorry for what I did. When the gardens didn't inform you, I truly believed I hadn't caused any harm."

He reached out to rest his hand over mine. "Please, Mari, I don't want you to cling to your guilt any longer. It's done."

I nearly cried in relief, not just for his forgiveness, but that he was being himself again in extending it. His expression gentled as he tenderly caught one of my tears clinging to the ends of my eyelashes.

"Please forgive yourself, Mari. It's in the past. All we can do from here is move forward."

I took a steadying breath and managed a nod. The corner of his mouth lifted slightly before he sobered again.

"Now to apprise you of the situation: the gardens are dying with no known way to reverse the process. What's more, shortly after our...incident, I received word that the crops in three additional areas of the kingdom have failed without warning. If we lose any more, our kingdom will face a devastating famine such as hasn't been seen in centuries."

I gaped at him. "More crops are dying? But how—"

"I have a theory that the land is connected to the enchanted grounds. Because they're dying, so is the rest of the kingdom."

I furrowed my brow. "The gardens are connected to the land? Is such a thing possible?"

He gave a wry smile. "I'm confident that it is, considering my experiences with my own curse."

Despite the seriousness of the situation, my heart gave an excited leap. "Are you going to finally tell me what it is?"

"I admittedly never planned on doing so, but after everything that's happened, you deserve to know."

I found myself leaning forward, eager for an answer to a mystery that had been mercilessly tormenting my curiosity ever since my arrival.

His half smile returned, dispelling some of the gloominess filling his eyes. "Curious, are you?"

"Of course, but not to worry—this curiosity won't lead me to pluck enchanted roses or unlock poisonous gardens."

He chuckled, and with it I realized that despite everything, things were alright between us again. "That's a relief. Now I'll satisfy your curiosity by telling you the entire story." He leaned back in his seat, as if preparing himself for a long tale. "Once upon a time there was a prince who was prone to wandering."

I lifted an eyebrow at such an unexpected beginning. "Is that prince you?" I asked, even though I already knew the answer.

"Indeed. Intrigued?"

"Very." I leaned even closer and rested my elbows on my knees. "And where did this wandering prince go?"

"Everywhere," he said. "While I've always loved the gardens, I've mentioned before that the rest of the castle never felt like home. I think I was always searching for something to fill that void, and I often found it while scouring the land discovering unique treasures. I enjoyed not only seeing more of Malvagaria and the surrounding kingdoms, but also tracking down both unique and seemingly ordinary things to add them to my collection." He frowned. "Naturally, Mother didn't approve."

"And your father?"

Briar's manner softened. "He always supported my unconventional hobby and saw it as an opportunity for me to see more of the kingdom and meet my future subjects. But he cautioned me that my wanderings could easily get out of hand and made me promise never to allow it to get in the way of my duties, a promise I did my best to keep. Mother was furious for his support and resolved to do whatever it took to keep me at home where I belonged."

My heart pounded as I realized what direction this story was going. "What did she do to stop you?"

"What she does best: she put a curse on me, one that bound me to the enchanted gardens. If I ever leave them, I'll wither away and die."

I gaped at him, half expecting him to crack a smile that revealed he was jesting, but his expression was quite serious. "Your own mother would do such a horrible thing?" I finally managed.

"I'm afraid so. She's cursed not just me, but all her children."

I continued staring, my disbelief making it difficult to find my voice. "You literally can't leave the grounds? I always assumed it was only your duties to your father and title that were keeping you here."

He shook his head. "Although there are exceptions. I was able to travel to Draceria last autumn, but only because the garden gave me one of its enchanted roses to sustain my life, keeping me connected to it even when far apart. I'm afraid that while it succeeded in that aspect, I wasn't quite myself. I was constantly exhausted and rather apathetic towards everything and everyone. That experience taught me the extent of my connection; even though I was technically able to be apart from the gardens, my thoughts were always focused on them and longing to return. I constantly felt like a plant in need of nourishment it wasn't receiving. It made for a very wearying trip."

I sat back in astonishment. Of all the theories I'd managed

to form about the curse afflicting Briar, none had even come close to the truth. "Can the curse be broken?"

He shrugged. "I'm certain it *can*, but I'm at a loss as to *how*. Even if I ever discovered the solution, part of me—the magic's doing, undoubtedly—makes me never want to break it. I feel as if I'd be severing a limb if I disconnected from the grounds now."

I frowned. "There has to be a way to overcome it, considering your brother succeeded in breaking his."

He sighed. "Unfortunately, our curses are drastically different. His came with conditions to fulfill—ones Mother put in place in order to bend him to her will—whereas her will for me was to keep me bound to the Malvagarian throne forever in order to more easily manipulate me once I became king. If there are any stipulations, I have yet to learn of them."

I shook my head in disbelief. It all seemed too fantastic to be real, but I'd seen enough magic in the past several months to believe anything was possible. "Why are you telling me all this?"

"So you'll more clearly understand that this garden's magic extends beyond the palace walls," he said. "I'm beginning to suspect that it's not just *me* that's connected to it, but also—"

I gasped sharply. "Your kingdom?"

He nodded gravely. "It seems too much of a coincidence that the kingdom's crops started failing without explanation at the same time the gardens began dying. If the crops are connected to the grounds, then they too are being afflicted by whatever poison is spreading."

It made sense, but knowing the problem didn't present any clear solutions. "So what can be done?"

He didn't answer right away. His eyes had suddenly grown wide, as if an epiphany had just struck him.

"What is it, Briar?"

He blinked rapidly, as if I'd torn his thoughts from somewhere far away. "Of course. The gardens...the weeds...the curse...I just realized what's happening, why I—" His mouth snapped shut and he stopped speaking. I watched as an internal struggle seemed to wrestle inside him before all at once his expression cleared. "Forgive me, I've gotten the conversation off course. What were you saying?"

I studied him intently. His face was calm, yet something different raged in his dark eyes. He clenched his jaw, as if fighting the impulse to share something. "What did you realize just now?"

He hesitated a moment. "Nothing," he said smoothly, and instantly the invisible wrestle seemed to pass. "Nothing important, at least. Now, we were discussing what to do about the gardens. The first step is to respond to the damage that's already occurred with the crops." He held up a sealed letter. "I've written to Drake asking him to begin overseeing the problem from his end of the kingdom, as well as begin working with some of our advisors in going over our food supplies so that we can better distribute them to the afflicted areas. But this solution is only a temporary one and can't take care of the core problem, one I fear there's no resolution to."

"So what you're saying is: we're on a sinking ship with no long-term relief in sight." At his nod, I groaned and buried my face in my hands. The situation was far worse than I could have ever imagined...and it was all my doing.

He rested a gentle hand on my shoulder. "Please don't be distressed. What's done is done."

"How can you say that after what I unleashed?" I demanded. "If all the crops fail, your people will starve."

"I'm not denying the situation isn't dire, but it's not entirely your fault."

My gaze snapped up. "What do you mean?"

"You may have unlocked the garden and hastened the spread of the dark magic growing there, but you aren't the one who initially planted the seeds of the sinister plants poisoning the garden. *Mother* did." His expression darkened as he rose. "Which means it's high time I pay her a visit so I can get to the bottom of whatever she created."

CHAPTER 20

*W*e walked through the corridors towards the abandoned east wing. After only a few hallways, Briar's fingers brushed my wrist, his shy eyes seeking permission. At my small nod his fingers wove through mine. I tightened my grip with a contented sigh. With his hand enfolding mine, I felt any lingering pain from his lost temper melt away.

"I'm surprised to learn your mother is within the palace," I said as we ascended the steps to the third floor. "I thought she was trapped inside a mirror."

"She is, but I thought it wise to keep her close, so I've left it inside her old quarters." He spoke with a distracted air, and when I glanced sideways at him I found him rubbing his temples with a wince of pain.

I stopped short. "Are you alright?"

He didn't answer for a moment as he massaged his forehead. "I've been getting terrible headaches, but it's nothing to concern yourself over."

That was most certainly *not* an order I'd obey. "When did your headaches start?"

"A few days ago."

My heartbeat escalated. *A few days ago*? But that was when… "You mean after we entered the locked garden?"

His brow furrowed. "Yes…I believe it was later that evening, but I'm afraid there's been so much going on since then I'm a bit fuzzy on the exact timing."

"And have you had similar migraines before?"

"No, this is the first time." He gently tugged my hand so we could resume our stroll and I followed reluctantly, my mind whirling.

It couldn't be a coincidence that Briar had started having headaches after entering the locked garden, but whether it was from the poison tainting it or from the stresses that came from discovering it I didn't know.

"You're looking rather serious." Briar's voice jerked me from my anxious thoughts.

"I'm concerned that your migraines are a result of whatever sickness is poisoning the grounds. You did claim that you're connected to the gardens…" Suddenly everything clicked into place. I gasped. "*Oh.*"

"What is it?" He suddenly looked rather apprehensive.

I didn't answer immediately as I hastily assembled the pieces from our conversation in his study to see if they all fit. They did. My excitement swelled. "If your curse connects you to the gardens, could that explain your faltering temper? The weeds are tainting the gardens, so perhaps they're also tainting your moods and causing you to—"

He didn't even give me a chance to finish. "Absolutely not."

I furrowed my brow. "What do you mean? Don't you think it's possible?"

He shook his head. "While my curse makes it so I can't leave the gardens, I have no reason to believe it extends so far as to connect me to them in such a deep way that their sickness becomes my own."

"But perhaps it's something to look into…"

"There's no need to waste our time chasing after an explanation that has no bearing on the situation." His tone was hardening with impatience even as he avoided my eyes, as if he couldn't make himself meet my gaze, which naturally aroused my suspicion.

I wasn't willing to give up my theory so easily. "Are you certain? For it'd explain everything: your moods, your headaches—"

"I told you they're not connected," he snapped impatiently. He noticed my startled expression and immediately softened. "Forgive me, I know you're only trying to help, but your theory is quite impossible. You've only known the details of my curse for a few minutes and must trust me that I know my own curse better than you do."

I pursed my lips, unconvinced. He noticed and sighed.

"I appreciate your having enough faith in me to seek explanations for my poor behavior, but I'm afraid I must take full responsibility for my actions. My recent tempers have merely been the result of the stresses of the crown, dealing with your horrible father, the crop failures, and of learning that you inadvertently unleashed Mother's dark magic into the gardens. As much as I wish otherwise, there's no other cause."

I continued studying his expression with a frown. He *seemed* sincere…yet I hesitated, especially when a foreign look suddenly filled his eyes, one I had no name for. I blinked, trying to assess it, but as quickly as it'd come, it disappeared, replaced instead with his usual strain.

As much as I yearned for my theory to be true, I saw no reason to doubt Briar; I'd never known him to be dishonest, not to mention he did know his curse far better than I did.

I finally nodded in acquiescence and he slumped in obvious relief before giving my hand a reassuring squeeze. "I appreciate your concern, but try not to worry; there are more pressing matters than my grumpiness, headaches, and lack of sleep."

I startled again. "You haven't been sleeping?" I'd noticed the exhaustion cloaking him from the moment I'd arrived at his study earlier, but had mistaken it as stress.

Briar looked like he wanted nothing more than to snatch his words back. "Not very well, but I've had a lot on my mind. I'm sure I'll rest well tonight." He forced a smile that did little to erase the tired lines surrounding his eyes.

I ached to ask for further details, but just then we arrived outside the entrance to the east wing. Briar turned to the guards that had been silently trailing us several paces back.

"We'll proceed alone," he said briskly. By the guards' responding frowns, I could see they didn't approve of such an order, but they simply bowed and took their places outside the entrance.

Briar picked up a nearby lantern to light our way, but its golden light did little to dispel the long corridor's thick darkness or the shadows stretching across the floor. Our footsteps were muffled by the dust-coated stones as Briar led me further in.

I shivered in the dank air. "How long has this section of the palace been abandoned?"

"Since last autumn, when Mother became trapped within her mirror while in Draceria. These are her private quarters, but without her here to use them, I saw little need to keep them maintained." He frowned. "I know we need to meet with her, but I fear it'll be futile."

"You don't think she'll know how to stop the poison from infesting the grounds?"

His frown deepened. "That's not my worry; she'll

undoubtedly know but likely choose not to cooperate. But I must try in hopes of saving my kingdom."

"How could she refuse?" I asked. "You're the king."

He gave a hollow laugh. "That makes little difference. Mother doesn't allow anyone to order her about, least of all me." He sighed. "I wish I didn't have to confront her at all, but there's just too much I don't know about Mother's magic and the weeds she created that are slowly choking the life from the garden."

We paused outside the door at the end of the corridor. Briar retrieved a key hidden beneath a dust-coated vase, but I rested my hand over his before he could insert it.

"The door is already unlocked."

He wrinkled his brow. "But it can't be..." He trailed off when I turned the knob and pushed the door open with an ominous creak. His look was immediately suspicious. "How did you know it was unlocked?"

"I discovered it when I was wandering the palace in search of which door the key opened."

I was wary to remind him of my previous foolhardy actions, but he only puckered his brow as he returned his attention to the door. "That's strange, for I always keep this door locked so that no one stumbles upon Mother. I must have forgotten to lock it the last time I was here."

He squared his shoulders, as if bracing himself for battle, and pushed the door the rest of the way open.

The lantern cast a golden pool across the room, which, like the rest of the wing, possessed an air of abandonment with its shrouds of dust coating the floor and furniture draped in cloths. The faint light was just enough to illuminate the accent table at the far end of the room, where the gold hand mirror covered in a design of black onyx gems rested facedown.

I immediately recognized it as the one I'd discovered the

first time I'd explored this room. "Is that your mother?" I whispered as we tiptoed nearer.

He nodded grimly before taking a wavering breath and reaching for the handle. "Mother? It's Briar." He forced a tight smile as he lifted the mirror and flipped it over.

I bit my lip to stifle my gasp, for within the glass was not Briar's reflection, but an image of a gorgeous, cold-looking woman with blood-red lips, raven-colored hair, and the most unpleasant of expressions.

Her eyes—dark like Briar's, but missing his warmth—immediately narrowed at her son. "It's about time you came to visit me. You've proven to be the most disloyal of sons leaving me stranded here alone."

Briar shifted guiltily. "I've been busy."

"That's no excuse. Your first responsibility is always to your mother."

Briar pursed his lips, undoubtedly to keep back any biting retorts he was tempted to give. Her eyes narrowed further.

"I see. You only visit out of duty...or as is more likely, because you're in need of me. Is that why you're here now?"

Briar hesitated.

"Answer me at once," she snapped.

He sighed, looking as if he wanted nothing more than to end this conversation as quickly as possible. "There's something I need to discuss with you."

She raised a smooth dark eyebrow. "I knew you still needed me. Do you foolishly believe I'll cooperate after your betrayal in Draceria when you allowed that pathetic Princess Rheanna to trap me inside this mirror?"

Briar sighed again. "You left us little choice; you were poisoning the crown prince and planning on annexing his kingdom."

"And you've been nothing but ungrateful for all of my

efforts to increase your power for when you ascend the throne," she said coldly.

"I've actually already ascended the throne. Father's dead."

For a moment his words hung in the dusty air. The queen's eyes widened before her cold composure returned. "So that's why you've come. Poor boy, are you already having a difficult time as king? You've always been weak, just like your brother."

Briar flinched and insecurity filled his eyes, causing anger to flare in my breast. The queen's triumphant smirk only stoked the flames, as if she knew how desperately Briar wanted to be a good king like his father and took great pleasure in attacking this vulnerability.

My previous resolve to remain silent cracked. "How dare you," I hissed.

The queen startled and whipped around to face me, but with the mirror's angle, I remained hidden from her view. "Who said that? Who's with you, Briar?"

He hesitated, clearly reluctant to introduce me to his vile mother. While his protection was sweet, I wasn't afraid of unpleasant people, especially when I had a rebuke to deliver. I motioned for him to turn the mirror to face me. With a sigh he did.

The queen's eyes widened when she saw me and she immediately sneered. "Who are you?"

I lifted my chin. "I'm Briar's guest, daughter of a merchant."

Her nose wrinkled in distaste as her gaze flickered over me. "You're absolutely hideous. What kind of company have you been keeping, Briar? A merchant's daughter...and such a homely one at that."

Briar glared at his mother. "She's most certainly not—"

I laid a gentle hand on his arm to calm him and his mother narrowed her eyes at it. I didn't need his kind defense, not when I'd long since grown numb to rude remarks and disdainful looks. And while no one had ever given me such a blatant insult before, my anger acted as a shield.

"It appears that rudeness is to take the place of decorum in this conversation," I said. "So allow me to make my own observation: I'm quite pleased you find yourself trapped inside that mirror, for in the few moments since I've met you I can tell you quite assuredly that you deserve your fate, and Malvagaria is much better off with you out of the way."

Her mouth fell agape. "How *dare* you address me in such a way. I'm the Queen of Malvagaria."

"Dowager queen," I corrected her with great satisfaction.

Her expression purpled and her gaze snapped to Briar, who seemed to be fighting a silent battle to do his filial duty by not laughing. "Who is this...this *creature*, and what is she doing in my palace?"

"*His* palace," I couldn't help mutter. Her eyes widened further at my continued impertinence.

"Tell me who this disagreeable girl is at once," she hissed.

"This is Mari...I mean Miss Maren."

His use of my nickname was clearly not lost on the former queen, nor was his blush and the rather tender way he looked at me. Her look became dangerous as she glanced between me and her son. "You haven't answered my question. I want to know who she is and what her relationship is to you."

Briar shifted beneath her icy glare. "That's a long story, and one we don't have time for."

"On the contrary, Son: being trapped within this prison has given me nothing but time," she said coldly. "Now enlighten me at once: where has your incompetence gotten you this time? Now that you're king, have you finally realized you're too weak to reign without me?"

Briar winced again and my burning anger returned anew, eager to be unleashed. "Considering you were foolish enough to become trapped in a mirror, you've seen nothing of Briar's rule, and thus don't have any right to pass judgement on him."

Once more her mouth fell agape and I couldn't resist smirking. I knew my disrespect was entirely inappropriate, but I refused to stand by and allow her to attack the man I loved. Several more biting comments begged for release, but I gritted my teeth to silence them, for as unfortunate as it was, we *did* need her help. Briar gave me a hasty look of warning not to antagonize his mother further until we had the information we needed.

She noticed this subtle exchange and her smirk widened. "It appears my assumption was correct: you need something from me. You may wear the king's crown, but I'll always be the true reigning force of Malvagaria."

"Not anymore; you're still the dowager queen," I couldn't resist muttering despite the wiser course of action being to keep my mouth shut.

She straightened herself up and lifted her chin with a regal tilt. "Ironic how the one who continuously corrects my title lacks one herself."

"Spoken by one who may be titled but finds herself a prisoner."

She glared and I met it with an icy one of my own. I'd spent my entire life standing up to bullies and I refused to stop now, regardless of the fact that she was the former queen.

She glowered at me a moment more before lifting her nose and turning back to Briar. "I don't like this girl. Send her away at once."

"I'll do no such thing," he said. "Mari is my guest and will be treated with respect. You no longer have any power here."

He lowered his eyes. "Although admittedly we do need your help."

"I knew it," she said. "You can't do anything without me. Unfortunately, I'm not inclined to assist you after the offensive remarks from your little *guest*."

I closed my eyes with a groan, silently cursing myself for losing my temper and goading the queen, never mind she'd deserved it.

"Regardless of how you feel about Mari or even me, as dowager queen you have a duty to your kingdom. We need information, which I'm confident you'll be able to provide considering it concerns your secret garden."

Her eyes widened in shock before narrowing darkly. "Elaborate."

"The garden has been opened and the weeds inside—"

Her sharp gasp cut off his remaining explanation. "You mean to tell me," she said through gritted teeth, "is that someone entered my garden and released the magic?" Her complexion reddened as she turned her accusing glare to me, instinctively knowing where to cast her blame. "You foolish girl. How dare you enter *my* garden and ruin the plants I've spent years cultivating?"

Her accusation doused my previous fire. Ashamed, I averted my eyes.

Briar stepped protectively in front of me to shield me from his mother's wrath. "It doesn't matter how the garden was opened," he said. "What matters is how we handle the situation from here. Since you're the one who planted the weeds, you must know how to stop them."

She glared at me a moment more before reluctantly returning her attention to him. "So they're already spreading?"

Briar nodded. "The entire garden is dying, as are many of the kingdom's crops."

"At least you're sensible enough to realize that the kingdom is connected to the gardens, which means you must also be aware that the situation is not only dire but that there's little to be done at this point."

"That can't be true," Briar said desperately. "They're your weeds. You have to—"

"Breaking curses is beyond my abilities," she said. "If I had that power, I'd have found a way to break the one trapping me now. As unfortunate as the situation is, it's your duty as king to face this harsh reality: Malvagaria is about to face a devastating famine from which it may never fully recover." Her expression twisted. "To think that mere weeks into your reign, my own son will be responsible for crippling a kingdom that took generations to build. I'm absolutely disgusted."

The devastation that filled his eyes at her pronouncement wrenched my heart and caused my temper to flare up again. I snatched the mirror from him and lifted it so I was eye level with the queen.

"You can't deflect your responsibility so easily," I snapped. "Whatever weeds are taking over the gardens are *yours*, and thus you must know more about them than you're telling us. If you have any love for your kingdom, you'll share what you know."

She met my gaze head on. "I may have created the poison but it was never intended for Malvagaria. I'm not responsible for your choice in allowing it to escape. Thus the blame lies solely at your feet."

Guilt squeezed my chest and only increased my desperation. I tightened my hold on the mirror's handle. "You're right in that I inadvertently caused this mess, and thus I'm determined to do everything in my power to atone for my mistake. I won't rest until I've extracted the information from you that we need."

She remained stubbornly silent as we stared each other down. I tightened my jaw. Fine, if this was the game she wanted to play, then I'd happily rise to the challenge.

I gave her a sickly sweet smile. "Still uncooperative? Then perhaps a bit of *persuasion* is in order. You know the myth about being cursed with seven years of bad luck should one break a mirror? I'd like to test that theory right now." I lifted the mirror as if to drop it onto the stone floor, taking delicious satisfaction in the fear filling her widening eyes.

Briar seized my wrist. "You can't break my mother."

"Why? She deserves it. No, stop—" But Briar had succeeded in wrenching the mirror away. I glared at him. "What did you do that for?"

"If you break my mother, then we'll never figure out how to stop the weeds."

I rolled my eyes. "We're not learning anything now, which was why I was *threatening* her. She may not be concerned about her people, but she cares about her own well-being, and now you've taken away our only leverage in getting what we want."

Briar eyed me suspiciously. "How can I be sure you were only threatening her?"

I pursed my lips. "Since you stopped me I suppose we'll never find out." It was rather disappointing not to be able to satisfy that particular curiosity.

"Whether you threaten me or not matters very little," she said. "Considering I've been robbed of my right to rule, I have no incentive to stop the weeds. Even if I could, I wouldn't even try. Let the Kingdom of Malvagaria become extinct, ruined by my incompetent son."

Briar's entire manner hardened as the darkness that had previously overcome him returned, completely distorting his features. "It disgusts me that you've turned your back on the people you once served."

The queen's eyebrows rose as she took in his cold tone and fiery gaze. "Well, isn't that...interesting."

"What is?" Briar snapped.

The queen only smirked. "That's my little secret. Now, to prove I'm not entirely without feeling, I'll confirm your suspicions: the plants growing in my garden were untamed weeds that spread easily once unleashed. There's really nothing you can do to prevent them from destroying everything in their path."

Briar's previous darkness melted into defeat. "We can't let that happen. We must stop them."

"You *can't,*" she said. "Dark magic is too powerful to be thwarted by the likes of you—it'd be like trying to stop the coming tide. Both are governed by natural laws whose course is impossible to alter."

My heart sank in despair. It was just as we'd feared: nothing could prevent the sickness from slowly consuming the gardens and thus the entire kingdom. The queen seemed to take great satisfaction in our somber expressions.

Briar set his jaw. "There's one more thing: we still haven't found Reve or Gemma."

"Unsurprising," the queen said without an ounce of sympathy. Briar's glare sharpened.

"Don't you care at all? They're your daughters."

"There's nothing to be done," the queen said dismissively. "I assume Reve will eventually come to herself and return home, whereas Gemma is protected within her tower."

"Where *is* her tower?" Briar demanded.

She wagged her finger at him. "I'm not going to tell you. Dear Gemma is much better off there than under your care."

"But she's trapped and alone, with nothing more than a single guard and a tower."

"An *enchanted* tower," she emphasized. "What could be safer?"

He scowled. "With the trouble your magic has brought to our family, forgive me for not better trusting your enchantments."

She rolled her eyes. "The tower won't go rogue if that's your concern. Would I ever do such a thing to my sweet, sickly princess?"

Briar's lips thinned, a sign of his clear doubts.

"You should stop worrying about your sisters' whereabouts and concentrate more on your kingdom...what's left of it. I am quite disappointed in you. You can barely run a kingdom without the gardens running amok and the crops dying. What makes you believe you'll take better care of your sister, especially when you're currently so...distracted?"

The look she gave me made my insides coil. Briar understood his mother's unspoken implication. "How dare you," he growled.

She sneered. "Your defense of the girl is as good as a confession. I'm surprised you chose her. Really, Briar, you can do *much* better."

Her latest attack crumbled whatever defenses had sustained me so far. Cheeks burning, I lowered my eyes.

Briar wrapped a protective arm around me. "You have no right to treat Mari in such a way. I no longer need your approval. You've always been too consumed with your vanity and lust for power to ever learn what's best for your children. Mari is perfect for me."

Despite the tension of the moment, my heart lifted at his words before he continued.

"Together we'll figure out how to stop the weeds, with or without your help."

With that, he slammed the mirror facedown, finally ending the unpleasant confrontation.

"Don't you dare just walk away; I'm not finished with you." The queen's voice was muffled but clearly furious. Briar ignored her, seized my hand, and stomped from the room, slamming the door behind us.

The lock made a satisfying *click* as he turned the key. "Good riddance," he growled, but his temper immediately vanished when he turned his attention to me, his eyes clouded with concern. "Are you alright, Mari?"

I managed a nod. He gathered me in his arms.

"She was horrible to you...but you stood up for yourself so well. I'm proud of you."

His arms tightened around me and I nestled deeper in his comforting hold. "I'm afraid I only made everything worse. We're no closer to a solution than before we confronted her."

He sighed heavily. "I should have known she wouldn't help us; her pride is of greater value to her than the welfare of her own people."

The worry already pressing against my chest grew heavier. "What are we going to do about your kingdom?"

"I have no idea."

We were just as lost as before. Nothing had come from our visit with the queen except a confirmation of our fears: whatever poison had been unleashed wouldn't rest until it had destroyed the entire kingdom.

CHAPTER 21

"*W*here are you taking me at such an hour?" My voice was quiet and breathless, both because the stillness of the night seemed to warrant a certain reverence and because of the wonderful, fluttery feeling that came from Briar's fingers laced through mine.

He gave me one of my favorite grins that caused his eyes to crinkle around the edges. "Inquisitive as ever, aren't you, Mari? I'm afraid you don't understand the finer points of a *surprise*."

I certainly did, for I was quite surprised when he led me through the front doors and into the evening air, slightly chilly but beginning to warm with the approaching summer. We rarely ventured into the grounds anymore now that the spreading sickness had almost completely consumed them, leaving little to explore.

"Are you taking me to a garden?"

His eyes lit up as he nodded, a welcome sight after the weariness that seemed to constantly cloak him from the stress, headaches, and exhaustion he'd suffered from this past week. "There's one special garden I've wanted to show you for weeks; it only appears at night. Thankfully, so far it's been untainted by the spreading weeds."

My heart lifted as we descended the front steps. Everything seemed so different when bathed in the silvery moonlight; it transformed the grounds, causing everything beneath its glow to appear enchanted, masking the sickness tainting the dying plants.

Briar led me down several unfamiliar cobblestone paths deeper into the gardens, all of which seemed foreign beneath the velvety night. Eventually he stepped off the path into wild undergrowth.

I wrinkled my brow. "Where are we—"

"You'll see." He gave my hand a gentle squeeze before quietly pulling me along, pausing when we reached a leafy archway woven not with flowers as I'd come to expect, but...

I gasped softly. "Are those *stars?*"

Briar only grinned as he took my hands and walked backwards, his gaze never once leaving my face as we stepped across the threshold.

My breath caught from the splendor that greeted me. The entire garden was aglow with dappled starlight. The silvery glow bathed the white lawn and illuminated plants, which flickered like hundreds of lit candles. Fireflies waltzed through the air, leaving different streaks of color against the velvety night. Flowers shaped like stars dotted the lawn, looking as if they'd been plucked and planted by the sky itself, while the real stars above reflected off the surface of the pond in the garden's center.

I stared in awe as I stepped further inside, wishing I had a dozen more pairs of eyes so I could fully take in the surrounding wonder. "It's magnificent."

Briar beamed, his smile aglow at my delight. "It only comes alive at night. I'm grateful you were able to see it before—"

He didn't finish, for talk of the garden's sickness had no place in a moment as magical as this, a world apart from all the stresses and fears of the past several weeks. Instead, this was a place where only Briar and I existed...together.

He laced his hand back with mine and led me deeper into the garden. Despite the beauty of the surrounding flowers aglow in a rainbow of colors, my gaze was repeatedly drawn to the man beside me, particularly the light that had returned to fill his eyes and his soft smile.

He glanced sideways and caught me watching him. "What is it?"

I found I couldn't speak, for the way he looked at me was with the same admiring look he gave the wondrous garden, except it was different...*deeper*. The thought was both beautiful and alarming, and made the secret I'd kept bottled inside my heart eager to escape.

I love you, I ached to whisper.

"Mari?" His tone was as tender as his expression. I couldn't answer, and he didn't press me to. Instead, he led us to the bank of the violet pond, where we settled on the lawn, so closely I could feel the warmth of his nearness. I ached to bridge the remaining distance between us to curl against his side.

I resisted the impulse and gazed out over the pond, mesmerized by the sight, although its beauty and the wonder of the moment quickly became tainted when I noticed Briar rubbing his temples with a wince of pain.

"Is your head still aching?"

He hastily lowered his hand. "It's nothing," he said.

I frowned. "Briar, it's not *nothing*. I'm becoming quite worried about these headaches of yours."

"Please, I don't wish to discuss them now," he said. "Not when there's something else I wish to speak to you about."

"And what is that?"

He became quite occupied with caressing the back of my hand with his thumb, each gentle touch igniting my heart and causing it to beat wildly, especially when he began stroking along each of my fingers, his movements slow and deliberate.

"Briar?" I asked breathlessly.

He took a deep breath and peered up at me, his eyes suddenly shy, but a new look also filled them, one that caused all the love I felt for him to swell within me.

Finally he spoke, his voice as quiet as the stillness of the night. "Are you happy here with me?"

"Yes," I whispered. "You have no idea how happy I am. I've never felt more joy than I have with you."

His tender expression softened further. "I'm glad. I'd do anything to make you happy. I'm so grateful you're here. Now that I've met you, I can't imagine life without you by my side."

My heartbeat escalated at the sudden turn in our conversation, while around us the flowers seemed to bristle with excitement. Could he be...confessing something deeper, or did that hope only come from my own longings? Regardless of whether or not this was his own confession, I realized it had to be mine, for the feelings of my heart couldn't be denied any longer.

"Briar, I—"

"Wait, Mari. Please. I...need to tell you something." The faint, silvery light illuminated the blush suddenly swallowing his cheeks.

"What is it?" I asked.

He opened his mouth to speak...before closing it with a sigh. He stared at me a moment before hastily looking away, his gaze unseeing as he stared out across the glowing garden. "What do you think of this garden?"

My brow puckered at the sudden change in topic. "It's truly enchanting."

"Do you also think it...romantic?" He suddenly appeared quite anxious.

My heart began to pound in an unrelenting tempo. I swallowed. "Romantic?"

He took a steadying breath before cradling my face, his eyes wide and earnest. "Yes, for I was hoping..." He paused, the blush staining his cheeks deepening as he lowered his eyes.

"Yes?" I prompted, barely able to speak with the hope suddenly filling my heart and clogging my throat.

He swallowed and peeked back up at me, his eyes still shy but determined. "You've become more than a dear friend to me. Ever since I met you...it took me a while to realize it, but what I feel...I'm hoping that you'd do me the honor of—"

My breath caught. Was he doing what I thought he was?

He paused and wrinkled his brow, looking almost frustrated with himself. "Wait, this is the wrong order. There's something I need to tell you first." He lifted my hands and rested them over his own pounding heart, his gaze wide and earnest. "I love you, Mari."

In that moment my entire world shifted. I gaped at him in disbelief, unsure whether I'd actually heard his beautiful words or had only imagined them. His hopeful expression faltered at my silence.

"Are you...disappointed I feel that way about you?"

I rapidly shook my head. "No, not at all. Can you...say the words again?"

His adorable blush deepened as he gave me a nervous smile. "I love you, Mari."

The words didn't feel any more real than they had the first time, but they were just as beautiful. At my continued disbelieving silence, he became nervous once again.

"I'm sorry if this is rather sudden, but with everything happening, I couldn't bear to keep silent any longer, so I—"

I flung myself at him, bridging the inches between us which had suddenly felt like miles. He fell onto his back as I tightly embraced him and burrowed against his chest. "You love me, Briar? Truly?"

"I do. So much." He wound his arms securely around me to sit us up and hold me close. "Does that make you happy?"

Happy was such an inadequate word to describe my current emotions; I felt so much joy I thought my heart would burst. Tears filled my eyes. "I never imagined anyone would ever say such sweet words to me, least of all my king."

His expression gentled as he carefully wiped away the tears clinging to my eyelashes before they could fall. "But why, dear Mari? You're so wonderful."

"Because I'm not—" The words trapped in my throat, but he seemed to understand what I couldn't say.

The most tender look filled his dark eyes. "But you *are* beautiful."

And in that moment I felt it, for no one had ever looked at me in such a way as he was looking at me now. His gaze was beyond loving...it was *adoring*, so incredibly soft and sweet, as if I was the finest treasure he'd ever discovered.

"No one has ever called me beautiful before," I whispered when I managed to find my voice.

He lifted my hands and pressed a kiss on the back of each. "Then I'll remind you every single day for the rest of our lives, for you're truly beautiful. I see it every time I look at you."

He traced each of my features, both with his caressing fingertips and his eyes, the adoration filling them growing with his perusal. His expression was far different than the appreciative way he examined the treasures in his collection and much deeper than the admiration he'd given the beautiful women he'd danced with at his coronation; it was as if he was seeing *me* completely...and loved everything that he saw.

"There are different types of beauty," he said. "There's the obvious beauty that comes from the world around us—the artistry of a fine painting, the wonder of nature—but there's also another beauty that's less obvious, one that must be felt more than seen. This beauty is found within a person's heart."

"And this is what you see?" I asked in a breathless whisper.

He smiled gently as his arms tightened around me to bring me closer. "I feel it whenever I'm with you. You're my best friend, Mari, one who is kind, loyal, supportive, brave... so many things. With the gardens dying, they likely won't be able to keep you a prisoner, but I'm hoping you'll choose to stay...with me."

My already full heart lifted further. "In what capacity?"

"The only one fitting. Doesn't every king need a queen?"

My breath hooked. Was this...a *marriage proposal*? Did dear Briar really want *me*, Maren, as his bride?

Worry clouded his eyes when once again I remained silent. "My apologies, I spoke in haste. I should have waited to propose until I was certain of your own feelings."

The vulnerability filling his eyes tugged on my heart. I cradled his face. "I love you, Briar. It would be my greatest honor to be your wife."

His wife. Surely this beautiful moment couldn't be real... but by the way his responding grin lit up his eyes and ignited my heart, I knew it was. Even the most detailed dream couldn't cause me such incredible feelings as I was experiencing now.

His fingers traced along my jaw to hook beneath my chin and lift my face towards his. I shivered as his warm breath tickled my skin as he leaned closer. His lips lightly caressed my cheek before trailing lower, pausing near my lips, where he lifted his gaze, seeking permission. In response I leaned closer, closing the distance between us to gently kiss him.

The kiss exceeded anything I could have ever imagined—it was soft, gentle, and full of such love as I'd never before felt. It was also shy, hesitant, and far too short. I'd barely started to kiss him back when he broke it and hastily pulled away, the shyness back in his eyes.

"Was that alright?" he asked uncertainly.

In response, I hooked my hand behind his neck and brought him in for a second kiss, desperate for another. While our first kiss had been nothing but gentle, this one fierce and eager. In it I assured this dear man that I cared for him deeply. My heart swelled as he kissed me back, and in that kiss all the pain that had previously scarred my heart faded away until I felt nothing but cherished.

My arms tightened around him and I melted deeper into his embrace. The excitement coming from the flora permeated the blossom-scented air, as if the gardens were rejoicing in this sweet moment as much as I was.

In this magical moment, I at last allowed myself to believe in the romantic future I'd always dreamed of, for I'd finally found someone worth spending my life with—a man who not only saw deeper into my soul, but loved what he saw. I hoped I'd be able to spend forever at his side showing him that his own heart was the most beautiful thing I'd ever seen.

CHAPTER 22

I lingered in bed the following morning, staring up at the velvet canopy in a daze as my mind drifted to the night before when I'd sat with Briar in the glowing garden and heard his sweet confession that he loved me... and wanted to *marry* me. My toes curled in pleasure at the thought and my heart swelled with happiness.

I closed my eyes to transport myself to the evening before after we'd broken our kiss—the time we'd spent cuddling in front of the lake with his arm around me and my head resting on his shoulder, walking hand-in-hand as he escorted me back to my room before saying good night outside my door with another kiss, and especially the soft, adoring way he'd looked at me as he pulled away.

Only the thought of seeing Briar again was enough to pull me from my memories and out of bed. I quickly dressed, eager to be by his side as soon as possible. There was so much to discuss about the future we'd chosen together, one that until yesterday had felt like nothing more than an impossible dream, but which was now mine for the taking.

I took more care with my appearance than usual before

pausing to admire it in the mirror with a contemplative air. I leaned closer to squint at my reflection. It was almost startling to see the change in myself, the beauty that came from not only my own confidence but the joy and love Briar had given me. I smiled in approval before hurrying down to the dining hall, where the man I loved awaited me.

Briar was already seated at the table, and judging by the dark circles beneath his eyes, he hadn't slept at all. With the way he rubbed his temples, he was clearly suffering from another migraine.

Worry knotted my gut as I hurried to his side and took the seat beside him. "Are you alright, dear?" I used the endearment shyly and hesitantly, but the moment I spoke the word I knew it was appropriate for our beautiful new relationship.

He looked up wearily, his exhaustion dissipating his usual adoration that had filled his expression last night. My heart wrenched in disappointment before I hastily locked it away. It had no place here, not when there were more pressing concerns, Briar being the most important.

"I'm fine, Mari," he said. "Did you sleep well?"

I'd never slept better considering I'd dreamed of him, but now was not the time for such a flirtatious admission. After all, love was more than whispering sweet nothings—it was being there for the man who possessed my heart in whatever capacity he needed from me.

"I did sleep well, but you clearly didn't. Does your head hurt?" I rested my hand on his arm and was pleased when he laid his over mine.

"The pain is excruciating, worse than it's ever been." It must hurt quite badly, for his eyes had an almost vacant look as he met my gaze. He stared blankly for a moment before managing a tired smile. "It's good to see you, darling."

Darling...my heart swelled at the endearment; it lifted

further when he laced our hands together and lowered them beneath the table to rest my hand on his knee.

"What matters of state do you have this morning?" I asked as the servants served us steaming plates of eggs, sausages, and toast.

It was the usual topic of our morning conversations so I could attempt to help lighten the burden he carried in any way that I could. And now that my future position was to be his queen and consort, this was a capacity I could serve forever. I thrilled at the thought, for no matter what Briar had to face as king, I wanted to be there for him.

To my surprise, rather than outline the day's task and seek my opinion as he usually did, he gave a jerky shake of his head. "I don't wish to discuss political matters now."

I furrowed my brow at this foreign reaction. "Very well, if you wish it."

"I do." His words came out stiffly. My frown deepened. He must be quite tired.

"Then what would you like to discuss instead? Our plans for the future?" I couldn't resist my girlish smile, but it faltered when he shook his head again, more rigidly than before.

"No, I don't wish to discuss such matters now. We have plenty of time to work out the details. In fact, I don't wish to converse at all." His tone was hardening, the complete opposite of the tender one he'd used last night. He caught the startled look on my face and his manner softened. "Forgive me, I simply don't feel well this morning, and thus am not up for conversation."

I relaxed at his gentle squeeze of my hand. "You do look rather miserable."

"But in a handsome sort of way?" His wink eased the sudden anxiety that had been twisting my stomach.

"Definitely." I leaned over to kiss his cheek, but my lips had barely grazed his skin when he jerked away so sharply he shook the table.

"Don't do that," he hissed. "Not here." His gaze flickered towards the attending guards and servants, looking almost embarrassed by my show of affection.

My cheeks burned. "I'm sorry, I—" The rest of my apology became trapped in my throat.

His disapproving expression remained for a second more before it faded. "My apologies, it's simply inappropriate for us to be so open with our affections until things are more official. With the crown comes necessary protocol. Do you understand?"

"Of course. Forgive me."

"Already done."

He squeezed my hand again under the table and I relaxed, but not enough to completely lower my guard, not when his mood had been unusually volatile this morning. But it was understandable considering how stressed and ill he appeared. Even so, I'd admittedly expected things to unfold much more romantically between us after last night, and it was disappointing that it hadn't.

In sickness and in health, I reminded myself firmly. I wanted to be with Briar for everything, and because of his own tender feelings, I'd get to. In the end that was all that mattered.

The remainder of breakfast passed in silence, yet quite pleasantly considering my hand was still woven through his and resting on his knee. I cast him several concerned glances, for he spent the entire meal slumped in his seat and picking at his food, not bothering to eat.

He did manage to drain his goblet, causing an attentive serving girl to come over to refill it. As the servant set the filled goblet down and withdrew, she knocked it over, spilling juice all over the tablecloth and onto Briar's lap.

His expression purpled as he leapt to his feet and spun on her. "Look what you've done, you clumsy girl."

She staggered back in shock at his yell. "My apologies, Your Majesty, I didn't mean to—"

He advanced another step, causing her to cower before his towering form. "Didn't mean to? Your insolence stained my clothes. How can such an incompetent girl be serving the king?"

I gaped, both at the fury twisting his expression and the fact that the man who'd never had any qualms about getting dirt on his clothes while he gardened was overreacting to a spilled drink now.

I brushed his arm. "It's just a stain, Briar. I'm sure the laundress will be able to—"

He flinched away from my touch and spun onto me. "Just a *stain*? This outfit is made from the finest imported velvet. And this girl"—he pointed accusingly at her—"just ruined it."

My frown deepened at the hardened lines filling his face. "It was just an accident."

"An *accident*?" He swept his arm across his uneaten breakfast, and the plates clattered to the floor, echoing throughout the massive chamber and causing the attending servants lining the wall to wince. "What about that? Was that an accident?"

I met his gaze head on. "No, that was a result of your temper."

His eyes narrowed. "Exactly. It was no accident...and neither was that clumsy girl's. I'm the king and demand only the best of servants...which clearly isn't her." He glared at the trembling maid, who looked on the brink of tears. "Get out. Now. I never want to see you within the palace again."

Alarm filled my heart. Surely he wasn't sacking her, was he? "Briar, what are you—"

He ignored me and advanced another furious step towards the frozen servant. "Didn't you hear me? I told you to get out. *Now!*"

I stood to intervene, but before I could even step forward, she swiveled around and ran from the room.

A thick, tense silence hung in the air. Briar stared at the broken dishes and spilled food he'd thrown onto the floor, fists clenched and breaths heavy. I waited for his usual calm to settle over him, but it never came.

Instead he glared at the remaining servants, who stood frozen, as if afraid to so much as breathe too loudly for fear of offending the king. "Don't just stand there. Clean this up, else I'll have no further use for any of you either."

They hastened to do his bidding, but he didn't linger to watch. He stomped from the room, brushing past me almost as if he'd forgotten I was there. For a moment I stared after him, numb with shock at how the morning had taken such a drastic turn.

I set my jaw determinedly. I refused to allow it to end on such a sour note. I forced a tight smile in gratitude for the servants cleaning up the mess before picking up my skirts and hurrying from the room.

In the corridor Briar was nowhere in sight, but I wasn't so easily deterred. My first thought was to check the gardens, but he hadn't spent much time there since they'd begun to wither, which left the study as the next most likely place.

I hurried up the steps, where at the top I saw him stomping through the hallway. "Briar!"

He slowed and glared over his shoulder, his expression just as fierce as it'd been downstairs. It softened slightly at seeing me, not entirely melting away the hardness filling it but dissipating much of it, especially in his eyes.

"Is there something you needed, darling?"

For a moment I simply gaped at him, his tender tone almost alarming after the anger which had previously filled it.

"I—" I wasn't sure what to say, still too startled by his display at breakfast to believe he could be himself again so suddenly; it was almost as if he didn't even remember what had happened. "How are you feeling?"

He approached and gently took my hands. "I'm still not feeling particularly well, but I appreciate your concern." He softly kissed my knuckles. "Now I'm afraid I must leave you to work, for I have many papers to go over. But it'd be an honor to spend lunch with you."

"Of course," I said.

His responding grin lit up his eyes and caused the remaining tension to disappear from his face. "I'm looking forward to it. See you soon, my love." And after a parting kiss on my cheek he departed.

I watched his retreating back until he disappeared around the corner before leaning against the wall with a heavy sigh, my mind whirling as I relived his moment of temper at breakfast. What could have accounted for it? Were his lack of sleep and terrible headaches to blame, or was there something deeper at work? He'd insisted it had nothing to do with the gardens, but how could he be so certain? And if they weren't to blame, what else could explain it?

Regardless, his behavior wasn't natural, for I knew Briar well enough to know that he was the epitome of kindness. But what had just happened…wasn't kindness at all.

My heart wrenched when I thought of the poor serving girl he'd dismissed. I'd have to speak to him about her later. Once he settled down, surely he'd realize he'd acted rashly, for he was a good and understanding man, not one who'd toss a hardworking servant out over such a slight.

The plan, as small as it was, helped calm some of the anxiety pressing against my chest. All would be well, especially after Briar calmed enough for me to get to the bottom of what was troubling him.

LUNCH CAME AND WENT, and Briar hadn't shown up, causing my worries not only to return but to escalate. It wasn't like Briar to skip meals or break his promises to me. My mind came up with all sorts of horrible reasons as to why before determining that he was simply busy and had lost track of time.

I stood outside his study holding a tray of food that I'd insisted on delivering myself—and after Briar's display this morning, the kitchen staff were all too happy to comply with my wishes. I adjusted the tray to lift my hand and knock. He didn't answer. I waited a moment before trying again. Still no answer. I frowned.

"Briar?"

I tried the knob. The door was unlocked and swung open to reveal an empty room, with no sign of Briar anywhere. My brow furrowed. Where was he?

"Briar?"

I set the tray on the edge of the desk and looked around. Piles of papers lay strewn all over the desk. I stole a peek at the top one and discovered it was a document outlining changes to the law. I began to look away when my gaze settled on an obscene number scrawled on the bottom—a proposed sum to raise in taxes, signed by Briar himself.

I gasped. What was Briar thinking raising the taxes so high, especially when the kingdom was in such dire straits? I had to speak with him. I swiveled towards the door, determined to find him and demand an explanation, when my gaze caught sight of something else. Curiosity propelled me to the fireplace, where a crumpled paper lay half-in, half-out of the hearth. Part of it had been burned, while the rest was scalded but had otherwise escaped the flames.

I crouched down to retrieve it and my breath caught as I unfolded it and read it. *No...it couldn't be.* It was the letter Briar had shown me the last time I'd visited his study, the one requesting Drake's help in sorting out the famine threatening to cripple the kingdom. He'd not only never sent it, but clearly had no intention of doing so.

But why would he do such a thing when he was fiercely worried for the welfare of his subjects and the trial they'd face this coming year from the impending food shortage brought on by the failing crops?

"What are you doing?"

I gasped and whipped around to find Briar glaring from the doorway. Gone was the tender look he'd given me when we'd departed hours earlier, leaving a fierce one in its place.

I swallowed and, after a wavering breath to gather my courage, I lifted the letter I'd found. "I brought you lunch and discovered this. I was curious, so I—"

"You're always curious," he snapped as he shut the door forcefully behind him and stomped towards me. I held my ground, refusing to cower before him. He was a good man and would never hurt me...but for the first time since I'd met him, he suddenly looked angry enough to.

What was happening to him?

He stopped in front of me, and after giving me another dark look, he snatched the letter from me. "What's this?"

I took another steadying breath. "It's the letter you wrote requesting aid from Drake. You never sent it."

He stared at it, looking almost confused, before he nodded rigidly. "Of course I didn't. I don't need his help."

I frowned. "So you have the situation with the failing crops well in hand?"

"Well enough." He crumpled the letter into a ball and tossed it into the hearth, where the fire finished consuming it. "All is in order, so you don't need to concern yourself with the affairs of my kingdom." He settled behind his desk as regally as if he were sitting on a throne. "Do you need anything else, or can I return to work now?"

I refused to be so easily dismissed. I rested my hands on the desk and leaned closer. "How is the situation with the crops? Is there enough food to evenly distribute amongst your subjects?

He sighed in clear annoyance at my meddling and leaned back in his seat. "Likely not."

Alarm twisted my heart. "Then what will we do?"

He shrugged. "Nothing. It's of no concern to me if a few people starve. It would only be the peasants who are already a drain to my kingdom. If I wish to build a prosperous empire, a few sacrifices have to be made along the way."

My stomach coiled in horror and I truly thought I'd be sick. "A few...*sacrifices?*" I frantically searched his expression, hoping to see he was in jest...but not only did he appear entirely serious, but the hardened lines were back, looking so much a part of him it was as if they'd never left.

He nodded briskly. "Indeed. Father was rather soft with his subjects. I'm wondering if Mother didn't have the right idea on how things should be done around here."

It took me a moment to recover my voice. "But...you admire your father."

"I used to, but..." He scrunched his brow, as if reconsidering his opinion, which was almost as alarming as everything else he'd been spouting during our exchange.

I jabbed my finger at the tax-increase document. "And what of this?"

His eyes narrowed darkly. "Snooping around my things, Maren?"

Maren...he only used my full name when he was displeased with me. Well, I was just as displeased with him, so at least we were on equal footing. "Yes," I said without any remorse.

His expression hardened further. "You have no right to do such a thing, nor do I have to explain myself or the affairs of my kingdom to you."

"You asked me to marry you last night," I said. "If I'm to be your wife, we discuss things. *Together.*"

He slowly rose so that he loomed over me. My heart gave a brief patter of fright, but I lifted my chin and met his stare head on.

"You overstep your bounds," he said darkly as he took a menacing step closer. I forced myself to stand my ground.

"You can't raise taxes, not when the kingdom is already—"

"You have no right to complain about my decision, considering the money I used to pay off your worthless father is one of the primary reasons the kingdom is facing a shortfall."

It was as if he'd slapped me, distorting what had previously felt like a precious gift into nothing more than a nuisance. I swallowed my threatening tears. "But—"

"Furthermore, how dare you presume to tell me what to do?" he growled, his voice escalating. "You won't interfere. Do you understand me?"

I tightened my jaw. "No, I don't understand anything. What's happening? This isn't you. You're behaving so abhorrently." And that was putting it mildly. My earlier suspicion returned, making more sense now than it had before. "Are you sure this has nothing to do with your connection to the poisoned gardens?"

For a brief moment his expression faltered and he looked as if were struggling to say something...but the brief battle ended almost immediately and he shook his head. "Of course I'm sure. I'd know otherwise."

I frowned, his insistent dismissal of the possibility only adding to my suspicion.

"My behavior has nothing to do with the gardens," he said. "I'm simply fulfilling my role as king. Mother's right— I've been weak, but that's all going to change from here on out." He looked at me sharply. "It's important that you understand who wields the true power. *I* am the king, whereas you'll be nothing more than my consort, and thus have no right to question my decisions."

I gaped at him. The memory of all our past conversations about how he much he relied on my support filled my mind, so different from this new, twisted version of how he viewed our relationship.

My shock quickly faded as my temper flared. "Is that what you expect from our marriage?"

"It's the way it must be," he said stiffly.

"No, it's not. Love is a partnership, not...*this*. Do you love me? Because I still love you."

Part of me was afraid he'd deny his love, even though it'd been only yesterday when he'd spoken the words...a magical moment his current mood had tainted. For a frightening moment he didn't speak, but then his fierce manner suddenly faltered, and he appeared almost confused. He looked at me as if really seeing me for the first time since he entered the study.

"Of course I love you, Mari. That's why I asked you to marry me."

He cupped my chin to stroke my jaw, but for once it didn't ignite a response in me; if anything, it almost felt...

wrong, almost as if he were merely going through the motions.

"I know you love me," I managed breathlessly. "And I love you. Dearly. That's why you're frightening me."

He immediately dropped his hand, his brows drawn. "*Frightening* you? How am I doing that?"

"You're not behaving like yourself." I took a steadying breath and stepped closer to wrap my arms around him. He stiffened before melting into my embrace; I sighed with relief as his arms enfolded me in return. "I want to help you," I whispered. "Please let me."

"There's nothing for you to do," he said. "All is well."

"No, it's not. Your attitude about the failing crops, your behavior towards me just now, your raising taxes—"

His dark mood abruptly returned. "I said all is well. Now stop badgering me." He released me and stepped away, as if he suddenly found it unpleasant to hold me.

Despite trying hard to be brave, my heart cracked. "I'm only trying to help. I—"

"I don't want your help, so you'd best leave. Now!"

I startled at his yell, but I refused to cower like the poor maid from this morning. I lifted my chin and glared at him.

"Very well, Your Majesty." I swept into an exaggerated curtsy, which seemed to startle him.

"Don't do that, Maren," he said stiffly. "It's Briar."

My glare sharpened. "Not at the moment it's not. I have no idea who you are right now, but you're most certainly *not* Briar." With a pounding heart, I turned and flounced from the room, fighting the tears burning my eyes.

I let them escape the moment I was safely in my bedroom, but I didn't have time to cry. I hurried to the desk and began rummaging through the drawers, searching for quill and ink before sinking into my chair and bending over the parchment, my hand shaking so badly I could barely hold the quill.

. . .

DEAR PRINCE DRAKE,

Please forgive my presumption in writing you, but I'm beginning to fear there's something seriously wrong with Briar and I need your help...

CHAPTER 23

The whole room seemed to be holding its breath at dinner. The servants watched their king apprehensively, as if afraid he'd explode at any moment. It hurt my heart to see his subjects so wary of him, but considering his behavior of late, they had a valid reason for their fear. It would have broken the old Briar's heart as well, but this man seemed entirely indifferent.

The last several days had felt endless. I'd sent my letter to Drake the moment I'd finished writing it and had received his reply the next day informing me that he'd arrive the following evening, which was tonight, a time that couldn't come soon enough.

I still hadn't informed Briar I'd gone behind his back and invited his brother to visit. With his increasing dark moods and the way he constantly snapped at the servants, I knew my action wouldn't be well received. But I'd been desperate, a desperation which only increased with each passing moment.

I clutched my fork in my white-knuckled fist as I watched Briar eat in his now usual stony silence. Since the incident in his study he'd not only grown grumpier but also colder and more distant. Tonight was the first meal where he hadn't held my hand in the way he'd had the habit of doing, but even though I missed the affectionate gesture, in his current state it was almost a relief.

Briar hadn't mentioned our heated exchange in the study, and he had yet to apologize for it, as if he saw nothing wrong with his behavior. That wasn't like him...*nothing* was. My heart slowly broke to see the man I adored become a strange, twisted version of himself, causing me to feel utterly helpless considering I had no idea how to help him.

A footman entered the room and tentatively approached, looking as if he'd rather do anything else than deliver his message. "Your Majesty?"

Briar's hardened gaze lifted from his food. "What is it?" he snapped.

"Forgive the interruption, Your Majesty, but Their Highnesses Prince Drake and Princess Rheanna have arrived."

Warm relief washed over me, and for the first time in days, some of the tension in my shoulders lessened. Finally I would no longer have to shoulder this burden alone.

Briar slammed his cutlery down, causing the footman to startle. "Excuse me?"

"The prince and princess are—"

"I heard you the first time," he said coldly. "What I want to know is why my brother felt the need to arrive unannounced."

The footman shifted nervously. "I couldn't say, Your Majesty, I—"

Briar's expression was reddening, and with it I sensed his simmering temper—always so close to the surface these days —on the brink of boiling over.

I laid a hand on his arm. "Don't be angry with him; I'm the one who invited them."

His narrowed gaze shifted to me. "You did *what?*"

I straightened further in my seat, trying to appear confident, the opposite of what I felt. "I invited them. I so wanted to see them."

"Then you should have sought my permission rather than go behind my back."

He glared at me and I met his gaze with an unwavering one of my own. Standing my ground softened his foul mood, albeit only slightly. He stood.

"I suppose there's nothing to do but greet them."

He offered his arm. I took it numbly and allowed him to escort me to the parlor where Prince Drake and Princess Rheanna awaited us.

The princess lay slumped against some pillows on the settee, looking both exhausted from their long, hasty journey and also slightly ill, while the prince paced restlessly. He spun on us as we entered, but before he could even greet us...

"What are you doing here?" Briar snarled.

Prince Drake blinked at him before casting an uncertain glance at me. "I—we heard—that is..." he trailed off.

I forced a smile. "I thought you'd be pleased to see your brother after all the strain you've been under, dear."

The prince's eyebrows rose at my endearment and the princess actually managed a small smile, but it faltered when Briar spun on me. "I warned you not to overstep your bounds, Maren. You have no right to invite guests without my permission."

"I didn't invite *guests*, but your *brother and sister-in-law*," I said as patiently as I could. "You've been quite stressed lately and could use their help in easing some of your burden."

"I don't need help." He spun onto Prince Drake. "And I especially don't want *your* help."

The prince studied him with a furrowed brow. "You do seem a bit tense. Are you sure—"

296

Briar muttered a curse. "Of course I'm sure; I—what are you doing here?" A timid maid had just stepped into the parlor bearing a tray of tea and sweets, looking as if she wanted to be anywhere else.

"Tea for His Majesty's guests?" she asked in a small voice before shrinking beneath the force of his glare.

"That won't be necessary. They're not staying."

Prince Drake's eyes widened. "You're sending us away? But we just got here."

Briar hesitated before shifting his attention back to the maid, who stood frozen, clearly unsure what to do. "I told you to get out. Obey me at once."

She left the tray before scurrying from the room. Briar rolled his eyes behind her retreating back.

"I have the most insolent staff in the entire kingdom."

"You need to stop treating them so poorly," I snapped as the battle with my temper finally faltered.

"I can treat them however I like; their purpose is to serve me." His narrowed eyes shifted to the prince and princess. "Why are you looking at me like that?"

They were gaping at him as if they'd never seen him before. Prince Drake opened his mouth to speak but seemed to think better of it.

Briar's eyes narrowed further as he advanced a step. "Do you have something to say to me, Drake?"

"Only that you seem a bit...off," he finally managed. He glanced towards the window, which overlooked one of the dead gardens. "Not to mention that the state of the grounds is far worse than we anticipated. Perhaps it's a good thing we came...despite the cold reception."

"You shouldn't have bothered," Briar said. "I don't want you here."

Prince Drake lifted his chin to a stubborn angle. "Regardless, we're not leaving."

For a moment the brothers had a silent stare-down before Briar turned his glower back on me. "This is all your fault for inviting them here when I clearly don't want them. You can't keep interfering in my affairs."

I pursed my lips. I didn't regret my interference, for the proposal to increase the kingdom's taxes wasn't the only alteration to the law I'd discovered these past few days, and would definitely not be the last issue I confronted him about. My constant disagreement with his actions as king had led to several fights, tainting the romance that had previously been so sweet but which was now riddled with nothing but tension.

"You can badger me as much as you want, but I refuse to back down from doing what's right." I gave him a challenging look, daring him to argue with me.

He stared at me a moment and for the first time in hours some of the hardness left him. "I could never badger you, my dear." He bridged the distance between us to cup my chin and I tried not to stiffen. His gaze flickered towards the prince and princess, watching us warily. "If you want them here, then I suppose I can allow them to stay. Will that please you, darling?"

Mouth dry, I managed a nod. He forced a tight smile that did little to warm the coldness lingering in his eyes.

"Wonderful. Then I'll discuss the arrangements with the housekeeper. I'll return in a moment." With a departing squeeze of my fingers he left.

The moment the door clicked shut behind him, Prince Drake spun on me. "What in blazes is going on?"

I glanced at the guards watching from along the walls and tipped my head towards the corner. He understood my need for discretion, and after giving his wife's shoulders a comforting squeeze he joined me there.

I leaned in close. "Briar is...changing."

ENCHANTMENT

"That's quite the understatement," Prince Drake muttered. "You were right to seek my help, never mind the timing was dismal, with dear Rhea..." He cast her a concerned glance before shaking his head, his expression darkening. "But it was clearly necessary, for Briar...I've never seen him behave in such a way. What's been happening?"

I summarized as quickly as I could so I could outline the entire situation before Briar's return. The more I spoke, the graver the prince's expression became. When I finished, it took him a moment to find his voice, for I seemed to have stunned him into silence.

He finally let out a low whistle. "It's worse than I feared."

I wrung my hands together. "It's been horrible. His dark moods have become more frequent and he doesn't seem to remember them later; it's as if he's two different people. I'm not sure what to do."

The prince shook his head, clearly at a loss. "I'm not sure what can be done. His behavior seems to be coming from more than just stress. If we could figure out what's triggering it, then perhaps we have a hope of helping him. Otherwise..." He shrugged helplessly.

My thoughts returned to my theory that the weeds were poisoning more than just the gardens, despite Briar's adamant denial. The more I considered it, the more unnatural his insistence that it couldn't possibly be true seemed, almost as if he *wanted* me to believe I was wrong. But with how he'd been changing and the timing of it all...I could see no other explanation.

"Have you ever known Briar to lie before?" I asked.

The prince immediately shook his head. "Never. He's always been the epitome of integrity."

I frowned. It was as I'd expected and why I'd tried to believe Briar's word that there was no connection between his mood and the dying gardens, but now he was behaving so out of character that I could no longer depend on the old Briar's virtues.

Prince Drake studied me. "Why do you ask? Has he given reason to doubt his word?"

Perhaps the prince would be able to shed some much-needed light on my hypothesis. "For a while I've been suspecting that the reason for Briar's foul moods is because of the curse connecting him to the gardens which are currently being poisoned—"

The door suddenly banged open, signaling Briar's return. We both startled and swiveled around. He stood in the door-way, glaring at the pair of us huddled together in the corner.

"What do you think you're doing?" he thundered, his dark gaze locked on the prince. Too late I realized we'd been leaning in rather closely in order to keep our whispered conversation from being overheard. We both hastily backed away from one another, but the damage had already been done.

My stomach tightened at the fury purpling Briar's expression, the telltale sign that his temper was once more about to be unleashed.

Prince Drake hastily held up his hands. "I promise it's not what it looks like. We were just—"

"Get away from Mari." In three strides Briar was in front of us. He shoved Prince Drake away with a look that promised more anger to come and immediately turned towards me, worry penetrating some of the fury lining his expression. "Did he hurt you?"

I rapidly shook my head. "Of course not."

"Are you sure?" In that moment *my* Briar was back, all tender and sweetness, concern filling his eyes as he sooth-ingly rubbed his hands up and down my arms. I was so relieved to see *him* that I instinctively wrapped my arms around him and burrowed against his warm chest, basking in the feel of his embrace as he enfolded me in his arms.

He rubbed my back, his touch so gentle, just like the man I loved, but when I tentatively peeked up at his expression, the gentleness hadn't reached his eyes, which were full of anger as he glared at his brother. "What are you playing at?"

"Nothing," Prince Drake said hastily. "We were only talking."

"*Talking?*" Briar snorted. "I know exactly what you were really up to—you were having a romantic tête-à-tête, weren't you?"

"No, I only—"

Briar looped his arm around my waist and advanced another step towards Drake, keeping me securely pinned to his side to bring me with him. "Why should I believe you? You already stole my first fiancée—never mind I didn't want her—and now you're trying to steal my second?"

"No, I—" Prince Drake's eyes widened. "Wait, are you two *engaged?*"

"Of course we are," Briar snapped. "And I won't have you ruining things. You stay away from Mari. She's *mine.*"

"Leave him alone, Briar," I said firmly. "Nothing happened. You're being completely illogical."

Briar glanced at me. His expression gradually changed as he stared, and the special look he'd always reserved just for me faded, replaced with...disgust. He wrinkled his nose and looked me over, as if seeing me for the first time.

"Perhaps I should let my brother have you; there's absolutely nothing remarkable about you." He unwound his arm from around my waist.

Pain clenched my pounding heart, and the sliver of control I'd maintained over my emotions broke as tears filled my eyes. He couldn't mean that. While he'd been changing,

I'd never doubted his devotion to me or that he loved me, thought me beautiful, saw me in a way no one else ever had.

"Briar—" I rested my hand on his arm, but he jerked away, as if my touch had burned him.

"It's *King* Briar," he snarled. "You will address me by my proper title."

I stared in disbelief, the anguish at his sudden transformation tearing my heart apart piece by piece. I searched his hardened eyes, no sign of the warmth I'd come to expect from the man I loved.

I knew he'd been drastically changing, but only now did I fully realize just how twisted he'd become, for the man before me was not the same one I'd fallen in love with—the one who'd sweetly whispered how beautiful I was to him, the one who adored me...a love that seemed to have disappeared.

Whatever strength I'd been able to miraculously maintain these past several days crumbled, breaking down the walls which had kept all my insecurities and heartache back. I fought to push through them before they could seize control. For despite the pain his words caused, I couldn't believe this was really him. Only this knowledge kept me by his side.

"This isn't you," I said breathlessly, my voice wavering as the last remaining fragile hold on my emotions faltered. "This is what the garden's poison is doing to you. Please, Briar."

"I warned you not to address the king in such an informal way," he said.

"You're not being a king, you're being a tyrant," Prince Drake said. "Miss Maren told me what you've been doing. Raising taxes, increasing the number of guards in the villages, refusing aid for the kingdom.... We won't stand by and let you rule in such a heavy-handed way."

Briar slammed his fist on the accent table lining the wall, causing the vase that had been resting there to tumble and shatter. "You're way out of line, Drake. I'll rule how I see fit, for *I'm* the king, not you, and what I say is law. I refuse to tolerate the presence of a traitor, even one in my own family. You will leave at once."

The prince tightened his jaw. "We're not leaving, especially not tonight. Not only are you in no state to be left alone, but the journey was especially long and taxing for Rhea, who was already feeling poorly after suffering yet another loss; if not for her own fierce concern for you, she wouldn't have come at all."

My heart wrenched for the princess. I hoped her tragic news would at least stir Briar's former compassion, but instead he only rolled his eyes. "Malvagaria is indeed fortunate it was spared from being saddled with a barren queen."

I gasped sharply while Princess Rheanna stared at him in horror for a shocked moment before her sob escaped and her tears spilled over.

Fury twisted Prince Drake's expression. "How dare you." He surged forward and tackled Briar to the ground. The guards reacted instantly and rushed forward to pull the struggling prince off the king.

Fire raged in Briar's eyes as he leapt to his feet and glowered at the prince. "If you were anybody other than my brother, I'd throw you in the dungeon this instant."

"Do what you must; no one speaks of my wife in that way."

The prince wrenched free from the guards' grasp and hurried to her side to gather her in his arms, but she only lingered there for a moment before hurrying from the room. The prince gave Briar a hate-filled glare before following her. The door slammed behind them with a resonating *thud*.

Briar's face darkened as he stared at the closed door. I waited with bated breath, hoping that he'd realize the pain he'd caused the princess and come to himself again. But he didn't. Instead he turned to me with the same hardened look that now seemed a permanent part of his features.

"Good riddance, now perhaps they'll leave."

My fists tightened. "How could you have said something so cruel to the princess?"

He shrugged. "It needed to be said."

Desperation replaced my hurt and anger. I stared at the man I loved, one who'd become nothing more than a shadow of his former self. "You must stop this, Briar. Please."

He rolled his eyes. "I told you before to stay out of my affairs, Mari."

Mari...I clung to his use of my nickname like a lifeline, even though there was nothing tender in his tone or expression. I seized his face with both hands to jerk his gaze down to meet mine.

"I will *not* stay out of this, not when you're becoming such a...a...*beast*."

The word seemed to startle him. Panic flickered across his fierce countenance before it twisted into disbelief and even confusion, both of which quickly faded into warning. "*What* did you call me?"

"A beast, which is exactly how you're currently behaving," I snapped.

He jerked away. "You dare address your king in such a way?"

I lifted my chin defiantly. "I don't care who you are. I made you a promise the day your father died to always be honest with you and to inform you the moment you ever abused your power, and I don't intend to break it."

His eyes narrowed. "Are you implying that I'm being a bad king?"

"Yes. Your father would be so disappointed in the way you're using your title to hurt and bully everyone around you."

That seemed to startle him. "I...promised Father I'd be a good king. I want to make him proud."

"Well, you're doing a terrible job."

He slowly backed away, his eyes wide with fear. "I'm not. I'm being a good king, the one I promised Father I'd be for our people."

"No, you're being a beast."

He frantically shook his head. "I'm not a beast." Desperation filled his previously fierce expression, his silent plea for my denial, but as much as his anguish hurt me, I couldn't lie to him. Tears clogged my throat. I hated the helplessness tightening my chest as I watched the Briar I knew and loved slip away from me beyond both of our control, no matter how hard I tried to cling to him.

"What are the gardens doing to you, Briar?"

The subtlest change flickered in his eyes, as if a candle had been lit where before there had only been darkness. He closed them and took a long, steadying breath before wordlessly extending his hand. I understood his silent invitation and rested mine in his. He held it tightly, as if I were his anchor in whatever storm was currently raging in his mind.

"I'm so sorry," he finally whispered. "I don't know what's wrong with me. My control is slipping away. I feel...as if I'm slowly being overcome..."

His eyes remained shut, as if afraid of meeting my gaze, but when he eventually opened them they swirled with a look so lost that it wrenched my heart.

"What's happening to me, Mari?" he whispered.

I brushed the hair off his brow before letting my touch linger on his cheek. The way he leaned into my hand was so like the Briar I knew, reminding me that despite the darkness that had overcome him, *he* was still here, even if at the moment he was buried deep.

"I'll find a way to help you," I said gently. "I promise."

I softly kissed his cheek. In one swift movement his arms wound around me to crush me into an embrace, his hold desperate, as if he was afraid that if he loosened his grip I'd slip away...or *he* would. And that thought was more terrifying than anything else.

CHAPTER 24

he princess and I sat side by side on my bed. Her eyes were still puffy and her cheeks streaked with tears, but she'd calmed considerably since the incident with Briar in the parlor, although with the way her lip quivered, I knew she was still hurting.

Outside the door, Briar's and Drake's yells had been echoing throughout the palace for the past hour, with no sign that their fight would end anytime soon. I found the prince confronting the king while he was in such a precarious state rather foolhardy but undeniably romantic. I just prayed that Briar still possessed enough of himself not to harm his brother.

"It's so sweet how His Highness dotes on you," I said in an attempt to distract myself from the dark direction my thoughts were taking. "I can tell he loves you very much."

Princess Rheanna twisted her wadded handkerchief in her shaking hands. "He does, but all the same I fear I'm disappointing him." Her hand lowered to her barren womb. "When Briar said that…it made me wonder if Drake secretly feels the same way."

"Of course he doesn't." I knew little about the prince, but I couldn't doubt the adoration he held for his wife, which filled his eyes whenever he looked at her. "And Briar doesn't either. You know him as well as I do—he'd never say such a hurtful thing if he were himself."

"Yet he *did*," she whispered. "And don't you dare defend him for it."

My own anger for his callous treatment of Princess Rheanna made defending him the last thing I wanted to do. Yet my knowledge that the man who'd hurt her wasn't the same one I loved made me long to stand up for him all the same.

"I certainly don't condone his beastly behavior of late," I said. "But we both know Briar enough to realize something is seriously wrong with him, and I believe that's the part of him that lashed out at you rather than Briar himself. Because of what I feel for him I must help him, somehow."

Princess Rheanna kept her gaze fixated on her lap for a moment more before she peered up at me with a watery smile. "I can't fault you for such a wish, especially considering it wasn't that long ago I experienced my own desperation to do all in my power to free the man I loved from his own curse." She wiped her eyes and straightened. "Briar is my friend, and you're right that his current behavior isn't typical of the man I care for, so I'll help you. Where do we begin?"

If only I knew. I stroked the lid of the secret box Briar had given me, which I'd held in my lap throughout our conversation in an attempt to quell the panic threatening to rise with each of Briar's foreign yells still emanating from the corridors. My fingers traced each nick marring the surface as my brain frantically tried to uncover a solution.

The princess's gaze lowered to it. "Is there something special about that box?"

"Briar gave it to me," I said. "It possesses a secret."

She reached for it. "May I?"

I handed it to her and she turned it around in her hands, her brow furrowed as she carefully examined it. "It seems rather unremarkable, but I know Briar—there must be something special about this box for him to not only have acquired it, but given it to you."

Her concentration deepened as she flipped it over to stare at the bottom. Her lips curved up.

"Is this what I think it is?" She slid aside the panel that covered the hidden knob and her dim gaze lit up. "Oh, how clever." She pushed the knob and the lid lifted to reveal the stunning jeweled rose within. Her half smile widened.

"Isn't it beautiful?" I whispered reverently.

"It is." She carefully stroked the ruby-lined petals and the emerald-studded stem. After a moment her forehead wrinkled. "There's another knob at the base of the flower."

She pushed it and we both gasped as music suddenly filled the air, a sweet tune that waltzed throughout the room and left us mesmerized; even the potted carnations swayed to the music. With each note a memory stirred, returning me to the day Briar had given me this box:

"Isn't it lovely?" he'd said. *"It took some time to discover its secret, but now that I have, I can only see it for what it contains. Most who look at this piece never discover it, which is unfortunate, for if they knew what's inside the box they'd realize that although it appears entirely ordinary, its value and unique beauty make it one of my most priceless treasures."*

That was the man I loved—a man with the ability to see deeper, whose own beauty I knew couldn't simply disappear so suddenly. Although his true self had been hidden like the rose within this box, I knew it was still there, just waiting for me to discover him again. But how?

The music box tune ended. I carefully set the box on my

nightstand beside the vase containing the rose I'd plucked from the garden months before, the half dozen petals that hadn't yet fallen only now just starting to wilt.

The princess stared at it. "Where did you get that rose?"

"From the garden," I said. "Do you recognize it?"

"I do. It's similar to the roses that grow on our palace grounds. I'd thought it one of a kind. May I see the bush this one came from?"

She'd voiced the silent yearning that had been prodding my mind for several days, as if the plucked rose whispered in words I couldn't hear, but which I felt all the same, urging me to return to the bush where everything had started. Could it possibly contain the answers we so desperately sought?

We gathered our shawls and made our way outside to the gardens. The air was frigid and a heavy mist hovered over the wilted foliage, black with decay and filled with thorny weeds. The bright magic that used to permeate the grounds had vanished, leaving nothing except death and shadows in its place.

I shivered and tightened the shawl around my shoulders before leading the princess towards the rose garden, where I'd been only once before. Even though it'd been months and I couldn't rely on the garden's guidance, I somehow knew the way, as if the knowledge had never left me. We picked our way through the dead undergrowth until we arrived at the familiar weeping willow, whose branches masked the clearing where the enchanted rosebush grew at its center.

I stared at it in disbelief, for unlike the rest of the gardens, it hadn't yet died, though the petals were beginning to dry and curl at their glittered edges, and many of the leaves had shriveled or fallen off completely.

But for now, the heart of the gardens hadn't yet been overcome by the poison, meaning there was still hope that we could find a way to heal the entire gardens. Relief flooded over me.

I ventured closer and stroked a petal from one of the living flowers. "You're still alive," I whispered. "How is that possible?"

I didn't expect an answer—for the garden hadn't spoken to me in weeks, not since the sickness had begun to consume it—but with every stroke of this rose, faint snippets caressed my mind.

Fighting...he's...fighting...it.

I startled and dropped my touch. "Did you hear that?" I asked the princess.

"Hear what?"

"The rosebush...it spoke. Didn't you hear it?"

She shook her head. "I've never been able to understand the gardens."

I wrinkled my forehead as I returned my attention to the rosebush. "Who's fighting? *What* is he fighting? Please tell me."

The flowers rustled, as if aching to be of service, but too weak to actually render it. I waited for it to say more, but it didn't speak again.

I frowned as I digested its brief message. I felt as if the answer hovered at the edge of my senses yet still too far out of reach for me to grasp.

Meanwhile, the princess circled the rosebush, examining it. "This is definitely the same type of rosebush growing at our palace." She paused and crouched in front of the severed stem where I'd plucked the rose that had trapped me here. She lifted her gaze to mine in a silent question.

I nodded. "That's where I plucked the rose."

She caressed the severed stem with her fingertip before her gaze settled on another only a few inches away. "There are two roses missing. These roses remind me of the one

Briar wore while in Draceria. I've wondered why he always had a rose with him. I bet it came from this bush. I'm surprised the plucked stems haven't regrown, but perhaps magical roses operate under different laws."

"Briar told me about that," I said. "His curse connects him to the gardens so that he can't leave. Only by the garden giving him one of its flowers was he able to do so."

Her mouth fell open. "He's connected to the gardens in such a way?"

"Yes, so much so that he said without them, he'd wither away and perhaps even..." I gasped sharply as the realization hit me.

"What is it, Maren?"

It took a moment to gather my thoughts. "For a while I've been wondering whether Briar's connection to the gardens has been poisoning him alongside them. The gardens have caused the kingdom's crops to die, and while Briar isn't physically dying, instead he's—"

"—changing," the princess finished.

I nodded. "Exactly. Although he claims his curse and the garden's condition have no connection, I've been certain he's wrong."

Briar's adamant denials had kept me from focusing on his connection to the garden as much as I should have, considering I'd so wanted to trust him. But either he didn't realize what was happening to him or he'd been lying. With the way the gardens had twisted his personality, I suspected the latter.

She hastily straightened, her eyes wide. "That explains his transformation. But what can be done? Is there any hope?"

"There is." My recent epiphany swelled within me, providing the light I'd been desperately seeking midst the recent darkness. "The rosebush is the heart of the garden and hasn't yet been overcome by the poison. Because of Briar's connection to it, he hasn't been entirely consumed by the dark magic. He's fighting against it, and so long as the rose-bush is still alive, there's still hope to save both him and the gardens."

We stared at one another for a disbelieving moment before we both lifted our skirts and hurried back to the palace. My heart pounded with each step, even as new hope swelled within me that with this revelation we could finally figure out how to help Briar.

Even after we reached the palace, it still took a moment to find him, for with the way his heated argument with his brother echoed throughout the halls, it was difficult to discern where the sound was coming from. We eventually found them in the crimson sitting room, standing inches away from one another with red faces and clenched fists.

Prince Drake held up a document that looked similar to the other horrible laws Briar had been drafting of late. "For the last time, you can't do this, Briar. I refuse to allow you to pull the last remaining guards from trying to find our sisters."

"Why should I continue to expend valuable men and resources trying to find them?" Briar asked. "I've spent months searching; the cause is hopeless."

The prince crumpled the document. "But they're our sisters. You can't just give up on them."

"Our sisters have become nothing more than a drain on my kingdom, thus—"

"*Briar!*"

My panting cry interrupted the argument and captured his attention. He spun on me. "Don't you dare try to interfere again, Maren. I won't be moved on this."

Still fighting to catch my breath, I stepped further into the room. "There's something I must tell you. You've refused to listen before, but you *will* listen now."

He snorted. "I care nothing for whatever you have to say."

Despite the cruel words and the dark way he delivered them, they couldn't hurt me, not when I now fully realized where they were really coming from—not from the real Briar, but the garden's poison that had infected him.

I ignored his attempts to back out of my reach as I approached and seized his face to lower it so he was eye level with me. He tried to wrench away from my grip but I held firm, searching his eyes, so dark and cold, and yet...

A flicker of the man I adored briefly filled his gaze. I sighed with relief. "There you are. I knew you hadn't fully left me."

It was gone in a moment. He pushed me away. "I didn't give you permission to touch me."

I stood my ground. "Your beastliness can't fool me, for I know who you really are. The rosebush isn't yet overcome by the weeds, and neither are you. I saw you just now. You're still here."

His anger faltered, revealing bewilderment. "What are you talking about?"

"Your curse connects you to the gardens, gardens which are slowly being poisoned...and thus you are, too."

Briar's confusion deepened before relief filled his entire manner, but it was gone in an instant. "I've told you before my curse doesn't affect me in such a way." The usual battle that always followed his denial reappeared in his eyes, only this time I recognized it for what it was—his fight against the garden that forced him to lie to me, for if I didn't know the truth, I couldn't help him. But this was one battle I refused to allow the garden to win.

"I can see you know it's true," I said. "You've known almost from the beginning, yet its power forced you to lie to me. It's what kept me in the dark for so long, but no longer."

His struggle to tell me the truth resurfaced, one he once

again lost, but I didn't need him to confirm what I already knew to be true.

I rested my hand over his heart. "Now I understand why you've been acting so beastly, but I can see who you really are, even if it's currently hidden...like the rose within the seemingly ordinary box. You're the one who taught me what true beauty means, so now I'll always be able to see it within you, even when you yourself can't. A rose is still a rose, even when it's consumed by thorns."

His fierce expression remained, but his eyes revealed the battle raging inside of him.

"You know this already," I said. "Even though that knowledge is currently buried. The rosebush told me you're fighting it, but it's becoming much more difficult, isn't it, dear?" I stroked his hair, half expecting him to flinch from my touch, but he not only let me but leaned against my hand when it lowered to his cheek.

"I both want you to stop and want you to keep touching me forever," he whispered. "How can I experience both emotions at the same time? I don't understand."

"The good man that you are is fighting against the poison trying to consume you and change you," I explained. "Please don't give up, and please don't push me away. Let me help you."

His brows furrowed. "Why would you want to help me? You called me a beast, and I called you"—he squeezed his eyes shut, as if the memory pained him—"I called you unremarkable, and thought something far worse."

I winced at that painful memory before forcing myself to push it aside; now was not the time to revisit it.

I stroked his face. "You're not a beast. The poison may be trying to make you believe that's who you are, but light is always stronger than darkness."

He shook his head. "There's too much darkness in me. I'm losing myself."

"It's not too late," I said. "For I can still see you, even if you can't. I love you, Briar. Please. Let me help you."

His arms wound rigidly around me, as if he was forcing himself to go through the motions. "I think...I love you, too. I sense this knowledge in my heart, even if I can't feel the emotion itself; it's buried too deeply."

He held me tighter, as if drawing strength from me. He searched my face, as if trying to find something he'd lost. His expression gradually softened, and with it I caught a glimpse of the man I loved.

"You have such pretty eyes, Mari, and they're not your only striking feature."

He continued staring, his gaze never wavering as he searched intently. He raised a hesitant hand and stroked the back of my cheek with his knuckles.

"There's something about you, something I feel I should know, as if from a long-forgotten dream...a dream I feel used to be a part of me, one I desperately want to recapture. One moment you seem unremarkable and quite plain, the next you're the most beautiful woman in the world. That's the image of you I always want see, but I feel it slipping away." Despair filled his eyes. "I don't want to forget how I see you, forget *you*. I think I do love you, but that emotion is nothing compared to the rage that feels a permanent part of me. How can I know for sure which is real?"

My helplessness returned to press against my chest so fiercely it threatened to crush me. "I don't know, but no matter what happens, nothing will change how I feel about you, even if you never remember that you once loved—"

A sob robbed my remaining words and I burrowed against his chest. I wasn't sure how he'd receive my close proximity, but to my astonishment and fierce relief, he

316

embraced me even harder, his arms shaking so violently it was as if he could barely keep himself together.

"I *will* remember," he said. "For despite everything, I can't fully forget that you're the most important thing in the world to me." His gaze slowly took in the room. "Everything seems so shadowy and lacks color...nothing is beautiful anymore." Fear filled his eyes. "I don't want to lose myself."

"I know," I said. "But you won't. Now that we both know what's happening, we'll find a solution, and even if we don't—"

My throat clogged with tears at the thought of that all too likely scenario. What would happen if the rosebush—the last thing connecting Briar to the gardens—died too? Would he be lost forever?

CHAPTER 25

$\mathcal{I}$ didn't want to leave Briar's comforting hold, afraid he'd slip away from me the moment I let him go. Within his arms I could sense the precarious hold he had on himself; with how much the gardens had died, it was a miracle he still maintained any sense of himself at all. How much longer would he be able to fight off the poison before it entirely consumed him?

Prince Drake cleared his throat, interrupting our brief moment of peace. "Is there a way we can sever Briar's connection to the gardens before he loses himself completely?"

"Not without breaking the curse," Briar said. "And unlike your own curse, I know of no stipulation that would free me from mine."

The princess pursed her lips in thought. "Instead of trying to break the curse, we should focus our efforts on trying to stop the poison from consuming more of Briar. When Liam was dying back in Draceria, Briar sacrificed his rose so we could create a healing remedy. Am I right to assume that rose came from the very rosebush you're connected to?"

Briar nodded rigidly. "Those enchanted roses are the lifeblood behind the garden's magic, and thus their powers lie in sustaining life."

"If the rose had the power to heal Liam, could it also heal the poison affecting you?"

My heart lifted as hope seized it. "Do you think it's possible?"

Prince Drake frowned doubtfully. "Briar's condition is a result of his connection to the dying garden, so I suspect we'd need to heal not *him*, but the garden itself."

My budding hope immediately died. Princess Rheanna eyed my crumpled expression.

"Perhaps the remedy will at least stave off the garden's effects on Briar until we can figure out a way to heal the source." She nibbled her lip. "But most of its roses have wilted. Would that dilute their power?"

Prince Drake's frown deepened. "I suspect it would. And there's another obstacle: there are consequences for plucking an enchanted rose, and the garden is in no state to provide such a gift itself."

My heart sank further at the discouraging direction the conversation was taking. Briar's arms shook as they tightened around me. "It seems so hopeless," he murmured. "What if nothing can be done and I lose myself forever?"

I clung to him, as if doing so would keep him with me. "You won't. I can't lose you."

Briar let out a weary breath and rubbed my back. His soothing and loving touch only confirmed that not only was he still with me, but that I couldn't live without him. There had to be a way to help him...

An idea struck me. "Since we can't use the enchanted rosebush, what about the rose I plucked? Although it's lost most of its petals and is slightly wilted, what remains is still in full bloom."

Briar shook his head. "Absolutely not. That rose symbolizes your connection to the gardens. I can't bear to think what would happen if we destroyed it."

"But her connection is different than yours," the prince said. "You're directly connected by a curse that prevents you from leaving, whereas her connection is of the garden's own making, one I suspect was arbitrarily created simply to keep her here for some unknown purpose."

"But we don't know for sure. I won't risk anything happening to her." Briar's expression twisted in his desperation to protect me, causing him to look more like himself than he had in a long time. My heart swelled at his sweet protection, but it was impractical.

"Your concern means everything to me, but if there's any chance my rose will help you, then I must try it."

Briar's hold tightened. "No, Mari, you can't."

Briar kept me securely pinned to his chest, making it impossible to wriggle free, so I turned to the princess. "Your Highness, will you retrieve—"

"Of course." She immediately rose and hurried from the room.

Briar's expression became frantic. "No Rhea, don't—" He cursed beneath his breath when the door clicked shut behind her. "I won't give in so easily. Even if she makes the tea I refuse to drink it."

"Then the effort would have been wasted," I said. "Now stop arguing with me, for this is a battle I will win, even if I have to pour the tea down your throat myself."

With his darkening mood of late, I half expected him to snap at me for my impertinence, but instead his manner softened and a glimmer of light returned to his eyes. "So stubborn, yet incredibly loyal. You're reminding me why I believe I'm in love with you."

"You remember?" I asked, my whisper filled with hope.

"I'm beginning to. But even if the curse entirely robs me of my feelings, it won't be difficult to fall in love with you all over again." He lightly kissed my brow. "Very well, you win; I'll drink the tea. Am I correct in assuming this is what I should expect in our marriage— you continuously getting your way despite my being the king?"

A teasing glint filled his eyes, another hint of the real Briar. The longer I remained in his arms, the more of him seemed to emerge, as if my presence was gradually healing him.

"I fully expect to get my way quite often," I said. "But since I love you, I might be persuaded to occasionally give in to your desires."

He heaved an exaggerated sigh, but his amusement remained. "Even knowing what I'm getting myself into, I refuse to let you go."

My heart warmed. "I don't object to that."

As if to make good on his promise, his arms tightened around me, bringing me even closer, and in this position we stayed until the princess returned with a cup of tea, whose floral scent rose with the steam. Briar accepted the tea and swirled it with a thoughtful pucker before taking a hesitant sip.

We held our breath and waited. My attention remained riveted to his eyes, for they were a measure of when Briar was with me or when he was a beast. Even after he'd drained the entire cup of tea, the darkness mostly remained, causing my suffocating despair to return.

"It's not working."

The princess rested a comforting hand on my arm. "Don't panic, it took some time for it to work for Liam."

I wrung my hands. "How long?"

She bit her lip. "Several weeks before he was completely

healed, but he began showing signs of improvement almost immediately."

Minutes ticked by, but the darkness didn't dispel from Briar's eyes, leaving us as lost and directionless as we were before.

I frantically searched my mind for another idea, desperate to come up with *something*. And gradually one slowly began to emerge, a bit fuzzy and uncertain, but an idea nonetheless.

I swiveled around in Briar's arms to face the prince. "You mentioned your doubts the remedy would heal Briar because you believe it's not him that needs to heal but the gardens themselves. Is it possible the rose could heal *them?*"

Prince Drake puckered his brow thoughtfully. "I believe that's more likely to work, but we're back to the original problem of how to do that."

My mind spun as I frantically tried to assemble my thoughts. "Briar said the rosebush was the lifeblood of the gardens. If we could somehow replant it, perhaps it'll heal the garden, and therefore Briar."

Princess Rheanna's eyes lit up. "Our palace grounds has an enchanted rosebush, one so far untainted from the spreading weeds. We can obtain one of its roses."

Hope blossomed in my heart. "We must go at once." I tried to wriggle from Briar's hold but he held fast. "You can't leave, Mari." The tender look I so loved filled his eyes, another glimpse of his real self the consuming beast couldn't completely steal. "If you leave the garden...I'm not sure what will happen to you, happen to *me*." His eyes widened with fear.

"You won't be alone," I said. "Prince Drake and Princess Rheanna—"

He shook his head. "I'm not myself around them. I can feel more of myself slipping away with each passing moment...except for when I'm with you. Please, you must stay with me. I need you."

His fear wrenched my heart. I soothingly stroked his cheek and glanced at the prince and princess. "Could either of you go instead?"

Princess Rheanna started to nod, but Prince Drake adamantly shook his head. "The journey was too wearying for Rhea to make it again so soon, and I refuse to allow her to take it by herself. And I can't go, for there's no way I'm leaving you ladies alone with Briar. What if he becomes violent?"

"He'd never—" But before I could defend him, Briar released me and hastily backed away, his eyes wide.

"He's right, we can't take such a risk. I could do anything."

"You won't." But a tinge of doubt lingered. I knew *Briar* would never hurt us, but as more of the weeds infested the garden, what if his remaining gentleness also died? His recently acquired temper was a testament that he'd already lost his easygoing nature. What more would the curse take from him?

I couldn't allow any more of him to be lost, which meant there was only one thing to do. I lifted my chin. "I must be the one to retrieve the rose."

Fear and desperation filled his eyes as he embraced me once again. "Please Mari, you can't leave. What if something were to happen to you? Or in the time you're gone I lose what remains of myself?"

I tried to tug free from Briar's hold but he held fast, his terror deepening. I stroked his cheek. "Nothing will happen to me or to you, nor will we allow the darkness to win. We must hold tight onto our hope, however small. Please trust me and allow me to do this, for I can't lose you."

His arms around me loosened. "But the gardens won't let you leave," he protested.

"The gardens are dead. They can't stop me anymore."

He moaned and pressed his forehead to mine. "But you could still be hurt. I can't lose you either."

My breath caught. "I thought you'd forgotten what you feel for me?"

He tilted my chin up so our gazes met, his filled with the special look I hadn't seen since our time in the glowing garden—the one where he truly saw all of *me*, both my virtues and my imperfections.

The corners of his mouth slowly lifted as his knuckles grazed my cheek. "I don't think I can ever truly forget my love for you. I can't believe that I ever thought I did. You're a part of me, Mari, making you the one thing I can't lose. I'll fight with all that I am not to lose myself, both for you and for my people."

He dipped down and softly caressed my lips with his, our first kiss since the darkness had begun to consume him. Despite knowing it still had a firm hold on him, in this moment there was only my Briar. I didn't waste the opportunity to give all of myself to him. He needed to know how much I loved him and believed in his goodness, even if he himself had forgotten.

"I'll save you," I vowed against our kiss. "I promise."

He kissed me more fervently, and in it I sensed his own promise to keep fighting, one which would give me the strength for what was to come.

THE GUARDS WAITED outside the gate as I approached the enchanted rosebush growing on the royal grounds of the prince and princess's palace, each blossom aglow in the early morning dawn. My limbs ached and exhaustion pressed against my senses, but there was no time to linger, and yet the roses' beauty kept me mesmerized.

It had been a long and arduous journey. Leaving Briar had been agonizing. He'd been in a foul temper as he made the travel arrangements, which only necessitated my need to go so that I could find a cure for his darkness as soon as possible.

But no matter how grumpy he became, he always had a special look for me, which assured my frantic heart that he hadn't yet lost the fight against the poison transforming him. This was further confirmed in his departing embrace, one that had been filled with his usual tenderness and love. I snuggled close, afraid of letting him go in case this was our last moment together.

He nestled against my hair. "Return to me."

"Stay with me," I whispered back before allowing him to help me onto my horse. He squeezed my hand once more before I rode away with my two accompanying guards, the dead vines making no move to stop me from exiting the gate.

We'd ridden nonstop for hours. I held one of the flowers from the bouquet the garden had gifted me several months ago close, as I'd promised Briar I would. He'd told me this gift from the garden would protect me. I also prayed it would speed my flight and provide the strength I needed to succeed in my quest.

We'd ridden through the night and had arrived at the palace as dawn lit up the horizon. I dismounted and, after giving the guards at the entrance the letter from Prince Drake granting me permission to enter, went alone to find the garden, while my guards lingered behind. Unlike at Briar's palace, this rosebush wasn't hidden, but was the centerpiece of the main garden. Each colored rose glistened in the sunlight, its magic emanating from each petal, magic I hoped would be able to heal the gardens and save Briar.

Despite the urgency of my quest, I couldn't help but stare at the roses, transfixed. Unlike the blossoms at the main palace who'd wilted from the sickness, these were vibrant, their glow a silent invitation to pluck one, yet I hesitated.

I reached out to lightly trace each glitter-coated petal of a crimson blossom, pondering what to do. I couldn't steal one, else I'd find myself at the mercy of whatever punishment this garden would inflict upon me. But any consequence, no matter how dire, was a small price to pay if I could help Briar. My love for him was stronger than any fear about what could happen to me.

I took a steadying breath. "Please forgive me for taking a rose," I said. "But the gardens at the main Malvagarian palace are dying, killing the kingdom's crops and causing the king to lose himself. I'll do anything to help him."

I hooked my fingers around one of the thorny stems, but before I could pluck it from the bush, the entire plant began to glow and the rose lifted from the bush as if controlled by an invisible hand, pausing to hover before me as an offering.

I stared at it before hesitantly reaching out to caress it. It quivered at my touch before pressing itself into my hand. The moment I held it securely, the rosebush stopped glowing. It took me a dazed moment to realize what had just happened—the rosebush had *given* me one of its roses.

Tears filled my eyes as I bobbed a curtsy. "Thank you."

The remaining flowers rustled in response, and then were still.

I carefully tucked the rose into my satchel before leaving the gardens. I paused at the threshold and looked around with a furrowed brow. The horses neighed nearby, shifting in clear agitation, but where were the guards? They—as well as the palace guards—were nowhere to be seen. My heart beat wildly in trepidation as I ventured a few steps beyond the gate, searching...until my breath hooked when I spotted their fallen forms several yards away, clearly unconscious.

Before my fear could take hold of me, scuffling footsteps sounded behind me and someone seized me from behind. I immediately began kicking in an attempt to break free, but the arms were firm and unrelenting, pressing me against an uncomfortably firm chest.

"Not so fast, girlie," a leering voice snarled in my ear. "You're not going to slip away from the master again."

He pressed a sickly sweet-smelling cloth to my nose. I held my breath for as long as I could before being forced to take a shaky gasp. Immediately I felt myself being pulled under as the world around me faded to black.

CHAPTER 26

*P*ain laced my pounding head as I gradually emerged from the penetrating darkness. It was a struggle to push through the thick fog pressing against my senses, and even as I did, my weighted eyes refused to open.

The first thing to pierce my incoherent awareness was the rough rope binding my wrists and ankles, as well as the wooden plank pressing against my cheek. I managed to pry open my eyes, but even after this small feat it took a moment to orient myself to my surroundings, made more difficult with the pain pulsating against my temples.

I lay curled in a fetal position. Faint light tumbled through the window, but it did little to dispel the shadows of the small room I was imprisoned in. I blinked, disoriented. Where was I? What had happened? I struggled to sort through my murky thoughts for a memory of some sort—a long and tiring journey on horseback, a rosebush of enchanted blossoms, a sense of urgency pressing against my chest and pushing me forward, someone seizing me from behind—

I gasped as the incident returned and I struggled to sit up, but my awkward, contorted position made it difficult.

"Ah, you're finally awake."

I swiveled around to face a paunchy, middle-aged man dressed in fine velvet, with thinning grey hair and matching cold grey eyes. He sat on a chair looking down at me with a hardened leer that caused icy terror to squeeze my insides.

"Who are you?" I asked shakily.

He gave a quick nod of his head. "I'm Lord Brone. We'd have become better acquainted if your father hadn't reneged on our engagement contract."

I lifted my chin, for I refused to give him the satisfaction of seeing my fear. "That engagement contract has been broken, so I demand to know why you've kidnapped me."

He raised an eyebrow. "*Demand*? Aren't you a feisty one. I'm a direct man myself, Miss Maren, so allow me to get straight to the point: your father cheated me."

"What does that have to do with me?"

His eyes narrowed. "It has everything to do with you, for you were the heart of the contract your father broke before suddenly disappearing. I sent out my spies to investigate and was met with good news: turns out that his daughter has been staying at the palace of the Malvagarian king."

My heart began to pound in an unrelenting tempo. "I still fail to understand why I should matter to you."

"Do you?" His eyes narrowed. "I'm a businessman, Miss Maren, one who doesn't appreciate when his deals fall through. When your father failed to uphold his end of our contract, I found it only appropriate to seize the goods he'd denied me. Since I was shut out of one profitable arrangement I've found another one, one which will be much more beneficial to me. I've had the palace watched for weeks, awaiting the day you ventured beyond the safety of its walls, and that day has finally arrived."

Anger seared through me. "I'm *not* goods you can simply steal."

"And yet...I just did."

I scowled and once again struggled to sit up, but couldn't quite manage it. "Whatever your motive for taking me, let me assure you that I most certainly won't marry you, no matter how much you threaten me. If that's your scheme, then it'd be in your best interest to—" His cold laugh cut me off. "What's so amusing?" I snapped.

"Your delusions that I would ever be interested in marrying *you*." He chuckled again, a dark, grating sound. "That's the last thing I desire. I admit that was the initial plan —we are betrothed, no matter the lengths your father went through to break it—but the moment I saw you, I realized your father had tricked me." He sneered in disgust as he raked his gaze over me in a way that caused me to shiver. I'd never been more grateful for my apparent lack of beauty than I was now.

"Since I obviously fail to meet your expectations, then there's no reason to keep me here." My voice wavered, betraying my attempt to sound brave.

He poured himself a goblet of wine resting on the nearby table. "Let you go? I think not. Despite your unfortunate appearance, you're too valuable a commodity; I'm much too clever a businessman not to recognize your monetary worth."

My heartbeat escalated as the fear I tried to contain escaped. "Why? What value am I to you?"

He leaned back in his seat and propped his legs up. "I'm a man of trade. I find goods others deem valuable and sell them to the highest bidder. As it turns out, you're a rather special good."

I clenched my tied up fists. "I'm *not* a good."

"On the contrary." He took a lazy sip of wine. "You see,

I've decided to sell you. I have it on good authority that a man of great power does want you, and therein lies your economic worth."

My breath caught. *Oh no.* For the first time since realizing Briar's feelings for me I regretted them, for as much as I relished them, they came at too high of a cost. The last thing Malvagaria needed was a wicked man using me as a bargaining chip against the king, especially with the dying gardens currently crippling the kingdom's finances.

I had to stop this. "You're mistaken," I said firmly. "The king cares nothing for me, which means you're just wasting your time."

He smirked. "I've been in the business too long to be so easily tricked, Miss Maren, and I'm much too savvy not to claim any commodity without first conducting the necessary research about its worth. Thus I know you're highly valued by the King of Malvagaria. If I'm correct, I'll trade you for a hefty price, and if I'm mistaken...well, then I'll have no further use for you, will I?" He sneered.

Icy terror clenched my heart. I was in grave danger... unless Briar complied with his demands. "You're going to try to extort ransom from the king? That's a very dangerous game to play."

His smirk widened. "Indeed it is, but risk comes with every mercenary endeavor. If I were Malvagarian it'd undoubtedly be a suicide wish, but considering I'm Bytamian and will be conducting the transaction from across the sea, out of reach of the king's influence, I feel confident in my own safety to take the risk." His eyes narrowed as his gaze flickered over me once more. "There are many surprising rumors spreading throughout the kingdom about how close you and the king have become. If there's even the slightest truth to them, I intend to fully use them to my advantage."

My stomach twisted in disgust as I glared at him in

hatred. I ached to correct the foul rumors concerning my relationship with Briar—he wasn't misusing me as everyone seemed to believe, but intended to marry me. If only I could use my future authority as queen to put this wicked man in his proper place. But if Lord Brone realized the truth, I'd find myself in even greater danger; I was already in quite the predicament. I refused to allow him to use my relationship with the king to feed his greed and thus further cripple the kingdom.

A new worry squeezed my heart—not that Briar would pay a ransom his kingdom couldn't afford, but that he'd have lost so much of his real self and his affections for me that he *wouldn't*. Had he already reached that point? How long had I been away and how much more had the garden's poison stolen from him during my absence? Had he been able to fight it, or had he succumbed to the darkness threatening to overtake him? I had to figure a way out of this so I could return as soon as possible with the healing rose and—

The rose! Where was it? I tried to sit up again and managed to get in an awkward, somewhat upright position, enough to lean against the wall and frantically scan the dim room, searching. I spotted my satchel near Lord Brone's feet.

He refilled his goblet and glanced lazily at my bag. "Oh, do you want this?"

I jerked my gaze away before he could see my rising panic and thus realize its contents were important. He drained his wine and set the goblet down before retrieving the bag. "I've already gone through its contents and am quite intrigued by the strange flowers I found."

Panic squeezed my chest as he withdrew the enchanted rose the garden had given me, which surprisingly didn't glow at his touch. He twirled it by its stem, his expression thoughtful.

"This is the most unusual flower I've ever seen. It's clearly from the enchanted gardens the Malvagarian Palace is rumored to possess. It'd undoubtedly fetch a high price, as would this one." He withdrew the glowing flower Briar had instructed me to keep with me, with a promise that it'd protect me. Whatever happened, I couldn't allow Lord Brone to take either flower from me.

I tore my gaze away from his triumphant gloating to look around the cramped room. "Where are we?"

"Ah, you're a curious one, are you? That would have proved quite the trial should our union have gone through." He swirled his newly poured goblet of wine pensively. "We're on the top floor of a warehouse near the coast, awaiting the ship that will take us to Bytamia."

My breath caught and it took me a moment to get over my numbing shock to find my voice. *"Bytamia?"*

He took another long swig from his goblet of wine as he leaned back in his seat, clearly amused. "Indeed. Staying here would result in all sorts of trouble if the king were to find you, but Malvagarian law can't touch me in my home kingdom."

My panic rose. He was right. Whatever happened, I couldn't get on the ship that would take me far away from Briar. Which meant I needed to escape. Now. But how?

As Lord Brone rambled on about what sort of price he'd be able to fetch for me, I slowly took in the room. Save for the table and chair Lord Brone occupied, it was sparse of furnishings; there weren't even any loose nails in the walls to use to cut away my bindings.

I was about to resign myself to having to break the window and use its broken glass when my gaze settled on the wine bottle Lord Brone was drinking heavily from. That would do. Now I just needed to wait for him to leave me alone so I could act.

Thankfully, it didn't take long for such an opportunity to

arrive. A quarter of an hour later a knock sounded. "Enter," Lord Brone said. The door opened to reveal two large, rough-looking men. Lord Brone took another sip of wine and nodded. "Update me on the travel arrangements."

"The ship is due to set sail in two hours," one of the men said. "But there's a slight problem."

Lord Brone slammed his goblet down. "Problem? Explain."

"There's been a double booking. The windowless chamber you'd arranged to transport your...latest acquisition"—the accomplice's gaze flickered briefly towards me with undisguised disgust—"has recently been acquired by someone else."

Lord Brone's face reddened as he snapped to his feet, leaving his now empty bottle of wine on the table. "This is unacceptable. I arranged for that chamber over a month ago to be available whenever I needed it. I must speak to the captain at once." He threw the enchanted flowers to the floor and stomped towards the door, pausing in the threshold to glance back at me. "I'd advise you to not try any funny business; I'm not a man to be trifled with. I'm locking the door and leaving my men to guard the outside. Escape is impossible."

Finally, a bit of good fortune, for little did he know that I was the type of escapee who didn't rely on doors. Perhaps whatever magic filled Malvagaria was working behind the scenes to help me escape so I could protect its king.

I lowered my eyes in feigned dejection until he'd left the room. I heard the key in the lock turn, followed by the welcoming sound of his receding footsteps. Then there was silence.

I didn't wait another moment to scoot towards the table. Standing proved more of a challenge, but by leaning against the wall I was able to balance myself enough to manage it. I nibbled my lip as I eyed the wine bottle. Breaking it would alert the guards outside the door what I was up to.

I quickly formulated a plan. "Let me out at once!" I cried. "You can't keep me here." I used the sound of my raised voice to mask the sound of shattering glass as I knocked the bottle against the table.

One of the men pounded on the door. "Shut up, girlie, or we'll gag you."

I ignored them, already working with the broken bottle-neck to cut the ropes. My restricted movements made me clumsy, and twice I fumbled and cut myself; I gasped at the sharp pain and felt blood streak my hands, but I continued sawing until the ropes broke free.

I allowed myself only a moment to examine the rope burns encircling my swollen wrists and my bleeding cuts. I tore fabric from my petticoat to bind my wounds before fumbling with the ropes at my ankles. Once free, I picked up the flowers Lord Brone had tossed to the ground, carefully put them back into my bag, and turned towards the window.

Luck was on my side, for it wasn't locked. I pushed it open and was greeted with cool morning air. Dawn tinged the sky, lighting up the coastal town. Not many were out and about so early in the morning, which would make fewer witnesses to my escape.

After checking the streets below for any sign of Lord Brone, I secured my satchel, hopped onto the sill, and expertly crawled onto the roof towards the eaves to drop down. I'd done this enough times that it was second nature, although my sore wrists and stiff limbs made maneuvering difficult. A hush settled below as several passerby noticed my escape, but I ignored them as I made my way to the edge of the sloping roof, where I twisted around and lowered myself to the ground.

My legs buckled beneath me as I dropped, and for a

moment I lay winded on the dirt path. As soon as my breath returned I hastily scrambled to my feet before any passerby could inquire after my well-being; the more invisible I stayed, the better.

I wasted no more time. I ran through the streets, away from the ocean and towards the outskirts of town. I had no idea where I was or how to return home, my only goal being to *escape*. I stayed within the shadows and obscure alleys, hoping to remain undetected, but whatever luck had guided me up to this point faltered before I reached the edge of town.

An angry snarl stopped me in my tracks. "There she is! Don't let her get away!"

I spun around to see the drunken Lord Brone staggering after me with his two cronies at his heels. I turned and bolted. I escaped the town and ran down the road, my breath already coming up short and my movements slow and clumsy from my sore limbs. Lord Brone was quickly gaining, especially when a stitch formed in my side, forcing me to slow, but I forced myself to keep going.

Approaching horses sounded in the distance and moments later riders appeared, bearing the royal insignia of Malvagaria. Fierce relief filled me, especially when the head rider pulled up beside me and Briar dropped from the saddle.

"Mari!" Before I had a chance to respond, he gathered me into a suffocating embrace. I immediately melted against him, basking in the love and relief I felt within his arms. However far the poison had progressed, at least it hadn't robbed me of him completely.

He pulled back just enough to cradle my face, his thumbs caressing my cheeks as he searched my eyes with the gentle look I'd come to adore and which I'd fiercely missed.

"Mari…oh, my dear, dear Mari."

He dipped down and kissed me—a hard, desperate one

that caused my toes to curl. He broke it too quickly for my liking and frantically looked me over, his touch incredibly gentle as he caressed my arms.

"Are you alright, love? Are you hurt?"

His gaze settled on the blood seeping from my makeshift bandages on my wrists and his entire manner instantly transformed. I watched Briar slip away as darkness filled his eyes and fierce lines appeared on his hardened countenance.

He spun onto Lord Brone, standing several yards away, he and his two men surrounded by Briar's guards. "You'll pay for hurting Mari." He immediately drew his sword and advanced, his twisted fury completely distorting the good man I loved.

I seized his arm. "Stop, Briar. This isn't you."

Briar's white knuckled hand clutching his sword shook as he pointed it accusingly towards Lord Brone. "He hurt you. He deserves—"

"No punishment he deserves is worth you changing into someone you're not," I said. "You're not a beast, so don't allow it to overtake you. Please."

His rage didn't dissipate, robbing him of any semblance to his real self. Fear clenched my heart. As much as I disliked Lord Brone, if Briar slew him, I feared he'd lose whatever part of himself remained. I couldn't allow that to happen.

Briar's breaths came out ragged as he seized me in an embrace and glared murderously at Lord Brone. "He deserves to die for what he's done to you."

"If you were in your right mind, you'd never choose such a harsh and irrevocable punishment so rashly." I soothingly stroked his back, and although his entire body remained stiff with tension, I felt him ease slightly against my touch. "The King Briar I know is merciful. Please don't allow your thirst for revenge to fuel the poison trying to overtake you. You're better than that."

He growled beneath his breath, even as his hold tightened around me, as if he was relying on me to maintain any sense of himself. The longer he stared at me, the more his darkness faded. Although his anger didn't completely disappear, enough calm penetrated it for him to sheath his sword.

"Tell me what happened. I must know the full extent of his crime so I can deem whether or not he even deserves my mercy."

I hastily summarized all that had transpired since leaving the palace. His expression darkened with each word, causing Lord Brone's delicious fear to escalate.

Briar's jaw tightened as he examined my red wrists. "He tied you up?" At my nod, he pressed the softest kiss on my wounds before examining my cuts with shaking hands. "I'm not surprised you managed to escape. You're so strong." His tenderness faded the moment he turned his murderous fury on my kidnappers. "You've committed a grave crime against the King of Malvagaria and will be punished."

Lord Brone paled. "Forgive me, Your Majesty, but I'm Bytamian and therefore your authority has no jurisdiction over me."

"Regardless of where you fare from, a crime against any kingdom's crown is a grievous offense," Briar said coldly. "You cannot escape punishment for kidnapping and harming the future Queen of Malvagaria."

Lord Brone blanched. "The *future queen?*"

I couldn't resist smirking. "Indeed. I'm sure you realize that it's in Bytamia's best interest to remain on good terms with the Malvagarian monarchy, so you won't be able to use their protection to escape punishment."

Lord Brone's expression twisted in panic, and I could almost see his mind frantically searching for a way to escape his predicament.

"Your Majesty, I believe there's been an unfortunate

misunderstanding. I wasn't kidnapping Miss Maren but *saving* her from these two ruffians after they kidnapped her." He motioned to his two accomplices, who immediately denied his accusations, but Lord Brone talked over them. "I'm an old friend of her father, and when I heard that she was in danger, naturally I rushed to her defense. You see, we used to be engaged and I couldn't bear to see any harm come to my former fiancée."

Briar's eyes narrowed. "Do you honestly think I can't see through your lies, or that I'd ever believe your account over Mari's? Nothing you say will allow you to escape the punishment you thoroughly deserve."

Lord Brone didn't give up so easily. "Please, Your Majesty, have mercy. I'm innocent of the charges against—"

Briar raised his hand, silencing him. "Enough. Another word from you and your punishment will be far more dire. For now, I'll leave it to your own king to decide your fate." His fierce look caused Lord Brone to swallow his remaining defense. He flicked his wrist towards his guards. "Lock him in the dungeon at Prince Drake's palace, apprise the Bytamian ambassador of the situation, and arrange for the scoundrel to be sent back for trial as soon as possible."

They bowed before escorting Lord Brone and his men away. The adrenaline from my ordeal faded as I watched them leave, replaced with relief, not just for having escaped but that Briar hadn't allowed his anger to overcome him and murder my kidnapper.

He gathered me back in his arms. "I was so worried," he murmured. "When the guards accompanying you returned and informed me that they'd been knocked out and woke up to find you missing—my heart broke at the thought that I'd lost you." He hooked his fingers beneath my chin and tilted my head up to frantically search my expression. "Are you sure you're alright, my dear?"

I managed a nod. "But how did you find me?"

"The glowing flower from the gardens." He pulled out his own, which he must have taken from the bouquet given to me by the gardens. "Since you still possessed this flower's match, its magic allowed it to lead me to you. I told you this was a very special gift from the gardens, given out of their love so that you can always return to me."

Worry penetrated my relief as I stared at it. "Does that flower connect you to the gardens for you to safely leave them?"

He hesitated before shaking his head. "No, it only works if I possess a rose they gift to me. It's been…a long journey."

I suddenly noticed how weary he looked…and how pale and sickly. Alarm filled my heart. "We must get you back to the palace immediately before—"

I hooked my arm through his to lead him back to his horse, but it was as if the fading adrenaline from his rescue had robbed him of the last of his strength, and he collapsed.

"*Briar!*"

I knelt beside him on the ground as the remaining guards hurried to our side. I turned him over to find his eyes closed and his breathing shallow. My heart wrenched. He was dying…and it was all my fault.

$\mathcal{T}$he carriage jostled as it hit another bump in the road, causing Briar to moan faintly. My spirits lifted for the first time in hours. Was he finally coming to? I stroked his brow, hot with a fever. "Briar?"

He moaned again but didn't open his eyes. My heart sank, but I tried to cling to this small bit of progress, for this was the first noise he'd made since suddenly collapsing following my rescue from Lord Brone. My chest squeezed at the memory.

It had been chaos as I'd knelt beside the king and barked out orders to the accompanying guards to arrange for a carriage to take us back to the Malvagarian Palace as quickly as possible. Horseback would have been much faster, but Briar was in no state to ride. So we'd been forced to settle for the slower means of travel, with arrangements made to change horses every few villages so we could ride through the night and hopefully reach the palace by dawn, a time that felt so far away.

The carriage dipped into another pocket in the road and Briar groaned again, only this time his eyes opened a sliver.

At first he looked rather disoriented as he blinked up at me before slowly taking in the carriage.

"Where are we?" he asked, his voice raspy.

"We're in a carriage on our way back to the main palace, where we'll plant the rose I got from the enchanted bush at Prince Drake's garden in order to save both you and the gardens."

I just prayed we weren't too late. I searched Briar's eyes in hopes of seeing any sign of how much man, how much beast resided in him, but he simply looked confused and rather miserable.

"How are you feeling?"

He didn't answer, but just continued to stare up at me. "You look like an angel, Mari." My knotted stomach flipped. His head shifted slightly from where it rested and his eyes widened as he registered our position. "I'm lying on your lap."

"You are."

His contented sigh and the faint smile that tugged on his lips as he closed his eyes showed that he found the arrangement more than acceptable. "No wonder I'm so comfortable."

He fumbled blindly until he found my hand, which he rested on his chest to hold, causing me to feel each pulse of his rapidly beating heart, as well as each shallow breath.

"How are you feeling?" I asked again.

He took another raspy breath as he peeked back up at me. "How far is the palace?"

"Not far." *Too* far.

I glanced out the window, where dusk tumbled through as the sky darkened. We were approaching nightfall, when it'd be difficult to monitor his condition, a task already proving challenging with his refusal to answer my questions regarding his well-being, a vagueness which caused my fear to cinch tighter in my chest.

I turned away from the window to find him still watching me. He managed a half smile. "I'm glad you're here, Mari. I love you, you know."

My entire heart swelled. "And I love you. So please don't leave me."

"We'll see." He closed his eyes with a defeated sigh. "Perhaps it's for the best. I'm tired of fighting the darkness inside me. My people deserve better...as do you. You deserve only the best."

A tear trickled down my cheek to land on his forehead. "You mustn't talk like that, Briar. Hold on a little longer."

He didn't answer, and a moment later his long, deep breaths filled the carriage, indicating he'd fallen asleep, leaving me little distraction from the icy terror encasing my heart.

But no matter how dire the situation seemed, I clung to my hope, however faint, that Briar would survive the trip back to the palace, that the enchanted rose would heal both him and the gardens, and that we would have a beautiful future together. This hope was the only thing that kept me calm as night fully descended, plunging the carriage into darkness, with nothing but the sound of Briar's ragged breaths and the galloping horses to keep me company. I kept Briar's head in my lap and stroked his hair and damp brow, my other hand still enfolded in his on his chest. His presence helped settle some of my suffocating anxieties, but only just barely.

After a seemingly endless night during which I occasionally dozed off, dawn finally arrived, and with it we finally reached the palace. I leaned out the window as we rolled through the gates. My heart sank at the black and wilted plants that greeted me—the entire garden was dead, having fully succumbed to the poison in the time I'd been away.

The carriage headed for the front doors. I carefully

shifted Briar's head in my lap so I could lean out the window and speak to the driver. "No, take us down that path."

I pointed to the one that twisted towards the hidden rose garden. If the carriage could take Briar most of the way, hopefully he'd have enough strength to continue to the garden on his own so we could plant the rose and finally end this nightmare.

The driver tipped his head in acknowledgement and obeyed me without question, just as the guards had done yesterday when I'd given orders following Briar's collapse, as if they already saw me as their queen. Now I needed to see it in myself so I could believe in that future with Briar, even though at the moment it seemed precariously close to slipping away.

"Mari?"

At Briar's weak voice I hastily ducked back inside. He was struggling to sit up, his eyes wild and his face deathly pale. His gaze settled on me and he extended his hand, his silent plea for me to hold it again. I rested mine in his before scooting closer and wrapping my other arm around his back to help him sit upright.

"Are you alright?" I asked again.

He shook his head. "I—need—gardens." He was so weak he could scarcely form the broken sentence.

I stroked his hair back. "Of course, dear." I tapped the ceiling to stop the carriage; it did with a hasty jerk that caused Briar to slump against me. I didn't even wait for the driver's assistance before pushing the door open and helping Briar stumble out into the chilly morning.

He immediately knelt down and burrowed his fingers in the dirt. He closed his eyes and took several deep breaths as he reconnected himself to the gardens. But would it still be able to rejuvenate him even though they were dead? I knelt beside him and wrapped my arm around his shoulders, a position we stayed in for several minutes, each one bringing a bit more color to his face.

"Should we go to the rosebush?" I asked when he looked well enough to stand.

His eyes slowly opened to take in the surrounding garden, where everything was wilted. His expression twisted. "It's dead."

He reached out to rub one of the nearby weeds between his fingers. With each touch, more of his pallor faded, as if these new toxic plants lent him strength where the garden could not. My heart pounded in trepidation. Was that a sign that whatever battle was raging in his heart was tipping in the poison's favor?

We needed to plant the rose in the heart of the garden as soon as possible. I wasn't sure it would help—indeed, the terror of the possibility that it *wouldn't* was almost paralyzing —but we had to do *something*.

I shifted, prepared to stand. "Are you ready to travel to the rose garden?"

He didn't look up from the weed, his expression rather peculiar as he stared at it, his eyes lit in recognition, as if he were greeting an old friend. I gently jostled his arm.

"Briar, we need to go to the enchanted rose garden. Now."

He blinked rapidly, as if I'd torn his thoughts from somewhere far away. "The rose garden?" His brows furrowed. "Oh yes, the rose garden. Did you get the rose?"

I withdrew it from my satchel. It was still in perfect bloom, its deep crimson and glitter-tinted petals such a contrast to the brown, black, and grey surrounding us, the only color in a place where the magic had been drained away.

A wild glint suddenly filled Briar's eyes, as if he wanted to snatch the rose and crush it. I held it out of reach. "Shall we go plant it?"

He blinked hastily again, causing the strange look to fade. "Plant it? Yes. We should." But he made no motion to move—whether due to the hesitancy that seemed to have suddenly settled over him or because he lacked the strength to do so, I wasn't sure.

I clambered to my feet and leaned down to help him up. "Can you stand?"

He nodded faintly and allowed me to tug him to his feet, where he immediately slumped against me, as if that small amount of exertion alone had exhausted him. I nearly collapsed beneath his weight but managed to remain upright. Before I could take the first trudging step, Briar dipped down to tug the weed from the soil.

"What are you doing?" I demanded. "You shouldn't touch it."

He curled it securely in his hand. "I need to. It's the closest I can currently be to the garden."

I didn't like the thought of him drawing strength from something so sinister. The sooner we planted the rose, the better.

I led Briar down the overgrown paths that twisted through the shadowy grounds, each step a struggle as he leaned on me to maintain his balance, causing my muscles to scream in protest. I nearly sagged in relief when I spotted the willow that guarded the rose garden's entrance.

"We're almost there." And not a moment too soon—my knees were beginning to buckle beneath Briar's weight and I wasn't sure how long I could keep him upright. I glared at the weed he clung to, as if it were responsible for his weakening condition. "You need to drop that weed. It's clearly not helping."

"It said it would," he murmured weakly. I frowned. *It?* Surely he wasn't referring to the *weed*, was he?

But I had little time to wonder, for we'd finally arrived at the rosebush. The grass surrounding it had yellowed and dried, as had many of the bush's leaves, but to my fierce relief most of the flowers were still in bloom, although more of their petals had either wilted or fallen.

I collapsed beside it and rolled over on the dead lawn to stare up at the grey sky, fighting for breath after the exertion of helping Briar all this way. I glanced towards him lying beside me; his gaze was riveted to a nearby clump of thorny weeds, seeming almost...*fascinated* by them.

"I think we should plant the rose here," he said.

That seemed logical—perhaps grafting the untainted rose amongst the others would allow them to draw the strength they needed to not only heal themselves but the rest of the garden. I prepared to dig a hole but paused at the sudden rustling breeze, as if the garden was agitated.

"What is it?" I asked. "Is there something you want to tell me?"

The roses managed to shift in a nod, weak but in clear distress, and whispers caressed my mind. But the words were indiscernible; all I sensed was a general feeling of unease.

"I don't understand." I touched the nearest flower, a bright violet blossom whose color was only just starting to fade. It wriggled against my hand, pressing itself more fully against my palm, as if the contact would help me understand its message.

Not...here.

I wrinkled my brow. "Not here? But this is the heart of the garden. Are you sure?"

Yes. Not...here.

I sat back on my heels and frowned at the rosebush. Its message didn't make sense, but it hadn't been wrong before, and it had no motive to mislead me...yet even so, I had to be completely certain it was correct, for we only had one rose and therefore no room for error.

I glanced at Briar to seek his opinion, but he'd scooted away from the rosebush and now hovered over the wildly growing weeds, his entire manner transfixed.

My stomach lurched. "What are you doing, Briar?"

He didn't answer, only continued to stare at the thorny thistles, as if hypnotized.

"Briar? I think we're in the wrong garden."

Still no answer. My unease grew.

"Briar? *Briar?*" I scooted close enough to nudge him and he finally turned away from the weeds to stare at me, his gaze unseeing at first, before it settled in determination.

"This is the right garden. The rose must be planted here."

I shook my head. "No, the rosebush says it's not. We must trust it."

I reached for the violet blossom again in hopes it'd confirm its instructions. Its whispered words were faint at first, but grew steadily louder in my mind the longer I remained in contact with the rose. It spoke only a single word: *source*. I frowned. *Source?*

"We need to plant the rose here," Briar continued firmly.

"But the rosebush—"

"I know my own gardens." His hardened tone warned against my arguing, even as the darkness in his haggard expression deepened, a sign that with his current exhaustion he was losing the constant battle within himself.

"Yes, but—" There was no time for fighting, especially when each wasted moment caused Briar to slip further and further away. "Come, hear for yourself."

He resisted and tried to tug away as I took his hand and placed it on the rose. The moment he touched it he stilled, his forehead furrowed in deep concentration. I used his momentary distraction to pull the weed from his loosened grasp. He didn't seem to notice.

"Can you hear its instructions?" I asked.

"It wants us to return to the source of the poison," he said. "There we must plant the rose." His gaze darted sideways to the flower in my hand with a fierce look like he wanted to snatch it. I tucked it carefully back into my satchel, and his dark look disappeared.

"Your mother's garden is where the poison started; if the rosebush believes we should plant it there, then we should."

He nodded and stood on his own, as if the contact with the rose had renewed his vigor. But before he took a single step, he bent down to retrieve the weed I'd taken from him.

"Briar, I don't think—"

"Come, we must hurry." This time he was the one to lead, striding slowly but purposefully in the direction of the dowager queen's garden. I hastily followed. We hadn't made it very far down one of the twisting paths when Briar suddenly stopped.

"What's wrong?" I asked.

He didn't answer as he tilted his ear to the side, as if he was listening to something. I strained my ears, but the only sound I could hear was my thudding heartbeat and the wind.

"Can you hear something?"

Again he didn't answer, but his expression was changing...hardening, like it did when he was a beast. My urgency increased. I tugged on his arm.

"We need to move faster."

He nodded and allowed me to pull him back into a hasty walk. I stole several side glances at his indiscernible expression, twisted in a way that caused trepidation to creep up my spine as my unease grew.

Despite our quick pace, it seemed to take forever to arrive at the hidden garden, where the hedge door was securely locked. I started to crouch down near the knot in the tree where I'd buried the key, only to remember that it was no longer there; Briar had taken it the last time we'd visited.

I glanced up. "Do you have the key?"

Again he didn't answer, his ear cocked towards the garden wall, listening intently, even though the only thing I could hear was the heavy breeze. His gaze slowly met mine. "The key? Of course I have it. I always keep it with me."

"Can you give it to me?"

He shook his head. "No. I should be the one to open it. You don't know the gardens as well as we do and can't be trusted with it." Yet he made no motion to retrieve the key himself.

Annoyance slipped past the barrier I'd created to restrain my escalating emotions. "It doesn't matter who opens it, so long as one of us does," I snapped.

He rolled his eyes as he pulled the key from his pocket. "Testy," he muttered.

I tightened my jaw in an attempt to keep back my biting retort as he inserted the key and unlocked the door. It creaked open, causing the air to suddenly chill and the scent of mold and decay to fill my nostrils and churn my stomach.

I stepped inside and was immediately swallowed up by the thick mist and heavy shadows hovering over the noxious weeds filling the walled garden. I felt all the hope which had guided me up to this point slip away, as if the evil garden was robbing me of every uplifting emotion, leaving nothing but darkness and despair in its place and causing whatever candle had been lit inside me to suddenly extinguish.

The rustling wind grew louder, brushing against my mind in harsh whispers, whispers I couldn't comprehend. But I could understand the suffocating feelings pressing against my thoughts: fear, worry, hatred, insecurity, worthlessness, and a strange simmering rage that yearned for its flames to be stoked so it could be unleashed.

I tried to push against these emotions as Briar shut the

door behind him and strode into the middle of the garden. There he extended his hand. "Give me the rose."

I cradled it protectively against my chest. "We should do it together."

"No, Maren. As the king who's connected to these gardens, I have to be the one to do it."

Maren...his use of my full name should have been a warning, but with all the negative emotions swirling within me, it was a difficult one to heed, especially when I felt emotionally exhausted, as if I were drowning in the darkest night, one absent of stars to light my way and with no hope of an approaching dawn.

Briar glared at me when I remained still. "Give me the rose, Maren. *Now.*"

My hand shook as I reluctantly held it out. Part of me realized I was being utterly foolish to hand it over so easily, especially when Briar's eyes had that wild, ferocious look within them, but that sensible part of my mind had been quieted by the other deafening voices raging within me.

Briar snatched the rose from my grasp, and the moment he'd taken it I realized I'd made a serious mistake, especially when a cold, triumphant smirk filled his distorted expression.

My heart pounded wildly. "Are you going to plant it?"

His smirk widened into a leer. "*Plant* it? Why ever would I do that?"

"To stop the—" His laugh cut me off, a chilling sound so unlike Briar. My trepidation increased. "What's so amusing?" I stuttered.

"*You* are. You're so naive, Maren. Planting this rose is the last thing I want to do, not when it'll destroy everything."

"But..." I tried to form an argument, but my head was foggy, as if the surrounding mist and shadows had robbed

351

me of all sense and made it impossible to think. "The rose will heal the gardens; it'll heal *you*. That's what we want."

"*No*." His entire manner twisted into the unrecognizable part of himself as he took a menacing step closer. "Don't you see? This rose will destroy the gardens, and do you know what will happen to *us* once it does? We'll die."

My breath caught. *Us*... "What do you mean?"

"What do you think?" he spat. "I'm part of these gardens. If I kill them, then I'll also die."

Fear clenched my heart, even as the surrounding wind grew to a steady roar loud enough I could finally hear what it was saying.

If you kill us you'll die too, if you kill us you'll die too, if you kill us you'll die—

"Stop it!" I screamed, pressing my hands to my ears, but it did little to drown out the sinister sound.

If you kill us you'll die too.

Briar quirked an eyebrow. "Can you finally hear the gardens? They've been whispering to me ever since we arrived back at the palace. We must trust them."

"We can't," I said, my voice escalating with panic as the taunting whispers continued to rage. "Whatever was once good and beautiful in the gardens no longer exists. We can't listen to them. We must trust the rosebush, the only part of the old gardens that hasn't been consumed by the poison from the noxious weeds."

He snorted. "The rosebush isn't part of us and therefore can't be trusted."

"But then why did you heed their advice to come here to—"

He laughed again and I shivered at the sinister sound. "You're so gullible."

My breath caught as his meaning hit me. "You tricked me into bringing you here?"

He shrugged. "Call it what you will, but it was effective, for this is where I need to destroy the rose."

He stepped towards a tall, thorny weed growing several feet high in the center of the grounds. It reached its claws out for the rose, eager to consume it. Icy despair rose in my chest. If the evil weed touched it, the rose would die, and with it our last hope of healing the gardens.

"Stop it, Briar! You can't give it the rose. Please!" I scrambled forward but tripped and landed on the cracked, dry ground. I twisted around to look behind me. During our conversation, the black vines infesting the walls had used my distraction to slither around my ankles, preventing my interference.

At the sound of my fall Briar glanced back at me. His eyes widened to see me sprawled on the ground, and a brief flicker of his true self flashed in his gaze. He stepped forward, away from the weed and towards me. "Are you alright, Mari? Are you hurt?"

Fierce relief filled me at his tender tone. *My Briar.* I had to seize this moment while he was with me before he slipped away again.

"Please don't do this, Briar. You're better than this."

He frowned. "How do you know?"

"Because I love you."

Another spark of light flickered in his eyes, softening some of the sinister lines etching his expression. "I love you, too." He took another step closer to me and away from the weed, which was reaching after him, trying to pull him back. "It's because I love you that I have to protect the gardens at all costs. Don't you see, Mari? If I die alongside them, then I lose you."

"You're not going to die; they're lying to you." But my stomach clenched in fear. The truth was I had no idea what would happen when we planted the rose, only that whatever was left of the enchanted gardens had instructed us to do it.

"You don't know that," Briar said.

"I don't," I conceded. "But I do know that the voice you're listening to is evil. If the weeds are telling you that planting the rose will kill you, then it must be a lie."

He paused in his advance, his frown suspicious. "How do I know *that*'s not a lie?"

"Because you know and trust me," I said. "You can't allow the evil garden to trick you, to change you into something you're not. Please, Briar."

His frown deepened. "They're not changing me. This is who I am."

"That's not true." My voice hitched with my escalating despair. "I see who you really are and it's not this; the true Briar is a man of compassion and gentleness. I don't want to lose you. If you want any life together with me, we can't let the dark garden win. Don't listen to it. Fight it. *Please.*"

He stared at me for a long moment, and within his dark eyes I could see the battle raging inside of him as he struggled to sort through both my words and the taunts of the garden still seducing him with their whispers.

I saw the moment when he emerged conquerer—the clarity and resolution that settled over him. He took a steadying breath as he bridged the remaining distance between us and crouched down so we were eye level.

He stared a moment more before the corner of his mouth lifted. "You have such lovely eyes, Mari, and that's not the only thing I love about you—everything about you is beautiful, good, and so wonderful."

He cradled my cheek and I managed to sit up so I could more fully lean against his touch. For one perfect moment it was just us—him caressing my face and staring into my eyes with his usual adoration, me seeing the man I loved returned to me. But it ended far too soon.

He tore his gaze away to focus on the rose he still held, twirling it thoughtfully by its stem. "The gardens are right— I've been so overtaken by the poison that killing the weeds will likely kill me. But you're also right; this will indeed destroy them."

My lip trembled. "It won't kill you." It *couldn't*.

His responding smile was wistful. "I'm part of these gardens, and therefore I'm part of the thorns that have consumed them. I can still feel them fighting to take over; soon there will be nothing left of who I once was. Which means I must stop this before they're victorious." Heartache filled his crumpling expression. "My biggest regret is losing the opportunity for a life with you. I wanted nothing more than to be your husband, to embark on all sorts of adventures and cherish you forever. But I made a vow when I became king to put my people first, no matter the cost. I just didn't realize it would be so high. To give you up and our future together—it's unbearable."

My tears escaped. "Don't talk that way, Briar. You'll be alright. You have to—"

He dipped down and pressed his lips to mine, silencing me. Despite the salt from my tears, his kiss was so sweet and tender. In it I felt his love, a love I wanted to keep forever. But I also felt a different love—the one that he had for the people he served, and I knew it'd be selfish of me to ask him to disregard that one, for it was part of what made him the remarkable man that he was.

His fingers dropped from my cheek as he pulled away, leaving me yearning for both him and his touch. "I hope that no matter what your life has in store that you'll find happiness." He pressed something into my hand. "Will you give this to Drake?"

I unclasped my fist to find Briar's royal signet ring on my palm. My panic rose, crushing me. "No, Briar." I scrambled for his hand, but he'd already straightened and stepped out of reach. I tried to stand to follow him, but the vines held me back. The terror at the possibility he would die consumed me. *"Briar!"*

He gave me a sad smile as he held up the rose. "I must plant this in order to heal the gardens and my kingdom. I want nothing more than to be a good king for my people, the one both you and my father believe me to be."

He knelt down and dug a hole, his movements blurred by my tears. He carefully planted the flower and paused, his ear tilted again as he listened to instructions I couldn't hear.

"I think that's the rosebush. It says that the enchanted rose requires one more thing—the greatest sacrifice a king can give his people." He met my eyes. "I love you, Mari. Always."

"Briar, please don't—"

I gasped as he dug his thumb into the thorn on the side of the rose. I watched as his blood slowly trickled down the stem to seep into the soil surrounding the flower, nourishing it. As Briar's blood touched the earth, the rose began to glow, slowly transforming from red to the purest white.

Briar withdrew his hand and watched as the rose glowed brighter and brighter. The moment it turned completely white, light extended from it to stretch across the soil, igniting everything it touched as it slowly grew closer to Briar. Just before it reached him, he lifted his gaze to meet mine, filled with the special, adoring look he always reserved just for me.

The moment the light seeped over him he collapsed. I screamed and tried desperately to break away from the vines confining me, anything to reach him, but they held fast. It wasn't until the spreading glow touched them that they shriveled and died, as did the thorny weeds filling the garden. But my only focus was on Briar, lying in a crumpled heap near the rose he'd planted.

The moment the dying vines' hold loosened I broke away and hurried to his side. My heart lurched as I rolled him over and saw his closed eyes and pale countenance. "Briar? *Briar!*" I shook him gently but he remained utterly still. I caressed his cheek, cold to the touch. "Oh, Briar."

I pressed my face against his chest and broke into shuddering sobs, clinging fiercely to him, as if by holding him desperately enough he'd be restored to me.

Several minutes passed. In my despair, I scarcely noticed the air warming and the mist vanishing, the suffocating emotions that had filled the garden slipping away, or the weeds continuing to die around me. There was only me, Briar, and the agony ripping my heart apart piece by piece at having lost him.

My breath caught as he suddenly stirred and his gentle touch caressed my back. I lifted from his chest to stare down at him. His eyes were open and filled with his usual light, a light I hadn't fully seen since I'd first opened the garden several months ago.

"Briar?" I stuttered.

He smiled and brushed my tears away with his thumb. "Hello, darling."

I continued to gape before I flung myself at him. "Oh, Briar." I squeezed him close and basked in the feel of his arms enfolding me, a place I wanted to remain forever. I tipped my head back to stare hungrily into his dear face, never wanting to look away in case this was nothing more than a dream.

I stroked his cheek. "You're alive."

He chuckled, a sound that was warm, familiar, and oh so dear. "I admit I'm quite surprised. I thought since so much of the weeds' poison had taken over me that I'd die with the poisoned gardens."

"I knew the gardens couldn't kill you." Even if in my moments of fear and grief I'd forgotten.

"Perhaps it was your faith that saved me." He kept me pinned securely to his chest as he sat us up and glanced around, his eyes widening. "Wow..."

I finally managed to tear my gaze away from him in order to look around. The garden had been utterly transformed— all the weeds had withered and died, leaving sprouts of green in their place. "It's been healed and is growing again." I returned my attention to him. "How are you feeling?"

He grinned widely. "Better than I have in a long time. And there's something else." His brow puckered. "I think my curse has been broken."

I gasped. *"What?"*

"I can no longer feel the connection that tied me to the gardens. Ever since my curse, the gardens felt like an extension of myself, one that I depended on. But now...it's gone, almost as if we'd never been connected in the first place." At first he appeared melancholy, as if he'd just lost a dear friend, but the look quickly transformed into relief and deep joy.

"Perhaps it's the garden's reward for your sacrifice. You gave all of yourself to save them and your kingdom, even without knowing the outcome of your choice." I lifted his hand and pushed the signet ring back in its proper place on his finger. "You've proven to be an amazing king, dear, and I'm so blessed I'll be able to watch firsthand as you serve your people in the many years to come."

Peace settled over him as he stared at his ring, as if he finally believed the words I'd been telling him ever since he received the crown. "You've always seen more in me than I could, even when I was losing myself."

"You never truly lost yourself," I said. "You were always there, for a person as good as you can never fully disappear."

Awe filled his eyes and his smile. "You see me."

"I do, just as you see me."

"Always," he murmured, his word the most beautiful promise. "I want to spend the rest of my life seeing you and being seen in return."

Mischief filled my smile. "As do I. Luckily for both of us, I think that can be arranged. You mentioned something about a long life as my wonderful husband, going on adventures and cherishing me forever…it sounded quite nice."

"It does." His arms looped more securely around me, drawing me closer. "Since I've been blessed with the future I thought I'd lost, I won't waste a moment not seizing it. Marry me, my beauty."

I'd barely nodded in acquiescence when he dipped down and captured my lips with his own. In his kiss I felt all of my Briar—his love, his goodness, his special way of seeing all that I was, as well as the hope of our bright, beautiful future at one another's side.

EPILOGUE

*T*he garden's joy surrounded us as we walked through them following our three-month wedding trip. I laughed in delight as a nearby elm used one of its branches to gently place a crown of daisies on my head.

"I take it you missed us?" I asked.

The plants all tittered excitedly in response, and a cheerful, floral-scented breeze tugged on our arms to pull us further inside. The beauty and splendor of the grounds filled my senses, and for a moment I was breathless as I took in all the flowers and colors that had regrown during our absence. Peace settled over me at the garden's vibrancy. All was well.

It had been an unusual wedding trip. Briar had wanted to use his newfound freedom to tour the kingdom, both to meet the people he loved so dearly and to see how the land fared after the gardens had healed. We'd traveled constantly, examining the farmland, helping to organize and distribute food, and even working in the fields.

But the greatest wonder had been experiencing Briar's fierce love and joy at meeting his subjects and witnessing the kind, gentle manner in which he interacted with them, especially the children. He'd been eager both to meet them and to show me off as his bride and queen. I'd admittedly worried how the people would receive me, but to my surprise I was welcomed quite enthusiastically, whether by my own merits or because the people could see the deep love their king felt for his queen with every word and gesture he bestowed upon me. Meeting them had helped me realize I'd finally found my place—at Briar's side.

Briar smiled at the crown of flowers the garden had given me before turning a teasing frown towards them. "A crown for your queen but not for your king? Have I been so easily replaced in your affections?"

They rustled as if giggling, and I joined in as I looped my arm through his. "It appears you have your work cut out for you to get back into their good graces."

"As if sacrificing everything for them wasn't enough. Unfortunately for me, any competition where you're my opponent has only one outcome, my beauty, and it's with you as victor."

I basked in the tender way he said my new nickname and the even gentler kiss that accompanied it. But it didn't last long before the garden interrupted us, using the wind to tug on our arms, as if urging us to go somewhere.

Briar broke our kiss with a glare. "Can't you let me enjoy my wife without wanting all the attention for yourselves?"

They only continued tugging, their movements pleading. I tilted my head, straining to hear their whispered response. *We have a surprise.*

I beamed. "A surprise? Who can resist that? Is it a wedding gift?"

Briar lifted his eyebrows at me, clearly pleased. "You understood them."

"Ever since becoming queen it's been much easier to do so without having to touch them. Now, shall we see what their surprise is?" I bounced on my toes impatiently and he chuckled, his look adoring.

"Curious as ever, darling?" His fingers stroked down my arm, leaving a trail of heat behind before he laced our fingers together. "Very well, I can't resist giving in to your every curiosity and whim."

We followed the garden's silent guidance, which led us through the gated entrance to the symphony garden. There we were greeted by the instrument plants, currently in the process of tuning themselves, the air filled with their palpable anticipation.

The moment we settled on the soft lawn, Hibiscus spotted me from his usual bed of hibiscus flowers and scurried over. I scooped him up and nuzzled him against my cheek. "Hello, sweetheart. I've missed you. Come sit with me."

Briar chuckled again as my pet eagerly settled himself in my lap. "Three months into our marriage and I've already been replaced by a topiary hedgehog."

"Never, dear. I can just as easily snuggle with you." I nestled against his side and had just cozily rested my head on his shoulder when his arm wound around my waist to pull me into his lap.

His heated breath caressed my skin as he nuzzled against my neck. "Much better. I was getting quite envious of that hedgehog."

I shuddered in delight, but while I fully welcomed this intimate position with my husband, my cheeks warmed. "In front of the plants, dear?"

He shrugged. "They'd best get used to it, for I see no end to my doting on you in the hours we'll spend in the gardens throughout our life together."

I glanced apprehensively at the nearby flowers, some of which were half turned away, while others seemed to be watching rather attentively. But all of them seemed quite pleased with themselves at our affection, a clear sign to them that their matchmaking had worked—which they'd finally unapologetically fessed up to as being the prime reason for tricking me into plucking the rose. The fact that our relationship had led to Briar breaking his curse was just an added bonus.

"They're watching," I whispered as Briar started to lean in. His grin became rakish as he burrowed his fingers in my hair and drew me into a spine-tingling kiss, which I happily melted into.

The garden allowed us this brief moment together before they once again rustled in annoyance and the wind pulled us apart, their protest over our lack of attention.

Briar sighed as he pulled away. "I hate sharing you."

"It's really not too surprising that they're making you; they've always thought themselves in charge."

"That they have." He stole one more kiss before reluctantly turning back to the agitated plants. "Fine, we'll cease being newlyweds. Now what do you want to show us?"

The nearby flowers bristled smugly, clearly pleased to have gotten their way, before the plant instruments launched into a lovely piece. My breath immediately caught. Words couldn't describe the beauty of the piece, one full of such wonder, hope, and enchantment.

"They composed a song for us," Briar breathed.

My heart swelled. "And it's so beautiful, just like our love story."

He snuggled me closer and I happily rested my head against his chest, basking in the feel of his heartbeat against my cheek as the garden's melody encircled us.

Memories of our time together ever since we met several months ago waltzed through my mind with each note—all of the beauty and struggles we'd experienced as we learned to see one another for who we really were and love that person with all our hearts. Each obstacle had only deepened our feelings for one another, feelings which had continued to strengthen in the time since taking our vows as we worked side by side for the people we served. Nothing had ever felt so right or brought me so much happiness. I'd been born to be Briar's queen.

He shifted me in his lap and hooked his fingers beneath my chin to lift my gaze to meet his own, one full of love, which only grew more tender with each passing day. It was quite wondrous having such a dear man look at me in such a special way, a way I'd always seen in myself but which someone else now saw in me, too.

"It's beautiful," I whispered. Whether I was referring to this moment, the garden's song, my husband, or just the magic of being cherished for myself, I wasn't sure. Perhaps all of the above.

He smiled, his eyes crinkling at the edges in the way I loved best. "It is." He leaned down. "My beauty." And he kissed me, continuing yet another day of our forever of seeing and adoring one another, with a lifetime of love, serving, and adventures ahead of us.

I couldn't think of anything more beautiful than that.

ALSO BY CAMILLE PETERS

Pathways
Inspired by "The Princess and the Pea" and "Rumpelstiltskin"

Spelled
Inspired by "The Frog Prince"

Identity
Inspired by "The Goose Girl"

Reflection
Inspired by "Snow White"

THANK YOU

Thank you for allowing me to share one of my beloved stories with you! If you'd like to be informed of new releases, please visit me at my website www.camillepeters.com to sign up for my newsletter, see my release plans, and read deleted scenes—as well as a scene written from Briar's POV.

I love to connect with readers! You can find me on Goodreads, Instagram, and on my Facebook Page, or write me at authorcamillepeters@icloud.com.

If you loved my story, I'd be honored if you'd share your thoughts with me and others by leaving a review on Amazon or Goodreads. Your support is invaluable. Thank you.

Coming Autumn 2020: Princess Seren's story, *Voyage*, inspired by *King Thrushbeard*.

ACKNOWLEDGMENTS

I'm so incredibly grateful for all the wonderful people who've supported me throughout my writing adventures.

First, to my incredible mother, who's worn many hats over the years: from teaching me to read as a toddler; to recognizing my love and talent for writing and supporting it through boundless encouragement and hours of driving me back and forth to classes to help nourish my budding skills; to now being my muse, brainstorm buddy, beta-reader, editor, and my biggest cheerleader and believer of my dreams. I truly wouldn't be where I am without her and am so grateful for God's tender mercy in giving me such a mother.

Second, to my family: my father, twin brother Cliff, and darling sister Stephanie. Your love, belief in me, and your eager willingness to read my rough drafts and help me develop my stories has been invaluable. Words cannot express how much your support has meant to me.

Third, to my publishing team: my incredible editor, Jana Miller, whose talent, insights, and edits have helped my stories blossom into their potential; and Karri Klawiter, whose incredible talent perfectly captured the feel of this story in yet another beautiful cover.

Fourth, to my wonderful beta readers: my dear Grandma, Charla Stewart, Susie Gerberding, Alesha Adamson, Mary Davis, and Emma Miller. I'm so grateful for your wonderful insights and suggestions that gave my story the last bit of polish in order to make it the best it can be. I also want to specifically thank Charla Stewart and Alyssa Meredith for helping me brainstorm the plot in its earliest stages. In addition, I'd like to thank all my ARC readers, who were so willing to give my book a chance and share their impressions. Thank you.

Fifth, to my Grandparents, whose invaluable support over the years has helped my dreams become a reality.

Last but not least, I'd like to thank my beloved Heavenly Father, who has not only given me my dreams, talent, and the opportunities to achieve them, but who loves me unconditionally, always provides inspiration whenever I turn to Him for help, gives me strength to push through whatever obstacles I face, and has sanctified all my efforts to make them better than my own.

ABOUT THE AUTHOR

Camille Peters was born and raised in Salt Lake City, Utah where she grew up surrounded by books. As a child, she spent every spare moment reading and writing her own stories on every scrap of paper she could find. Becoming an author was always more than a childhood dream; it was a certainty.

Her love of writing grew alongside her as she took local writing classes in her teens, spent a year studying Creative Writing at the English University of Northampton, and graduated from the University of Utah with a degree in English and History. She's now blessed to be a full-time author.

When she's not writing she's thinking about writing, and when's she's not thinking about writing she's…alright, she's always thinking about writing, but she can also be found reading, at the piano, playing board games with her family and friends, or taking long, bare-foot walks as she lives inside her imagination and brainstorms more tales.